Shr___ her head, looking at me in a way that
_____ ___

"No. You are a change-bringer. Whatever choices
you make lead to change for the rest of us. But it is not
something you chose." Then she said, "When you leave
this place, we shall not meet again."

I shivered, my skin rising to goose flesh. Because
I could see from the vacant look in her eyes that she had
sunk into a futuretelling trance. I did not want to ask,
but I had to know. "What do you mean?" I whispered.

"Before the next Wintertime ends, you will bid
farewell to all that you love and you will journey far
over land and sea to face the beast."

"All that I love?" I echoed.

"All," Dell said, serene and implacable.

BOOKS BY
ISOBELLE CARMODY

◆

THE OBERNEWTYN CHRONICLES

THE GATEWAY TRILOGY

◆

LITTLE FUR

ISOBELLE
CARMODY

THE
STONE KEY

Random House 🏠 New York

Copyright © 2008 by Isobelle Carmody
Cover art copyright © 2008 by Penguin Group (Australia)
Map copyright © 2008 by Penguin Group (Australia)

All rights reserved.
Published in the United States by Random House Children's Books,
a division of Random House, Inc., New York.

Random House and colophon are registered trademarks of Random House, Inc.

This is a slightly modified version of the second half of a work originally
published by Penguin Books Australia Ltd, Camberwell, in 2008. Published here
by arrangement with Penguin Group (Australia), a division of Pearson Australia
Group Pty Ltd.

Visit us on the Web!
www.randomhouse.com/teens

Educators and librarians, for a variety of teaching tools, visit us at
www.randomhouse.com/teachers

Library of Congress Cataloging-in-Publication Data
Carmody, Isobelle.
The stone key/Isobelle Carmody. — 1st American ed.
p. cm. — (Obernewtyn Chronicles ; bk. 6)
Summary: Elspeth must find and stop the person infected with the plague before
sickness—and ultimately death—threatens everyone in the Land.
ISBN 978-0-375-85772-0 (pbk.) — ISBN 978-0-375-95772-7 (lib. bdg.)
[1. Orphans—Fiction. 2. Extrasensory perception—Fiction. 3. Human-animal
communication—Fiction. 4. Plague—Fiction. 5. Science fiction.] I. Title.
PZ7.C2176St 2008   [Fic]—dc22   2008025197

Cover and map design by Cathy Larsen
Cover background artwork by Les Petersen
Cover photographs by Getty Images

Printed in the United States of America
10 9 8 7 6 5 4 3 2 1
First Random House Edition

for Mallory,
who found me on a table
and read me on a plane,
and for Daywatcher Whitney
and Moonwatcher Nick,
who were my guides on this
unexpected and unexpectedly
enchanting quest

✦ CHARACTER LIST ✦

Angina: Empath guilden and enhancer; twin brother of Miky

Ariel (aka H'rayka, the Destroyer): sadistic enemy of Obernewtyn; distorted Talent; allied with the Herder Faction and Salamander

Atthis (aka oldOne): Agyllian or Guanette bird; blind futureteller

Avra: leader of the Beastguild; mountain mare; bondmate to Gahltha

Blyss: Empath guilder

Bram: Sadorian tribal leader

Bruna: Sadorian; daughter of Jakoby

Brydda Llewellyn (aka the Black Dog): rebel leader

Calcasuus: horse; companion of Jakoby

Cassy Duprey: Beforetimer, later known as Kasanda

Ceirwan: Farseeker guilden

Daffyd: former Druid armsman; farseeker; brother to Jow; beloved of Gilaine; unguilded ally of Obernewtyn

Dameon: blind Empath guildmaster

Dardelan: rebel leader of Sutrium

Darius: Twentyfamilies gypsy; beasthealer

Dell: Futuretell guilden

Domick: AWOL Coercer ward; former bondmate of Kella

Dragon: powerful Empath guilder with coercive Talent; projects illusions

Druid (Henry Druid): renegade Herder Faction priest and enemy of the Council; charismatic leader of a secret community that was destroyed in a firestorm; father of Gilaine; presumed dead

Elspeth Gordie (aka Innle, the Seeker): Farseeker guildmistress; powerful farseeker, beastspeaker, and coercer, with limited futuretelling and psychokinetic Talent

Fian: Teknoguild ward

Gahltha (aka Daywatcher): Beast guilden; bondmate to Avra; a formidable black horse sworn to protect Elspeth

Garth: Teknoguildmaster

Gavyn: Beast empath; beasts call him adantar

Gevan: Coercer guildmaster

Gilaine: mute daughter of the Druid; farseeker bound to Lidgebaby; beloved of Daffyd; slave in the Red Queen's land

Gilbert: former armsman of Henry Druid

Grufyyd: bondmate to Katlyn, father of Brydda

Gwynedd: Norselander; rebel leader of Murmroth

Hannah Seraphim: director of the Beforetime Reichler Clinic

Harwood: powerful coercer

Helvar: Norselander and shipmaster of the *Stormdancer*

Iriny: halfbreed gypsy; half sister to Swallow

Jacob Obernewtyn: Beforetimer; wealthy patron of Hannah Seraphim

Jak: teknoguilden; bondmate to Seely

Jakoby: Sadorian tribal leader; mother of Bruna

Javo: Obernewtyn's head cook

Jik: former Herder novice; Empath guilder with far-seeking Talent; died in a firestorm

Jow: former follower of the Druid; brother to Daffyd; beastspeaker

Kader: Healer with empathy and farseeking Talent

Kasanda: mystical leader of the Sadorians; left signs for the Seeker to help in her quest

Katlyn: herb lorist living at Obernewtyn; bondmate to Grufyyd, mother of Brydda

Kella: Healer guilden with slight empath Talent; former bondmate of Domick

Lark: Norselander from Herder Isle; son of shipmaster Helvar

Lidgebaby: powerful coercer-empath; an infant bound to the Druid's Misfit followers at birth

Lina: young, troublemaking beastspeaker

Linnet: coercer-knight

Louis Larkin: unTalented highlander; inhabitant of Obernewtyn; honorary Beastspeaking guilder

Malik: traitor to the rebellion, allied with Herders

Maruman (aka Moonwatcher, Yelloweyes): one-eyed cat prone to fits of futuretelling; Elspeth's oldest friend

Maryon: Futuretell guildmistress

Matthew: Farseeker ward with deep probe abilities; slave in the Red Queen's land

Merret: powerful coercer with beastspeaking Talent

Miky: Empath guilden; twin sister of Angina; gifted musician

Miryum: AWOL leader of coercer-knights

Pavo: Teknoguild ward; died of the rotting sickness

Powyrs: rebel sea captain

Rasial: white dog with powerful coercive abilities; second to Avra in Obernewtyn Beastguild

Reuvan: rebel seaman from Aborium; Brydda's right-hand man

Roland: Healer guildmaster

Rushton: Master of Obernewtyn; latent Talent

Salamander: secretive, ruthless leader of the slave trade

Sallah: rebel mare; companion to Brydda

Seely: unTalented caretaker of Gavyn; stranded on west coast

Straaka: Miryum's Sadorian suitor, killed in the rebellion

Swallow: Twentyfamilies D'rekta, or leader

Zarak: Farseeker ward with beastspeaking Talent

PART I

◆

STONEHILL

◆ 1 ◆

I OPENED MY eyes to find a young gull perched on my chest, peering at me with a speculative black eye. When I moved, it gave a startled squawk and flapped away. It stopped atop a rock and watched me.

"Give up, for I am too big for you to swallow, little brother," I croaked, and struggled to sit up. The night's storm might have been a dream, for there was not a cloud in the dazzling blue sky that arched overhead. The sun was hot enough to have dried the exposed part of my hair and clothes. I had drunk as much of the brief flurry of rain as I could, but I was thirsty.

Indeed I had woken thirsty for the last few days, and it was doubtless thirst that had woken me.

Or maybe the gull had pricked me with its claws. I looked around and found it was still watching me like a small baleful sentinel. But then my gaze went past it, for beyond it in the distance, only half visible through a dense golden haze of sunlit sea spray lay the city that had occupied most of my thoughts since I had awakened the first time on the sand. While I had rested in order to give my body time to heal, I had come to feel certain that the city was Morganna, but it was impossible to be sure at this distance. I could see that it was

3

walled, but I could not tell if it was a complete wall or merely overlapping sections of wall.

I had asked the ship fish Ari-noor to bring me to Murmroth, at the other end of the west coast from Morganna, but the currents and shoals in the strait were such that any ship wanting to travel to Murmroth had to begin its journey on the coast just past the mouth of the Suggredoon, so it could very well be that I had lost hold of the ship fish not far from Morganna.

The thought of ships had preoccupied my mind the last few days: somewhere on the sea sailed the *Black Ship* with its deadly cargo of plague that the Herder leader intended to unleash upon the west coast. I had come to the west coast with the sole desire of finding the plague carrier before his sickness became contagious, but I had no idea where he would be left ashore. In a city, certainly, and in my estimation a large city, but which one I had been unable to discover.

With luck, it would be Morganna, but it might as easily be Aborium or even Murmroth. For this reason, my plan had been to call at every city and ask if the *Black Ship* had recently put in anchor there. But I had not reckoned on losing contact with the ship fish that had borne me across the treacherous strait or on smashing my head on a rock in a shoal and nearly drowning. Indeed it was only the aid of the mystic Agyllian birds, who had come to me on the dreamtrails, that had enabled me to reach the west coast alive. The Elder of the Agyllians had warned me that I must rest so the curative capacity the birds had taught my body could heal me swiftly. And I had obeyed.

Other than my apprehension about finding the plague carrier in time, it had been far from unpleasant to sit on the sloping white sand and gaze out to sea. Spending such long periods of time in the water with the two ship fish and hearing the wavesong, or feeling it, for it seemed as much to be felt as to be heard, had given me a deeper appreciation of it. The wavesong had flooded me with appreciation for those I loved, for those who had come to my aid.

The thought of love brought to my mind an image of Rushton, but it was too painful to let my thoughts dwell on the Master of Obernewtyn, given our estrangement. I thought instead of my two protectors, Gahltha and Maruman. I missed them terribly, though I knew they were aware that I was safe because Atthis had sought assistance from their spirits in order to save me.

I turned my head to look out to sea. Despite the day's clarity, I could not see even a shadowy outline of Herder Isle. Two Islands, I reminded myself, for although the Herders had long ago destroyed the isthmus once connecting the two islands, the link had been renewed when the high wall surrounding the Faction Compound had fallen into the channel, creating a stone path from one to the other.

The dangerous, terrifying period I had spent inside the Herder Compound, first at the mercy of the Herder priests and then through the fall of the Faction on Herder Isle, seemed as if it had happened ages ago, rather than only a few days earlier. There had been much still to be done to secure victory when I had left for the west coast. I wondered for the hundredth time what was happening there and whether the Norselanders, the shadows, and the renegade novices had managed at last to overcome the ruthless captain of the Hedra force and his remaining warriors. I wondered if the *Stormdancer* had been repaired yet. I had meant to travel across the strait in the ship, but it had been damaged when the Herders tried to invade the Land, and the shipmaster, Helgar, had told me it would take at least a sevenday to make the ship seaworthy. I had felt such despair hearing his words, knowing it would be too late then to cross the strait and find the plague carrier in time to stop him from infecting anyone.

Only later that night had I thought of calling to the ship fish, Ari-noor, who had rescued me already. She had not come, but her pod-sister, Ari-roth, did.

Against all odds, I had reached the west coast. I reckoned that since the *Black Ship* had to travel from Norseland, having first provisioned itself and made whatever repairs it needed after its last trip, before weaving through various shoals and currents to reach the west coast, the *Black Ship* was only just now likely to be setting its plague carrier ashore. And it would take some days for the plague to become effective. So I had a few days in which to act.

The thought that the ship might even now be anchoring on the west coast made me uneasy. I was glad that I had left instructions for the *Stormdancer* to travel straight to Sutrium so the rebels could be alerted as to what had happened on Herder Isle and to warn them that no one must cross the Suggredoon, in case I failed.

I had ensured that the plague would be contained if I failed. But it sickened me to think of how many would die on the west coast.

"All," had said the One, the supreme leader of the Herder Faction. "All will die."

The memory of these words was enough to thwart

my attempt to relax. I sat up and massaged the stiffness from my muscles while looking out over the shimmering waves. I thought of the true dream I had experienced when I had almost died, of Cassy Duprey and Hannah Seraphim's first meeting.

It had been fascinating to see Rushton's Beforetime ancestor Hannah Seraphim, for my Beforetime visions of the past had always centered on Cassy Duprey, a Beforetime sculptress whose father had been director of the Govamen program working on the computer-machines that had caused the Great White holocaust that had destroyed their age. I had known that Cassy and Hannah Seraphim had met, but I had not previously seen them together.

I pictured Hannah's pleasant face with its striking brown eyes and expressive smile and felt suddenly that Jacob Obernewtyn *had* loved her, and this was at least partly why he built Obernewtyn and funded her research into the Beforetime Misfits' Talents, called paranormal abilities by the Beforetimers. I had hoped to dream of Hannah again as I lay hour after hour, drowsing rather than waking or sleeping, but past dreams were not something I could control.

I had mulled over the dream endlessly, though.

The meeting between Hannah and Cassy had obviously taken place before the young woman had invaded her mother's mind to prove that she possessed paranormal abilities. The vision held no trace of the grief I had witnessed in Cassy, and I guessed from this that Cassy's Tiban lover had not yet died when she had met Hannah.

The gull's caw startled me from my reverie, and I

looked up to see it flap into the air, just escaping the sharp claws of the plains cat that had been stalking it. I sent a greeting to the cat, and she came gliding over.

"Red meat would strengthen ElspethInnle," said the tiny black cat with its enormous tufted ears and wild eyes. "Better than ubu." She dropped next to me several of the prickly cactus fruits that she and her mate had been bringing me since I first beastspoke them for help. She sat down to clean herself.

"My thanks, Mitya," I told her, feeling my heart seize with longing for Maruman, who had cleaned his ears in exactly the same fastidious way.

The plains cat ceased her ablutions to watch me as I rose carefully to my feet, her nose twitching daintily. I walked back and forth, testing my strength. For two days I had been practicing standing and walking, but this was the first time since I had awakened on the beach that I felt neither pain nor dizziness, and the double vision I had suffered since waking had finally abated. My heart quickened at the realization that I was finally well enough to begin my quest. Despite my fears about the plague, I thought eagerly of reaching the city that had been so tantalizingly out of reach, because it meant food and water. My stomach rumbled loudly.

"ElspethInnle should eat some bloody meat," said Mitya again.

I said nothing, for I had already made vain attempts to explain to the single-minded little plains cat that I did not eat the flesh of anything that lived, for I could live well enough on fruits and vegetables and grains. She and her mate had not believed me, and they had brought me several tiny dead furry plains mice. I had finally convinced them to eat their kill. They had departed with it and returned an hour later with some of the prickly ubu. The cactus fruits had ensured my survival, but they had little taste and scant nourishment; even as I ate those Mitya had brought with her, I thought longingly of a hot bowl of vegetable stew with fresh baked bread and a bowl of rich honeyed milk. It made me salivate like a starved dog.

"I will go to the city now," I beastspoke the plains cat when I had finished my brief meal.

"Many are funaga-li that dwell there," said Mitya disdainfully.

"Nevertheless, I must go there to find my friend," I told her. "Where is Guldi? I wanted to thank both of you for helping me."

"Guldi prepares a den, for soon I will have kits," Mitya sent. She gave me a look of glimmering pride, and I told her they were certain to be as beautiful and clever as their parents.

"Of course," she said complacently.

I cast one last glance around me, needlessly, for I carried nothing at all with me; then I bid the little cat farewell again.

I set off toward the city, glad that I was able to walk along the sand, for I was barefoot, having left my shoes from Cinda on the shore at Hevon Bay on Herder Isle. It angered me that I had not had sense enough to tie them to my waist before I entered the water. Aside from needing them to walk, there was a real danger that, barefoot and utterly bedraggled as I was, I would be judged a beggar and refused entry to the city. Of course, I could coerce my way out of any trouble, but given that I was still weak from my ordeal, it would be better to do nothing that would require exertion beyond walking. Certainly not before I managed to find some food.

It would be best to slip into the city along the shoreline, thereby avoiding the guarded entrances, but it would depend upon where the tide was when I arrived.

Driftwood lay scattered along the beach, and I began to gather it, reasoning that if I had to go through a gate, I could claim to be bringing wood into the city to sell. Once inside the walls, I would simply leave the wood somewhere and coerce shoes and some respectable clothes from a storekeeper. I needed to smarten my appearance if I did not want anyone to question my possession of a horse when I tried to leave. I would have to steal the horse, of course.

But first I would find food and water, and then I would go to the waterfront and find out whether the *Black Ship* had anchored there recently.

By the time I was close enough to see that the town was fully walled, I had a good-sized armful of wood. This was fortunate, since the tide was high enough to make it impossible to enter at the shore. The walk had fatigued me, but it had not left me shaking and sickly as even a short walk had done two days past. My body seemed to have finished healing itself, and I was sure that once I had some proper food and water, I would be completely renewed.

Coming along the shore meant that I was approaching the city from the side and would enter through one of the lesser side gates. I had assumed that it would be scrutinized less closely than the city's main entrance gate, for important people and most travelers would come along the main coast road and so enter the city by its imposing main entrance. The only people who used a city's side gates were its poorer denizens—fisherfolk and foragers of various kinds. This was all to the good, for my bedraggled appearance would cause less comment in such company.

As I made my way slowly along the stony ground beside the wall, I found myself so thirsty that there was little else on my mind save reaching a well. I had endured thirst constantly since awakening on the west coast, but somehow it had become harder to bear the nearer I came to the city. Nevertheless, before I reached the gate, I forced myself to stop in the shade cast by the wall and set down my pile of wood. I rubbed my sticky face vigorously to remove the salt, combed my fingers through my hair, and plaited it as best I could. I then wove some strands of the spiked grass to bind the wood together. A real wood carrier would also have a woven shoulder pad, but I did not want to waste any more time.

Taking a deep breath, I shouldered the wood and joined those waiting to be admitted to the city. I was immediately relieved to notice that the bent crone at the front of the queue carried wood, too. I entered her mind to confirm that the city was indeed Morganna, but unfortunately she knew nothing of which ships had anchored here. Nor did the two boys behind her, leading horses. Both were grooms for the same stablemaster, and it occurred to me that I could easily pass for one of them if I pushed my hair under a cap, hunched down, and left the city the same way. Behind the grooms, a big man sat on a cart drawn by a bullock. The cart was piled high with ubu and a brown nut, which his mind told me he had gathered some distance from the city.

The nut meat was inedible raw, but once boiled, it could be reduced to a mash and used to thicken stews and soups. Directly in front of me were several poor-looking travelers with thin packs, ragged clothes, and pinched faces. A swift probe revealed they were from the tiny farms where people eked out a living along the narrow belt of less barren land that fringed the Blacklands. Their last crop had failed after a mysterious blight had attacked the farms following one of the winds that occasionally blew in from the Blacklands. They meant to seek work and amass enough coin to buy seed and return with provisions before the next planting season. They had come to this gate to avoid the entry tax required at the main gate.

When I came close enough to see the soldierguards inside the gateway, I farsought the bigger of the two but was dismayed to encounter the unmistakable buzzing rejection of a demon band. I cursed my stupidity in failing to realize that the soldierguards would be demon-banded. Hadn't Brydda told me that all soldierguards this side of the Suggredoon wore the bands?

It was too late to leave the line without drawing attention, and I had to enter the town anyway. I would need to coerce a diversion if there was any trouble. To my intense relief, the guards barely looked at me before waving me through.

There were several wheeled stalls and carts set up on either side of the wide street running back from the gate. The man with the bullock and cart had stopped and was haggling with a stallholder over the price of the spiked fruit. A number of men with creels were selling fish to another stallholder, and I realized that the stalls must absorb a good deal of the produce that entered the city.

I edged through the small crowd examining the fish and produce, managing to anger several people by prodding them with the sticks I had collected. Cringing and apologizing, I wondered how any real woodgatherer ever managed to move along a crowded street without poking someone in the eye.

Desperate to leave the press of people, I turned into the first street running off the wider gate road, only to find the way ahead blocked by three surly young men playing a game of stick and stone. Rather than coercing them to turn their brutish attention away from me altogether, I took the less exhausting step of channeling their aggressive energy into sneers and threats. I had not felt any real danger, yet I was thankful to come to a square where women and men sat on porches sewing or peeling vegetables with children threading about their legs.

I crossed the square diagonally and entered a lane that headed toward the sea. It occurred to me that selling the wood would not only earn me some coin, but it would also allow me to engage in a conversation that might enable me to ask more general questions, such as whether anyone had seen the *Black Ship* of late. Of course, I could delve into people's minds for what I needed, but asking aloud would be quicker and less wearying.

First I needed to find some water, for my thirst was acute. I asked a young woman about a public well, but she spat at my feet and muttered a curse to drive off beggars.

It took another half hour to locate a large public fountain in the center of a busy square surrounded by stalls and barrows. By now my head ached so badly from thirst that I felt ill. Throwing down my bundle, I took up the wooden dipper chained to the fountain, held it under a gush of water, and drank deeply. I dippered and drank two more before forcing myself to stop. I was still thirsty, but I would vomit if I simply drank my fill. I waited a moment and then drank two more dippers. Only then did I notice disapproving glares from the men and women seated about the rim of the fountain. A brief probe told me that I looked too near a beggar to be drinking from any but the beggars' wells in the poorer parts of the city. Ironically, the troublesome bundle of wood prevented those watching me from demanding to see a beggar's coin. This, I had learned, was the coin that proved one was *not* a beggar. In that sense, I thought sourly, the coin was misnamed. Anyone failing to produce a beggar's coin could be reported to the soldierguards, whereupon the poor soul would be beaten and thrown out of the city. I heaved the wood onto my shoulder again, resolving to acquire a beggar's coin promptly.

Leaving the tiled area about the well, I crossed a grassy circle to a small cluster of braziers. Blue smudges of smoke gave me hope that I could exchange the wood for coin, but the first seller I asked offered a bowl of shellfish stew in exchange for the wood. My stomach rumbled, urging me to accept, but I dared not risk being without wood or coin. Shaking my head, I said I needed a coin, and the man shrugged and gave me a copper. Relieved to be free of my troublesome bundle, I went straight to a shoemaker's stall and coerced him into seeing a silver coin rather than a copper, which enabled me to buy a rough pair of sandals and a threadbare but decent cloak from the next stall. I could have made both stallholders see coins where there were none, or made them give me what I needed, but this was safer and required less energy. In truth, I was weak with hunger.

I had two coppers from the cloak seller, and I used one, again transformed coercively into silver, to buy a comb, cheap woolen trousers, and a shirt. I coerced another trader to let me use his changing tent and discarded my rough, salt-stained clothes in favor of the new garments, regretting that I could not bathe first. Once dressed, I used another coerced copper to buy a water bladder, a small knife, and a chunk of fresh onion bread. The latter smelled so delicious that I ate it standing by the baker's stall. He was a sociable man, and it did not take me long to learn that the *Black Ship* had not called at Morganna in recent days. Indeed, the baker wondered why, saying that it was more than six sevendays since Salamander had come to clean out the Councilcourt cells and take his slaves to Norseland. I also learned that he knew nothing of the attempted invasion of the Land, which suggested that the Council truly had been kept in the dark about it.

I asked if the *Black Ship* might have called at Port Oran and was delighted to hear that big ships never went there because of too many hidden shoals. This meant that I need not backtrack toward the Suggredoon before going farther up the coast.

Bidding the baker a casual farewell, I decided to try to find a horse and ride out of the city as soon as possible. The next settlement along the coast was Halfmoon Bay, a city only slightly larger than Port Oran. I was almost certain that the *Black Ship* would choose a larger town in which to release its deadly plague, but it would not do to bypass it and find later that I had been wrong. I remembered that Halfmoon Bay had a sectioned wall, which meant that I could simply ride in one side, check the piers to make sure the *Black Ship* had not been there, and then ride out the other side. If I could leave Morganna within the next hour, I could conceivably reach Halfmoon Bay by nightfall.

I walked, farseeking anyone I passed until I found my way to a public stable. Unfortunately, too many customers and workers provided no opportunity for theft. Rather than wasting time locating another public stable, I decided to try taking a horse from the holding yard of an inn. I had passed several already and had noticed that the smaller ones did not trouble much with attendants. As I searched for a small inn, I sent out a general probe in the hope of encountering any of the Misfits I had sent to the west coast to work with the rebels there. I was not surprised when it did not locate.

At last I spotted several horses in an inn's holding yard. I was initially disappointed to see two grooms talking to each other, but they were so deep in conversation that I decided to sidle up to the yard's outer fence and beastspeak the strongest-looking horse among them, a lovely, long-legged mare with a sand-colored coat. As I had hoped, she recognized me as the Seeker as soon as I beastspoke her, saying that it would be an honor to aid ElspethInnle. I was pleased to learn that her owner was a feckless young mistress who would likely remain drinking at the inn until dusk, though it was now barely noon. Indeed, the horse, whose name was Rawen, assured me that her mistress would be so drunk that she would have difficulty understanding that her horse had been stolen, let alone making anyone understand her. The theft of her horse would be reported eventually, of course, but there would be enough of a delay that we need not worry about being stopped.

Asking the mare to wait, I coerced the yard's sole occupant, a serving girl, to fetch me some bread, cheese, and apples from the kitchen and a simple saddlebag from the tack room. When she returned, I bade her keep watch as I stripped off my new clothes, sluiced myself and my hair with icy water, and used the cloak to dry myself before dressing again: It was a rudimentary bath, but I felt wonderfully clean and refreshed as I carried the food and newly filled water bladder back to the holding yard.

Once there, I saw that one of the grooms had departed. I coerced the other to fetch Rawen's tack and fill a saddlebag with oats and hay. When he returned, I had him saddle up the mare, and I thrust the food and my few possessions into the saddlebag, buckled it up, and mounted. I was unaccustomed to a saddle, but I could not ride bareback without drawing unwanted attention.

I bade the lad lead Rawen from the yard and dismissed him after erasing all memory of our dealings and inserting in its place the memory of having seen an older man with blond hair and a furtive manner hanging about the yard.

To my relief, Rawen knew the way to the main gate, which she said was much closer than the side gate. In a short time, we were approaching the city's busy main entrance. I asked Rawen to stop and dismounted, pretending to adjust her saddle as I studied the best way out. A swift probe told me that the six soldierguards on duty here wore demon bands. Five were concentrating on the long line of incoming travelers while the sixth dealt with people leaving the city. He gave only a cursory glance to each, and, reassured, I was about to mount Rawen again when a man leading two horses reached the gate. The soldierguard held out his hand, and the man produced what were clearly the horses' papers. I was dismayed, and sensing it, Rawen asked what the matter was. I explained as best I could, but she assured me that no one ever asked for anything on the rare occasions when her mistress had taken her out of the city to exercise. This sounded so odd that I asked if I could enter her mind to watch a memory of her last departure from the city. She agreed, and it took only a moment to discover that her mistress was the daughter of one of the city's more important traders.

I was appalled, but it was too late now to return the mare to her stable, and if I simply released her, she might come to harm. Then I would still have to find another horse, with papers, thereby losing all chance of reaching Halfmoon Bay by nightfall. I might even find myself locked inside the city. All things considered, there was nothing to do but go on boldly.

Once again, my fears proved groundless, for when it was our turn to go through the gate, the soldierguard looked at Rawen rather than me and advised gruffly that I had better be quick if I wanted to exercise my mistress's horse and return before the gates closed. Under other circumstances, I would have been alarmed that the soldierguard had recognized the mare, but this enabled us to leave without papers. The moment the horse was reported missing, though, the soldierguard would remember me, so I needed to put as much distance as possible between us and the city.

Once away from the gate, Rawen willingly broke into a canter. It was wonderful to ride again, and I was pleased to find that Rawen enjoyed the gallop as much as I did. Mindful of the need to find the null swiftly, I bade her gallop as long as she could comfortably do so, and as we progressed, I conveyed my recent adventures.

We alternated between a canter and a walk, but I had miscalculated the distance to Halfmoon Bay, and it was dusk before we saw the city in the distance. There was little point in entering after dark, so I told Rawen that we would camp near the city. She asked if I might ride her along the sand beside the water, for she liked the sound and scent of the waves. I agreed, and when we reached the sand, I bade her stop, and I dismounted and walked beside the mare. It was pleasant, and by the time we were close enough to the city to make camp, it was quite dark. But even as I removed Rawen's tack, the moon rose and transformed the sea into a sheet of undulating silver that I stopped to admire. The horse rolled in the sand with voluptuous delight, and then she galloped into the waves, rearing and splashing like a child at play.

After she emerged and shook herself vigorously, she devoured the oats and hay I set out for her while I ate cheese and bread. We both drank sparingly from the water bladder. I had no means of starting a fire, and as it grew cold, I began to worry about Rawen, for she had told me that she had never spent a night in the open. Removing my cloak, I would have thrown it over her, but she suggested that she lie and then I could sit beside her, and the cloak could cover us both.

Lying against her warm belly, I gazed out at the sea, which unrolled its waves like silken rugs threaded with silver. My thoughts turned inevitably to Gahltha, for I had often sat in this way with him, sharing warmth and friendship. Where was he now? I wondered. Back at Obernewtyn or in Sutrium? And what of Maruman?

"You are bound to these beasts?" Rawen asked curiously, for she had seen their images in my thoughts.

"We are friends," I sent. "But what of you/your friends?"

"An equine owned by funaga does not have friends," she told me mildly. I asked about her life and learned that she had been bought unbroken as a filly by an owner who had trained her with care and gentleness. After he died she had been bought as a gift for her present mistress. Despite being feckless, it seemed the girl had not been unkind to her horse, for she regarded Rawen as a possession that enhanced her own beauty and value.

I asked how the mare thought her mistress would react to her loss. Rawen said that it did not matter how her young mistress reacted, for her owner was the girl's father, and he would be furious. This disquieted me, for a furious and self-important trader might complain loudly enough that soldierguards would be sent to hunt the thief. Of course, they would search initially for a fair-haired, furtive-looking man, but it would not take long for the soldierguard at Morganna's main gate to give an accurate description of me. And persistent questioning of those who had entered the city might reveal that I had departed in the direction of Halfmoon Bay.

20

The only way to prevent their finding me would be to enter Halfmoon Bay without the mare. I explained my concern and asked Rawen if she felt able to make her way alone to the other side of the city. I told her that I did not expect to be inside the city for more than a few hours, and when I left, I would summon her. Rawen agreed to the plan, and I decided that we must leave her saddle and bridle. If she was spotted saddled and riderless, she would be pursued as a runaway. It was a pity I could not take the saddle with me to sell, but aside from being too heavy to carry, it was distinctive, and its description might be circulating with that of the mare. I would bury the saddle in the sand, I decided, but the bridle was small enough that I could take it with me into Halfmoon Bay and sell it. With the coin it fetched, I could buy a plainer bridle with which to lead Rawen, more food, a horse blanket, and a tinderbox.

I yawned and was about to close my eyes when I realized that I could send a general farseeking probe into at least part of the city because of the gaps in the wall. I sent out a coercive probe searching for recognizable mind signatures, just as I had done in Morganna. To my complete amazement, I immediately brushed against a mind I knew! I was so startled that I lost contact too soon to identify whose mind it had been, and try as I might, I could not locate it again. But I had not the slightest doubt that I had touched the mind of an Obernewtyn Misfit. Whoever it was must have either been on the verge of sleep or had moved behind a section of wall. The moment I entered the city, I would farseek again. The thought of being able to speak with a Misfit filled me with excitement, and it was some time before I could calm myself enough to sleep.

The night grew steadily colder, and I worried again about Rawen, but hearing my thoughts, the mare sent equably that she was content. Turning to look at her long face, silvered by moonlight, I saw her prick her ears at the sound of the waves breaking on the shore, and then she turned her head and sniffed the air blowing across the open plain. I was close enough to sense that her mind was truly untroubled, and I marveled yet again at the ability of beasts simply to be. Rawen was not wondering what would happen next or regretting the pampered life she had led in Morganna. She was simply *being*.

Envying her serenity, I knew that it was not in me to emulate it. I turned my eyes to the waves and found myself thinking of the null. Lark and Elkar had both told me that Ariel chose his nulls from among the intake of novice boys, so I had to suppose that he had deliberately chosen an older null specifically for this task. It made sense, but why a null at all? Why not simply someone who could be infected by the plague? Or had Ariel wanted someone with no personal desires or intentions to interfere with whatever he had been bidden to do?

There were no answers, and at last Rawen's warmth and the song of the waves lulled me to sleep. I woke not long after dawn, feeling deeply refreshed. Turning out the last of the oats, I left Rawen to her meager firstmeal while I set about digging a hole deep enough to accommodate the saddle. Once it was buried, I tied the ornate bridle under my shirt and ate an apple with pleasure, giving the other to the mare.

She crunched it up, then nuzzled me and bade me

be careful before she cantered away along the beach. I watched her until the sunlit haze of sea spray swallowed her up, and then I rolled the empty saddlebag tightly, wrapped my cloak around it, and set off toward Halfmoon Bay.

✦ 2 ✦

"WHERE HAVE YOU come from?" the soldierguard asked
the older man.

He was first in the short queue of people waiting to
enter Halfmoon Bay at the gap gate nearest the water.
Like the three before him, he had come from a grubber
farm in the badlands, whose crops had mutated after a
series of storms that had blown in from the Blacklands.
I knew from conversations with Seely, who had lived
most of her life on the west coast, that although the strip
of land that ran along the Blacklands was slightly more
fertile than most of the west coast, there was a high inci-
dence of mutated crops and livestock. Anything abnor-
mal was supposed to be destroyed, though in practice,
life on these farms was harsh enough that many muta-
tions were passed off as normal. When it could not be
concealed, the grubbers had no choice but to burn their
crop or livestock and abandon their farms to travel to the
nearest city. Some never went back, but most tried to
earn coin enough for new seed stock and untainted livestock before returning.

I had thought to be a grubber in search of work, but
now I feared my tale would sound too similar, so I invented a sick grandfather in need of medicine. My story
thus refined, I turned my attention to what I could see

of Halfmoon Bay through the section gate, which was little more than a guarded opening between two sections of wall. Instead of the well-stocked stalls and the bustle of trade inside the gate at Morganna, the open area beyond the gap was narrow and dirty, and the buildings appeared to be on the verge of tumbling down. A group of ragged-looking men playing a card game on the back of a cart stopped occasionally to cast furtive glances toward the gate, and a swift probe told me that they were keeping watch for a traveler wealthy enough to follow and rob in the maze of narrow streets leading away from the gate. I was glad my clothes were simple and that I carried only an empty saddlebag and cloak. Even so, I wished that I had gone into the city a different way, for clearly this gate led to one of the city's poorer areas.

The older man was admitted, and as the soldier-guard turned his attention to the two men before me, a group of soldierguards strolled up and lounged against the wall. I could not probe any of them because of their demon bands, but I needed no Talent to realize they must be drunk, for their eyes were glazed, and they laughed often and foolishly at nothing. I half expected the soldierguard on duty to reprimand them, but he merely cast them a frowning look before returning to his questions.

The two men claimed to be tailors from Port Oran come to buy special cloth from a weaver. The soldier-guard admitted them and shifted his gaze to me. I offered him my story demurely, suddenly very aware of Rawen's bridle tied around my waist.

"*Medicine*, she calls it," crowed one of the drunken soldierguards. "That's a good one, Pyper."

"What skills do you offer?" asked the soldierguard, ignoring him. It was a question he had asked the others, and I had an answer prepared.

"I am hoping to cook in a tavern or maybe tend horses in a public stable, for I am good with beasts," I said.

The soldierguard nodded, and just as it seemed he would bid me enter, the other soldierguard said, "She don't speak like any grubber I ever heard, Pyper."

I was dismayed to realize that he was right. I had not thought to affect the slow, almost singsong speech of the grubbers who had gone before me.

"My mother was city born," I said quickly.

"Did she come from Halfmoon Bay?" asked the soldierguard named Pyper.

"What is her name? Perhaps I knew her," called one of the drunken soldierguards with a leer.

I ought to have been afraid, but suddenly I was angry. I was seeking to save the lives of these men as well as the lives of my friends, and I had no time for their foolish hectoring and sly hints. I gave my mother's true name and said that she had come from Morganna. As I spoke, I reached out to beastspeak a thin, swaybacked horse standing placidly by the cart where the men were gaming. I identified myself as ElspethInnle and asked if she would rear up and create a diversion so I could slip into the city. She said that she would be beaten unless there was a good reason for her alarm, so I beastspoke a dog drowsing in a doorway. He agreed at once to help, and he even offered with a sparkle of mischief to froth at the mouth so the funaga would think he was rabid. Without waiting

26

for me to agree, he sprang up and catapulted across the street, barking wildly.

The soldierguards swung around in surprise to see a snarling dog worrying an apparently terrified horse, and while everyone was thus distracted, I slipped through the gate and down the nearest lane. It was empty, and I sped along it and turned into another intersecting lane. There were people here, so I slowed to a walk, listening for the sound of pursuit.

Continuing on, I noticed that the houses were less dilapidated than those about the gate, but they still had an unkempt, neglected look. Crossing a square, I spied a public well and stopped to drink. Only then, as I re-filled my water bladder, did I remember my midnight encounter with the other Misfit mind. Incredulous that I could have forgotten, I sat on a stone bench beside the well, closed my eyes, and sent out a probe. I searched for some time, concentrating hard, but to no avail. My spirits plummeted, since the probe had most likely failed to locate because the person it sought had left the city.

I shook my head and told myself that the sooner I could get out of the city the better, for it had an unlucky feel about it. Setting off again, I found myself in a street where an open gutter ran down the middle, streaming with privy water and all manner of refuse; it was all I could do not to vomit. The stench was vile, yet people passed along the street or stood by it talking to neighbors, and children screamed or fought or played next to it, all of them apparently oblivious to the noxious mess running by their feet.

I left the street with relief, only to find myself in

another just the same, save that the people here all wore rags, and several gave me looks of sullen resentment that made the hair on my neck prickle. I was dressed so plainly that I had given no thought to being robbed, but now it occurred to me that the poverty here was advanced enough to make me a worthy mark. As if summoned up by the thought, a big dull-faced man and a squint-eyed woman stepped out to block my path. Before I could even begin to shape a coercive probe, the dog I had farsought at the city's entrance came charging past me to snarl meaningfully at the pair.

"'Er's got a doggie," the big oaf said, beaming down.

"Shut yer neck, yer gollerin' sheep," hissed the woman, and dragged the big man back into the doorway from which they had emerged.

"Thank you, but I could have managed," I beast-spoke the dog when we had passed out of sight of the pair.

"Of course you could, ElspethInnle, but it is an honor to aid you," he sent so amiably that some of my tension abated. I asked if he would lead me to the sea, and as we went on together, he shared, in the highest of good humor, what had happened at the gate. One of the soldierguards had tried to club him, but he had given the funaga-li a bite for his trouble, and instead of being whipped, the horse had been praised by her master for defending herself so bravely against the vicious mad dog. Best of all, he said that as far as he could smell, it was assumed that I had fled in terror, and no one had seemed to care if I had run in or out of the gate.

"Won't your human be angry?" I asked, for a description would be circulated of a rabid dog.

"I call no funaga master," he answered with cheerful contempt.

"A wild dog who lives in a city?"

"I am free, not wild," he said, adding that a city offered good pickings for a smart, free beast. Then he told me that his name was Fever.

"Fever?" I repeated aloud. He barked assent so pertly that I laughed and shook my head. Then I sobered and sent, "I am surprised to hear that there are good pickings here, for this funaga settlement seems poor to me."

"Pickings are not good for your kind," the dog agreed. "But there is plenty of good rubbish for a dog to eat, and water and lots of fat rats as well."

I shuddered, realizing that of course a dog's notion of a good place to live would differ greatly from that of a human. We came to another street running with filth, and, sickened, I asked Fever if we might go some other way.

"This is the quickest and the safest way to the waves," he assured me, untroubled by the squalor.

I struggled on, batting flies away from my mouth and eyes with my free hand and wondering that this city had not sprouted its own plague. Thinking of plagues made me remember the frail teknoguilder Pavo, who had once told me that the Beforetimers had used sickness as a weapon. He had said that they harvested the seeds of sickness and preserved them, just as one would with fruit or maybe seed and grain, so that they could be planted long after and still germinate. Pavo would never have imagined that Ariel would unearth some of these dire seeds and try to unleash an ancient plague in the Land.

I wondered where the Beforetimers had discovered seeds of sickness in the first place. It was hard to imagine plague in the Beforetimes of my past dreams, where everything seemed so smooth and clean and shining. But maybe there had been places like Halfmoon Bay in the Beforetime, where the squalor and poverty had produced a crop of sickness for the taking. It was a strangely horrible thought.

A breath of fresh air blew into my face, redolent with the sweet, clean smell of the sea. Moments later, we came out onto a boardwalk. The dog turned to follow it, and I noticed a scattering of small fishing vessels anchored in the water ahead, but no greatship. On the shore, a large sea market thronged with traders and buyers despite the early hour, and Fever sent that he had a funaga friend who worked on the far side of the market. He offered me a mental picture of a big, powerful-looking man with springy black hair, a direct searching gaze, and a ready smile.

I was startled to hear Fever describe a human as a friend, for it was seldom that unTalents cared for beasts that they did not regard as their possessions. Perhaps this man could tell me whether the *Black Ship* had recently called at Halfmoon Bay. If I failed to learn what I needed to know before I reached the other side of the market, I decided I would find and speak to Fever's friend. I would buy provisions and a tinderbox, and with luck, I might even manage to sell Rawen's bridle, all as I sought information.

Pushing my way into the crowd, I was struck by the festive attire and jewels worn by many market-goers. Half of them looked as if they were going to a ball, which was strange, because under normal circumstances, the wealthy did not shop for themselves; they sent servants to do it for them. Yet here they were, shopping in a sea market and showing every sign of enjoying it.

"What is going on in this city?" I muttered under my breath.

Fever must have smelled my confusion, for he said, "It is not always like this."

Before I could ask what he meant, he spotted another dog that bristled and offered an immediate challenge. "My friend is on the other side of the market where the trees are," the dog sent, and abandoned me unashamedly to take up the other dog's challenge.

I edged and elbowed my way laboriously toward the end of the market, where two trees grew close together. I tried probing a couple of passersby to find out if the *Black Ship* had put in recently, but none were thinking about the ship. I did learn in my probing attempt that the city was preparing for its moon fair.

I was in the process of exchanging some more transformed copper coins to buy a tinderbox, a pack to carry it in, some food, and fodder for Rawen when I spotted Fever's friend. He looked exactly as Fever had shown him to me, save that his cheeks were smeared with soot. He was sitting at a stall set up between two trees, wearing a leather blacksmith's apron and stoking a small brazier. Not until I was right in front of the stall did I notice that he had one leg thrust out stiffly, showing a wooden knob instead of a foot.

"Do you want something mended?" he asked in a pleasant, rasping voice.

"Will you buy a driftwood bundle if I gather it?" I asked, saying the first thing that came into my mind, since I could hardly say that Fever had sent me.

"Driftwood is not the right sort of wood for my fire, lass," he told me. "It burns too swift and bright. Metalworking wants a fire that will burn very hot and show little flame. There is an art in the making of fire for metalwork."

"Where do you get wood for such a fire?" I asked.

The man gave me a speculative look that made the hair stand up on the back of my neck. "You are not from the west coast," he said softly.

"I was born in Rangorn," I said, letting myself sound slightly defiant. I could imagine people might not be too willing to admit they had come from the other part of the Land, but there must be many on the west coast who had not been born there.

"Don't be afraid," he told me. "I am not one of those who thinks every person born the wrong side of the Suggredoon ought to be reported to the Council as a spy. But for your own sake, I would not tell anyone else here where you hail from. You ought to get some boot-black or hoof polish and rub it over your skin to darken it a bit. It is your pallor that gave you away as much as your accent."

"Thank you," I said. I hesitated and then forced myself to smile a little. "To tell the truth, I am more afraid of Herders than soldierguards."

"There are stories enough about Herder doings to freeze the blood of any maid or man," the metalworker said soberly.

"I came here to buy medicine for my grandfather," I said. "I have a bridle to sell, but it is a family treasure,

32

and I fear that I will be charged as a thief if I go to the wrong buyer."

"A wise apprehension," the man said gravely. "I can recommend a good buyer, but he will not do if the bridle is stolen."

I felt my cheeks redden, and he continued expressionlessly. "There is also a man in a closed tent farther along the boardwalk. He will cheat you but less than other such men, and he is discreet."

I entered his mind to see that he took me for a woman who had fled an abusive bondmate or possibly a brother or father, because he had noticed faint bruises on my face and arms. He thought the stolen bridle belonged to whoever had hurt me and that I had courage to have stolen it and fled. Far from despising me for the theft, he was trying to think of a way to help me without frightening me. He had thought of his sister, who sent him off each morning with a cheerful smile and "Have a pleasant day, Rolf." He grimaced at the thought of someone mistreating her. As always when I had steeled myself to face darkness and hatred, the unexpected sweetness of compassion undid me. I withdrew from his mind, determined not to enter again, for he was no foe.

He said, very casually, "As you might have noticed, I am crippled. If you will take a coin and buy me a bannock or two for my firstmeal from that stall yonder, there will be enough remaining for you to buy one for yourself. You can leave whatever it is that you are carrying so I know you will return." I did not have to read his mind to know that he had added this last sentence because he felt I would fear his intentions if he seemed too generous. I laid down the cloak and saddlebag and took his coin, wondering what this man's spirit would look like, were I to see it through spirit eyes.

I made for the stand he had pointed out where the smells made my mouth water, though the woman behind it had a sour expression. I ordered the bannocks and watched her take them hot from the little oven on wheels beside her. She wrapped them and named a steep price. I told her the man at the metalworking stall had given me the coin and that I would have to go back and tell him it was too little. I was backing away when I noticed a wry smile twisting her thin lips. She glanced toward the metalworker and shook her head.

"Aro sent you, then. And I suppose you're to keep one of my bannocks for yourself, for fetching them for a crippled man, even though I always take them over to him?" Dry amusement tinged her voice.

"I . . . He is very kind," I stammered, more taken aback by her transformation than her words. I also found myself confused by her calling the man Aro. His sister had called him Rolf.

"He is that, the dear fool. There is not a stallholder in this wretched place for whom Aro has not done some kindness. Indeed, if gratitude were coin, he would be a rich man. Well, have the bannocks, then, and give me the coin." Her voice had gone back to being cool, but there was now humor in her eyes.

"You are kind, too, I think," I said on impulse. She had not the metalworker's natural generosity of spirit, but his sweetness had seeped into her.

"Get along," she scoffed.

Strangely heartened, I returned to the metalworker, who bade me sit awhile if I liked. As he ate his bannock with dirty hands and evident relish, I thanked him

34

between bites, and then I told him the same tale I had told the soldierguards at the gate. I asked casually if he had noticed the *Black Ship* pass by recently.

"It anchored nightfall the day before yesterday," Rolf said.

I stared at him, frozen midbite. I choked down the mouthful and stammered, "Y-you mean Salamander the slaver brought his ship here?"

He gave me a warning look. "In Halfmoon Bay, we call him the Raider. Both him and his ship. But you need not fear his collectors, for this time he did not empty out the cells, and he stayed only long enough to deliver Councilman Kana's spiceweed. It seems he had not the time to empty out the cells, but he did hand out coin enough to pay for all who are in them, else the soldierguards might not have let him go."

"He pays the *soldierguards* for the prisoners he takes?" I asked.

"Let us say he pays bonuses to show he is pleased with the number of prisoners available when he comes to fill his hold. The bonuses have made him a favorite with the soldierguards."

Trying not to sound too anxious, though my heart hammered so loudly I thought he must hear it, I asked if he had seen the *Black Ship* anchor with his own eyes.

"I was finishing off a late job," he said. He stopped abruptly and glanced about. Then he said, "Listen, I have an idea. You need coin for medicine, and there is a better way to earn it than gathering driftwood. A laundry down the way belongs to a friend of mine named Metta. She might have something for you if one of her regular women is off sick. Or maybe she will get you delivering. She has a couple boys, but they are shiftless.

35

Tell her the metalworker from the market sent you. Even if she has no work, she will know where else you might try. And she will also know a good herbalist who can prepare something more useful to your grandfather than patent medicines, and at a reasonable cost. You might as well find out how much you have to earn."

Despite my need to know more about the *Black Ship*, I was struck by his generosity. Rather than probe him, I asked, "Why would you help me? You do not know me at all save that you judge me a thief."

"I do not judge you at all, lass," he said gently. "The world is full of people all too ready to perform that service for everyone and everything they meet. Maybe this leg makes me feel the suffering of others and wish to alleviate it, if I can. Or maybe it is that I see no evil in your face; therefore, if I can, and if you will allow it, I would help you."

I stood up and reclaimed the cloak-wrapped saddlebag before looking into the metalworker's face. "It is strange and wonderful to hear you speak so in this city, which *my* instinct tells me is full of cruelty and misery," I said softly. "I thank you sincerely for your kindness, and I regret that I have lied to you. In truth, I am not seeking medicine or coin. I need information."

His expression shuttered, and I held up a hand. "I am not a Council spy. I just want to know if you saw a young man come off the *Black Ship*. He is about my age with long blond hair and a very handsome, striking face. He would not have worn Herder attire, and he was not shipfolk."

"Who are you?" the metalworker asked.

"No one of any importance," I said. "But I came here

for something more important than you can possibly imagine, not only for me and my friends, but for all who dwell on this coast. Please, the fair man. Did you see him?"

After a long searching look, Aro nodded slowly. "Happens I did see a blond man come from one of the ship boats. I did not mark his face, but my friend who sold you the bannocks said that he looked handsome. Una had packed up and was waiting for me, for we generally walk home together. She saw them first."

"Them?" I interrupted, unable to hide my growing excitement.

"The fair man and the Herder," the metalworker said.

"A *Herder*!" I echoed. I understood that disguising his plague carrier as a Herder would be a stroke of brilliance on Ariel's part. No one would dare harm or harass a priest, and he would be able to go anywhere he liked without being questioned. Unfortunately, it also probably meant that he was in the local cloister.

"Where is the Halfmoon Bay cloister?" I asked.

"Some distance outside the city wall, near the main road," the metalworker said. "But I doubt the Herder I saw could have walked so far."

"Why? Was he injured or . . . ill?"

The metalworker shook his head. "Neither, by my eyes. But there was something wrong with him. There was a look in his eyes of . . . I can only call it confusion. He would walk a few steps and then stop, almost as if he had forgotten what he was doing. In each case, his companion led him on until he walked of his own accord again."

"Do you have any idea where they went, if not to the cloister?" I was almost stammering with excitement.

He shook his head. "I am sorry."

"I must find out where he is." I stopped abruptly, for something the metalworker had said struck me. He had spoken of *seeing* the Herder's expression. That meant he had seen the null's face!

It was too good a chance to waste. I formed a probe and entered his mind again. This time I did not confine myself to the upper levels of thought, which run just under speech and merely echo it. I fine-honed my probe and plunged deeper, through the strange mists and half-dreams and phantasms of the subconscious layer of his mind, down into the great body of memory and dream. To enter that level in another person's mind was dangerous, because the compulsion of other people's dreams and memories was even more powerful than one's own. Fortunately, I had long mastered the means of shielding myself from the pull of such dreams and memories. I sought a particular memory, and as I had hoped, our conversation had stirred it to the surface, so it was very bright and easy to find.

I entered the memory, being careful to retain a thin, coercive shield. I saw the market where I stood, but now it was night and most of the stalls were closed or closing, save an ale shop on the other side of the square and a man hawking fried bits of fish to the other stallholders. The enticing odor was making the metalworker think a bit of fish would please his sister with whom he lived. He imagined her delighted expression—"Rolf! My favorite!"—when he arrived home. The bannock seller was packing up as she waited for her last rolls to bake, and Rolf was finishing a special order for a seaman who had paid handsomely for the work to be completed before he went home. The fellow would come soon, and he wanted to be ready.

Una approached Rolf's stand with a swagger and threw a package on the bench, saying brusquely that he might just as well have them since she had overbaked for the morrow. He thanked her, taking her offering for the generosity that it was.

"You should not work so late, Aro," she scolded.

"I promised," Rolf told her, continuing to work. "Wait a little, and I will walk you home."

She shook her head in irritation. "I am not afraid to walk alone. But someday your determination to keep your word will see you dead."

"Unfortunately, keeping your word is the point of giving it," Rolf said, with a smile to soften the sting.

"Well, let us hope your fine and hasty seaman keeps his word and pays you well for this late work," Una retorted tartly.

Rolf decided not to tell her that he had already been paid. Una liked pretending to be tough and cynical, and he liked playing the naive fool for her.

He finished the last buckle and was polishing it when Una bade him look, in a low voice that caught his attention. She was gazing out to sea where a ship boat was rowing in from the *Raider*. Rolf felt the same disquiet he always did at the sight of the *Black Ship*, for he could not help but think about its wretched cargo. Still, a ship boat rowing ashore from the *Raider* this early was odd. Usually no one came from the ship before midnight, for the slaves were brought out of the cells early in the morning to avoid marching through a crowded market. Not that anyone was like to protest, even if babies and older women were being taken, but the Raider's ways were always secretive. The man himself never set foot ashore save to look over the penned slaves, and once he had approved, he immediately reboarded his ship boat and returned to the *Raider*, leaving his men to complete the transaction.

As he and Una watched, a burlyman caught the tether ropes thrown up from the ship boat, and in a moment, two men climbed onto the nearest jetty. One of the new arrivals wore Herder robes, which was nothing unusual. The *Raider* and its smaller sister ships often brought Herders or carried them away while collecting shipments of slaves or bringing spiceweed for Councilman Kana. But this Herder was not alone, and the man with him, with his long fair hair and fine white cloak, was no Herder. As the pair made their way along the pier, Rolf noticed that the fair-haired man was half-supporting the Herder, who limped and kept halting. Rolf began to industriously polish his buckles, and Una pretended to be utterly absorbed in the activity when the two neared Rolf's stall. It was unwise to take too obvious an interest in the Raider's affairs. But right opposite the stand, the Herder tripped. His hood slipped back, and his face was momentarily illuminated in the brazier fire's ruddy glow.

For an instant, Rolf had looked into the Herder's dark blue eyes, and it was as if someone had punched him hard in the gut. The Herder's eyes had been utterly devoid of intelligence or thought, yet his expression had been one of unimaginable horror. It was, Rolf thought, as if he had seen something so indescribably awful that reason had fled, leaving only the frozen shell of horror etched into his face. He had seen such

40

expressions before on those unfortunates taken from the cloister to Herder Isle, but he had never seen a Herder look like this.

Inside his memory, I was reeling with my own shock, for the gaunt and haunted face of the Herder *was that of the Misfit coercer Domick.*

✦ 3 ✦

"WHAT IS IT, lass?" Rolf asked, looking concerned.

I blinked into the sunlit day, feeling as if I had staggered from a dark tunnel. I tried to make some answer, but the discovery that *Domick*, the coercer who had vanished under mysterious circumstances the previous year at the same time the Herders had taken Rushton prisoner, was the person Ariel had infected with a deadly plague—the person I had come to the west coast to find—was beyond any imagining. I understood now that it must have been Domick's mind I had touched the previous night, and I thought with anguish of the coercer, whom I had known for as long as I had known Rushton. Brydda had always claimed it odd that both men vanished at the same time, and I realized now that they had been taken together. One of the Threes had said that Ariel had had plans for Rushton, but he must have been mistaken. It had been Domick around whom his plans had been formed, unless he had originally thought to use Rushton as his plague null. Perhaps that explained the state of Rushton's mind when we found him. Ariel might have tried to use him and failed, so he had taken Domick to Norseland, leaving Rushton in the Sutrium cloister cells, where we had found him.

"Lass, are you well?" Rolf asked, beginning to rise awkwardly from his stool.

I nodded, realizing I must have been standing there for long moments, pale and gaping. I shook my head with a sobbing laugh. "I must seem mad to you. But it is only that I have . . . I have had a shock."

"Sit down again and catch your breath. You look ill, truly," Rolf said in concern.

"I am not ill," I said, and then gave a wild bleak laugh at the knowledge that soon everyone on the west coast, including this man, would be ill if I could not find Domick.

And what to do when I did find him? I wondered. But that question was too dark to contemplate.

"You must not sit here laughing and weeping," Rolf said sternly. "You will call too much attention to yourself, and someone will trot away to tell the soldier-guards there is a wild creature at the market that wants locking up. The cells may be full, but the Councilmen won't want any trouble on the eve of the festival."

That I might bring suspicion on him, after his kindness, enabled me to master my emotions. "I do not want to endanger you, Rolf," I said hoarsely.

He frowned. "How is it that you know my name?"

"The . . . the bannock seller spoke it," I began, but he shook his head.

"Una calls me Aro, which is short for Arolfic Smithson. Only my sister calls me Rolf." His voice was steady, and his eyes looked into mine.

I drew a long breath, forcing myself to be calm. "How I know your name is part of a much greater and more complex story, and I have not time enough to tell it to you. Yet I hope you believe that I would tell it if I could, for I trust you. Why I trust you is also part of that larger story. Let me say only that you offered help, and I accept it. I need to find the Herder who came ashore with the fair man, as swiftly as can be, and get him out of the city. It is more important than you can possibly imagine."

Rolf held my gaze for a long moment, knitting his brows slightly. Then he said, "The Herder is known to you?"

"He . . . was once a friend." I choked out the words. "He is only disguised as a Herder but is not really one. But the Herders have done something to him that could bring deadly harm to all who live here on the west coast. I have come to prevent that."

He nodded slowly. "You are a rebel, then. I guessed as much. Well, I may be a fool, but as you say, I offered help, and help I will give. I don't know where those two went, save that they went north from the market, but that is not the way to the cloister. I have a friend who can help you locate them. Go to Metta at the laundry and tell her I said to introduce you to Erit. Say my name to him—Aro, not Rolf—and tell him I want him to help you. Tell him what you have told me." He gave me clear directions to the laundry, but when I moved to depart immediately, he caught my wrist in a gentle but powerful grip and added that if I needed further help or a refuge, Erit would show me where he lived with his sister by the fifth gate.

"I can promise you a safe, clean bed and a good meal, and then after, I will help you and your friend leave the city."

"I thank you," I said, unable to tell him that Domick

44

was infected with the plague and was, therefore, the last person he would ever want as a guest.

I hurried in the direction he had indicated, weaving and elbowing my way through the increasing press of laughing, chattering people. I reached the street Rolf had described, to find it deserted, and I could not resist stopping to send out a probe shaped specifically to Domick's mind. I did not expect it to locate, so I was not disappointed when I failed.

The laundry was thick with steam and bustling with activity. Amid the smells of soap and boiling washing, I approached a young girl up to her elbows in suds and asked for Rolf's friend Metta. She pointed to a merry-faced woman stirring a steaming boiler of white clothes. She was middle-aged, with enormous splendid breasts, a mass of treacle-brown curls, and the mischievous, flirtatious eyes of a much younger woman. Seeing me approach, she asked courteously what my need was. I spoke the words Rolf had bidden me say, and her smile faded, but into concern rather than animosity.

"I hope Aro knows what he is doing," she sighed, wiping the suds from her hands and arms and drying them. Undoing her apron, she bade a young girl to stir the bleach until she returned. Then she led me out the back door into a crooked lane hung with washing. A little way along it, she stopped and pointed to a narrow passage between two buildings, saying I would find Erit there.

I peered into the weed-clogged opening, which seemed no more than a gap between buildings, wondering if she was joking. But when I glanced back, she only nodded encouragement at me, so there was nothing but to push into the opening. Aside from the first part, the narrow passage had been cleared. It led me to a large angular space at the back of several buildings mounded high with weed-embroidered rubble, but beyond the rubble was a small clearing where a rough lean-to had been cobbled together. Some small, very dirty boys were squatting near the entrance playing a dice game. I hesitated, then went over to them to ask if they knew a man called Erit.

"Who wants to know?" asked the smallest of the boys truculently, a filthy urchin with a gap between his front teeth that made him whistle comically as he spoke.

"Ro . . . Aro sent me to speak with him. I am to collect a favor."

"Aro, eh?" said the whistling boy, looking owlishly around at his ragged companions. Then he looked back at me, his expression suddenly serious. "All right, I'm Erit. You can talk in front of them. What do you need?"

I stared at him, touching his mind to confirm that he was indeed Erit. Then, suppressing my misgivings, I told him that I needed to find a man in Herder robes who had been brought ashore from the *Raider* two nights past by a handsome, fair-haired young man. I described what Rolf had seen.

"Sounds as if the Herder was sick," Erit said. "No doubt his friend took him to the healing house."

"He wouldn't have taken him to the healing house," said one of the other urchins. "Herders have their own healers in the cloister."

"True," Erit said. "On the other hand, something tells me the man she wants is no true Herder, else she would have named him so rather than saying he wore

46

Herder robes." He was looking at me as he spoke, a question in his eyes.

"He is not a Herder," I agreed, my confidence in the urchin rising at this evidence of his sharp wits. "His name is Domick, and he is . . . a friend."

Erit nodded in a slightly absentminded way. "All right. Bally, you go nose about the city healing house. Gof, you and Grim go out to the main gate and see if this pair went out toward the cloister. Might as well make sure they are not in the obvious places first."

I interrupted his instructions to say that I was almost certain that the fair man would have left the city, having taken Domick somewhere safe but innocuous. Erit asked for a description of Domick, and I gave it as best I could from what I had seen in Rolf's mind, adding, "Do not approach him. The Herders may have tampered with his mind, and there is no telling what he will do. Just locate him and come and tell me where he is."

Erit nodded and turned back to his companions to give further directions as to where they might search. At last he gave a decisive nod, and all the boys departed purposefully save for their diminutive leader. Erit turned back to me, an assessing look on his face. "If this man is in Halfmoon Bay, we will find him, but this better not set the Raider upon us or Aro."

"It will not," I promised.

"If Aro trusts you, well and good," Erit finally said. "What will you do once you find your friend?"

I swallowed sorrow. "I must get him out of Halfmoon Bay as soon as possible. I have a horse waiting outside the city, which reminds me I will need some water and fodder for her."

He nodded. "Time enough for that later. Wait here now. There's food and water in the hut. Help yourself."

He was gone in a flash, and after a brief surge of frustration at having to wait while others acted, I relaxed, guessing that my presence would only have hindered the urchins if I had insisted on accompanying them. I ate some of the apples and bread, and I tried again to farseek Domick. When I failed, I paced for a time before spreading out my cloak. It was most sensible to rest in readiness for whatever the night would demand.

Later that day, Erit explained that the famous and ancient masked moon fair lasted three days instead of the customary single day. It had been held in Halfmoon Bay for more than a hundred years and still drew visitors from all along the coast. The fair's fame was not just that it lasted three days and involved an elaborate game of masks, but the Councilman of Halfmoon Bay always presented a real solid gold crown to the wearer of the finest mask, who would become the fair's king or queen.

Erit also told me that although the merriment was now focused on the wealthy area and the better markets, when the fair proper began at midday the next day, the town's entire population would be involved, for anyone seen unmasked thereafter during the fair must serve his or her finder as a slave for a day or forfeit a gold coin. Erit added wickedly that the fair was a great occasion for pickpocketing and gulling fools.

I was unable to smile. His explanation told me exactly why Ariel had brought Domick to Halfmoon Bay.

He had known of the masked moon fair, known that people would come from all over the west coast. He had chosen this city and this occasion as the swiftest means of spreading the plague. Domick would probably become infectious on the morrow or the day after, and because the people he infected would not become contagious for some days, they would have time to return to their own cities. Once the deaths began, it would be too late to close any city, for there would be plague carriers in all of them.

In order to allow a margin for safety, I had to get Domick out of the town before midday the next day.

Erit and his friends had not found it difficult to track the coercer. Within an hour of leaving me, the leader of the little band of urchins had returned to say that a strikingly handsome blond man and a sickly-looking Herder had gone to a Faction house at the edge of a prosperous district not five streets from the sea market. Erit's informant was a maid who worked in a private house opposite the Faction house; the same girl had seen Ariel leave, alone, several hours later.

Erit explained to me that the house was used primarily by priests awaiting a ship to Herder Isle and was operated and guarded by Hedra, those warrior priests whose numbers had grown so alarmingly in recent times. It was strange to think that although we had defeated the Hedra on Herder Island, I must face them here again. Ironically, they were in as much danger as the poorest beggar, for the plague Domick carried would take all who dwelled in the west, no mother their allegiance.

Erit began to describe the interior of the Faction house, saying that there were several sleeping chambers on the ground floor, as well as subterranean cells for prisoners destined for Herder Isle, but I was sure Ariel would not have allowed Domick to be locked up as a prisoner. He needed to be free to roam if he was to spread the plague, and Ariel would have wanted to ensure it without exciting too much curiosity in the Hedra guardians, given that they were also to die. Most likely, Ariel would have suggested that Domick had a specific mission to perform at the behest of the One, which required him to move about freely.

Erit took me to a lane that ended in the street of the Faction house. He pointed out a soldierguard barracks at the end of the street. Its entrance faced away from the Faction house street, but the soldierguards who marched up and down the street in guard duty came every few minutes to the corner, and they glanced at the Faction house regularly enough to see anyone approaching or leaving it. They would also hear any commotion and come to investigate.

"The best thing is to wait till your friend comes out and then speak to him," Erit suggested quietly.

"He may not come out alone, and I need to see him as soon as possible," I said. I tried to farseek the coercer, but not unexpectedly, the walls were tainted. A message-taker entered the street. As we watched, he went to the Faction house and rapped on the door. A Hedra answered and, after looking at some paper proffered by the message-taker, ushered the man inside. When he came out a few minutes later and marched away, I probed him. Unfortunately, he had only stood in the foyer, so I was unable to get any sense of where Domick might be.

"Are you thinking of sending him a message to draw him out?" Erit asked, misunderstanding my interest in the message-taker.

"I do not know if Domick will be capable of responding to a message," I told him. "The message ought to go to the person in charge of the Faction house. And who would it be from?"

"The fair-haired man who brought him here?" Erit suggested. Then he asked if Domick would come willingly with me, once outside the Faction house. I had to admit that I did not know.

"Are you saying that you will have to capture, bind, and gag him?"

"I fear it will come to that," I admitted.

A group of people emerged, laughing and chattering, from one of the fine houses between the accommodation and the barracks at the end of the street. Erit watched silently until they had gone out of sight, then he said that his gang would keep watch on the Faction house to learn its routines and gather information about its denizens and about Domick. "It will be best if you return to the hut to wait," he concluded.

I shook my head, saying I would help keep watch, but Erit said it was not a good idea, for although the moon fair would not begin officially until midday the next day, there was a long tradition of boisterous pre-fair celebrations that would continue deep into the night. During this time, almost every soldierguard in the city would be patrolling the streets. Erit shot me a glance as he added that one of his boys had heard a rumor of a young woman fitting my description who had stolen a valuable horse in Morganna and had been seen riding toward Halfmoon Bay.

"By evening, every soldierguard in the city will be looking for the thief, for a reward has been offered," Erit said. "It would be a great pity if you were taken for her."

"True," I conceded. "All right, what if I leave the city for the day and return after dark? I need to tend to my horse anyway. If you can get me some suitable clothes, I could pretend to be a boy."

Erit approved the plan, suggesting that, since I had some hours to spare, I might ride Rawen to Stonehill, where there was good grazing and a well besides. I had never heard of Stonehill, but Erit said it was a one-hour ride along the coast, and I could not miss it. Since I was leaving the city, he also suggested that I remain outside until the tide was low enough for me to enter by the sea gate, for it had no permanent guard. It would also be well after midnight, so there would be little danger of encountering fair revelers.

I fretted at this, for it left mere hours before the start of the fair, but Erit pointed out that the safest time to rescue my friend would be early the following morning when the fair revelers, and most of the soldierguards, would be snoring abed. In the meantime, he would speak to Aro and see if he could suggest any plan to wrest Domick from the Herders' clutches without bringing them down on our heads.

Thus it was that I left the city attired as a lad with a small bag of food for myself and directions to Rolf's house, just in case Erit was unable to meet me at the sea gate as we had arranged. I left by a section gap opposite the one I had entered, passing a great chattering crowd of people lined up and waiting to enter the city. By their clothes and fine horses, most were festival-goers, like those I had seen at the sea market. The rest were the usual sort of sellers, wheeling their carts or shouldering great bundles of goods, all waiting to sell their wares in Halfmoon Bay.

As Erit had promised, the soldierguards were intent on incoming visitors and traders, so my exit from the city among a group of lads set on collecting shellfish to hawk was swift and smooth.

I trailed after them to the water's edge, noting many other poorly dressed people fishing or picking through the sand. I noted, too, that the tide was washing so high against the wall's end section that it was hard to imagine it would later withdraw enough to open up the space between the wall and the waves, known as a sea gate.

I set off slowly along the water's edge, shying the occasional pebble into the waves as if I were a lad. The heavy boots that Erit had given me to match my boy's attire were several sizes too big and already rubbing my heels.

"Was there anyone ever with worse luck when it comes to shoes?" I muttered, exasperated that I had forgotten the sandals I had bought in Morganna. Then I thought with a pang of the beautiful handmade and dyed slippers that Maryon had gifted me, sitting at the foot of my bed in my turret room in Obernewtyn, and indulged myself in a moment of passionate longing for that small, well-loved room and its comforts. Then I thought of Rushton and knew that Obernewtyn could never again be the beloved refuge it had once been for me. However should I tell him that he had been on Herder Isle at Ariel's mercy? No wonder he did not wish to remember what had happened to him.

This dark thought distracted me for a time, but my heels hurt dreadfully. Finally, I glanced back to be sure that I was too far for anyone to see me clearly and removed the offending boots. Their unpleasant odor made me wonder exactly where Erit had got them. Tying the laces, I rose, slung the boots across my shoulder, and walked into the waves to cool my feet.

Standing in the cold shallow froth, I turned inland to watch some young stable hands exercising their charges with an enthusiasm that might have alarmed the horse's owners. Clearly I could not summon Rawen until they had retreated inside the city walls, for a lone and unbridled horse would certainly be pursued, and these lads might have heard the rumor of a horse thief from Morganna. I sent out a probe to locate the mare and found her some distance inland on the other side of the main road. I asked her to meet me after the sun set, explaining that I was walking along the coast away from the city toward a place with both grazing and water. I apologized for having no other directions, but Rawen said if there was fresh water, she would scent it when she was closer.

Bidding her be careful not to be seen, for her mistress had offered a reward for her return, I withdrew and set a swifter pace, wondering if Stonehill would be high enough to gain any farseeking advantage. For some reason that even Garth could not yet explain, it was easier to farseek farther when higher than the person whose mind you wished to reach. The greater the height, the farther the reach. Of course, Stonehill was probably not high at all, for what heights had west coasters to compare it with? The so-called mountains upon whose feet Murmroth stood were really only the tail end of a string of peaks running away from a great range of Blackland mountains. Still, it was worth trying to farseek the Misfits at the Beforetime ruins, for now that I knew the null was Domick, I was more anxious than ever to have Jak's advice on how Domick might be treated.

It was close to dusk before I saw what I first took to be a mass of smoke some way down the beach but which soon revealed itself as a great tower of rocks. Realizing this must be Stonehill, it was not until I was closer that I could see that it was not a mound of stones but a single massive tor, which reminded me of the stone pinnacles where the Agyllians dwelt in the highest mountains. Garth had once said that such pillars were actually the insides of ancient mountains and that these rocks had burst up from the fires at the heart of the world and cooled to such hardness that they had remained when the earth surrounding them had worn away. This hill of stone was higher than the wall about the Herder Compound on Herder Isle and looked to have the surface area of Obernewtyn's farms, but how would one scale such a sheer monolith?

The sun set just as I reached the foot of the immense tor, and I stopped to farseek Rawen. She told me apologetically that she had been delayed trying to cross the road unseen but that she was even now galloping toward me. I sent her a mind picture of Stonehill, and it was not an hour before I heard the sound of hooves coming up behind me. Rawen pranced to a halt, her mind anticipating the heady and unaccustomed pleasures of the fresh grass she had scented atop the tor. There was a hectic excitement in her mind that had been absent when I had first entered it, and it occurred to me that her easy acceptance of captivity and the saddle, and her readiness to do the bidding of others, might have ended now that she had tasted freedom. Nevertheless, she insisted I mount her for the ride up to Stonehill, saying that she had scented a way up but that it was very steep at the outset.

The place she brought us to was so sharp an incline that I doubted any horse would be capable of scaling it. Rawen assured me so confidently that she could do it that I mounted up, telling myself that Erit would not have suggested I come to Stonehill unless it was possible to climb it.

Rawen cantered back some distance from the hill, explaining that she needed a run-up to gain speed enough for the first part of the climb. My heart leapt into my mouth as she turned and galloped full pelt at the dark bulk of the hill, for although she radiated confidence, at that speed, bones would be broken—hers and mine—if we fell. But Rawen did not falter, despite the steep incline. She leapt like a mountain goat from jutting stone to jutting stone, her sure-footedness surpassing anything I had ever seen. After a short terrifying period in which I did little more than close my eyes and cling to the mare's back, the way flattened slightly, and Rawen's speed decreased. I opened my eyes and saw that we had reached a narrow switchback ledge that soon widened to a trail. I did not dare look down, but gradually I relaxed and began to feel the beauty of the sea-scented night.

At length, Rawen stopped, saying she needed to rest. Dismounting carefully, I looked up and noticed that the hill flattened out only a little higher up. Refusing

Rawen's offer to carry me again, I bade her go on at her own pace. I would climb up directly and meet her at the top. She obeyed and was soon lost to view.

At first the way was steep and difficult, and I wondered if I had made a mistake in not staying with Rawen, but in a short while, the slope flattened. When I stopped to catch my breath, I decided to try farseeking the Beforetime ruins. Some impulse made me shape a probe to Merret's mind as I sent it in the direction of the ruins. To my surprise, it veered away toward the coast and located. I was immediately conscious of Merret's amazed disbelief.

"Elspeth?!" The strength of the coercer's clumsy but powerful farseeking probe made me clutch my head in pain.

"Ouch! Of course it is me," I sent sharply.

"Sorry!" she sent just as loudly, then I felt her make an effort to restrain her mind—never easy for coercers. "Sorry," she said again. "I was just so . . . But where are you?"

"I am on the west coast," I sent. "I came by sea, and I am just outside Halfmoon Bay on the Aborium side. I was trying to throw my mind to you in the ruins and the probe veered sideways."

"I am on my way to Aborium," Merret sent, her mindvoice again growing strident with excitement. "But what do you mean you came by sea? How many of you are here? How many ships?"

"There are no ships," I told her. "You know, of course, that the rebellion was won on the other side of the river?"

"We know a good deal more than that because of

Dell's foretellings, though not all is clear. Is it true that Rushton was found in the Sutrium cloister cell and is once again Master of Obernewtyn?"

"It is, but let me give you some memories. It will be quicker than trying to explain; then we will talk."

Merret made her mind passive, and I evoked a series of memories that covered the main events since I had left Obernewtyn. I concluded with a vision of the One's revelations about Ariel's plague null.

Merret's anger swelled so strongly that it almost dislodged me. "I am sorry, Elspeth," she sent. "But why would even Ariel do such a foul thing?"

"I do not know," I said. "But that is not the worst of it." I showed her the memory I had taken from Rolf's mind, of Domick passing through the sea market with Ariel.

Merret's mind boiled with emotions, but she swiftly mastered herself to say, "So it is Domick who carries this plague, and he is in Halfmoon Bay.... Ye gods! The masked moon fair! Half the coast is headed there!"

"I am sure Ariel realized that," I told her bleakly. "But don't worry; I do not think that Domick is contagious yet. Ariel would not have wanted to risk the sickness incapacitating his carrier before the moon fair begins. I think he probably infected him in Halfmoon Bay. The girl who saw them enter the Faction house together said he was there for several hours."

"Then we are all doomed anyway," Merret sent.

"No," I said. "If you gather the others and go to the Beforetime ruins and remain there, you will be safe even if the plague does break out, so long as you allow no one to join you. It will be less than a moon before it will be over, because eventually a plague that kills everyone will kill all carriers. If you act quickly, you will have time enough to warn the rebels. But you need to tell them that unless they can convince or force the Councilmen to close their cities immediately, they had better ride out with supplies and set up desert camps away from everyone until it is over."

"You are going to stay to find Domick?" Merret guessed.

"I know where he is," I sent. "The man whose mind I showed you is helping me. He has a friend who has located Domick in a Faction house not far from the piers. I do not know whether he is a prisoner or a guest, but they promised to help me reach him. They say it will be best to act in the very early morning, for half the population will be abed, sleeping off tonight's indulgences."

"The city is a cesspit, because Councilman Kana is greedy and unscrupulous and will stoop to anything to line his pockets," said Merret in distaste.

"It does not matter," I said. "It is my intention that by midday tomorrow, with their help, I will be well away from Halfmoon Bay with Domick."

"This Erit is a child," Merret protested, for she had seen him in my mind.

"And what were we when we took over Obernewtyn?" I snapped. "Erit has already proven himself by finding out where Domick is staying."

"He and this metalworker know everything?"

"So far they know almost nothing. They think I am a rebel trying to rescue another rebel who has some sort of weapon. But tonight I will tell them that I am a Misfit, and I will tell them about the plague that Domick carries."

"You trust them." A statement rather than a question.

"Without their help, I would still be seeking Domick, for his mind is closed to me."

"Even so, I will ride to Halfmoon Bay. I can be there by tomorrow morning," Merret sent decisively.

"No," I said. "I need you to warn the others and the rebels."

"I can do both," Merret replied. "I am riding to Aborium to meet Gwynedd and some of the newer rebel leaders. All the original rebel leaders were killed in the Night of Blood, save Serba, Tardis, and Yavok. Then Yavok was murdered, Tardis died not a month after, and Gwynedd became the leader of what remains of the rebel network."

I did not bother to explain that I knew about Gwynedd saying only, "It is extremely fortunate that you are about to meet Gwynedd."

"Not truly," Merret responded. "We have been meeting once every sevenday this last twomonth."

"Then we are fortunate that this is the day. Tell Gwynedd that Dardelan would have come to their aid sooner, but all the ships were burned during the rebellion, and when the rebels built more, they, too, were destroyed, probably by Malik's men."

"I do not think Gwynedd will be much surprised by Malik's new treachery. No more am I. But though he will be interested to hear of what has been happening on Herder Isle, I think he and the other rebels will be more concerned about what you intend to do with Domick once you have him."

"I will ride with him out onto the plain on the other

60

side of the main road where there is no danger of anyone running into me by chance. Then I will make camp and care for him."

"But, Elspeth, if you are with him when the plague becomes contagious . . ." Merret began.

"Someone must be. Why should it not be me?" I said tersely. I knew that I could not avoid the heroic light that would be cast on my actions, but I was probably the only one who would survive the plague because of what the Agyllions had taught my body. I went on, "Tell Jak everything and see what he advises as treatment for Domick. If there are medicines that will ease his pain or heal him, you can leave them some distance from the camp, and I will walk out to get them."

"Elspeth, this is absurd. You cannot do this alone. As soon as I speak to Gwynedd and the others, I will come to Halfmoon Bay to help you. Blyss is already in Aborium, and she can ride back and speak with Jak."

I wanted to refuse, but in truth, I might need help. "Come, then, but remain outside the city. I will farseek you if necessary," I said, growing mentally exhausted now. It was always a battering business to sustain a far-sought conversation with a coercer. And sharing memories was tiring with anyone.

"Where are you now?" Merret asked as I was about to withdraw from her mind. I told her, and she said, "How strange that you should find your way to Stonehill, given that it was not where I told you it was."

"I don't understand," I said, unable to remember her ever mentioning Stonehill to me.

"I thought it was on the other side of Aborium," Merret said.

"We can speak of this later," I said, for I was becoming fuddled. I bade her ride safe and withdrew from her mind.

I rested for a time and, drowsing, found myself remembering a vision I had once had of Domick lying slumped in what I had thought was a Council cell, his hair long and matted, his body covered in sores and filth. I had no doubt now that the vision had been of Domick on Herder Isle or Norseland, and I wondered what Ariel had been doing to him all this time, given that he could not have been infecting him with plague.

At last thirst forced me to climb again, and it was not long before I reached the top of Stonehill. A gentle slope rose before me, covered in long grass that swished pleasantly in a slight wind. It was very dark, for the moon had risen behind a tattered veil of cloud and was only fitfully revealed, but I walked steadily, eager to reach a place where I could see the ocean. The wind grew stronger, and I was so intent on leaning into it that I was almost on them before I noticed the outline of buildings near the top of the slope. Drawing closer, I saw that they were ruins. I entered the nearest dwelling. There was no roof at all, and whatever had once been laid down as a floor had gone, too. But the grass growing there was soft, and I was delighted to see a pile of the brown rock that was used for fires on Herder Isle. All I needed were some twigs and dried grasses to start a fire, and I could cook the potatoes Erit had given me.

Once outside, I remembered that I wanted to see the ocean and continued up the slope until I reached the top. The hill flattened out and ran to a cliff edge where the stone looked as if a knife had sheared it off.

The moon was shining through the clouds onto the sea, and I stood for a long time looking at it and thinking of Ari-roth and Ari-noor and of Dragon and her mother and of Harwood and the others upon Herder Isle. But the wind that flowed from the sea was chilly, and soon I turned to head back to the ruins. I had one clear glimpse of them and the land about them before the moon vanished again, but I had seen enough to discern that the ruins were not merely a few buildings but a proper small settlement. I wondered why Erit had not mentioned it when he suggested I ride to the top of Stonehill. If there had once been a settlement here, there must be some easier way up the hill than the perilous path I had taken with Rawen.

In looking for some twigs to start a fire, I noticed a hollow to one side of the ruins that had once been walled. Within it grew the remains of a substantial orchard. Queerly shaped stumps were all that remained of the trees, all thickly distorted trunks with little branches. Dead, I guessed, the branches long ago broken off for firewood.

I headed toward the nearest gap in the wall, wondering why Halfmoon Bay had not been built about this hill. It would have provided a magnificent lookout and given the city true distinction.

Then the clouds shifted, and moonlight bathed the thick stumps in a light that transformed them into stone.

I GASPED, FOR even at that distance and in the moonlight, I recognized in the stone forms the work of Kasanda, who had once been D'rekta of the Twentyfamilies gypsies. That meant that the ruined buildings must be the first and only home of those gypsies before they had struck their safe passage agreement with the councilmen and become nomadic. If I was right, this was also the site of the school for stone workers that Swallow once told me about. Now I understood why Merret had made her cryptic comment about Stonehill. Hearing of my interest in statues, she had once told me that she had heard of a stone garden where sculptors were trained, built upon a sea cliff on the other side of Aborium. She had got the location wrong, but I recalled her saying that she wanted to visit the stone garden. I wondered why I could not remember her telling me about it. Then I realized that had been the last farsought conversation I had had with Merret before the Suggredoon closed.

I stopped dead, my heart beginning to race, for I was remembering the fourth line of clues that Kasanda had carved into the panels that had become the doors to Obernewtyn.

*"Who [would/must] enter the [sentinel/guard/
watcher] will seek the words in the house where my
son was born."*

Sentinel was the name of the Beforetime project
that had been set up to develop a worldwide retaliatory system of weaponmachines that would deal indiscriminately with any aggression between countries. But
something had gone wrong, and these weaponmachines
had brought about the Great White holocaust that
had destroyed the Beforetime and poisoned most of
the world. These were the weaponmachines I was to
find and render helpless. And if the clue meant what
it seemed clearly to say, words in these ruins would
help me gain access to the Beforetime complex without
harm.

As if in a dream, I turned back toward the ruined
buildings. Whatever message I found here must have
been carved during Cassy's time in the Land, yet the
clues on Obernewtyn's door panels had to have been
carved after Cassy had journeyed to Sador, for how
else could she have learned the gadi in which they had
been scibed? But if she had made the panels after she
went to Sador, how had they fallen into the hands of
the gypsies Louis Larkin had seen bringing them to
Obernewtyn? Was it possible that Cassy, now Kasanda
of Sador, had sent them back to the gypsies who had remained in the Land, and if that were so, why hadn't
Swallow mentioned that the revered Sadorian seer had
once been D'rekta of the Twentyfamilies gypsies? Or
had he known but not mentioned it to me?

Setting aside the puzzle, I looked about and tried to

envisage how the ruins had looked when they were whole and occupied. A number of smaller dwellings had been built in a semicircle, facing a larger building of which little remained. The larger building had most likely been communal: an eating place or maybe a sculpture hall. I methodically went through all the smaller buildings, checking what remained of the walls and patches of flagged floor, seeking the words Cassy had left for me.

I found none, though I did discover a well with a stone cauldron beside it between two of the huts. I drew up a bucket of icy water and drank thirstily, wondering again why a settlement with water and fertile ground in a desert land had been left abandoned after the Twentyfamilies gypsies had left. Pouring some water for Rawen into the stone cauldron, I continued searching the remaining smaller buildings and then inside and outside the walls of the larger building, but I found no carved words.

I went back to where I had left my bag, took out the potatoes and the battered tinderbox Erit had given me, and set to making a fire. When the brown rock glowed hotly, I pressed the potatoes into the embers, took a stick of lighted wood, and revisited the walls of the ruins to see if I had missed any small carved words, but still I found nothing.

The moon was shining brightly now, and the sight of the thirty or so statues glowing in the pallid light made the hair on my neck stir, for it came to me that the Cassy of my past dreams, whom I had seen commune with flamebirds and mourn her lover and fight with her parents, had once stood in this very place as a grown woman. She would not just have been a woman, but a

66

mother. An even stranger thought occurred to me. She had known my face as she stood here, for had she not carved it from glass in the Beforetime? And perhaps she had thought of me as she stood here with her little son in her arms. Or maybe she had thought of her friend the Red Queen, and the queen's brother, who had fathered the child. It struck me forcibly then, for the first time, that Cassy's bond with the queen's brother meant that her son was a distant cousin to Dragon! Was *that* why Cassy had dreamed of my meeting with Dragon *even before* she left the Red Queen's land? She must have, for why else would she have left something there for me that Dragon alone could reveal?

I thought of what I had seen in Dragon's Comatose mind. Her dying mother had bidden her remember the grave markers of the first Red Queen and her brother. The dream had been a vision dream, full of symbolic images, but I had no doubt that this part had been true. Dragon's mother had spoken of the grave markers of her ancestors, who had known Cassy.

I summoned from memory the sixth line from the Obernewtyn doors.

> That which will [open/access/reach] the darkest door lies where the [?] [waits/sleeps]. Strange is the keeping place of this dreadful [step/sign/thing], and all who knew it are dead save one who does not know what she knows. Seek her past. Only through her may you go where you have never been and must someday go. Danger. Beware. Dragon.

Despite being sure that the "one who did not know what she knows" was Dragon, there was still much in the clue that mystified me. But all at once it occurred to me that what Kasanda had left for me in the Red Queen's land might not be a thing but words, and if that was true, then the obvious place for the words would be on the grave marker of the Red Queen's brother. Indeed, what would be more natural than for Cassy to have sculpted a stone for the grave of her dead lover? But would she truly have been capable of using his grave to leave me a message? Perhaps it had been his sister who had suggested the stones, for Cassy must have spoken to her of the Seeker and the need for her ancestor to know that I would someday come to the Red Land to find the sign left for me.

I shivered and realized I had been standing as still as the statues before me. Thrusting my numb fingers under my arms, I went to look more closely at them. The nearest was a cloaked man and was less refined than the wall friezes Cassy had created in her latter days as Kasanda in the Sadorian Earthtemple but was more subtle than the glass form she had made for the Reichler Clinic foyer in the Beforetime. I bent to look at the base for any words carved there, but there was nothing but a faint *C*.

I went to another statue and then to others, stopping to study the faces as much as the stonework that shaped them, wondering if they had been people whom Cassy had known. From what Swallow had said, the workshop and school she had established here had been very successful in the early days, and in addition to the many ordinary young Landfolk who had come to learn Cassy's technique, many more had come to have their forms sculpted. Some of the stone figures were clearly Twentyfamilies gypsies, judging from their attire and facial characteristics. One, the statue of an older gypsy woman, had an expression of great pride but also a hint of stern sorrow.

Some of the pieces were not Cassy's, though it was clear she had taught the maker. And although these were fine, none surpassed the mastery of their teacher. Several of the better pieces were inscribed with an *E*, and I wondered who "E" had been.

In one corner, I came upon several groupings of children that seemed sentimental. These were not Cassy's work, and I guessed they had been done by her novices or acolytes, but in their midst was a statue that Cassy had obviously done, of a boy about Erit's age, posed in sitting position, hands clasped loosely about his knees. This boy lacked the tough, good-natured brashness that animated Erit's engaging face. He looked more vulnerable and reminded me somewhat of the Norse boy, Lark, whom I had met on the way to Herder Isle. I stood for a long time, marveling that Cassy had been able to capture the nature of a boy's yearning so well and so tenderly. It came to me that this might be Cassy's son, who had taken over the Twentyfamilies when she had left the land.

How had he felt, I wondered, when his mother had vanished? Swallow had told me once that, although many of the tribe had believed their D'rekta had been stolen away from the Land against her will, her son had always insisted that she had known she would be taken and had allowed it. If she had known what would come, she must have told her son, who went on to make the pact with the Council that had brought the Twentyfamilies to their nomadic existence. This enabled the gypsies to watch over and protect the messages and signs for me that she had strewn about the Land. Maybe Cassy's son had even distributed some of them.

Had he lost that gentle yearning once he became responsible for the Twentyfamilies, I wondered, and what had he yearned for as a youth anyway?

I left the statue and went farther down the field than I had gone before. There was more novice work here, but there was still the occasional form that could only have been wrought by Cassy. I came to the statue of a girl about my own age, standing and gazing into the middle distance, frowning slightly. She had lifted one hand as if to shade her eyes from the sun's glare, and like the statue of the boy, the face had been modeled with great care. Some moments passed before I realized that it seemed familiar. The person it resembled most was Hannah, whom I had just seen for the first time in a vision when I come to the west coast. It was curious that Cassy had chiseled Hannah as a girl, given they had not met until Hannah was middle-aged. Had she dreamed of her mentor as a younger woman? It might be so, for the likeness was not exact. The brows were wrong, and the mouth was more full then those of the older Hannah, the chin softer. Whatever it might lack in accuracy, the statue was an exquisitely rendered work that showed its maker's affection for the subject. Both the young woman and the boy had been posed gazing outward, but where the boy's expression had been poetic and full of yearning, the statue of the girl was characterized by determination and strength. It was as if she, unlike the boy, was looking for something very important and very specific. Certainly this was not the face of a dreamer.

70

I heard a sound and turned my head, expecting to see Rawen, but instead I saw a woman coming toward me, her face hidden in shadow. Stumbling backward in fright, I caught myself from falling by grasping the hand of the stone girl whose face I had been studying. The woman did not speak, and for one wild moment, I thought she was a ghost. Then I saw her face and my shock subsided, for I recognized the strong, willful face of Swallow's half sister, Iriny, whom I had once saved from burning, though she had cursed me for it.

"You!" I gasped.

"I," she agreed caustically, her odd two-colored eyes gleaming. "I gather that is your fire back there? Your potatoes."

"I . . . Yes. And there are apples and bread," I stammered, made foolish by astonishment. She quirked a brow, saying that if this was an invitation to nightmeal, she accepted, but we had better go back and rescue the potatoes, for they smelled well and truly done to her. Not until we reached the ruin and were out of the wind did I pull myself together enough to ask, "Iriny, however did you get here?"

"The plast suit," she said simply, kneeling and rolling the potatoes out of the fire with a stick. She knocked one toward me and set aside another to cool for herself. "The Master of Obernewtyn brought it the night he returned Darius to us. That was when we learned of the Herders' attempt to invade the Land with the help of the traitor Malik."

"How is Darius?" I interrupted, stupidly trying to open my potato when it was still too hot. "He was so ill when I saw him last."

She reached into the bag Erit had given me and

withdrew the dark loaf, tearing a piece and wolfing it down before she answered. "He was sick when I left, though your healer Kella was treating him." She shrugged and ripped off another piece of bread before handing me the loaf.

I tore off a piece and ate it, asking, "You used the plast suit to cross the Suggredoon? Why?"

I was thinking of Atthis, who had told me that she used Swallow, among others, to save me when I had been near death trying to cross the strait. It would not be the first time the D'rekta of the gypsies had saved my life at the behest of the seer.

Iriny said, "Swallow dreamed that one of us needed to come here. He said it was a matter of the ancient promises. He wanted to come himself, but the elders would not permit the D'rekta to put himself at such risk when he has yet to father a child to take his place." She gave a sour grin. "I volunteered to come, and the elders agreed. We needed a diversion to draw the attention of the watchers, so we used the rafts we had prepared for the day that we might cross the river again. Not to cross the river, for anyone trying that would be an easy target, rather, we stuffed clothes with straw and set them afire as we pushed them out into the water. It was night, and they made a wondrous bright diversion that let me slip unnoticed into the river wearing the suit.

"As soon as the soldierguards on this bank spotted the rafts, there was an uproar. I waited in some rocks until some of the soldierguards on the bank opposite me moved downriver slightly to see what was amiss, then I swam across. I am a good swimmer, and because the suit has a tube that enabled me to breathe while underwater, I did not have to expose myself."

She pulled out a knife and skewered her potato, deftly cutting it open and scooping out its steaming contents.

She went on. "The soldierguards soon realized the burning rafts were a diversion, but they were looking for an unlit raft carrying a spy, never imagining a person would immerse herself in the tainted water. In all the commotion, it was a simple matter to reach the barrier the soldierguards have set up to keep people from the old ferry crossing and slip over it, because of course it was designed to keep people out, rather than in.

"Once I had crossed the open space between the barrier and entered a rough sort of village, I knew no one would catch me. All I had to do was get rid of the suit, so I skirted the village and went some distance onto the open plain to bury it. Then I made my way back into the settlement and mingled with the folk there."

She leaned forward and flicked out two more potatoes from the embers. While they cooled, she went to get some water, saying that she had found herbs with which she could brew a hot drink.

Left alone by the fire, I ate one of the apples from the bag and thought of the first time I had seen the half-breed gypsy. She had been tied to a pole, yet she had dared taunt the Herder torturing her. I had intervened on impulse, spurred on by her courage, yet the act of saving her had brought me to Swallow. Almost every meeting with the D'rekta had been somehow connected to my role as the seeker, and in a sense, Swallow knew more about that part of me than any other human. And Iriny had come here at Swallow's insistence . . .

I stopped midbite and cursed myself for a fool, for surely he had sent Iriny here because Atthis had revealed to me that I would need someone to tell me exactly where the D'rekta's son had been born so I could find the sign Cassy had left here for me!

Iriny returned but before I could speak, she said, "I should tell you. Before I left, my brother told me that you are the one referred to in the ancient promises. That he told me violates the ancient promises, and it troubled me. But I guess now that he knew you would be here, and he sent me to give you aid. If my brother is right and you are truly the one to whom the ancient promises refer, it must be that the end days are here when all promises will be fulfilled. Therefore, I will serve you in whatever capacity you require."

I drew a deep breath and said, "As it happens, I do need help. I must find words that were carved where your first D'rekta's son was born. I think that one of the statues in the stone garden must have once stood in the house of your D'rekta, for I have searched the ruins and can find nothing on the walls . . ."

She was shaking her head. "Evander was not born here."

I gaped at her. "Isn't this the first and only settlement your people had in the Land?"

"It is, but the D'rekta's son was born in a rough hut constructed at the front of a cave in the base of Stonehill. It was built when my ancestors first came ashore, to shelter the D'rekta who was very near to her birthing time. They did not build atop Stonehill until later, after they had constructed the road. Not until the boy neared manhood did the D'rekta make a carving in the cave."

"Take me there," I said, half rising, but again she shook her head.

74

"A rockfall destroyed it just before my ancestors brought Evander here to die. When he learned of the avalanche, he commanded that the cave be dug out. But too much stone had fallen, and in the end, he carved the words from the cave into a stone and invoked the ancient promises when he bade the Twentyfamilies set the stone into his death cairn and tend it as if it were one of his mother's sacred carvings. He spoke at length to his son in private, to pass on what needed to be told, and thereafter, he died."

"Where is the cairn?" I asked with excitement, hardly able to believe that in the midst of all that had happened, when my quest was far from my thoughts, I had stumbled on another sign from Kasanda.

Iriny had risen, and now she took up a stick from the fire and went out into the night. I followed her past the walled stone garden. The night had gone still, as if the world held its breath in anticipation of what I was about to see. The cairn rose up out of the grass, formed from many rocks shaped and fitted together so perfectly that they needed no mortar to bind them. Iriny went around to the side of the cairn that faced the sea. The glow from embers at the stick's end allowed me to read the two groups of words carved into one of the stones. The first said that these words had first been carved in the cave where Evander had been born, and under them, in a more ornate script, was carved

I come unto thee, Sentinel. Judge my hand and let me pass, for all I have done was in your name.

"Do you know what the words mean?" I asked Iriny as we made our way back to the ruins.

"I do not know nor do I think the Twentyfamilies who made the cairn knew. Once I heard a seer say that the words in the cave referred to some infamous event that had happened in the past, but they did not say what it was, for the ancient promises instruct us never to speak of the days before our people came to the Red Queen's land. My brother may understand the meaning of the words, though, for each D'rekta has passed on his secrets to his successor through the generations."

As Iriny added brown rock to the fire, I asked what sickness Evander had died from.

"It was not sickness but an accident," she answered. "Our people had come from the highlands down to Sutrium to make the yearly tithe at the Councilcourt. There was a storm, and just as our wagons entered the city, a great shaft of lightning struck a building, setting its roof ablaze. Evander's horse was young, and it reared. Though he was a good rider, he fell, and it was a bad fall. At first it seemed that he would recover, but some weakness crept into his broken body, and he began to waste away. When the healers had done all they could, it is said he smiled and announced that he was glad, for he might now return at last to the only place where he had been truly happy, for that was where he would be buried. And he bade them bring him here."

"What if he had been killed immediately when he fell?" I asked curiously. "He would not have passed on his knowledge to his son."

She shook her head. "One of the seers would have warned him. It happened once with another D'rekta. A seer visioned that he would die suddenly, so he told his son what was needful. A sevenday later, he died during a firestorm."

"What if a D'rekta has no son?"

"Then his brother or sister or his daughter becomes D'rekta, and if there were none of these, the seers would have warned of that, and he would have adopted a son or daughter by the blood rites and passed on his knowledge. If the child was a babe, the knowledge would be passed to a guardian D'rekta. That, too, happened once. The seers named an old woman as the babe's guardian D'rekta."

I marveled at the determined fidelity of the gypsies to their vows as Iriny wiped her knife on the grass and put it away. I wiped my sooty fingers and thought of Evander calling Stonehill the only place where he had been truly happy. "I suppose Evander must have loved his mother very much, and that is why he wanted to come here at the end."

Iriny shrugged. "I think it would be an uncomfortable thing to have a mother so full of destiny and so preoccupied by a future that she and no one else could see. My father . . ." She stopped, licking her fingers. "Well, those who must love their duty have little left for other things, and the first D'rekta had a very great and terrible duty."

Her words made me wonder if Evander had meant that he had been happy on Stonehill because his boyhood had been free of that heavy duty he had been forced to assume as a young man. It was sad that his life had seemed an exile from his golden youth.

"Did you notice the carving of a girl shading her eyes?" asked the gypsy. I nodded. "She is not a

Twentyfamilies gypsy, but she came to the Land with my ancestors from the Red Queen's land as a toddler. It is said that the D'rekta loved her like a daughter and that Evander loved her, too, though apparently not as a brother loves a sister. She went away to the mountains after his mother was taken by slavers. Some say she went because Evander desired her and she felt toward him only sisterly love. Still others say she went to the mountains to seek her own mother. Whatever the truth of it, Evander sought her out whenever the Twentyfamilies' wanderings brought them near the place she settled in the highlands, but in the end he bonded and bore a child to a Twentyfamilies pureblood as he was duty-bound to do."

There was sadness in her face, and I knew she thought of her own halfbreed mother, set aside by Swallow's pureblood father for a Twentyfamilies girl when he was forced to become D'rekta after his brother died childless. Suddenly, Iriny rose to her feet, as lithe as a snake at the sound of hooves.

"It will be Rawen," I told her, and we went to greet the mare, who was drinking thirstily from the stone cauldron I had filled. I shaped a probe to tell her who Iriny was, but as I did so, I noticed that Iriny was making rudimentary beastspeaking signals to the mare.

"She does not know beastspeech," I said aloud, conveying the meaning of my words to Rawen. "We met in Morganna, and I suppose no beast has ever been there who knew it."

I was surprised when Rawen lifted her dripping muzzle and disagreed, commenting that some creatures in Morganna had spoken of a special sort of signaling some humans used to communicate with beasts, but she had thought it a myth. Then she asked if I still wanted to go back to Halfmoon Bay. That made me realize that I had not yet told Iriny about Ariel and Domick.

I told her as succinctly as I could of the overthrow of the Faction on Herder Isle and of Ariel's journey to the west coast to deliver someone whom he had deliberately infected with a deadly plague. Painfully, I explained my discovery that it was Domick, whom she had met. Iriny's frown deepened as my tale unfolded, but she did not interrupt. I concluded that I was going back to Halfmoon Bay to take Domick from the city before his sickness became infectious. "In case I fail, you should go to a safehold we Misfits have here until the plague runs its course, for all who contract it will die."

"I will remain with you and give what aid I can," Iriny said in a voice that brooked no argument.

I replied, "You understand that Domick might be contagious now."

"I will come with you," she reiterated simply.

Seeing that she would not be swayed, I suggested we descend. We did so using the road the Twentyfamilies had built, which was somewhat less precipitous than the path I had taken earlier.

"Evidently, they had some special device from the Beforetime that enabled them to cut through rock as if it were butter," Iriny said, explaining the impossible smoothness of the road spiraling down. She glanced at me and asked why the Herders wanted to kill all who lived on the west coast. "Are not their own people here as well?"

"I think the priests regard their order as more important than any individual priest, or even any cloister.

But it was the One who rules the Faction who desired this terrible thing, and he was a madman. Mind you, it was Ariel who shaped the notion in his mind." I looked at her to see if she understood who I meant, and she nodded. "As to why he would want to kill so many people, I cannot say. But he is defective, so perhaps it is foolish to try to come up with a rational reason for his actions."

"There is still reason in madness, though it be flawed," Iriny pointed out.

I shrugged. "In one of his fits, the One said something about the destruction of all life here being a wonderful example of Lud's power and wrath."

"But it would be the Herders' might that would be shown, *their* power."

"The One did not see it so, and if the other priests had known what he planned, I think many of them would have approved and called it Lud's judgment," I murmured. "Or maybe I should say that it would serve the Herders to see it so. The Herders preach that Lud made people in his image, though we are flawed and so must strive for perfection. But I think the Herders made Lud in their own image, to serve as scapegoat and excuse."

"How can people make Lud?" Iriny asked.

"I do not know, but look at the Lud of the Gadfians who regarded women as less than beasts and beasts as nothing. The men of that race believed that Lud made women for no other purpose than to beget and nurture more men who would worship Lud. As the men believed, so their Lud was said to believe, and if he disagreed, he never told anyone so."

"Did their Lud not desire the worship of women?"

I shrugged. "According to the Gadfians, Lud desired only fear and obedience from women, not love or worship. That is why the women and a few men left and formed a new exiled race in Sador. They rejected their ancestors' Land and Lud. And how should a Lud be left behind like a land from which one has sailed, unless he was no more than the invention of the men of that land?"

Iriny looked thoughtful. "Even if this Lud had some hand in the making of humankind, as the Herders preach, might not he have planted us like a gardener plants a seed, tending it for a time and then leaving it to grow as it will?"

"That is an interesting idea," I said. "But if there were such a Lud, I wonder what it would make of the intolerant Lud of the Gadfians or the punitive Lud of the Herders."

"It would not think of them at all," Iriny said.

Once at the base of Stonehill, Rawen, insisted she could carry both if us as long as we did not ask her to gallop, and we rode slowly to Halfmoon Bay. It was nearly four in the morning when I bade the mare stop and let us down. A quarter league from the city, I could hear the muted sounds of laughter and music as we dismounted, which suggested that many were still celebrating the coming masked moon fair in advance. Rawen cantered briskly away along the sand, promising not to stray too far so that she could come swiftly when I summoned her. Then we walked the rest of the way along the shore on foot. I had no fear that we might be seen, because the moon had set now and it was very dark.

The sea gate was not completely open when we

reached it, for waves still nibbled at the base of the wall, but I decided not to wait. When I turned to say as much to Iriny, I saw that she was already unlacing her sandals. I took off my own boots, wincing at the blisters on my heels, and followed her as she waded through the water around the end of the wall and into the city.

"What now?" Iriny asked after we had replaced our shoes.

"We will go to Rolf's house. Erit must have been delayed," I said. I had told her in more detail, as Rawen plodded along, all that had occurred in Halfmoon Bay before I had come to Stonehill.

The sound of boots marching in unison on the cobbles made us exchange one swift glance and then dive under the boardwalk that ran along the seaward edge of the city. When the tide was in, the waves would run right up under it, but now it was dry enough, though the sand was too wet to sit on, so we crouched down to wait.

I held my breath, listening as the boots came closer. Iriny lifted four fingers to indicate four walkers, and I rolled my eyes. Then there was the sound of wood thudding. The boots came to a halt almost directly over our heads, and I sent out a probe. That I could not reach the minds of any of the walkers told me they were soldierguards wearing demon bands. They began to speak of the morrow, one congratulating the other for having managed to be off duty on the first day of the masked moon fair. The other grumbled that women were much more inclined to smile at a man in uniform. Better if he had the last day of the fair off, having had the chance to flaunt himself first in his uniform. The other laughed, sneering at him for needing such trappings.

Iriny grimaced at their crude boasting, but I thought it better to listen to the utterances of fools than to have them looking about attentively. Once they had marched away, we decided to wait before coming out.

"This city has a bad feel to me," Iriny muttered. I asked if it had always been so, and she said that she had never been here before, which surprised me. She shrugged, saying, "I have been to Stonehill several times since my brother permitted halfbreeds to join the Twentyfamilies, but I never came into Halfmoon Bay. Swallow did, of course, and others of the tribe, for there was always a good market for our more complex and costly work here, but I do not enjoy cities."

Again we heard footsteps, but these were light and quick, and when I sent out a probe, I found Erit wondering where I was. Iriny and I emerged to find him standing a little distance away scratching his head. I called his name softly, and he swung round. His eyes widened at the sight of Iriny.

"You are a gypsy," he said when we approached, the bluish radiance of predawn slicking his ratty little dirt-streaked face.

"I am, and what sort of burrowing animal are you?" Iriny asked, sounding amused.

The boy bridled and stuck out his chin. "I am Erit and I'm not afraid of you."

"Good," Iriny said. "I am not afraid of you either. But I hope this house we are going to has something more than bread and potatoes, for I am fearfully hungry."

"There is no time to waste in gorging ourselves," I said, knowing it was mere hours now till midday and the start of the masked moon fair.

"We can do nothing until the sun has risen and the city begins to stir," Erit said.

"Aro has a plan, then?" I asked eagerly.

He nodded but said he would let Aro explain it. "Is she coming with us?" Erit asked, looking at Iriny. "I suppose you found her visiting their ghosts?"

"Ghosts?" I said, puzzled. "You mean the statues atop Stonehill?"

"The stone garden is said to be haunted by the ghouls of dead gypsies," he said.

That explained why no one else lived atop the hill, I thought. "Why did you tell me to go up there, if there are ghouls?" I asked as Erit turned and beckoned for us to follow.

He looked over his shoulder at me. "It is said the ghouls only drink the blood of those who are treacherous and evil-hearted."

I blinked, startled to realize that I had been tested.

✦ 5 ✦

IT WAS NOT far to Rolf's house, which stood at the end of a row of small dwellings. No light showed at the windows, but the moment Erit knocked, the door was opened by a woman so like Rolf that she could only be his sister. She was older by perhaps a decade, and her hair was gray-streaked where his was dark, but her smile had the same warmth as she bade us enter the main room before we introduced ourselves. Rolf was waiting there, sitting at a scrubbed wooden table, his face and hands clean and his hair combed. He urged us to sit, too, for he could not easily stand. We obeyed, and I introduced Iriny.

"I am Arolfic and this is my sister, Mona. Erit you have met, though probably he had not manners enough to offer his name to you, or ask yours," Rolf said in his rumbling voice.

"She is a gypsy," Erit said.

"I do have eyes enough to see it, boy," Rolf said. He looked at me. "I once heard that rebels across the Suggredoon have had some dealings with the Twentyfamilies."

"It is true. But Rolf, before we go on, I must tell you the truth about myself and the danger my friend

Domick poses to you and the west coast. My name is Elspeth Gordie, and I am a Misfit."

He shrugged. "I know that Misfits worked with the rebels. Indeed, I once heard the rebel leader Serba speak out passionately against those who regard them as lesser beings because they are different."

"Domick, whom we hope to rescue, is a Misfit, too. But some time ago, he was captured by the Herders. We did not know this until recently when I learned he had been delivered to Ariel, who is not a priest but serves them and is high in their councils. That is the blond man you saw bringing Domick from the *Black Ship*. When you spoke of seeing the man with him yesterday, I used my Talents to look at your memory. That was when I saw that the man with Ariel was Domick. That was why I was so shocked. Until that moment, I did not know the person I followed was a friend."

"But if you did not know, then why were you following him?" Rolf asked.

"Because I learned that the blond man, Ariel, had brought a man here from Herder Isle whom he meant to infect with a deadly plague that would spread to all who came into contact with him, once it became contagious. I know the west coast has endured plague before, but this will be worse, for all who contract it will die. I came to find the man Ariel had brought here, because I wanted to stop the plague."

Rolf's face had gone pale, and I saw that his sister had pressed a hand to her mouth in dismay.

"You said *once it became contagious*," Erit said.

I nodded, once again appreciating his quickness. "There is a delay of several days between when a person is infected and the moment he can infect others. Domick is infected, but there will be a few days before he can infect anyone else. The trouble is that we do not know the exact length of the delay or when Domick was infected. I think that Ariel brought Domick specifically to Halfmoon Bay because people come from every town on the coast to attend the masked moon fair and that means that the plague will spread so swiftly that no city will be able to close its gates to isolate itself. Since the moon fair begins today, and since Domick has not yet left the Faction house, I am assuming that the plague seeds he carries will not ripen until today at the soonest."

"You should have told us," Erit said accusingly.

"Now, boy," Rolf said soothingly. "Maybe she could have told us sooner, but I don't suppose she had any malicious reason for failing to do so." He looked at me. "It is hard to understand how a sickness can be carried about and dispensed like a patent medicine, yet if you are correct, it seems as if you might be right about the timing of this foul business, for Erit and his friends have learned that your Domick is to be escorted by the Hedra at the Faction house to the first-night festivities as a special envoy from the One. That will put him at the heart of the crowds for several hours, and although there will be feasts each night of the festival, this is always the best attended and most lavish, for it is when Councilman Kana will crown a masked moon king or queen."

"How did you learn this?" I asked Erit, who was scowling at the table. He glared at me.

"I talked to one of the kitchen maids. She told me about this queer priest over from Herder Isle who was to be a special envoy from the One and who would attend every event, starting with the first-night feast, to pass among the people and grant them Lud's blessing. She said she did not see how he could manage it, since he seemed quite mad. She thought it a pity the handsome fellow who had brought him was not to be the envoy." Erit looked suddenly at Rolf. "We will need a new plan."

Rolf nodded, saying to me, "I had thought to take your friend during the first-night's festivities, but I see now that we must take him as soon as possible. Erit, go over what you learned again and let me have a think."

Erit obliged. "The maid said the Hedra think your friend mad. She said the priests complain that he has not come out of his room at all since the handsome blond man had helped him into it. He will open his door only a crack to admit plain fruit and water. He has been offered bathing water but refuses it with the terror of a man being offered a mug of poison. She said she had heard his moans and shouts, even though her sleeping chamber is on the other side of the Faction house from the guest chambers."

"From what I heard of the last plague, lack of appetite and delirium are the first symptoms," I ventured.

Rolf's face had become set, and he glanced at his sister before nodding. "That is so, and most often this is followed by a period when the temperature drops almost to normal and it seems as if the person is recovering. That can last as much as a day before the temperature rises again, and this time there is nausea and vomiting, then fits. Once the buboes come, the end is near."

His detailed description indicated that he had seen plague victims in the last epidemic. I said, "One of our healers told me that the last plague became contagious at the vomiting stage. Since we know nothing of this plague, I am going to assume it is the same, and I wager, if it is possible to time it so well, that this period of seeming health will coincide with the time of the festivities tonight."

We were silent for a moment, and then Rolf said, "Tell me of your Misfit powers."

I swallowed my impatience and said, "I can read minds, though Misfits do not enter the minds of allies without permission except in matters of life and death. I judged it such a matter when I entered your mind to learn what the plague carrier looked like. As to my other Talents, once in the mind of another person, I can influence his or her actions. Also, I can pick locks and communicate with the minds of beasts."

"Useful skills, I imagine," Rolf said mildly, though his sister and Erit stared at me as if I had grown a second head. "Do you need to be looking at a person—or touching him—to enter his mind?"

"I need to be in physical contact only if the person I want to probe is asleep or if it is raining, for water inhibits our Talents," I said. "So does tainted ground."

"Can you not reach the mind of your friend, then, and make him come out?" Erit demanded.

"When you showed me the Faction house, I tried, but the walls of the Faction house are tainted with small amounts of Blacklands material," I said. "The Herders do it deliberately, because they know it blocks Misfit Talents. But even if I could reach his mind, I am sure Ariel will have left instructions with the Hedra to keep Domick inside until this evening."

"Can you reach your friend's mind when he emerges from the Faction house?"

"Unless he is wearing a demon band. Or unless Ariel has set up a block in his mind to make it impossible." Seeing the puzzlement on their faces, I explained about Ariel's block in Malik's mind and in the minds of the One and the Threes.

"You are saying he is a Misfit, too?" Rolf asked slowly.

"He is a defective Misfit with the ability to manipulate minds and emotions, and he sees things that have yet to happen," I said.

"I think we ought to use a message-taker like you were thinking yesterday," Erit said. "We send a message pretending to be from this Ariel, ordering Domick to be brought out of the Faction house to him. Then you can enter his mind and make him come to you."

Rolf said thoughtfully, "The message is a good idea, but even if he is able to leave, he will probably be escorted by Hedra, and they'll have to be dealt with. And there is another thing. You will have to be masked, because masks are worn from dawn today until dusk on the final day of the festival. If you are found unmasked, you will be co-opted as someone's festival slave for the day."

"But where can we get masks?" I said worriedly.

"There is no shortage of them in this house," Rolf murmured. He reached up and took his sister's hand. "You see, our sister Carryn was a gifted mask-maker. She died in the last plague, along with both her children and her bondmate."

"I am sorry," I said, appalled.

"Yes," Rolf said. "But we have masks here that

Carryn made for customers who perished in the plague. It is fitting that you will wear them to help prevent another plague."

"I will get the masks," said Mona, her eyes shining with tears.

"Do you have any idea how many Hedra will escort Domick?" Iriny spoke for the first time.

Rolf looked at her. "At least two," he answered. "Can you fight?"

"I can deal with two men," she said calmly.

Erit stared at her, fascinated, as Rolf asked, "What if there were more?"

She shrugged. "Then I will need help."

I saw Rolf relax and realized he had been testing Iriny to see if her words were empty boasts.

"I can fight, too," Erit put in eagerly.

Rolf shook his head. "I think that we had better avoid setting ourselves up for an open confrontation. What we need is a diversion that will allow Elspeth to spirit her friend away from his escort. One advantage is that they will not regard him as someone who would escape, for they think he is one of them."

"Will there be enough time to set up a diversion?" I asked worriedly.

Rolf smiled, and for a moment he looked very like Erit. "I will arrange the diversion."

"What if he refuses to come with you?" Erit said to me.

"We could use a sleep potion," Rolf told them. "I know of one so strong that the fumes will render him unconscious for a short time. Still, we will need to separate him from the Hedra to manage it. I assume your mind powers will enable you to deal with anyone who sees what is happening?"

"I can manage two or three but not at the same time," I said.

"Well and good," Rolf muttered. "Can you scribe the letter to Domick? A metalworker's hands are not fit for a quill. Better also scribe a covering letter to the Hedra who are to take him to the festivities this evening." As he spoke, he rose and hobbled across the kitchen to rummage in a cupboard. He withdrew a quill and some parchment. "Scribe that Domick is to be brought to the pier to collect a special gift from the One, which he is to present to Councilman Kana this evening. Ask the Hedra master of the house for an escort or two. That ought to waylay any suspicions."

By the time I had completed the letters, Mona had returned with a wicker basket filled with beautiful hand-painted boxes. As she began to unpack them reverently, Rolf took the letters from me and read through them, sealed both, and went to some trouble to make a mark that would pass for an identification stamp that had been damaged or worn away. "If the message is delivered by a reputable message-taker, it is less likely the seal will be scrutinized."

"If Domick is unconscious, how am I to get him out of the city?"

"I will have Golfur close by, my greathorse," Rolf said with a fleeting smile. "I have asked Erit to prepare a bundle of supplies, which will be lashed to Golfur's saddle. I will also have a canvas sheet and ropes ready to truss Domick up so we can lay him over the saddle and make him look like a carpet, and a few false parcels to lash atop him and hide his shape."

Overwhelmed with gratitude for his thoughtfulness and generosity, I apologized to Rolf for being unable to reimburse him for the supplies, but he interrupted to say that since I was ready to sacrifice my life to save his city, he could hardly begrudge me a bit of food and water. "Now I will also put Golfur's papers into his saddlebag, for you may be asked to produce them when you leave the city. Once you have no more need for him, you can return him to me."

I said awkwardly that Rolf ought not to lend me any horse, for I would not return it to him unless the beast wished it. "You see, we Misfits believe that beasts should not be owned by humans. If Golfur comes with me, it will be as a free horse."

Rolf laughed. "Bless you, lass, but a stolen horse is useless unless you can also steal his papers, and there is no time for that. Better to take Golfur, and if he wishes to be freed of my company, I will not oppose it. But you will discover his will soon enough if you truly can speak with beasts. That is a Talent I might envy," he added wistfully.

"When this is all over, I will teach you to communicate with beasts," I promised. "There is a language of signals that can be learned by men and beasts, which allows them to communicate. These were devised by a man who once ran the Aborium rebel cell."

"You speak of the Black Dog?" Rolf asked.

"You know him?" I asked eagerly.

"Regrettably, I did not meet him, for I was never a rebel, though I have given them aid from time to time. But I heard he was a good man."

Erit had returned, and Mona began to remove a series of exquisite masks from their boxes.

"They are very beautiful, but they are all masks for wealthy folk," I said.

"Not necessarily," Mona replied in her soft voice. "During the masked moon fair, there is much play upon deception and the wealthy delight in wearing their servants' clothes with a jeweled mask, or they will wear their own attire but have a cheap mask so that none can be sure of their status or their identity. They derive much hilarity from seeing their friends bow and scrape to a potboy or croon to a washer lass. Or even an urchin." She reached out and took a splendid, bright-red mask, enameled to a high gloss and sewn with shimmering jet beads, setting it on Erit's dirty face. The urchin offered us a wicked gap-toothed grin. The effect of such a smile with such a mask was as alarming as it was comical. Mona spread out other masks and bade Iriny and I choose our own.

Iriny selected a splendid yellow and gold creation that resembled the metal masks the soldierguards sometimes used to protect their faces during confrontations. I chose a dark green mask with emerald beading about slanted eye slits and beautifully realistic cat's ears, wondering what Maruman would make of it. Mona went out again and returned with a hooded green cloak of thick velvet, which she said I ought to wear until I mounted Golfur, for no one seeing a girl in a green velvet cloak and cat mask would think her the same as a simple lad riding a laden greathorse from the city. Uneasy about being given so much, when my gift to this house had been news of a potential catastrophe and a reminder of an old and painful tragedy, I said, "What if some harm comes to it?"

"Better that harm should come to a cloak than a

94

courageous young woman," Mona said with unexpected firmness. "Take it and wear it now. Return it to Rolf if you can. I will put those clod-stamping shoes you wear now into Golfur's saddlebags, for you must wear something more dainty with the cloak. Your feet are too big for my shoes, but Carryn's feet were bigger. Wait."

Again she withdrew, only to bring back a pair of leaf-green embroidered slippers as exquisite as the mask. Again I tried to refuse and again she stood firm.

"I am afraid you may as well give up," Rolf laughed. "For all her meek manner, she is a virago when crossed."

Despite everything, I laughed out loud to hear the gentle, soft-voiced Mona described in such a way. "I will take the cloak and the shoes and the mask, and you have my thanks for them," I said.

Mona smiled and Rolf kissed her on the cheek. Then he took a deep breath and said, "I think we must begin. Elspeth, you go with Erit to the message-taker's house and follow him to the Faction house. I assume you can use your powers to reach me?"

I nodded and bent down to remove my heavy shoes before stepping into Carryn's slippers. They were a little tight but very soft and well made. I bade Mona farewell then, knowing I would not see her again before I left the city, and donned my mask and cloak. Erit put on his, too, and we left the house together. The shutters on the windows had kept the sunlight out, and I blinked at the day's brightness.

The streets were already busy with servants and tradefolk bustling about, and all wore masks, though none so fine as the ones Erit and I had. It did not take us long to reach the message-taker's house with its winged shoe suspended above the door. I hung back in a shadowy doorway, pretending to empty a stone from a slipper, as Erit hammered at the front door and explained to the red-cheeked man who opened it that he had an urgent message for some Hedra. I had already probed the man, so I heard his thought that he would refuse the missives, because his head ached from the ale he had drunk the previous night, and anyway he did not like the Hedra.

Controlling a surge of annoyance, I forced him to accept the messages, and then I constructed a little web of fear, replacing Erit's image with Ariel's and dredging his memory until I had enough to construct a false memory of a meeting at the waterfront during which Ariel had given him the missives he would deliver to the Hedra. It was not a deeply bedded or particularly well-constructed memory, but it would serve when he was questioned, since I could not manipulate his answers to the Hedra's questions once he entered the house. I coerced him to deliver his message promptly, and it was not long after he closed the door on Erit that he came bursting out of it, still buttoning his vest. Erit had already left me, saying he would follow the message-taker across the roofs. He almost fell off the drainpipe he was climbing when he heard my voice in his head.

"How did you think I would communicate with you?" I asked.

"I did not think of it," Erit admitted sheepishly. "I thought you would just make me know what I was supposed to know."

I told him that was coercion rather than farseeking,

and Misfits did not coerce friends without their permission.

"I thought the message-taker was going to refuse the hire at first," Erit reflected as he watched the man from the rooftops.

"He was," I said. "I changed his mind for him."

I lost sight of the message-taker when he entered the street where the Faction house stood, for I had to backtrack to the little lane that was to be my vantage point. By the time I was in place, the message-taker was straightening his small half mask and knocking at the door. The door opened, and fleetingly, I saw in his mind an echo of the cold, stern face of the warrior priest who opened it. The Hedra demanded the message-taker's documents and studied them, then gestured for the missives. He broke the seal on one without looking closely at it, read it, and asked the message-taker to describe the man who had paid him. His mind dredged up the memory I had built, and he gave an unmistakable description of Ariel. The message-taker was discomfited by the interrogation and the Hedra's badgering manner, so I loosened my control and let him speak naturally. "Is something amiss, sirrah?"

The Hedra frowned. "This missive asks that one of the Herders staying here meets with the man who hired you, yet that same man bade me strictly to keep the Herder here until this evening, and as I understood it, he meant to travel on with the Raider."

"Perhaps the Raider will collect the blond man after performing some other errand up the coast," I made the message-taker say. "In any case, I have fulfilled my duty." He gave the bow of his calling and withdrew, and for a moment I had a clear view of the Hedra watching him march away, a preoccupied expression on his hard features. He closed the door, and there was nothing to do but wait.

I sent a probe after the message-taker, erasing his memory and grafting in its place another memory of having delivered a message nearby some days earlier. This done, I farsent Rolf to tell him what had happened. Mindful of the fright I had given Erit, I was careful to announce my presence. But Rolf welcomed me with an openness that startled me. I had just begun to describe the exchange between the message-taker and the Hedra when Erit gave a thin whistle from above. I looked up to see him pointing frantically in the direction of the Faction house where five Hedra had emerged with a hooded figure.

Certain it was Domick, I stretched out my mind to him, but as I had feared, he wore a demon band.

"Follow them!" Erit hissed, and I looked up to see him leap like a cat from one roof to another.

I set off back along the lane at a run, at the same time warning Iriny and Rolf that there were five Hedra, not two, and that Domick was demon-banded, which meant I could not coerce him. Fortunately, Rolf had had the foresight to give me a small bottle of sleep potion and a pad of cloth, though he had stressed that, if possible, it would be better to get him out of the market area on his own two feet. If it proved impossible, I was to summon Iriny to help carry him.

Rolf asked me to name the street I was on so that he could figure out which way we would enter the sea market. "That narrows it to two routes," the metalworker said after I told him I was on the Street of the Dancer. "How does your friend look?"

"He seems to be walking slowly, but he is hooded, so I cannot see his expression. He is not masked, though, and neither are the Hedra."

"None of the Faction mask themselves," Rolf explained.

The streets were busier now, and I guessed they would become busier still with each hour that passed. Even so, I stayed well back, for I did not want the Hedra to mark me. At one point, I lost sight of them when a small crowd of people spilled out of a door into my path, laughing and singing and reeling against one another. They were all masked and clearly had not yet finished celebrating the night before the fair. One of the men leered at me and caught me by the arm, but one of the women spat a curse at him, and he released me as if I had turned into hot embers.

I hurried on, probing Erit to find out where the Hedra had gone. In a few minutes, I had them in sight again, and Erit told me to let Rolf know they had taken the longer route. I obeyed.

Rolf told me to inform him when the Hedra had moved from the Street of the Fishmaid to the sea market. He also suggested I move closer to the group there, because a great throng of people would prevent the priests from noticing me and also keep them from moving too quickly. I needed to be ready to catch hold of Domick the moment Rolf created a diversion. I was to bring Domick to the Lane of the Weaver, next along from the Street of the Fishmaid, where Rolf would wait with Golfur.

I wanted to ask what the diversion would be, but a group of men arguing heatedly blocked my way, and I needed to concentrate to coerce my way through them. By the time I had done so, I had lost sight of the Hedra again. Once more, Erit directed me to them, just as the hooded figure stumbled and fell to his knees. The Hedra stopped and hauled Domick to his feet, and I felt a stab of pity for the coercer, who had suffered so much abuse. If only I could safely remove him from Halfmoon Bay. Then I was struck by the sad and dreadful irony of applying the word *safe* in any form to Domick, for there was no refuge or rescue or escape from the plague seeds multiplying in his blood. All the horror and danger the world had to offer had been planted inside him with only the leanest of hopes that Jak would know how to cure the plague, or at least slow its progress.

When I saw that we had reached the Street of the Fishmaid, I farsent Rolf, who asked me to warn Iriny. I found her pretending to consider the purchase of a knife from a trader and told her that Domick and the Hedra were just now entering the market.

My probe dislodged when Erit suddenly leapt down beside me, his eyes glittering through the slits of his mask. "Quick," he said. "We need to get close to the Hedra before Rolf gives the signal."

"What signal?" I asked, but Erit was already sprinting away. I raced after him, wishing I had asked Rolf more about the diversion.

The market looked almost exactly as it had the previous day, save that it was slightly more crowded and everybody but the small children wore a mask. For a moment, I could do nothing but stare until I remembered myself and began to edge and coerce my way through the masked revelers.

As the Hedra pushed more deeply into the crowd, they were forced to slow down, and soon I was near enough to hear them barking brusque instructions for people to move aside. Those in the crowd were trying to obey, but those behind were pressing forward to see what was happening.

"Any second," Erit hissed into my ear. "Get right up behind the Hedra *now*. The Lane of the Weaver is behind those two stalls." He pointed discreetly back the way we had come.

Too anxious to speak, I nodded and coerced two bird-masked men to draw apart so I could slip between them. I was close enough to Domick that I could have reached between the Hedra to touch him, when suddenly I heard a piercing whistle. Instantly, there was pandemonium. At first I thought the crowd had turned on the Hedra, but then I realized the commotion arose from some market stalls right next to us. It was hard to tell, for it seemed that a fight had broken out between two stallholders, but then one of Erit's urchin friends darted by with a big man pursuing him, screaming with rage.

Then it dawned on me that the hullabaloo was Rolf's doing. I remembered the bannock seller saying how much Rolf had done for other stallholders, and if I was right, the whistle must have been his signal. I could not imagine how so many people had agreed to help him in the short time since Erit and I had left his house. But as a diversion, the ruckus was impressive and very clever, for it would appear to have nothing to do with the Hedra.

Erit suddenly darted past me and gave the Hedra directly in front of me a hard blow before diving through the legs of the masses of people. The warrior priest snarled a curse and surged after him. He had drawn his metal-shod staff, and now he began to strike at people indiscriminately, driving them back. There was now no one between Domick and me but the remaining Hedra holding fast to his arm.

"Be ready," Iriny said, slipping past me. I did not see what she did to the Hedra, but he fell like a stone. I darted in and caught Domick's arm in the same place the Hedra had held him and drew him gently backward. To my intense relief, he came obediently, seemingly unaware that his keeper had changed.

Heart hammering, I managed to steer him toward the two stalls Erit had indicated, but to my dismay, three soldierguards stood at the end of the Lane of the Weaver, clearly trying to see what was going on. Not daring to show any hesitation that might awaken Domick to the fact that something had changed, I led him to the next street. It was the Lane of the Ropeman, and I farsought Rolf immediately. He bade me go along it to the nearest crossing road and turn left. He would meet me there as soon as he could. The quiet of the lane seemed to reach Domick, and he lifted his head.

He looked exactly as he had in Rolf's memory, his expression fixed in a rigid mask of horror, save that his deadly pallor was now accentuated by eyes bright with fever surrounded by bruise-dark circles. Something stirred in his expression, a muddy confusion. Was it the mask? I wondered, trying to decide if I ought to remove it and show myself to him.

"Where is . . . my master?" he mumbled.

Sickened by the knowledge that he could only mean Ariel, I said quickly, "He waits to speak with you."

"They . . . they said so. But he said I would not see him again. . . ."

"There has been a change of plans," I said with sudden inspiration. Clearly, I had hit the right note, for suddenly the muddiness gave way to a feverish excitement.

"Where is my master?" Domick demanded. His voice was louder now, and I realized that it was not Domick's voice I heard, yet the voice seemed strangely familiar.

"I will take you to him. Come," I said, drawing him along the lane. We had not gone more than a few steps before Domick wrenched himself out of my grasp.

I turned to face him. "What is the matter? We must hurry."

"I know you!" Domick cried, and he reached out and snatched the mask from my face. His face contorted in horror. "Elspeth Gordie! The beloved."

Confounded by his words, I stared at Domick. He was not the broken null I had expected, but he was not himself either. He had recognized my voice and my face, but why did he look at me with such violent revulsion? All expression in his face died, and he reached out to me. For one bewildered moment, I thought he meant to embrace me, but then he closed his hot hands about my neck. He was thin and gaunt and ill, but there was a sinewy strength left in him that crushed my throat. He brought his face close to mine, his breath foul, and I felt the heat of his fever like a blast from a fire pit.

"You will not interfere with my master's plans," he said. Grief and rage and terror shuddered over his features in maniacal progression, and then the blankness returned and he squeezed. "I am the instrument of my master!" he bellowed in my face, and even while I fought to tear his fingers from my neck, I was afraid of the noise he was making. I struggled hard, trying to claw Domick's hands to loosen their deadly grip, but they were slick with sweat, and I could not get any purchase. Shadows began to flutter at the edge of my vision.

Desperate, I struck out at Domick's face. He flinched instinctively, letting go of me with one hand. I caught the flying hand and clung to it, though the fingers of his other hand still dug into my throat.

"We were friends, Domick!" I rasped, now that I could get a bit of breath.

Domick flinched. Then he snarled, "Shut up! I am not Domick. Domick is dead. I am . . . I am Mika," Domick said, his fingers slackening slightly.

I stared at him in disbelief. I had been with Domick once when he had taken on his spy persona of Mika, and it had chilled me to see how much he became that cold arrogant man. Obviously, whatever Ariel had done to Domick had destroyed his mind so only this invented self remained. That was why I had recognized the voice and manner.

Suddenly, Domick's face blazed with anguish, and he threw me away from him so violently that I fell to my knees. By the time I had scrambled to my feet, he was running awkwardly along the lane away from the square. He had almost reached the crossroad when a man stepped out leading the biggest horse I had ever seen. He wore a simple mask of black inlaid with metal, but his powerful shoulders and wooden leg told me it was Rolf.

I could not cry out to him, so I beastspoke the startled horse. "I am ElspethInnle! Do not let the running funaga through!"

Domick seemed not even to see the enormous beast who lowered its great shaggy head and butted him backward into a door. His head struck it with a sickening crunch, and he crumpled unconscious at its base.

As I reached him, a woman opened the door and gaped down. Before she could scream, I coerced her ruthlessly and sent her back inside. Rolf knelt by me and bade me give him the sleep potion. He dribbled a few drops onto the pad and held it over the coercer's mouth. Rolf then fetched a length of canvas from Golfur's back and, unfurling it, rolled Domick onto it. He wrapped him up in a neat parcel, open at his head so he could breathe, and between us we lifted him onto Golfur's back. I would never have managed it without the metalworker, for the horse was even bigger than he had looked from a distance. I had thought the term *greathorse* was the name for a west coast breed, but now I realized it was merely a description. I dug in the saddlebags for my heavy shoes and the cap Erit had given me. There was also a simple mask to replace the distinctive cat mask. I removed the cloak. Exchanging the delicate slippers for my heavy shoes and retrieving the mask that Domick had knocked away, I wrapped them in the cloak.

In the meantime, Rolf arranged bundles and parcels on Golfur's back until Domick's form was all but concealed. "How is he?" the metalworker asked when he had finished.

"I don't know if he is infectious," I said, handing him the mask and slippers wrapped in the cloak.

Rolf shrugged. "I suppose we will know soon enough." He took the bundle and shot me an inquiring look. "You beastspoke Golfur to ask his aid?"

I nodded, glancing anxiously about us to make sure no one had entered the lane. Rolf shook his head in wonder, then looped his hands and bade me climb up onto the greathorse and go.

"Iriny . . ."

"I will make sure she is safe. You concentrate on your friend. Get him out of the city. If we live, I expect to have your story someday."

I put one foot into his hands, and he hoisted me up into the saddle.

"Thank you," I said with a rush of gratitude for this good man.

"Go!" Rolf said again, slapping the greathorse. The beast turned to administer a large affectionate lick before ambling off along the street. It was not a moment too soon, for even as we passed into a wider street, a troop of soldierguards came hurtling along, bristling with weapons.

✦ 6 ✦

To my relief, Golfur knew the way to the nearest gate, so I had no need to remember the instructions Rolf had given that morning. I had only to sit on his back as he moved through a crowd that parted to give him room and seemed to accept his size more readily than I could. As we made our stately progress through the streets, I calmed down enough to send a probe to Erit, who immediately began to crow with delight at hearing I was leaving the city with Domick. When I expressed my concern for the trouble I had left behind, he assured me with high good humor that the fracas in the market had abated as mysteriously as it had begun, leaving puzzled revelers and some furious and dismayed Hedra who were now ranting to a troop of soldierguards about the loss of a priest they had been escorting to the piers.

Erit explained that the signal Rolf had given was actually a long-established signal to all stallholders that one of their number was under threat. They had discovered that direct intervention, especially if soldierguards or Hedra were involved, would end up in the person trying to help being imprisoned, too. It had been Rolf's idea that if there was enough unrelated confusion, the person in difficulties would have a far better chance of slipping away. Each of the stallholders had come up with his or her own specialty when help was needed, and each could be evoked with a different signal.

I marveled at Rolf's cleverness and wondered that such a man could be a mere metalworker, yet in the end, a man was not his trade or craft. Erit went on to tell me that the soldierguards, who had raced to the market believing they were to face a violent rebel outbreak, were more amused than anything else by the anger of the haughty Hedra, for there was a niggling sort of rivalry between them. Naturally, the ill-concealed amusement of the soldierguards incensed the Hedra, just as it was meant to do. Now the Hedra captain was shouting at the soldierguard captain, Erit reported, demanding their help in finding Domick.

I left Erit and sought Iriny and Rolf. Failing to find them, I returned to Erit. The boy was still absorbed by the confrontation in the market. I bade him give my thanks to his urchin friends for their help and my regrets to Iriny that there had been no time to bid her a proper farewell. Then I withdrew and concentrated on what to do when we reached the gate.

I had no fear that there would be anyone looking for Domick when we passed through. It was too soon, and from what Erit said, the bad blood between the Hedra and the soldierguards would cause even greater delay. I ought to have been as elated as Erit at our success, but Domick's fever and grogginess made me fear that the plague might be nearer to becoming contagious than we had guessed. After all, we knew nothing about this disease.

Golfur ambled into another street, and I was surprised to see the gate. Only one man was waiting to leave with an empty cart, and he passed out even before we reached the gate. A great long line of people and horses and wagons waited to be admitted, and all of the soldierguards at the gate save one were tending them.

Beyond the gate, the tawny plain stretched away under an enameled blue sky unmarred by a single cloud, and I felt a surge of eagerness to be out in the open and away from the press of people and the reek of the squalid city. Even so, I beastspoke Golfur, asking him to slow down, for I wanted to try one last time to reach Rolf or Iriny. I still could not locate the metalworker, but this time when I sought Iriny, my probe located. To my horror, she was in the hands of the soldierguards, because several people had witnessed her striking the Hedra, and she was unmistakably a gypsy.

I cast about wildly, and this time I found Rolf. His serene mind calmed me.

"Do not think of turning back or waiting to see what happens," he warned me. "I have told you that I will take care of the gypsy. You must trust me and do what you need to do now, for if you fail, Iriny may as well die at the hands of the Hedra or soldierguards."

He was right. I sent, "I leave her in your hands, then. I am about to go through the gate. I just . . . I wanted to thank you again."

"You can do that in person when all of this is over."

"Good luck to you."

Drawing near the gate, I studied each of the four soldierguards. There was little urgency in their manner or voices, but they were thorough. There were no horses saddled and ready to give chase, and I made up my mind that if there was any trouble, I would ask Golfur to pretend to bolt through the soldierguards, and I would screech in pretended terror. With any luck, the soldierguards would laugh and give no thought to chasing after us, but even if they did, no normal horse could match the giant strides of the greathorse, however fleet of foot they were. I hoped fervently there would be no need for it, as I did not want to subject Domick to such a ride. Indeed, I was worried about how well he could breathe, trussed up as he was.

I was now close enough to the gate to hear one of the soldierguards demand trading papers from a man bringing in rugs from Port Oran. The mention of the city seemed to galvanize the soldierguards, who asked if he had seen any women traveling alone. At first I thought they must be seeking Rawen, but then one of the soldierguards spoke of an older woman with different-colored eyes and named her an assassin from the other side of the Suggredoon, and my heart almost stopped, for I realized it was *Iriny* they sought. Someone must have seen her at the river after all. Whatever order had been given concerning her must not have been circulated completely, else the soldierguards at the sea market would not be bandying words with the Hedra. But it would not be long before they learned who they had.

I was about to farseek Rolf when one of the soldierguards finally noticed me waiting and beckoned me. Biting my lip, I shook the reins, and Golfur ambled forward to stop before the gate.

"Dismount," ordered the soldierguard in a bored voice. I slithered down ignominiously, landing hard enough to jar my ankles painfully, and then I realized my fine escape plan of getting Golfur to bolt was useless, because how on earth was I to mount him without help? The soldierguard snapped his fingers, and I realized that he wanted the horse's papers. I dug them out of the saddlebag, hoping he would not notice that my hands were trembling, for he was standing right alongside Domick. If the coercer so much as sighed, we would be undone.

"What are you carrying?" asked the soldierguard at length, passing the papers back to me. He tapped at the parcel that was Domick.

"I am taking new leather to be worked to softness, dyed, and cut into belt lengths by grubbers. Once it is brought back, my master will create silver buckles and stamp a design into the leather that he will inlay with silver." I had concocted this tale on the way to the gate, but beads of sweat dampened my forehead, for the soldierguard was now resting his hand solidly on Domick. Growing desperate, I began to cast my eyes and mind out for someone who could create a diversion.

But the soldierguard shrugged. "Go on, then, and take care of that beast, for if he is harmed, I suppose your master will want you hide for his belts."

He roared laughing, and I was on the verge of walking out through the gate when a cold voice spoke behind me. "Wait." Both the soldierguard and I turned to face an older soldierguard whose yellow cape proclaimed him a captain.

"This horse is yours?" the captain demanded of me, flicking his fingers impatiently. Too frightened to speak in case he realized I was not a boy, I shook my head and handed him the papers.

"Hoy there, how long is this going to take?" someone called from the line outside the gate in a hectoring, impatient tone. The soldierguard captain turned to scowl at the queue.

"Who asks?"

No one answered, and the captain took a threatening step toward the line before noticing that he still held Golfur's papers. He turned and thrust them at me, telling me to be on my way, and then he began to lecture the waiting people. Did they think he was only here to check for traders trying to evade the city tax? No! Didn't anyone realize that there were no rebels in Halfmoon Bay precisely because the soldierguards were vigilant? Were they not aware that the three-day festival and the crowning of the masked king or queen would make the perfect target for a violent rebel scheme? As it was, a dangerous murderess had crossed the river and had been seen heading toward Port Oran.

Trembling with relief for myself and fear for Iriny, I led Golfur through the gate. The greathorse plodded steadily past the soldierguards and the people crowded at the entrance, none of whom seemed to find his appearance odd. I wished passionately that I could simply ride off, but absurdly, I could truly think of no way to mount the enormous horse. There was no alternative but to lead him along the waiting queue, which stretched for a good distance along the road. A cluster of makeshift stalls had been erected outside the gate, selling water bladders, pastries, and all manner of other things to those forced to wait in a long queue in the sun. Every stall also sold a selection of cheap and not so cheap masks for those who had forgotten them or had not brought one.

As we passed the last stall, I noticed a mound of rocks that I could possibly use as a mounting block. I led the greathorse to it, and spotting me, the stallholder observed in a friendly bellow that he would swear that was the greathorse of Aro the cripple.

I ignored him and muttered a curse under my breath, for the mound was not quite high enough. Gritting my teeth, I tried jumping from the top of the mound onto Golfur's back, but he was too tall, and I slipped back and only just managed not to topple from the rocks.

"Now, that must be the most inelegant attempt to mount a horse that I have ever witnessed," said a mocking voice. "You had better let me give you a leg up, young master."

I turned to see Merret grinning as she leapt down lightly from the back of a stocky, muscular white horse. In all the drama of taking Domick from the Hedra and escaping the city, not to mention what had happened on Stonehill, I had completely forgotten that she was coming to Halfmoon Bay. I was overjoyed to see her, but I dared not greet her openly with so many watching eyes. I meekly let her boost me into my seat. Then she mounted, too, and we rode on together casually. "You have him?" she farsent with painful force.

"He is under the packages with a canvas wrapped around him." I farsent my response with pointed gentleness. "Golfur—that is the name of this greathorse— had to knock him out, and we had to use sleep potion on him."

I said nothing more, having noticed two riders sitting motionless at the side of the road. I sensed they were watching us, and I was about to say so, when I recognized the coercer-knight Orys, though he now wore his hair in the Norse style, with side plaits. The other rider was the empath Blyss, who had been a fragile child when she left for the west coast. She had grown into a lissome, blond beauty with pale gold hair that was cropped short, so it flew about her head like pale feathers, and she was riding black Zidon, whom I had last seen ridden by Merret when they left Obernewtyn for the west coast. I beastspoke the horse with pleasure, but on the heels of my delight at seeing them all safe came a darker thought.

I glanced about to make sure there was no one close enough to hear me, and then I stopped Golfur some little distance from them and said loudly and clearly, "Blyss, Orys, I am more glad than you can imagine to see you are safe. But now you must ride away, for I am sure you all know that Ariel infected Domick with plague. Merret has already come so close that if Domick is contagious, she is doomed, but you are safe yet."

"Have no fear for us, Guildmistress," said Orys. "Dell foretold you contacting Merret and heard all that you told her about Domick, so she did a casting focused on him. She saw that although Ariel had intended and believed that Domick would become infectious today, he will not be capable of passing on the plague before dusk on the morrow. She bade me ride to Aborium at once, and I did so, arriving only shortly after Merret had told the rebels what she had learned from you. Dell asked me and Blyss to ride to Halfmoon Bay with Merret to escort you and Domick to the Beforetime ruins, where Jak can care for him without his sickness endangering anyone."

"What else did Dell foresee?" I asked, for the

futureteller was one of those whom Atthis had used to save me from drowning.

Merret shrugged. "That you would come out this gate closer to noon than dawn; that you would have Domick with you, and that you would need help. It is lucky for you that we came, too, for who else would have made that man in the queue shout at the soldier-guard?"

I said softly, "Merret, you know as well as I do that no futuretelling is ever absolutely set. Dell might be wrong about Domick not being infectious until tomorrow evening."

A ghost of a smile touched Orys's lips. "Dell said you would say that. She said to assure you that she checked her futuretelling about the course of Domick's sickness a dozen times."

Merret said, "We will camp at dusk. We will be on the main road by then."

"I would rather ride straight through," I said.

"I too. But Dell told Blyss that we must make camp at dusk, for a great troop of Hedra will ride out from Halfmoon Bay cloister then, searching for a woman of your description, last seen leading a missing Herder into a lane. Half of the Hedra will ride toward the Suggredoon, and the other half will go toward Murmroth. Apparently, every traveler with horse or cart will be searched, but Dell says they will initially ignore those camped, because no sane fugitive would blithely pitch a tent so near the scene of a crime. We have food and medicines to ease Domick, as well as fodder for the horses."

"Then we are well provisioned, for I have those things, too," I said sharply. Then I chided myself for my lack of gratitude. Dell had foreseen enough to send the help I needed, and it was wonderful to know that Domick was not infectious yet; better still, to know that Jak would be able to help him, for I had truly feared he would die.

We rode at an easy pace up to the main coast road, but there was no chance to talk properly because of the number of travelers we passed. It was easier to ride in silence, thinking our own thoughts. But when we reached the main road and began to make our way along it, I took the opportunity of a gap in the travelers to ask Merret what had happened when she had broken my news to Gwynedd. Domick had bruised my throat badly enough that it hurt to talk, but that was far less painful than enduring a farsought conversation with a coercer as strong as Merret.

"He was appalled, of course," Merret said. "They all were. But Gwynedd quelled the fuss by saying calmly that we Misfits have shown ourselves time and time again to be competent and honest, and that you were one of our leaders and had performed dangerous rescues many times over the years. He said that your Talents would aid you in finding Domick and that panicking was a waste of time. One of the others asked if he advised them to do nothing, and he said, 'Warn everyone of the attempt by the Herders on Herder Isle to start a plague that would kill Councilmen, Herder priests, and ordinary folk alike, leaving nothing but a barren wasteland, and prepare all rebel groups to evacuate the cities with their families and enough supplies to set up isolated desert camps.' Then Orys arrived with Dell's futuretelling that you would succeed."

"Did Gwynedd accept the futuretelling?"

Merret gave me an odd look. "You will find that the rebels here are a good deal more ready to accept our abilities and their benefits than many on the other side of the river. Maybe because so many of us died along with the rebels on the Night of Blood. Once Gwynedd told the rebels what Dell had seen, they began to talk of what else you had told me—the invasion of the Hedra and the overthrow of the Faction on Herder Isle. Which reminds me, Gwynedd is very keen to speak with you of what has been happening on Herder Isle. You know, of course, that he is a Norselander?"

I nodded.

"Guildmistress," Blyss broke in shyly, "I know there is much to tell of what has been happening here and on the other side of the river, yet it would please me—all of us—if you would give us news of Obernewtyn."

I obliged, speaking for a time of small matters as well as large. I told them of the powerful bond that had grown between Gavyn and the white dog Rasial and of Kella's tiny owl, Fey, that now rode on his shoulder. I told them of the Teknoguild house in the White Valley, with its lack of doors and floors, and of the opening of Jacob Obernewtyn's tomb. I told them of Dardelan's request that I journey to Sutrium to make formal charges against Malik and of the proposal that Obernewtyn become a village. Orys asked me about finding Rushton, and I was not sorry to have my tale interrupted by the arrival of a group of riders who galloped up and then slowed to match our pace.

A gray-haired man asked if we had heard of the gypsy assassin the rebels had dispatched across the river to kidnap a priest from Herder Isle sent to officiate at Halfmoon Bay's masked moon fair. I left Merret and

Orys to gossip with them and asked Golfur to move slightly ahead, telling myself I ought to be glad rumor had bypassed me. But I could not bear the thought that I might be the reason Iriny would suffer yet again at the hands of the Herders.

After a time, the newcomers set off again at a gallop, but almost at once we were overtaken by a portly man and his wife riding equally portly ponies. Once again, I left them to Merret and Orys and rode wrapped in silence until dusk fell and Merret announced that we would stop to make camp. She had chosen a place between two noisy groups of people already camped by the wayside, and while I understood that we were safer amidst these folk, I wished we might have camped alone. There was a tense moment while the couple contemplated joining us, but finally the wife said she would rather go on and sleep in a real bed.

Merret heaved a sigh of relief after they had ridden off, and she and Orys swiftly erected a dun-colored tent. By the time this was done, the sun had set. We carefully untied Domick's canvas-wrapped body and bore him inside the tent where Blyss had laid out a blanket and lit a lantern. As we laid him down, she went out to start a fire to boil some water, and Orys went to tend the horses, leaving Merret and me to unwrap the coercer. Loud laughter and snatches of song rose from the surrounding camps, and I was glad of it, for as we lifted Domick to slide the canvas out from under him, he moaned loudly.

Merret said, "If he is still like this when it begins to quiet down, I will visit both camps to see what news they offer and mention that we have a companion with terrible constipation." Catching my look of indignation, she shrugged. "It is better to have them laughing than suspicious, Elspeth, and Domick is in no position to feel humiliated."

I sighed. "I know you are right. It is just that he has suffered so." I was unfastening the small ties down the front of Domick's Herder tunic so we could remove it and cool him down. I glared with loathing at the demon band he wore, wishing I could unlock it, but the taint in it was simply too potent.

"Don't worry about the Demon band," Merret said. "Jak can remove it easily once we arrive." I nodded and pulled open Domick's Herder tunic. I was sickened to see that there was almost no flesh on his body without cuts or burns, and many of the scars were puckered and angry-looking, as if they had never properly healed. Blyss was just entering the tent again and gave a cry that was as much a reaction to our horror as to the savage scarring on the coercer's pale, emaciated torso.

"Hush," Merret said, leaping up to lay her long arm around the shoulders of the slender blond empath.

Orys looked into the tent worriedly, having heard Blyss cry out. He grimaced, seeing Domick's body. "I will bring in the water to clean him once it is boiled," he said, grim-faced, and withdrew.

His words had been directed at Blyss, who now came to kneel on the other side of the coercer. Brushing away tears, she slipped a woven bag from her shoulder and removed a pouch from it. It was a small but efficiently composed basic healer's kit such as Kella prepared for each of her guild. Except Blyss was an empath, not a healer. Yet there was no doubt that the instruments were hers and that she knew how to use them as she began to examine Domick's wounds.

Merret came to sit cross-legged beside me, saying softly, "We have had to turn our hands to many additional duties since we were cut off from the other part of the Land, Guildmistress. As you will see, Blyss has become a very competent healer." She smiled at the golden head bowed in concentration, and the tenderness in her eyes made me wonder what else had developed in the months of their isolation.

Once Domick had been cleaned and made as comfortable as possible, Blyss laid a damp cloth over his brow and another over his body to reduce his fever. Then she bade us go and eat, as she would take first watch. Outside, Orys had begun to prepare a stew, regretting the lack of bread. I suggested that there might be some in the parcels that Rolf had packed, and Merret offered to fetch it. When she returned, she handed Orys a loaf of dark bread, which he set about slicing. I excused myself, for I had just remembered Rawen. Shamed to have forgotten about her, I farsent her at once to invite her to join us, saying there was water and fodder aplenty as well as equine companions. She accepted eagerly, with no reproaches for my forgetfulness. Warning her to stay well away from the road, I withdrew.

The meal was not yet ready. Casting around for a way to distract myself from the memory of Domick's ravaged body and my fears for Iriny, I wandered to the horses and beastspoke with several, who told me of the freerunning herd that, on occasion, lent their aid to the funaga who dwelt in the Beforetime ruins, in exchange for water and fodder when grazing was sparse. I saw Ran, the white stallion who led the freerunning herd, in close conversation with Golfur as they champed on the hay Orys had put out for them. Curiosity made me open my mind to their communication, and I heard Ran urging the greathorse to join the freerunning herd, saying there were two other greathorses among them, both of whom were mares.

Golfur answered in a slow, deep mindvoice that he must return to Rolf, who was his little brother and would certainly get into difficulties without him. Ran was clearly struggling to understand how a funaga could be regarded as kin to a horse, and Golfur seemed entirely unmoved by the suggestion that he was a slave. I remembered Rolf's comments about the greathorse and thought that, whether or not the crippled metal-worker understood beastspeech, he certainly knew Golfur.

Rather than interrupt the conversation, I asked Sigund, the charcoal mare that Orys had ridden, to let Ran know that another mare would join them later, then I returned to the camp in time to hear Domick groan loudly. I strode across to the tent and entered it to find Blyss leaning over Domick, who was writhing horribly, his face twisting in agony.

"What is it?" I asked.

Blyss looked up at me, white-faced. "I am no true healer, such as Kella, but my empathy tells me that Domick is dreaming of what was done to him, and the memory is so deep and powerful that he feels the pain of his torture all over again."

"Is there nothing you can do?" I asked.

"I have done all I can for his body. If I had some sleep potion, I could use it to deepen his sleep so that he will not dream."

"Wait!" I cried, and withdrew the bottle Rolf had

given to me. The empath unstoppered the bottle and carefully dribbled a few drops onto a kerchief and held it over Domick's mouth, just as Rolf had done.

Coming out of the tent again, I heard the drumming of hooves approaching. Orys and Merret were gazing along the road toward the Suggredoon, as were the people in the adjoining camps. Soon the riders came into view, grim-faced Hedra who thundered past without stopping. A chill ran down my spine at the realization that if Dell had not warned us, we would have been overtaken and searched. I came to stand by Merret as we watched the darkness swallow the troop.

"We will break camp before dawn and head directly toward the Blacklands, taking care not to be seen," she said. "We will ride right to the badlands that run in a narrow strip along the edge of the Blacklands. There are mutated plants and shrubs that grow high enough to give us some cover. Then we will ride for the ruins, being careful to go slowly enough to raise no telltale dust."

"Because they will come back?" I asked, nodding after the riders.

Merret inclined her head. "Dell says they will be angry, and they will tear apart every camp beside the road, looking for Domick and for the woman who took him," she said.

As we ate the stew Orys had prepared, I told them about meeting Iriny and of the danger she now faced for helping me. "Rolf promised to help her, but he did not know she was being hunted for crossing the river, and now they think it is she who took Domick," I said.

"Do not trouble yourself," Merret said, "I will return

122

to Halfmoon Bay after I have brought you to the ruins. If nothing else, we should let these people who helped you know that they are safe from plague. I assume you told them about it?"

I nodded, and then I asked if she would take Golfur with her, because the greathorse wished to return to Rolf.

"This Rolf must be quite a man to impress a great-horse."

"He is," I said.

Orys offered me a bowl of dried fruit softened with hot water and sweetened with honey, saying how odd it was to think that Rushton and Dardelan and all those on the other side of the Suggredoon knew nothing of the plague threat or of Domick's part in it.

"Or mine," I murmured. "Unless Maryon has future-told it. But they will know it when the *Stormdancer* sails from Herder Isle." I thought of Yarrow and Asra and wondered if the Hedra master had surrendered yet.

"They will know of the plague, but they will not know we have Domick," Orys pointed out.

"I wonder if *they* know Iriny came across," Merret said thoughtfully. "From what you say, it was entirely a Twentyfamilies venture, yet the rebels must have seen the burning rafts. I must tell you that I am impressed that she got across the Suggredoon. We have been try-ing for months from this side." She stretched, her joints making loud popping noises. "You said that Iriny buried the plast suit she used. Perhaps it can be recov-ered, and we can use it to send a messenger to Dardelan, letting him know that we managed to pre-vent the outbreak of plague. I will speak of it to the gypsy when I go to Halfmoon Bay . . ." She trailed into silence as Orys threw some shrub wood onto the fire and went to relieve Blyss.

"How do you think the Council and the Herders here will react when they learn that those on Herder Isle have been overthrown?" I asked.

Merret prodded at the embers and said, "The Councilcourt will be pleased to discover they no longer need to dance to the Faction's tunes, for much of the Herders' power rests upon the fact that there are so many more of them just across the strait. The soldier-guards will be elated, because if you count Hedra and soldierguards here on the west coast, I would say the numbers are similar. It may even be that there are more soldierguards, but the Hedra are more deadly and dis-ciplined fighters."

"Are you saying they would clash?"

"I think that a war between them is inevitable," Merret said. "I would not lose sleep over the idea of their killing one another, except both sides will con-script ordinary folk to fight with them. We are nowhere near prepared to rise here, but we may have no choice if the soldierguards go to war against the Hedra."

"You speak of the soldierguards, but what of the Council in all this?" I asked.

"The truth is that their power always rested on that of the soldierguards and the terror invoked by the Faction," Merret said. "I think, though, that they will have to back the soldierguards simply because the Faction will have no use for them at all."

"There is another thing to consider," I said. "I told you of the weapons I saw in the Herder Compound armory. If demon bands were shipped here, why not weapons as well? If even some of the vile weapons I saw there are stored here in the cloisters, this war you speak of could be far more savage than anyone could imagine, and the likelihood is that the priests will win."

Blyss emerged from the tent and sat down wearily on a blanket Merret spread out for her. The coercer asked how Domick was, and Blyss answered that he was sleeping soundly and that his fever had fallen slightly. Merret solicitously filled a bowl with stew and gave it to her.

As the night wore on, I asked what had happened on the west coast following the closing of the Suggredoon. Merret replied that Serba had escaped and gone to warn the rebels on the other side of the river while Yavok and a few of his men survived simply because the rebel had been late collecting them for the meeting. Tardis survived, along with all of her people, only because Merret had ridden out to farseek a warning to the healer Kader. He had been stationed with the Murmroth rebel group, and Tardis had immediately commanded that all rebel haunts be abandoned. She then convened what came to be known as the Cloud Court: a meeting place that changed constantly. For a time, it looked as if Murmroth would be the rallying point for all rebels left on the west coast, but then Yavok was murdered by one of his own men, and the Murmroth rebel group under Tardis responded by closing ranks, rejecting all the rebels from outside Murmroth and ejecting Alun and even Kader, who had saved them.

"It was a sore point with Tardis that we refused to

divulge the location of our safe house, you see." Merret sighed. "In truth, while Tardis was not as fanatically prejudiced against Misfits as her father seems to have been, she did not feel comfortable around our kind and was glad of an excuse to cut the connection. So we Misfits who had survived retreated to the ruins to live as best we could and to wait, for we knew you would come eventually."

"It was a time of terror," Blyss whispered, her eyes unfocused as if she looked into the past. "The Council was not satisfied with having killed most rebels on the Night of Blood. They searched for survivors and killed them publicly and horribly whenever they found them, along with whoever had sheltered them. The Councilmen arrested and tortured anyone known to have sympathized with the rebel cause, and it became a crime even to voice any criticism of the Council. The torture of people resulted in more arrests and more torture, often of innocent people."

"The Herders were equally fervent in their search for Misfits," Merret said in a low voice. "They knew that we had helped the rebels, and they held services reviling mutants as damned creatures and demons, and they demanded ritual cursing. Anyone who did not show enough fervor was taken and interrogated, then burned for having Misfit sympathies. People attended as never before because to be absent was to be suspect. Also, hundreds of people who may or may not have had Misfit tendencies were burned after being reported by neighbors."

"It sounds hellish," I murmured.

"It was. The soldierguards who had fled across the river were enraged at having been forced to abandon their homes and families. They demanded an immediate offensive on the rebels, but the Councilmen refused. We later learned that the Herders had warned them not to invade until they were equipped to wipe the rebels off the face of the earth. I am sure the Councilmen took the Herders' advice, because only the priests' warning had prevented the rebels from taking over the west coast as well. And the Council readily accepted the Faction's offer of demon bands to protect all Councilmen and soldierguards against mutant possession. The soldierguards from the other side of the river were absorbed into the various city troops, and the Council set up the barrier and river watch. But the soldierguards from the other side of the river remained volatile, and their grievances added an unruly, dissatisfied element to a group that was already difficult to control. That the Hedra were openly contemptuous of them did not improve the relationship between the two groups. Nevertheless, for a time, the Council and the Faction settled into their old uneasy relationship, secure in the knowledge that the rebel network had been broken on the west coast and that no one could cross the river. Both poured their anger and energy and frustration into ensuring that no one would ever dare to rebel again. In a way they succeeded, until Tardis died and Gwynedd became the leader of the Murmroth rebels."

"I gather he made contact with you," I said.

"He wished to do so, but he knew only that we had a secret desert camp," Merret said. "It was chance alone that had me in Aborium foraging for information when one of the Aborium rebels I knew recognized me. She told me that Tardis was dead and that Gwynedd had taken over the rebel group in Murmroth. She said he had begun to resurrect the rebel network, contacting survivors, encouraging them to re-form proper cells with elected leaders, urging them to recruit new members. People were receptive, because they knew that most soldierguards were greedy for Salamander's bonuses. They were weary of their children and friends being arrested on the slightest pretext, especially if they looked healthy, and being taken away across the sea to be sold as slaves. She told me that Gwynedd wanted to communicate with us, so I rode to Murmroth to speak with him.

"Thus we began to work with the rebels. Their numbers began to grow after Gwynedd staged several operations with our aid to rescue prisoners from Councilcourt cells. We also attacked the Faction. Priests out to collect tithes were robbed and sent stumbling naked back to their cloisters, and the coin was used to buy the freedom of young men and women taken by the soldierguards. During many raids, rebels rescued groups of boys destined for the cloisters. The lads could not return to their homes, of course, but remote grubber farms began to have visits from distant cousins. Some of those saved remained in Murmroth and began to train as rebels under Gwynedd, whom they naturally revered," Merret said.

"Did the Council and the Faction realize all of their troubles were emanating from Murmroth?" I asked, curious.

"No," Merret said. "Gwynedd made sure we operated along the coast in all the towns and outside all cloisters. He knew a good deal about the Councilmen of the other coastal cities because of the information Seely had given him, so the Council was convinced there was another full network in operation, however much they might deny it publicly."

"I don't understand," I protested. "Tomash questioned Seely, and her information about the west coast was unusable."

"Useless to us because we knew too little about the west coast to fit Seely's idiosyncratic knowledge into any sort of framework that would give it meaning," Merret said. "But Gwynedd *has* the framework, and he also knew what questions to ask. It seems that Gavyn's father was very sociable, and both high-ranking citizens and Councilmen alike were his guests. Once he bonded with Lady Slawyna after Gavyn's mother died, he often had Herders visit as well, for his wife's son was a Herder. Being part of the household and yet also a servant of sorts meant Seely was in the perfect position to gather information and gossip." The coercer chuckled. "It is a nice irony that Seely has been the most useful of us to the rebels."

I smiled and wondered if becoming useful had altered Seely's shy diffidence.

"How do things stand now with the rebels?" I asked.

Merret shrugged. "As I have told you, there are too few of us for a proper uprising. Indeed, Gwynedd has never suggested wresting control with so few rebels. He seeks only to weaken the Faction and the Council as much as he can and to prepare us to aid Dardelan and the other rebels when they come for the west coast."

I wondered if Merret had any idea how often she included herself when she spoke of the rebels under

Gwynedd. Something in my expression seemed to convey my reserve, for she said mildly, "I do not think it a betrayal of Misfits to admire a man who has no Talent yet is gifted and honorable."

"What made you trust Gwynedd, given that he had served Tardis?" I asked.

Merret considered the question. "In part, it was that he insisted upon being taught Brydda's fingerspeech, and he encouraged all of his people to do the same. But the true moment of revelation came when it struck me that Gwynedd had never offered freedom to the horses with which he communicated. I wondered why until I realized that he never saw it as his to offer. From the first moment he communicated with them, he has regarded horses as fellow freedom fighters. 'When *we* are free,' he always says, to them and to us and to his own people. But I do not seek to convince you, Elspeth. You will judge him for yourself soon enough. Needless to say, he sees your arrival as a sign that we will soon rise against our oppressors."

I laughed without much amusement. "A meager sign since I am only one, and instead of coming on a ship, I was washed up on the beach like a piece of flotsam."

Merret shook her head. "If only one could come, who else should it be but you, Elspeth Gordie?" She laughed in faint exasperation at my uncomprehending look. "Think about what you have told me! You stopped the Hedra from invading the Land. You went to Herder Isle and defeated the Faction on its own territory. You rode a ship fish across the strait, found Domick, and brought him out of Halfmoon Bay before he could begin a plague."

"You exaggerate," I protested. "I did none of it alone!"

"No," Merret said, casting me a serious considering look. "No, it is never you alone, yet think how often you have been the pebble that begins the avalanche."

◆ 7 ◆

"ELSPETH?" BLYSS WHISPERED. "Merret said to wake you."

I sat up. It was very dark, but the stars were fading, so it must be near to dawn. The others moved about quietly, preparing to leave. I got up and folded my blanket, and Blyss took it to Orys to stow as I stepped into my ill-fitting shoes and drew on my cloak. My stomach rumbled, but I ignored it, for we had decided the previous night not to eat before we left. Merret and Orys were now dismantling the tent, and I asked Blyss softly where Domick was. She pointed to Golfur, and I realized they had created a pallet along the length of Golfur's broad back, upon which the coercer lay. A blanket had been laid over him, and when I reached up to tuck it in more securely under the ropes binding the pallet to the greathorse, I was dismayed by the heat radiating from Domick's body. Blyss had said the previous night that his temperature had dropped, but it seemed he was hotter than ever.

Someone nudged me, and I turned to find Rawen gazing at me. She looked a good deal less a fine young lady's horse than she had when I had first set eyes on her. Her coat was dull and dusty in patches, and her mane and tail were badly tangled, but her eyes sparkled as she told me that I was to ride her, since Golfur carried a burden already. I thanked her and would have mounted, but Merret called softly that we would walk at first.

As we crossed the road, I glanced along it in the direction of Murmroth and then in the direction of the Suggredoon, but there was no sign of movement. I wondered how long it would be before the Hedra returned. The people who had camped near us would speak of us when questioned, but Merret had spent some time the previous night coercing memories into key people in the groups, one of whom had us heading toward the ocean at about midnight, and another would swear to have seen us angling back toward Halfmoon Bay. I noticed Orys and Blyss carefully brushing away our tracks with swatches of cloth to disguise our true direction.

By the time Merret gave the command to ride, my heels were bleeding and painful. Before I mounted, I removed my heavy shoes with relief, pushing them into one of Golfur's saddlebags just in case I needed them.

We had spoken little while we walked, and we continued in silence, conscious that voices carried far on the plain, but soon we were approaching the fantastic and distorted shapes of vegetation on the badlands: bizarrely shaped giant shrubs and spiked green tubers rising above the ground. I had never been here before, and the reality defied any description I had heard of its strangeness. But it was a narrow enough strip that allowed me to see the dark jagged form of the immense mountain range that ran along the Blacklands.

Blyss rode up on Zidon to offer some small hard

twigs of food. "We will have a proper firstmeal a bit later, Merret says, but these will take the edge off your hunger," she promised.

I did feel uncomfortably hollow, so I took two of the graying twigs and crunched one gingerly. I was about to comment on its tastelessness when Blyss asked why Ariel and the Herders would unleash a plague on the west coast when so many of their own people would die as well.

"It is a question I have asked myself many times," I said. "There is no satisfactory answer. The One approved the plan, but Ariel was behind it."

"And the Raider approves?" Orys asked. "Surely he would rather have people alive so they can be sold as slaves?"

Before I could answer, Merret said, "Who knows truly what the Raider desires? With all the slaves he has traded, he must have amassed wealth enough for several lifetimes. And yet his slaving continues. At least it did until recently. So maybe his desire is not for coin."

"I think both he and Ariel gain pleasure from the suffering they cause," Orys said, nodding to Domick's prone form on Golfur's back. "And if hurting one person is pleasurable, imagine how much more delicious the suffering of thousands."

"Stop it!" Blyss whispered, white to the lips. "I have never heard anything so ugly."

"Forgive me," Orys said remorsefully. He looked at me. "I fear I have become somewhat obsessed with Salamander—the Raider as we have come to call him, like those on this coast. I have made it my business to try to learn more of him, and there are stories aplenty of his readiness to kill and maim."

"Tell me what you have learned," I said.

"That he is fanatically secretive and instinctively deadly and always seems to know if treachery is intended or if he is being lied to; that there are rules he seldom breaks; that his entire head and body are always covered, of course, and that these days he only comes ashore in a ship boat with an enormous mute to inspect the Council's offering. Then he gets aboard the ship boat, the mute rows him back out to his ship, and someone else comes to strike the bargain and load the slaves."

"We know most of this already," I said.

"Exactly," Orys said. "In all the months I have worked on trying to learn more about him, I have discovered almost nothing. And I wonder why he maintains such secrecy."

Conversation lapsed again for a time, and at length dawn broke. I watched birds pass across the silver-gray sky in arrowhead formations. Above, high skeins of cloud shifted constantly in a wind that slowly descended to scour the earth. There was sand enough in it that I was glad of the cover of the misshapen bushes and weirdly oversized plants, but eventually it was so strong that we stopped to tie cloths about our mouths and those of the horses. Gahltha had once told me horses had a hundred names for the wind, which could not possibly be translated into human speech. According to the stallion, funaga senses were too dull to pick up minuscule but important differences between degrees of dryness in the wind or slight shifts in angle or direction, or even the smells carried on the wind, all of which required a specific name.

We struggled on for another hour before Merret shouted that we must stop, for Ran had signaled to her that the wind was about to whip up a series of small but dangerous dust demons. Having no idea what these were, I dismounted hurriedly because of the tension in the coercer's voice and the speed with which Orys and Blyss reacted. I went to help untie Domick's pallet, but Merret said there was no time and signaled Golfur to get down. The other horses did the same, and Rawen took her place alongside the enormous Golfur, her skin twitching with excited apprehension. Orys and Merret quickly distributed blankets with ropes at the corners, which I was bidden to grasp as tightly as I could. By the time the dust demons struck, we were all huddled beneath the blankets.

For half an hour, we were buffeted but unharmed by a shrieking wind that wailed so loudly my ears hurt. I did not know what dust demons looked like, but their voices were dreadful.

Then the wailing stopped abruptly, and the wind was gone. Merret and Orys threw off the blankets and began shaking them free of dust and refolding them while the horses stood and shook themselves. All save Golfur, who knew what he carried and stood still as Blyss checked on Domick. None of the others seemed shaken by the dust-demon assault, but my legs still trembled as I stood and brushed away the fine powder of sand that had seeped through the blankets.

Merret suggested that we might as well have a bite to eat and wash the dust from our throats. Without ceremony, we ate rolls with cheese that we had prepared the night before and passed around a small bladder of water while the horses ate some oats and drank water from the wooden bowls Orys prepared.

I was eating and gazing absently across at the Blacklands when Blyss came to stand with me, asking, "You know what I think about when I see them?" I realized she was speaking of the Blackland mountain range and shook my head. "I think of how they are part of the same range that encircles Obernewtyn. You cannot imagine how I have sometimes missed greenness and misty rain."

"We even missed the snows of wintertime," Merret laughed, coming to stand beside Blyss and ruffling her flyaway golden curls.

Ran lifted his white head and whinnied. As he stamped and twitched his ears to explain to the others what he sensed, I impatiently entered his mind to find that the stallion could smell a host of riders moving back toward the Suggredoon.

Orys knelt down and pressed his ear to the ground, and he sat back on his heels and nodded. "Thirty riders, I'd say."

"The Hedra who rode toward Murmroth, by my guess," Merret said with satisfaction. "Now that they have passed, we can go more swiftly, for there will be no one to see our dust."

Two hours later, Domick began to groan and strain at his bonds, and I knew that the sleep potion was wearing off again. We stopped long enough to check the ties, and Blyss reluctantly administered another small dose from Rolf's bottle. When we rode on, the empath's expression was full of anxiety, and she admitted that Domick's fever had been mounting since morning and was now dangerously high. I suggested Orys ride ahead to warn Jak we were on our way, but Merret pointed out that Dell was likely to know exactly when we would come.

To take my mind off worrying about the coercer, I rode up beside Merret and asked her if Dell had dreamed of Matthew.

She gave me a sharp look of interest. "As a matter of fact, we have all dreamed of him at one time or another. Enough were true dreams for us to piece together that he is a slave in the Red Queen's land and has been trying to rally the people there to rise against the slave owners who occupy the Land. Only they refuse to rise because they believe they must wait for their queen to return. But Dell claims that it is Dragon whom Matthew is waiting for."

I took a deep breath, and on impulse, I spoke aloud for the first time of what I knew. "Dell is right," I said. "Dragon is the daughter of the Red Queen."

"What!" Merret cried, and the other two looked equally astounded.

"I went into her mind to try drawing her out of her coma, and I learned that it was the memory of her mother's death and betrayal that initially sent her into a coma—or rather her need to deal with the memory that she had repressed. Inside her mind, I saw her mother betrayed and stabbed by her advisor, and then she and Dragon were given to slavers with instructions that they be sold or thrown overboard. But something happened. Dragon's mother beastspoke whales that attacked the ship. She was dying even as she and Dragon entered the water. Then she summoned a ship fish and commanded it to take Dragon ashore. I believe the ship fish brought her to the west coast, and somehow she made her way to the ruins and lived there until we found her."

"It explains her fear of water," Orys said, shaking his head.

"Of course, that was a dream, so the real events might be rather different. Remember, she would have been younger and very frightened and confused. But my own dreams tell me that Matthew knows who Dragon is," I said. "At first he wanted to free the Red Land and come for Dragon, but now he wishes to fetch Dragon to the Red Land to fulfill the legend so the people there will overthrow their oppressors."

"We knew from Dell's futuretelling dreams that Dragon had awakened, but it was not until you offered me memories of all that transpired in Saithwold that I understood that her memory was flawed," Merret said.

"Kella and Roland say her memory will return, but even if it does not, I will ask Dardelan to send a ship to escort Dragon to the Red Queen's land. Perhaps the sight of her true home will remind Dragon of what she has forgotten."

Merret gave a shout, and I looked up to see the low broken walls of the Beforetime ruins.

After so long, it was strange to ride again into the grid of streets and piles of broken rubble remaining from the Beforetime settlement that had once stood here. Close to the edge of the ruins facing the Suggredoon, I noticed a square broken tower rising above the other buildings that I did not remember. It was ruined, yet surely there had been nothing so high when I had been here last. The others must have built it and made it look like a ruin, to serve as a lookout tower.

When I asked Merret, she grinned at me. "Fortunately, these west-coast folk are not as observant as you," she said. "They still think of these ruins as haunted, and we do all we can to support the legend Dragon began with her coerced visions."

As we neared the tower, I saw that there was a good solid lookout post atop a set of sturdy steps, hidden inside the corner where the two walls had been repaired. I farsought the lookout but found it empty.

The ground under the horses' hooves was now sand, and I remembered that from Aborium to Murmroth there were patches of true desert like those in Sador, and from time to time, dunes drifted slowly from these like slow strange nomads. It seemed that one had invaded the ruins some time past, for our passage, slow as it was, raised a gauzy cloud of fine sand, which the wind and sun spun into an opaque haze of gold.

We entered a narrow street and traveled single file, Merret in the lead on Ran, followed by Blyss on Zidon, Orys on Sigund, and Golfur behind them bearing Domick. I brought up the rear on Rawen. We passed a corner that stood at about the height of the horses' chests, the stone wall cracked and crumbling where a dry scrub grass had taken root, and it looked familiar. We were close to the central square where we had first dismounted years past, when I had come here with Pavo. How the discovery of the vast, dark Beforetime library had thrilled and astonished me. Since then, Teknoguild expeditions had come many times before the rebellion to gather more books, and I knew they now believed that the library was the very top level of a building that went deep beneath the earth. How deep, they had never been able to say, because they had been unable to access the other levels.

Looking around, I saw no sign of any settlement, save the broken tower. Not a smudge of smoke existed, nor anything else that would prompt someone riding past the ruins to investigate, and this made me wonder if Dell and the others had made their refuge beneath the ground in the library level. Or perhaps deeper. I asked Orys if they had managed to find a way into any of the levels beneath the library.

"We have entered all thirty levels below the surface," he answered blithely.

Thirty levels of books! I cried in disbelief.

"Not books," Orys said. "They were only on the first level. Dell says the building that housed the library was not a keeping place for books or a place to work, as most of the Beforetime buildings were. She thinks that the library existed only to hide the true purpose of the levels beneath, which were intended to house people in an emergency. There are sleeping chambers for more than three hundred, though they are very small, and there is a vast kitchen and eating area. Pretty much all the other space on the kitchen level and the next two is taken up with storerooms containing food enough for years."

"It was meant to be a refuge?" I managed to croak.

"It was, only no one ever came here for refuge. We found the bones of a single person in one bedroom, and Dell said that some bodies found on the upper levels were probably trapped when the Great White came. Jak thinks that is probably what happened to the man whose bones we found in the lower levels; he would have had no choice but to stay there."

I felt as if one of the dust demons from the plain had blown into my head. I wanted to think about what I had learned, but we were now approaching the central square. The last time I had seen it, it had been at night, and moonlight had given the broken walls and streets a ghostly look.

Lost in memory, I gasped as a column ahead of us moved, until I saw that it was Dell. She had been sitting atop a broken pillar watching our approach. Merret called out a greeting as the lean futureteller slipped from her perch and approached us. I saw with astonishment that she wore queer blue trousers in a fabric and design I had never seen before and enormous black boots, rather than the traditional beautifully dyed sweeping gowns and tunics favored by those of her guild. And she had cut her hair very short. But her cool, tranquil expression was unchanged by her months of exile, and as her pale eyes settled on me, I felt the same shiver of apprehension I always felt in the presence of a powerful futureteller, half fearing that she would make some dreadful pronouncement. At the same time, I longed to ask exactly what Atthis had said to solicit her aid in saving me from drowning. She merely gave me a formal bland greeting.

"It is good to see you safe," I said, dismounting and striving to appear at ease. She smiled and turned aside to watch as Merret and Orys took Domick's pallet from Golfur's back. I fetched out my clodhoppers, pulled them on, and straightened.

"Poor man," Dell murmured in her soft voice. "He has suffered much."

Seely appeared behind the futureteller, and I was startled to see that she wore exactly the same clothing as Dell, but her thin hair had grown, and now she had it plaited on either side of her face. Seeing me, she smiled and raised her hand, but her expression grew serious as her eyes settled on Domick, whose pallet the others had laid on the cobbles.

"Is Jak ready for him?" Dell asked.

"Of course," said Seely without looking away from Domick's gaunt face. Dell gestured to Merret, whereupon she and Orys lifted the pallet and bore it away carefully in the direction from which Seely had come. Dell suggested the younger woman go and help them with the doors, and she obeyed at once.

"Shall we go?" she asked me.

"We should tend to the horses," I said, for they were all still saddled save for Rawen. "There is also food in the saddlebags. . . ."

Dell smiled. "Pellis will be here in a moment to give them fodder and offer them a rubdown if they wish it."

"Pellis?" I asked, not recognizing the name.

"Merret found him. He is a Misfit. There are seven others who have joined us here since the Suggredoon closed, all children. They delight in tending the horses, for all except Pellis have learned Brydda's signal speech. Pellis does not need it, for he is a beastspeaker. But you will meet them soon enough." She strode away, obviously expecting me to follow, and I did so, wincing as the boots pressed against my blisters and realizing that, contrary to my expectations, Dell rather than Jak or Merret was leader of the library refuge. Her every gesture and word had the authority of leadership, and the others clearly accepted this. It seemed utterly uncharacteristic, for futuretellers were usually far too preoccupied by their inner worlds to bother with the real world.

Belatedly, I sent a probe back to Rawen promising my return and asking her to tell Golfur that I had not forgotten my promise to send him to Rolf.

Dell turned into a long street, which brought us to a labyrinth of broken and tumbledown walls. After wending our way through them, we reached a doorway that was almost intact and was in a bit of wall that, when I looked closely, appeared to have been rebuilt. It had been done subtly so it would not immediately be obvious to passersby. Through the door was the great pile of rubble that I had climbed with Pavo so long ago. At the top was the trapdoor that had led us to the Beforetime library. We had simply come to it from another direction.

At the square opening in the ground, I looked down at the metal steps I had last seen with Pavo. I looked up to find Dell watching me. But instead of speaking, she again made a slightly peremptory gesture, and I climbed down the steps.

Only when out of the daylight did I realize that some eldritch light source was illuminating the stairs. They led to a passage with smooth white walls extending in both directions. I knew from the last time I had been here that the passage led in one direction to vast vaults of books. Pavo, Kella, Jik, and I had gone that way, but Dell turned in the other direction, passing me to take the lead. I followed, remembering with a shudder the bones we had found. Pavo had speculated even then that the complexity of the locking mechanism we had released suggested the building's use as a refuge

144

for the Beforetimers. From what Orys said, that had been the building's true purpose. Obviously, the people whose bones we had found had not managed to enter the refuge before it had been locked.

Quite suddenly we came upon the others standing together in a group. At first I thought they had stopped to wait for us, but as we drew nearer, I saw their attention was fixed on a metal door set into the side of the passage. It met the edges of the wall so smoothly that I might not have noticed it if they had not stopped, but I wondered why the others did not open it. I would have asked, but even as I stopped beside Dell, I noticed that the metal door was humming softly. The metal split open, and each side slid into the wall to reveal a small chamber lit from above. I stared as the others crowded into the tiny space, arranging themselves carefully around Merret and Orys and the pallet they carried.

"Come," Dell said, and I entered the chamber, where there was barely room to move, let alone do anything else.

"I thought we were going to see Jak?" I said.

"We are," Dell answered calmly as the metal doors slid back to seal the opening.

I began to feel I could not breathe, being pressed into such a small space with other people, but Dell laid a hand on my shoulder. Then I realized that nobody else looked alarmed or even surprised. The chamber began to hum softly and vibrate, and I had the strange and terrifying sensation of falling. A heaviness filled my limbs, but before I could gather my wits enough to ask what was going on, the metal door split and slid away again.

I stepped out into the passage on trembling legs,

suppressing nausea. Merret, Orys, and Seely set off along the passage, but I caught Dell's arm just as the metal door closed again. "Why did we shut ourselves in there? Don't you know how ill Domick is?" I demanded, and heard the anger in my voice.

"That was an elevating chamber," Dell said mildly. "It has brought us to a passage on another level of the building. Look at the color of the light." She gestured to the walls, which I realized were now emanating a green light. "The chamber travels up and down the levels of this building through a vertical chute on thick ropes of twisted wire," she added.

"We are below the library level?" I asked incredulously.

She nodded, beginning to walk after the others. "To be precise, we are seventeen levels under it," Dell said. "The elevating chamber is very swift."

"We . . . we are *seventeen levels* under the earth?" I asked, my mouth drying out.

"You get used to it," Dell said lightly as we caught up with Seely.

"Jak will be waiting," Seely said, and set off again along the green-lit passage. As we followed her, I thought of my dream of Hannah and Cassy meeting for the first time. Hannah had brought Cassy to just such a shining metal door in the foyer of a Beforetime building, and they had stood waiting outside it just as we had waited in the passage. Had not Hannah even spoken of an elevating chamber? And certainly the Reichler Clinic Reception Center had been some floors above ground level.

We turned into another passage that led to a metal door marked with a yellow and black symbol. As we approached, the door slid into the wall to reveal a continuing corridor with a red line painted on the smooth floor. Jak stood there, speaking to Orys and Merret. He beckoned to Seely and bade her show them where they were to lay Domick. Then he greeted Dell and me, clasping my hands with a warmth that surprised me. Maybe Dell and Seely had not been the only ones changed by their time in exile.

"It is very good to see you, Elspeth," he said. "When Dell told me you had come here alone, with the help of a ship fish, I was amazed."

I was in no mood to speak of my journey, however amazing. "Jak, Domick . . ."

His expression became grave. "Yes. Let us go and see how he is."

He led me to an enormous room whose walls were lined with Beforetime machines such as I had seen in the Teknoguild cave, only there were ten times as many machines. What astonished me more than the number was that *several of the screens glowed with life.*

"How did you do this?" I whispered incredulously.

"Wait," Jak said gently, and I followed him into a circular room lined with glass chambers and centered around a large computermachine. Each chamber was brightly lit and contained an identical flat, hard-looking white bench rising on a single metal stalk. Beside it stood a metal construction as tall as a man and incongruously fitted with four great hinged arms, each ending in a different tool. All of this so astonished me that it was a moment before I saw that Domick had been laid out on a bench.

Seely was inside, removing Domick's clothes, and I heard her gasp when we saw the extent of the scarring on his body. Orys and Merret turned away, the latter saying she would clean up, eat, and sleep a few hours before riding back to Halfmoon Bay to check on Iriny. I thanked her and noticed that Dell had already slipped away. Her cat-footedness had not changed.

"The Beforetimers called this a biohazard laboratory," Jak said, speaking these strange words with ease. "Each chamber can be completely sealed off, for it has its own air supply. That machine alongside the bed can be made to administer food and medicines and even various treatments, as well as carry away waste."

He looked at me to see that I understood, and I nodded.

"Once the plague becomes contagious," Jak continued, "we can care for Domick and speak to him, and we will not catch the plague so long as he remains within the chamber."

"How can that feed him?" I asked, pointing to the metal construction.

"He will be fed nourishing liquids through tiny tubes that fit into the ends of needles, which are inserted into the veins inside his arms," Jak said. I gaped at him, and he laughed slightly. "Forgive me. You must find this very bewildering. It is hard to find simple words to explain the wonders in this room, let alone the levels of this incredible place."

Seely called out, and Jak muttered an appalled exclamation when he caught sight of Domick's ravaged naked form.

"Shall I wash him?" Seely asked Jak, her voice echoing oddly in the glass chamber.

"There is no danger yet, Dell says, but let us seal the chamber and show Elspeth what Pavo can do."

"Pavo?" I echoed faintly.

He pointed to the tall machine beside Domick. Seely emerged from the chamber and closed the door. Jak went over to the computermachine in the center of the room, slid into a chair, and began to tap at the letters laid out in lines.

"Watch," Seely instructed, pointing to the chamber where Domick lay. I turned again to see the tall machine unfolding its arms like some sort of metal mantis. When it leaned over the unconscious coercer, I held my breath, for it looked so cruel and ugly, but the plast hand reached out silently and, with startling delicacy, removed the sheet. Then it ran its hand over Domick's body with infinite gentleness, and where the hand went, water and soap suds flowed, running off him and drawn away by narrow runnels carved into the white bench. The water flow eased to a trickle when the hand smoothed over his face and increased again when it touched the black stubble on his head. Then the water ceased altogether, and the plast hand lifted and moved over him again without making contact. I realized that air must be flowing from the hand, for soon Domick was completely dry. The hand gently replaced the sheet and withdrew. Not until it stopped did I recognize that my face was wet with tears. I hardly knew why, save that he looked so utterly lost and vulnerable lying in the glass chamber. Brushing the tears impatiently away, I turned to look at Jak.

"As well as washing him, Pavo has been taking his temperature and making various small tests. But we will have him conduct some more complex tests and take some blood to learn more of this plague." His words were for me, but his eyes were fixed on the glowing face of the computermachine.

I looked into the glass chamber and saw the plast hand attaching small flat circles of what looked like plast to Domick's forehead, his chest, and the insides of his wrists. Each circle had a thin plast line attached to it, which coiled back to the tall machine. I gasped to see another of the metal hands insert a shining metal spike into the crook of Domick's thin, scarred arm, but Seely laid a light hand on my arm, saying, "Do not worry, Guildmistress Elspeth. Pavo will be far gentler than any of us could be. I know, for I was brought here when I broke a bone in one of my legs."

I stared at her, in awe of the fact that she and the others had been living among these machines and artifacts of the Beforetime for many months, learning how to use them.

"Now Pavo is taking some blood," Seely said, and I watched in horrified fascination as the plast hand inserted another spike into Domick's other arm, and the plast tube turned red as his blood began to dribble through it. I noticed now that transparent straps lightly attached Domick's wrists, ankles, and forehead to the bed, and while I knew these prevented him from moving and hurting himself, it ached me to see him bound up as must have been his fate at Ariel's hands. If he woke . . .

"The blood will tell us what sort of sickness Domick has been infected with," Seely said.

"Jak is controlling that?" I asked, pointing to the machine tending Domick, because I could not bring myself to call something so ugly by the name of my old friend.

"Jak could control Pavo manually using the computermachine," Seely answered. "But mostly it is better to leave it to Pavo, for he knows a great deal more than even Jak. You might say that Pavo is deciding what to do and Jak is agreeing."

I stared at Seely, for she had spoken of the machine as if it were a live creature.

Jak came to my side. "The air in the chamber is being heated to exactly the right level that is needed. Domick's fever is high now, and Pavo is administering various potions that will help to cool it."

"How does the machine know what is needed?"

"It is designed to heal. In a way, it *is* a healer, but you have to tell it to heal and agree to its suggested treatments. In Domick's case, I have asked it to examine the blood being taken and look into its memory to find out if it has any record of the same sickness so it will know how to treat it. If it is a Beforetime sickness, as Dell says, we will soon discover its nature, for Pavo's memory contains knowledge of all the Beforetime sicknesses. Although Pavo is swift, the records to which it has access are impossibly vast, so it will take some time."

"How did you figure out how to use this place? That elevating chamber . . . ?" So many questions clamored to be answered.

Jak laughed. "I daresay you did not like your first experience in it. We would not have been able to operate any of this, of course, without the computer-machines. Fortunately, computermachines remember everything, and once you can make a computer-machine work, it can tell you how to use it better. *It can teach.* You don't even need specialized knowledge. You can ask questions every step of the way. Of course, communicating with computermachines is no simple matter, because a computermachine can only answer in the words it knows, and it can only understand questions put to it in words it will understand."

"You are saying that *computermachines* taught you how to work the lights and the elevating chamber and this machine? But how did you make the computermachines work?"

"We did not have to make them work. They were working all along. Their power source is buried deep under all the levels of this place, and *it was never switched off*. Once we learned to communicate in a way that the computermachines could understand, we had the means of learning everything we needed to know. Of course, a lot of our discoveries were pure accidents, because while the computermachines could answer most questions, they could not tell us which questions we failed to ask.

"For instance, initially we used a long and exhausting set of metal steps to go from one level to the other. I set up a bed here, rather than running up and down the levels. Then I thought about it and realized that Beforetimers clever enough to create all of this would surely not have traipsed up and down so many steps. So I asked the computermachine how else I could reach the surface, and it told me about the elevating chamber. As you can imagine, I had not the slightest notion what an elevator was, but with persistence and lots of questions, I finally understood the gist of it. Nevertheless, that first trip was extremely horrible."

"Seely said you have used these chambers to heal on other occasions," I said, noticing that the girl had slipped out.

"Many times," Jak said comfortably. "We have never had to seal the room before, though. Indeed, I did not know that was possible until I began asking questions to prepare for Domick's arrival. Poor wretch," he added, and flung a look at the pale coercer. "I have had the computermachine produce all the information it can about such sicknesses. Apparently, plagues are ancient Beforetime sicknesses that had been wiped out long before the Great White—until some Beforetimer had the bright idea of resurrecting them to study their effects. It seems incredible that the fools would choose to wake such lethal diseases merely to study them. There must be some limit on the pursuit of knowledge."

"Garth would be surprised to hear you say that," I said.

He gave me a startled look, then frowned and nodded. "Maybe he would. But all of this changes a person, Elspeth."

He moved back to the computermachine, and I watched him tap the rows of small numbers and letters scribed on squares in the tray before the screen, aware that this was how he spoke to the computermachines. I had seen it done before in the caves of the Teknoguild, but again I marveled that spelled-out words could be understood and responded to by something that was only metal and plast.

"Domick's chamber is now completely sealed," Jak said after some moments. "No one will enter the room until he is healed."

I looked at the coercer again and gasped to see bars of plast emerge from the side of the white bench and move lightly over his torso to fasten themselves on the other side. Then the plast hand drew a white cloth over him.

"He is like to become restless because of the fever, and the straps will keep him from throwing himself off the bed. There are also things in that strap—I do not understand what, exactly, that will feed constant information to Pavo and help him tend to Domick's needs." He frowned at the screen in concentration, then he turned to me. "He has been drugged?"

I nodded and explained about Rolf's sleep potion.

"It has done no harm to him, but I have asked the computermachine to tell me what it is made from, just in case. Did you speak with Domick before you gave it to him?"

I told him what had taken place in the sea market and in the lane, concluding, "He remained unconscious from then, because we were giving him the potion."

"So he spoke in the voice of his spy persona," Jak said. "That is strange, but I suppose the fever made him hallucinate."

"Is there any way to get the demon band off him?" I asked. "Once he wakes, I would like to be able to probe him, if he is unable to speak to me."

Jak nodded. "I have sent Seely to get a key. Dell has one, but she must not have foreseen that he would be wearing a demon band."

"But you said the chamber is sealed."

"We can put the key into a tiny drawer from which all air can be drawn, and then push it into the larger chamber where Pavo can take and use it," Jak said. "However, as far as being able to question him, I am afraid he is unlikely to wake naturally for some hours, unless you want me to force it?"

I shook my head.

"Good. His body has been savaged enough. Why don't you go rest? A sleeping chamber has been prepared for you, and I will send for you the moment there is anything to tell."

I shook my head. "I will stay here in case he wakes."

Jak sighed. "Very well. There is a chair over there. Drag it over to the chamber and keep watch. I must work in another room, but don't worry—Pavo will watch over Domick." He added gently, "It is not your fault that this happened to Domick."

Is it not? I wondered bleakly after he had gone. Whatever Ariel had done to Domick, we at Obernewtyn had begun the harm by allowing him to spy, even after it had become clear that it was affecting him badly.

Suddenly the chamber's blinding white light dimmed and turned a soft rose. Whether the computermachine or Jak had changed the light, I was relieved. I sat back in my seat and wondered why I was not cold, so deep under the earth. Doubtless, Jak had asked a computermachine to make the air warmer. How comfortable he seemed amidst the machines and instruments of a lost age. And it was not only the teknoguilder; Dell was the same. "You get used to it," she had said of the elevating chamber. And Seely seemed not only confident in her new surrounds but also content. She had lost her tremulous uncertainty, blossoming into a quiet, competent young woman with steady hands.

Domick moaned, and I leapt to my feet, my heart thudding hard against my ribs. Misty ghost hands formed where I rested my hands against the glass, and my mind raced as I tried to think what to say to the coercer. But his eyes remained shut.

He moaned again and writhed, and the machine reached out its plast hand to touch a circle that must have been loosened by the coercer's movement. Again Domick stirred restlessly, rocking his head from side to side. I watched, fascinated, as bolsters rose slowly from the bed on either side of his head to cushion the movement. He fell quiet again, and after a time, I sat back down.

This time when I relaxed, fatigue flowed through me, and my eyes began to close. Despite willing myself to stay awake, each blink seemed longer than the one before, and it was harder and harder to open my eyes. My mind was beginning to drift. I thought about Rolf, Erit, and Iriny, and I hoped they were safe. Had Merret left yet for Halfmoon Bay? No, she had said she would sleep and go early in the morning. Besides, I had yet to tell her how to find Rolf. I leaned my head against the glass and looked at Domick's glowing white body. How dark his brows and lashes seemed in that gaunt, bone-white face.

I must have slipped into a dreamless slumber sitting like that, for the sound of steps coming lightly toward me wakened me. It was Seely with a tray of food, and I wondered how she managed to walk so lightly in her heavy boots. "Perhaps you do not feel hungry, Guildmistress, but you ought to eat," she said, and without waiting for an answer, she set down the tray on the floor beside me. Instead of leaving me, she moved closer to the glass to gaze through it at Domick.

"Kella used to talk about him sometimes when I was back at Obernewtyn," she said softly. "I wonder what happened to bring him into the hands of the Herders."

"When he recovers, he will tell us," I said, realizing

that the others were probably discussing such questions over a meal. I pictured them, sitting in a room with a warm light and the scents of food, speculating. Most of all, they would be relieved that the threat of plague had been averted, elated that their time of exile might be nearly over. I envied their comradeship and closeness, but I did not truly yearn to join them. The sight of Domick lying so still and wounded by all that had befallen him made it impossible to contemplate talking and laughing and eating.

"Jak is in one of the other laboratories," Seely said, turning from the glass wall, "where the computer-machines are looking at Domick's blood. He said he will come soon. It will take time to find out anything."

"You seem so calm," I said. I was commenting on her tranquility, but she misunderstood me.

"I am not afraid," she said. "If Dell is wrong, then we will die. Being afraid will not change that."

"You are right," I said. "But fear does not usually heed reason."

"Fear produces its own reasons," Seely said. "I know because I have heard its craven voice so many times. Sometimes I feel that I have been afraid for most of my life: afraid of losing my mother and then afraid for my friend, and then afraid for Gavyn and for both of us when we were runaways and Lady Slawyna and her son wanted Gavyn dead. Then I was afraid of coming to Obernewtyn. But it turned out to be a true refuge, and Gavyn belonged there. But there I learned a new and more subtle fear. I was frightened of being pointless. You see, I am not a Misfit. I have nothing special about me that would let me belong. I realized there that I had made looking after Gavyn my reason for existing. And when that was gone and he did not need me . . . Well, in truth, he never truly needed me. He is not like that. But we had a purpose together. . . ." Her voice trailed off.

"Working with Jak has helped you not to be afraid?" I asked softly, wondering what she would think if I told her that Gavyn and the white dog Rasial had entered a merge with Dell and others to save my life.

She gave me a quick look. "At first, he was just kind, letting me help him. I knew that, but I liked being with the teknoguilders, for they did not seem so . . . so impossibly Talented. They were only passionate about their research, and I could be useful, because although I did not have their passion for knowledge, I liked doing things, sorting and making careful observations. It was peaceful and I was good at it. It was so nice to feel useful. Then . . ." Her cheeks flushed a little in the chilly light. "Then he suggested I come here with him, with the expedition. I knew there would be danger, but I didn't care. I would be useful."

"And now?"

"I am happy," she said, radiant. "I almost feel ashamed to say it when so many people have died here or have been taken away. Merret and Orys and Blyss . . . The others often speak of Obernewtyn with longing. But Jak does not long to be anywhere save where he can pursue his work, and I am happy to be of use to him. Of course, I will never be like him—so lost in curiosity and so hungry to discover. But I am interested, and I am good at thinking and doing practical tasks." She gave me a sudden, direct look. "I love him," she declared, almost defiantly. She laughed softly. "He would not allow it to begin with. He said he was too old. But"—a shimmer of pure mischief lit her eyes—"I convinced him."

"I am glad you are happy," I said gently.

"That is why I am not afraid of the plague," Seely said earnestly. "If I must die for what I have had, then I will die. Jak and I will not be parted, and I will not be afraid."

"Who is there?"

We both swung to face the glass, and I saw that Domick was awake, leaning up as far as the restraining bands would allow.

"I will get Jak," Seely whispered, and hastened away.

✦ 8 ✦

"DOMICK?" I SAID, wondering if he could hear me.

He squinted in the direction of my voice, but the central room was dimly lit, and I realized he was unable to see me from within his red-lit chamber. He struggled to sit, only to discover that he was restrained. He struggled hard at his bands for a moment and then sank back, saying hoarsely, "That is not my name. I am Mika. Domick was a fool and a coward." He squinted again, struggling to see me. "Who are you? I recognize your voice. You hide in the shadows."

"I am not hiding," I said, pressing my face to the glass. "We are friends. Don't you remember? Can you see me now?"

He glared toward me, and then something flickered over the gaunt pale features, a kind of pain, and the slyness faded from his expression. "Elspeth? Guildmistress?" There was sorrow in his voice, but he sounded himself. My heart leapt, but before I could shape any response, his face clenched and he gave a groan. Again he fought against the bands binding his forehead and wrists, trying to break them. When he grew calm again, sweat gleamed on his brow and upper lip. He smiled ferociously at me, a vicious baring of teeth. "Of course! He knows who you are. He thinks you will rescue him. He is a fool. My master understood that perfectly."

I felt as if I were in the elevating chamber again. "Who is your master?" I asked.

The mad smile widened. "He knew you would want to know. He told me you would ask." I stared into his glowing face, the dark eyes like small black pits of wickedness and malice, and I told myself that it was not possible that he meant Ariel; that Ariel had known what I, specifically, would say in this moment. For that to be true, he would have to have foreseen that Domick would be here, with me. If he had foreseen that, he would have known his attempt to spread the plague had failed.

"Tell me what your master sent you here to do," I said.

The slyness became a demented exultation. "I am the instrument of Lud. I come to punish the wicked. All who sin will fall ill and die. The seeds of Lud's divine retribution are planted in me."

These words matched the rantings of the One, but Ariel had been in control of the One. Striving to think how to reach Domick, I asked, "Have those at Obernewtyn sinned? Has Kella sinned?"

The gaunt face twisted at the name, becoming Domick's face. "Kella." The word came out a half-strangled sob.

"Domick," I whispered, frightened of drawing forth Mika again. "How did they catch you?"

"We were talking, and they were suddenly all around us. They had demon bands on, which was why

161

I had not felt them. Rushton fought, and so did I, but there were too many. They took us to him. To . . . Ariel." Fear shimmered in his eyes.

I had to fight to breathe slowly, to calm myself. Rushton *had* been taken at the same time! "Where did they take you?" I asked, wondering if they had been parted immediately or if both had been taken to the Sutrium cloister before Domick was taken to Herder Isle.

"They took us to the *Black Ship*. Ariel was waiting. The ship took us to . . . to Norseland, to his place. To *their* place." He was beginning to tremble now, and his fists were clenched. I had the feeling he was striving to hold on to himself, to hold Mika back.

"Us?" I asked softly. "*Rushton* was taken to Norseland?" My mind was racing, because how could we have found Rushton in the Sutrium cloister if he had been taken to Norseland?

"Rushton would not . . . would not open his mind to Ariel," Domick croaked. "He fought. I . . . I was . . . weak. . . ." Domick arched his back horribly and shuddered violently from head to toe. If the plast bands had failed, he would have hurled himself to the floor. One of the circles fixed to his temples had been torn away, and the metal form twitched its hands and pincers but did nothing. Perhaps it was waiting for him to be still again. Domick stayed arched like a taut bow for a long, terrible moment. He whispered hoarsely, "Ariel . . . entered my mind. I am strong, but he . . . he is an empath. He uses empathy in some twisted, dreadful way. Like coercing but worse. It hurt. . . . I could not stop him. . . ." He flopped back, and when his eyes opened again, Domick was gone. The bloodless lips stretched into a sneering smirk. "He has gone," he sneered.

"Mika."

He snickered, and his expression grew petulant. "You helped him take control. You should not have done that. I shall not allow it again."

"He spoke of Rushton," I said. Mika made no response. "Rushton was taken to Norseland, too, wasn't he? But then Ariel sent him back to the Land because he defeated your master."

"He was useless. He went mad rather than submit," Mika said. Alarm flickered in his face. "You will not trick me again," he snarled.

"I couldn't trick you," I said, letting admiration tinge my voice. "You survived, which means you must be smarter than Rushton or Domick. They were the fools."

His eyes narrowed, and he gave a shivering laugh. "Mika is no fool. Mika understands the necessity for suffering. For failure."

"That is why your master trusted you, isn't it? Because you are no fool. He sent you, knowing he could trust you. He couldn't send Domick, because he would not obey. Ariel has no need of guards or manacles, because you serve him faithfully." I spoke swiftly, obeying my instincts. "What were you to do?"

"I was to come to the west coast to bring the wrath of Lud," Mika said. Exultation died in his face, and he went on sullenly, "Then master told me he had found out Elspeth Gordie would be there. *You*," he hissed. "He said you must not be harmed, because he needed you." He glared at me. "He said it was Lud's will that you would stop me and that we must not question Lud's will."

I stared at him, utterly baffled. "Why did he send you, if he knew you must fail?" I asked.

"He sent me because of you, Elspeth Gordie. He said that you would ask who my master was, and I was to say it was Ariel. He said I was to tell you that you are his tool, no matter what you believe, and that you will pay for interfering with his plans." All of this was said in a mumbling sulky voice, which trailed off uncertainly. Domick seemed unaware that he was trembling and sweating copiously, and I was certain that the plague was now infectious.

"How am I to pay?" I asked.

He giggled horribly. "He said you would ask that, too. See how clever he is? He said I must tell you that you will pay in pain."

"Guilden Domick," I said sharply and with authority.

Mika stared at me, his mouth slackly open, and then he closed his mouth, and there was pain in his eyes. "Elspeth," Domick rasped. His voice was stronger than before. "You must not . . . enter my mind. He has . . . set up traps. You would not die, but you would suffer, and that is what he wants. He hates you. . . . You can't imagine how he hates you. And he sees so much. More than Maryon and Dell. More clearly. But there are gaps! There must be since he did not know I would be able to take control and talk to you. He did not see that you would make me strong."

I was afraid to say Ariel's name in case it brought Mika back. "Tell me about Rushton."

"It is as Mika told you. The Herders got us. Ariel told the warrior priests where to find us. Rushton was trying to make me come . . . come back to Obernewtyn. I was . . . I could not. I told him that. What Mika had done was too . . . I could not go back to Kella with blood on my hands. If she sensed what I had done . . ."

"So the Hedra took you to Ariel, and he took you both to Norseland. What happened then?"

"Ariel has a machine that gets inside your head. Noises and colors and pain come from it . . . He used the machine to try to open our minds so he could empathise us. He is a weak coercer, you see. But Rushton would not let him in. I fought, too, but he found Mika, and he summoned him and made him strong. Mika opened my mind for Ariel. He . . . came inside my mind with empathy, but—Elspeth—he is like an empath turned inside out. He . . . he made me feel such terrible things. He made me imagine hurting Kella. He made me take pleasure from it. I fled inside myself, which left Mika. It was what Ariel wanted. Mika coerced Rushton, and Rushton had no defense against him because they had been . . . we . . . were friends." The last words were spoken in a sobbing hiss. "Ariel entered Rushton's mind, but still Rushton fought. He used your face and form as a shield against hatred and despair and pain and all that Ariel used on him, but with Mika and the machine, Rushton could not hold out forever. When Rushton broke, Ariel took his revenge. He made Mika help him to . . . distort Rushton's memories so whenever he thought . . . of you, of Elspeth . . . he would feel pain and he would see the most dreadful . . ."

"Why would he do such terrible things to Rushton?" I asked through clenched teeth, sickened to the heart by what he was telling me.

"Ariel said Rushton must suffer for opposing him. But in truth, his anger at Rushton is small compared to his hatred of you. I . . . Once I asked him why he hated you so. He said that he had dreamed you would find something he greatly desired, something from the Beforetime. Only you could find and claim it, and no matter how many times he sought for another outcome, it was always the same. You found what he desired. He realized that the only way for him to possess what he wanted was to let you find it and then take it from you!" Domick almost screamed this last word. Then he lurched forward and vomited thin yellow bile onto the white sheet. Two more of the circles had been torn away, and I heard a muffled beeping sound. Domick laughed, a thread of saliva hanging from his lower lip. "See? He is a thing I can vomit out." It was Mika's voice, crafty and malicious.

"That is because you are stronger," I said smoothly.

Mika nodded eagerly. "Domick had locked me away. I was hidden in the darkest place in his mind, but the master let me out and made me strong. He laughed and laughed when he discovered me, and Domick wept." There was contempt in his tone. "The master gave me power, and I obeyed him. He locked Domick in the darkness where he had hidden me."

"He used you," I said slowly. "He used the plague to make me find you so you could tell me what he had done to Rushton."

Mika's eyes glowed blackly in his ashen face. "He trusted me to do his will—me, not Domick. I wanted him to kill Domick, but he said that he could not be killed or I would die." His face twisted with rage. "But he said Domick would never get out. Never." The triumph in his face dwindled to an irritable fretfulness. "But you made Domick want to come. You tricked me."

Now there was anger again, but I ignored it, for I felt that something still eluded me.

I said coldly, "Your master failed you. Because he made a mistake about Domick's strength, and he made a mistake about Rushton, too, didn't he? He took him to Norseland and tried to use him, and in the end, he could only hurt him."

Mika sneered. "Rushton held you before him like a shield, but we broke him and then the master gave Rushton to the Herders to let him rot in a cell."

"But Rushton is not in the cell. He is free and works against your master. That was a mistake, too, wasn't it?" Some part of me was sickened by my cruelty, for it was Domick I was taunting. Mika was just a poor twisted part of his mind. I forced myself to go on. "You were supposed to be the instrument of Lud, bringing plague, but instead you are just Ariel's messenger boy."

"It is your fault." Mika's face was as confused as a child's.

"Yes," I said. "The seeds of sickness in you will flower and you will die, but only you. Why did Ariel infect you with the plague when he knew you would never be allowed to spread it to another person? Why didn't he trust you to pretend?"

"He . . . he said it would change things if he did anything differently. He said . . . he said he must act as if . . . as if he had seen nothing. It was the only way. . . ."

"So you alone are to die from the plague you carry? Maybe he kept that from you. Maybe he didn't trust you after all. . . ."

"He did! He trusted me. He said I must wait, and you would find me. He said you had to find me because of the plague." The words became a labored gasping and a breathless sobbing. Then he was still, his head hanging down. When the face lifted, Domick's eyes looked out at me, tortured and bleak.

"I am so sorry, Domick. I needed to weaken him," I whispered. I could feel sweat trickling down my spine.

"Elspeth, listen to me," Domick rasped. "Ariel wants you to live, because he needs you to get something that he wants. . . . I . . . Elspeth, I think it might be a weapon. Something terrible. That is the center of Ariel's mind, and all the rest is a chaotic whirl of madness and brilliance and cruelty. I felt it when he bound himself to me so he could enter Rushton when I did. The One is mad, but Ariel is worse."

I heard a movement behind me but did not turn. At any second, Mika might again take over. My whole body ached from tension, and I hoped whoever was behind me would have the sense not to speak. But it was already too late. Domick gave a cry and seemed to struggle with an invisible assailant before sinking back. Mika leered at me, panting. "You think you are so smart! He tells you things he should not, but my master is stronger. You think he failed with Rushton? You are wrong! He serves my master yet!" His white face shone like polished marble in the bloody light, and his eyes seemed to bulge. He continued speaking, but now there was only a mad babble. Then he convulsed again and fell back, unconscious.

The plast hand reached out and began to wash the sweat from his body.

"It begins," Jak said. He was behind the bank of computermachines. "He is obviously delirious."

I swallowed, tasted blood, and realized I had bitten the inside of my cheek. I asked, "Did you hear what he said?"

"Some of it, but I would not strive to find meaning in the mad babble of delirium. After all, he said that Ariel took Rushton to Norseland, but Dell foresaw that he had been found in Sutrium."

"He was, but it is possible he was taken to Norseland first. It would . . . explain much if it is true," I said with difficulty. "What did you mean by saying it had begun?"

"I meant that the first stage is ended. Domick is contagious now."

I had guessed it, but the words said aloud made me feel as if he had struck me. "Have you found a way to heal him yet?"

"We have still not been able to identify the plague," Jak said. "Elspeth, you should get some food and rest. Pavo has given Domick something to make him sleep now, for his pulse was racing dangerously, and there was a risk that his heart would give out. He will not wake again for some hours. Seely will come for you the minute there is something to tell."

I shivered and nodded, and he took my elbow and made me sit down, saying that Seely would return soon to take me to my sleeping chamber.

"I do not think I will be able to sleep after this," I said.

"I could give you something to help," Jak said, "but I know you eschew such remedies. Why not bathe and eat and have a look around if you cannot sleep immediately. This is truly an amazing place, Elspeth. You might find Dell and ask her to tell you how she began to communicate with the main computermachine here. Without that, none of this would have been possible."

That got through the haze of confusion I was feeling. "*Dell* communicated with computermachines?" I asked.

He smiled. "Not just any one. Dell communicated with the central computermachine, which masters this entire complex and all of the lesser machines." Then he sobered, looking past me to Domick. "We have named the computermachine that runs this healing center 'Pavo' in tribute to my old master, but I do not truly think of it as a live being. Dell has taken the opposite point of view. She believes that a computermachine is simply a different kind of being. This approach enabled her to do what I could not, for all my rational theories. Indeed, it was her struggle to communicate with it as one life-form to another that led to the discovery that it can both speak and listen."

"Speak and listen?" I said in flat disbelief. I stood and Jak led me to his machine.

Jak nodded. "The Beforetimers gave computermachines voices. The one here sounds like a woman. I learned to communicate with computermachines by tapping on the scribed letters, and I continue to communicate in this way, making instructional sentences on the screen. But Dell speaks to it aloud, asking it to explain words and concepts and explaining her own questions. I would like to do as she does, for I see her results. But although I am a teknoguilder with machine empathy, I simply cannot make myself regard a computermachine as a live thing. I see it as a tool, but Dell sees it as a living thing with its own intelligence and ideas, and that approach has allowed her to do far more with it. Dell made the computermachine grow crops of hay and wheat and lucerne in vats on the thirteenth level, which we give to the wild herd. But her true interest is in what the computermachine will *not* explain or show us. You see, there are whole areas on some levels that we cannot enter, because we need code words or sets of numbers that we do not have.

"That ought to be the end of it, but Dell has the idea that if she interacts with the main controlling computermachine for long enough, teaching it, stimulating its intelligence, and developing its reasoning ability, she will eventually be able to convince it to allow us access to deeper programs that will tell us more about the Beforetime and give us greater knowledge and power."

Seeing my look of consternation, he went on to explain that a program was a set of instructions given to a computermachine, which told it what to do. In the case of the dominant computermachine in the complex, its program gave it access to other computermachines. In a sense, it was the program that was the computermachine. "Unlike all the other computermachines here, such as Pavo, the main computermachine in this complex can learn new information and integrate it with old information. That is why Dell is so certain it is capable of eventually understanding why it should give us access to its deepest secrets." He shrugged. "I admire all that she has accomplished, but I must say that I think Dell is wrong in imagining a computermachine program can alter itself enough to sympathize with our need. On the other hand, when I think about what her approach has managed to accomplish, I am prepared to be proven wrong."

"Do you know what the purpose of this place was in the Beforetime?" We were now walking along the green-lit passages toward the elevating chamber.

"It was constructed specifically as a shelter in case of exactly such a world-changing disaster as the Great White. I do not know why the Beforetimers did not use it. Maybe the end of that time came too swiftly. But unless Dell succeeds with Ines, we will never know the truth of it."

"Ines?" I echoed, my skin prickling, for in one of my visions, the Beforetime Misfits had spoken of contacting Ines at Obernewtyn.

"INES are the letters representing the specific type of advanced program contained in the central computer-machine, but Dell uses it as a proper name."

"Where does Dell speak with the main computer-machine?" I asked, trying to keep the excitement from my voice.

"You can address it from anywhere within the complex, and it will respond," Jak said. "You only need give an order using its letters as a name. I will show you. Ines, can you produce some music?"

"Do you have a preference, sir?" asked the attractive voice of a woman that came from everywhere, like light. This was the voice I had heard only recently in the recurring dream of walking in a dark tunnel and hearing the drip of water!

"Just something soft and soothing," Jak said.

Music began, of an exquisitely complex type I had never heard before, but I was still reeling at the voice.

"Ines, stop the music now, please," Jak said, and the music stopped.

I was about to ask why he had stopped it when I

saw that Seely had arrived with the key to the demon band. Jak took it from her and bade me farewell, saying he needed to return to Domick. Seely led me on to the elevating chamber, asking me anxiously how Domick was. I muttered something, still too astonished by Jak's demonstration to concentrate on anything else. At the elevating chamber, Seely pressed her palm to a square panel in the wall alongside the door. When we entered, she touched one of the listed numbers on the wall and one in a row of colored buttons. This time I felt myself grow heavy, and when the chamber's vibrating ceased, I felt myself become light.

Out of the elevator, Seely led me only a few steps to a gray door in a corridor filled with gray doors. She touched the door, and it slid open to reveal a small square chamber containing a bed, a table and chair, and a glass box about the height of a tall man in one corner. There was a single door in the room, and Seely said with a slight blush that it led to a privy where I could relieve myself. She pointed to the glass box standing upright in the corner. "You bathe there, and drying sheets and some clothes are there." She pointed to a cupboard. She indicated a panel against the wall and said I had only to lay my hand on it if I wanted the lights out. Pressed again, the light would be restored.

After she left, the door hissed closed. I stretched out on the bed, knowing I ought to clean myself but feeling unable to face the intricacies of the bathing box. I thought of Domick's claim that Rushton still served Ariel. He probably meant that Ariel had foreseen that Rushton would reject me, which would cause me pain. Despite the light's brightness and my thoughts' churning, I slept without dreams.

I woke groggy and needing desperately to relieve myself. I went reluctantly to investigate the small room beside the bed. The light flickered on as I entered what was little more than a small cabinet containing a seat with a hole in the center. It looked like a privy, but it was so smooth and clean and sweet smelling that I sat down uneasily. When I stood, a great jet of water burst out and cleaned the bowl. The loud and unexpected noise made me stagger backward from the cubicle, trip over the threshold, and sit down hard. For a moment I sat there, gaping with shock, then I burst out laughing, thinking how utterly foolish I must have looked.

But I sobered as I remembered what Ariel had done to Rushton and Domick. I had felt too overwhelmed to make any sense of it before I slept, but now it seemed sheer lunacy that Ariel would prepare Domick physically and mentally to bring plague to the west coast if he intended only to taunt me. Surely he could have gone through the motions of sending Domick with plague, without infecting him. But Domick said Ariel was convinced that what he had seen would alter if he did anything differently. Yet he *had* done something different. He had told Domick the truth, and he had bidden him taunt me with it. I had long thought him to be defective, but Domick had called him mad. Perhaps his madness, like his hatred for me, arose from the knowledge that I was the Seeker and that he could not fulfill his destiny as the Destroyer without my first attempting to fulfill my quest.

I had never thought of it before, but Atthis had always said that *only if I failed* would the Destroyer have his chance. Perhaps what I had always regarded as a

174

race was in fact a complex game in which the Destroyer must wait for the Seeker to make a certain move before he could make his own. Certainly Domick's words suggested that Ariel intended to allow me to find the Beforetime weaponmachines that had caused the Great White and then prevent my destroying them. It was little wonder he hated me, then, for it meant he must protect the very person who stood in the way of what he most wanted. I had always thought of him as my nemesis, but for the first time, I understood that I was also *his* nemesis. Even when he knew I would thwart him, he had to allow it, for fear that he might prevent my doing what I needed to as the Seeker!

The ironic notion made me shiver, because I could imagine the towering rage Rushton would have unleashed in opposing Ariel *with an image of me!*

I became aware of a stale odor rising from my body, composed of human and horse sweat and sheer uncleanliness. Revolted, I sloughed off my filthy clothes and padded across the smooth floor to the glass cabinet. I stepped into it with some trepidation and saw three circles on the wall: blue, red, and yellow. I touched blue hesitantly and gave a shriek as icy water cascaded down. I slapped at the red circle, and the water became instantly a boiling torrent. Pressing myself to one side of the cabinet, I pushed the yellow circle. Deliciously warm water flowed out, and I stepped into it and hastily pulled the glass door closed.

I stood for a long time under the miniature waterfall, turning and sighing with pleasure, as the sweat and dirt of my long journey sluiced away down a small round drain hole in the floor. Marveling at the constancy of the flow and temperature of the water and wondering without too much urgency how to turn it off, I noticed three small transparent levers against the wall. Curious, I touched one warily. A gleaming blob of scented matter fell to the floor of the closet and washed away, releasing a soft cloud of perfume. Guessing it to be soap, I pressed the lever again, catching the scented blob and rubbing it over my hair and body. The scent of roses enveloped me. The other two levers had different scented matter.

Once I had washed the bubbles from my body, I pressed the yellow lever again, and to my relief, the water ceased immediately. Pleased to have mastered the cabinet as well as rendering myself clean, I opened the door and took a drying sheet from the cabinet, noticing several pairs of the same blue trousers that Dell and Seely wore and three different-sized pairs of boots. I disliked the smooth stiffness of the cloth, but I could not bear my own clothes. Dressing in the queer trousers, I noticed a second pile of short-sleeved shirts made of some thin, very fine, white material. I put one of these on and pulled on a pair of soft thick socks. The boots looked heavy, but in fact they were light and very soft, and the sole was spongy to the touch. I found a pair that fit and put them on, marveling that something so ugly could be so comfortable. Then I worked the tangles and snarls from my wet hair with a comb I found on another shelf. Leaving it loose to dry, I undertook the difficult business of washing my filthy clothes in the water cupboard. Before long, they were squeezed out and hung around the room to dry. Seely had not come back, and after trying the door for a moment, I gave up and lay on my stomach on the bed.

I thought of Rushton with sorrow and guilt,

knowing that he had been tortured simply because he had loved me. I could not bear to think how he must have suffered whenever he looked at me, despite suppressing the memories of what had happened to him. No wonder he had turned away from me. I shuddered to remember that Dameon had pressed me to force Rushton to look at me and speak with me and face me, so certain had he been that Rushton loved me! He had not known, as I now did, that love had been most cruelly bonded to pain and fear and torment in the Master of Obernewtyn. Every time Rushton had to deal with me, it must have rocked his sanity. Perhaps Ariel had hoped that the sight of me would eventually drive him mad, and this might have happened, had I remained in the Land and taken the Empath guildmaster's advice. Maybe *that* was what Mika had meant by saying that Rushton still served Ariel.

Before I saw Rushton again, I must think well and long about what to do.

I must have dozed, because I started awake when I heard a soft tap at the door. I called out as I rose, and Seely burst in, saying, "I'm so sorry, Guildmistress, but you need to come at once. The sky is full of smoke. Dell wants you to see if you can farseek Merret to find out what is happening."

"Merret? But where is she?"

"She went last night to take the greathorse back to Halfmoon Bay and to see if your friends are safe."

"Last night . . . but wait! Are you saying there is a fire in Halfmoon Bay?" I asked as we went back out into the purple-lit passage.

"We do not know, but there is a great deal of smoke

coming from that direction. Blyss is frightened for Merret," Seely said.

"How long have I been asleep?" I asked as we hastened down the passage.

"Since yesterday afternoon. It is very early in the morning now," Seely answered.

We were soon entering the elevating chamber, and I experienced almost as much nausea and alarm as on the previous day. Unable to help myself, I asked Seely what would happen if the chamber broke and we were caught between levels. She gave me a slightly uneasy look but said that Ines would know how to fix it.

"Ines," I echoed.

She gave me a measuring look, then said, "I know Jak does not like us thinking of a computermachine as being alive, but I find it hard not to do so. Ines speaks to me and responds to me. She remembers what I have said to her, what I like and do not like, and she asks many questions of me. When I ask *her* questions, she tries her best to answer me and to explain when I don't understand. I feel like she cares about me."

I did not know how to respond, for was it not a computermachine that had once tortured me and Rushton and that had helped Ariel destroy Rushton's love for me? Was it not a computermachine that had caused the Great White? Had those computermachines all had names and soft, soothing voices that could be evoked?

The elevating chamber came to a halt, and the doors slid open; the scent of fresh air seemed intoxicating. I almost ran to the metal steps, and as I mounted them two at a time and burst out into the chilly sweetness of the predawn air, I thought of Hannah telling Cassy that the false sunlight that lit Newrome was not as sweet as true sunlight. I stopped to wait for Seely, relishing being outside. The wind riffled my hair, and I was glad I had not braided it.

Seely joined me and then took the lead as we wove our way through the ruins toward the watchtower. She told me that Alun had first seen the smoke.

We crossed the square, but there were no signs now of the horses or the saddles and packages they had carried. Someone stumbling into the square would not have the slightest clue that people lived close by. At the watchtower, I followed Seely through a door and up the steps, thinking how cleverly they had been constructed. The top platform was screened by the jagged outer wall, and here sat the beastspeaker and empath Alun, eating an apple. With an exclamation, he leapt to his feet and greeted me with delight. But I could only gape, for beyond him, an immense column of gray smoke was billowing into the pale blue sky.

"Ye gods, that looks as if a whole city is on fire!" I said, aghast.

"The amount of smoke suggests it, but it looks to me as if the smoke is coming from too far inland to be any of the cities," Alun said.

I had been studying the smoke and said, "If I did not know better, I would say it was coming from the Suggredoon."

"I was thinking the same thing," Alun admitted. "Except whatever was burning is still burning, and the shantytown that serves the camp of soldierguards would have gone up in less than an hour."

"I will try to reach Merret, but if she has reached

Halfmoon Bay, it is too far," I said. I strove fruitlessly and shook my head. "Maybe I can use Kader and Orys in a merge."

"Orys rode out last night, too, to let Gwynedd know you have brought Domick in safely," Alun said. "Seely could go and get Kader, but perhaps you can use me, Guildmistress. I have some farseeking ability, though it is not as strong as my other Talents."

I thanked him and linked with his mind. Again I cast my probe, shaped to Merret's mind. I had not extended my reach much more than a furlong or two, yet the probe located. But it was not in the direction of Halfmoon Bay, and the contact was tenuous. Merret understood at once and poured her own energy into strengthening the connection as I told her about the smoke and asked what she knew. She had seen the smoke from inside Halfmoon Bay and had ridden out to investigate.

"So the smoke is not coming from Halfmoon Bay?" I farsent.

"No," Merret responded. "It is coming from the Suggredoon. In fact, it looks as if it is coming from the other side of the Suggredoon."

"From Sutrium?!" I was so startled that I almost lost contact.

"I am not there yet, and there is so much smoke that I cannot be sure," Merret sent. "Many soldierguards have galloped by wearing the colors of different cities, but I can't probe them because of their demon bands. Some of the gossip on the road says that the Faction has invaded the Land and is fighting with the rebels, but that's impossible, given what you told us," Merret observed.

I felt a sick lurch of alarm. "It is not impossible," I

told her. "You see, when Harwood and the others left the Land to board one of the invaders' ships, there were still hundreds of Hedra at large. Maybe they managed to avoid capture and regroup, or Malik might have had more support than we realized. How close are you to the Suggredoon?" I asked.

"I am within sight of the ramshackle village that has grown up near the barrier the soldierguards set up. But if I go another step nearer, I will lose you. It is taking all my concentration to keep contact."

"You'd better go nearer, then, and see what you can find out, but first, are there any priests about?"

"I have seen quite a number heading toward the old ferry port, but they all wear demon bands. They look as puzzled as the soldierguards, which makes me think that the fire must be on the other side of the river.

"Oh, there is something else—I met your Iriny! She was dressed exactly as Rolf had described when she left Halfmoon Bay. She felt me enter her mind, and it did not take me long to explain who I was. She repeated what Rolf had told me, that he had used his connections to get her out of the Councilcourt cells before the Herders could make enough fuss to get their hands on her. She said that she wanted to cross the river to give some important information to her brother. She said the smoke would provide the perfect opportunity to cross, and she must act while she had the chance. I bade her—"

Without warning, the probe broke free and rebounded with painful abruptness.

"Are you all right?" Seely asked anxiously as I staggered back.

I opened my eyes, and the radiance of the newly

risen sun seemed to claw at the inside of my head. I squinted and looked at Alun, who was pale and sick-looking. He laughed shakily and said, "I hate it when that happens." I apologized, but he waved away my words, saying that if Merret suddenly moved out of range, there was nothing I could have done. He asked if I really thought that the fire was the result of a Hedra force warring with the rebels across the Suggredoon. Of course, he had heard the whole exchange.

"If it is, then they are clearly winning," I said grimly. "For rebels would not torch the city."

"It might be the Raider," Seely suggested. "Maybe Ariel convinced him to bring some more Hedra from the camp in Norseland, and they sailed across the strait to attack the rebels."

I considered her suggestion seriously, but at length I shook my head. My instincts told me that Yarrow had been right: Ariel had severed his connection with the Faction when he had abandoned Herder Isle.

"Do you think the gypsy will make it across the river?" Alun asked.

I studied the billows of smoke and envisaged Iriny flitting between the tents and soldierguard patrols to slip silently into the dark water. "If anyone could manage, she will. But my concern is that if she does cross, she might be leaping from the pan into the cook fire if there are Hedra on the other bank, for the Faction has no love for gypsies."

PART II

◆

SANCTUARY

✦ 9 ✦

IT WAS WELL past midday before I returned to the Beforetime complex. Seely had gone back down earlier to let Dell know what I had learned, but I had wanted to try to contact Merret again. I had not managed it, however, even when Kader appeared to take the watch from Alun and allowed me to draw on him.

Puzzled and uneasy about what might be going on over the river, I went below with Alun. As we descended the metal steps, he said with cheerful relish that we ought to arrive in time to sample one of Dell's delicious midmeal soups. I raised my eyebrows. Many futuretellers at Obernewtyn had chosen domestic tasks to busy their bodies and leave their minds free, but the meals they prepared were invariably bland or peculiarly spiced.

Dell laughed at my expression when I stepped from the elevating chamber into a large, pleasant room that smelled deliciously of the soup she was pouring into a tureen. "I have learned to like cooking and to enjoy doing it well," she said.

"You have changed," I could not help saying as she ladled me a bowl of soup and pushed a platter of thickly sliced, fragrant hot bread toward me.

"Our time of exile has changed all of us here," Dell

185

said seriously. "I think we have become closer than people of different guilds do at Obernewtyn, because danger always seems to stalk us, and we rely on no one but ourselves." She changed the subject then, questioning me closely about what Merret had told me.

I concluded by saying I would try again to reach Merret in an hour, for surely by then she would have garnered some useful information and be heading back in our direction.

The elevating chamber doors opened, and Blyss ushered in a flock of boys and girls. Realizing these must be the Misfit children Dell had mentioned earlier, I smiled as they approached and touched their minds lightly to confirm their Talents. The futureteller gave each of them bread and soup and bade Blyss and Alun help themselves. Then she untied her apron and laid it aside, excusing herself and asking me to join her once I had finished my meal. I was puzzled that she had not stayed to eat with us, but then Blyss introduced me to Pellis, who had a startling shock of carrot-colored hair sticking out in all directions. At twelve, he was older than the other children he introduced, who ranged from ten to four.

In normal circumstances, I would have drawn their stories from them, but I was anxious to farseek Merret again, and before I could do that, I would have to see Dell, which made me uneasy. The moment Blyss had finished her soup, I asked her to take me to the futureteller. It was odd, I thought as we entered the elevating chamber. I had felt perfectly comfortable with Dell the cook, but now I feared an interview with Dell the Futuretell guilden.

My discomfort with futuretellers centered upon the fact that, while Atthis had warned me never to speak of my quest, futuretellers often dreamed of it in a fragmentary way, which inevitably led to questions I could not or would not answer. The Futuretell guildmistress, Maryon, had more than once referred obliquely to my quest, but she had never spoken of it outright to me. Indeed, she had seemed to understand the importance of not speaking of it. But Dell was second in rank and skill to the guildmistress, and Maryon might have discussed me with her before Dell had left for the west coast. Perhaps she had made up her mind to abandon any squeamishness about my quest. *What would I do*, I wondered, *if she asked me about it directly?* And yet was there any need to remain silent with her when Atthis had drawn Dell into a spirit merge with Maruman, Gahltha, and others in order to save me?

As she led me along a yellow-lit hall on the building's thirtieth level, Blyss broke into my thoughts. "The Futuretell guilden cooks, but she never eats her meals in the great hall. She prefers to eat alone in Sanctuary. I think you will see why."

"What is sanctuary?" I asked.

She gave me a shy smile. "It is better for you to see Sanctuary rather than have someone tell you about it. But it is also what we call this complex now. Sanctuary, for it has proven so to us, and it was created in the first place to be a sanctuary for the Beforetimers."

I wanted to say that it had not served them well since almost no one had managed to get there before the Great White destroyed their world, but it would have been harsh to say. I glanced at Blyss again, and she

187

was smiling softly. I contemplated asking about her relationship with Merret but decided it was none of my business and turned my attention to my surroundings.

The corridor we had entered on this level was smooth and bare, like all those I had passed along in the Beforetime complex, but unlike the rest, it curved, and now that I thought about it, there was something odd about the yellowish light flooding the passage.

I had just realized that, instead of coming from both walls, the light here came only from the inside wall of the curving passage, when suddenly that wall became transparent. I stopped abruptly, astonished to see trees growing on the other side of the glass! The more I looked, the more I realized that it was not just a few trees in some sort of underground garden. There were more trees behind the ones I had seen first and more beyond them. I was looking at a forest, and astoundingly, above the trees was a blue sky!

"Come, there is a door just along here," Blyss urged. She touched the transparent wall, and like the door to the elevating chamber, the glass split open and the intoxicating scent of hot greenery and damp rich earth flowed over me.

"Welcome to Sanctuary," Blyss said, clearly enjoying my reaction.

"What is this? H-how . . . ?" I stammered.

Blyss shook her head and smiled. "Let Dell explain." She pointed to a track weaving away from the opening in the glass and through the trees. I followed the empath along it, feeling as if I had stepped into a dream. After we had been walking long enough for me to feel warm, I realized that things were not quite as natural as they seemed. There were no bird or animal cries, nor the sound of insects, and there was not a breath of wind. The light, which seemed at first to be so like sunlight, was too yellow, quite aside from the fact that there was no sun. The light emanated from the blueness, which, I realized after my first shock, must be the blue-painted roof of an immense cavern.

"Here," said Blyss triumphantly, and I saw that the path ended in a clearing at the open door of a small dome-shaped hut half obscured by foliage. "This is where Dell spends most of her time," Blyss added.

As we came closer, I saw that the hut was not a rounded dome but merely many sided. It had only two rather small windows, one on either side of the door, and when we entered, I saw why. Shelves that groaned under the weight of hundreds of books covered the other walls, and on a table in the center of the room sat an enormous computermachine. A chair faced it, but Dell sat in a more comfortable-looking chair beside the window.

Hearing us enter, she rose with a smile, saying softly, "Thank you, Blyss." It was a dismissal, and Blyss smiled at me and withdrew.

"How did you do all this?" I cried the moment we were alone.

The futureteller burst out laughing. "Of course, I did not do this. It was here when we came; it is a living seed store, maintained by Ines. But I should not laugh. My own astonishment was great when I first came here, though Ines had told me what to expect. I thought I was misunderstanding her."

"Jak told me about you and Ines," I said.

Again she laughed. "You make it sound like a love affair."

"You used not to laugh so much," I said, rather foolishly.

This rendered the futureteller serious. "You spoke before of change, and I have been thinking of your words. True, I have become less . . . somber than I was at Obernewtyn. I have noticed it in myself. I will not go back, even if that turns out to be possible. I belong here now."

"Here?" I said in disbelief.

She nodded. "There is enough in this complex to bewitch the mind for several lifetimes. Jak feels the same. For him it is the information and the laboratories, and for me, it is Ines."

"You speak of a computermachine as a person."

Dell sat down at the seat behind the computer-machine and bade me draw up a chair. "I think of Ines as something that lives. In some way, our relationship has an element of a beastspeaker and beast in that the two communicate but are essentially different kinds. Because of that, there will always be gaps in their understanding of one another. The secret of harmony is to accept those gaps."

"Jak says you believe that you can make the computermachine let you enter forbidden areas of its . . ." I stopped, groping for a suitable word.

"Her program," Dell said. "A computermachine is only a machine. The program is what allows her to think. It is the mind that inhabits the plast and metal body. But as for *making* Ines tell us the secrets she is keeping, that simply would not be possible. The forbidding is built into her programming just as the instinct not to jump off a cliff is built into us. However, while we could be forced off a cliff, Ines cannot be forced to go against her programming. But she might be brought to reason well enough to see that her program needs to adapt and grow."

"Do you really think it is possible for a machine to change its mind?"

"What I know," Dell said, "is that Ines can learn. That is part of her programming. The whole time we have been here, she has been teaching me, but she is also taking in what I tell her as new knowledge, which can be compared to old knowledge. She is changing me, but in a sense, I am also changing her." Dell lost her lecturing tone and said with a sudden, almost girlish, burst of excitement, "Elspeth, you cannot imagine what Ines knows of the Beforetime."

"Then she knows about the Great White?" I asked, suddenly aware that Ines might know the location of the computermachines that had caused it.

But Dell shook her head. "I asked about the Great White, but the last thing she remembers before my waking her is the command her human user gave to put herself to sleep. That is not the same as being switched off. All of the lesser computermachines that she can manipulate continued following their programs, but there was no mastermind. Think of our hearts pumping and our lungs breathing while our mind sleeps." Dell smiled. "Jak accessed the lesser computermachines not long after we arrived, but Ines woke only after I spoke her name and bade her wake."

"What made you think of doing it?" I asked.

She shrugged. "I do not know. The letters scribed upon her formed a name, so I got into the habit of thinking of the computermachine as a female. Then one day I was thinking of that storysong that Miky and Angina made about a sleeping princess, and it suddenly seemed to me that the computer was like a sleeping princess. Some mad impulse made me command her to wake and speak to me. I did not expect her to answer, and when she did, I near fell over with shock." She chuckled. "Of course, if she had truly been switched off, as the Beforetimers say, it would have been like trying to waken a dead person."

"Why was she made to sleep? Does she know?"

"She knows that before she was put to sleep, she was cut off from the other Ines programs. There were many computermachines in the Beforetime with the Ines program. Because they could all learn and adapt to what they learned, that might mean they are all different, with different information from different human controllers. But they were all linked as well. Indeed, that was their virtue and their specialty. They linked and were able to share information. So what one knew, all knew. This made them incredibly accurate and knowledgeable, but also identical. Then, just before the Great White, all the Ines programs were isolated from one another. That is when *this* Ines, and I suppose all the other computers with Ines programs, became unique, for after this time, they learned and thought alone. Ines does not know why the links between them were blocked, but she says that only Govamen had the power to close down their etherlink."

"Govamen," I echoed, fascinated.

Dell gave me a quick look. "Interesting, isn't it? The computermachines with Ines programs were cut off from one another by the very organization that made prisoners of the Beforetime Misfits kidnapped from the Reichler Clinic. It is difficult not to see Govamen as a sinister body, and much that Ines has told me confirms this impression. I asked her once if we could reconnect her to the other computermachines, and she said it would be possible but they could only be reconnected by using one of the central Govamen computermachines that control the links, and only three of those existed. I think it unlikely any of them survived, because they would certainly have been targets in whatever conflict led to the Great White. In any case, it would be dangerous to do it, because Ines believes it is likely, given the suddenness of the Great White, that many of the computermachines containing her programming were not put to sleep by their human users. This meant that when their users perished, they remained awake but isolated from their sister units and lacking any contact with their human handlers. Since the Ines program focuses so much on the acquisition and exchange of knowledge with other Ines units and with human users, the isolated programs would have suffered a gradual distortion, a sort of madness that would immediately infect any other computermachine connected to it."

"Almost like a computermachine plague," I murmured.

Dell looked startled and nodded. "Being effectively Ines's human user now, I understand very well how a computermachine program would suffer, for she has an insatiable hunger to know things. Lacking that connection to her sister computermachines, she has no other source of new information but what we give her. Fortunately, that seems to satisfy her. Most fascinating is that when I tell her something that does not agree with the knowledge she possesses, she is able to consider both sets of knowledge and decide which to believe.

193

Sometimes she decides that neither is completely correct, and she formulates a modified or merged version of the information. This capacity for assessing information and discarding those parts she has judged obsolete or irrelevant makes me certain that the right argument or piece of knowledge could make her discard the imperative that requires certain keys and codes before she will allow me to know all that she knows. Then she will simply open her deeper self to me."

"What do you hope to learn?" I asked.

"I do not know. But I am curious about why certain information in her memory was considered to be so important or valuable or dangerous that it had to be kept secret."

She got up from the stool and crossed to the window. Without turning, she said, "I care for Obernewtyn and the people there. But I have found a true purpose for my life with Ines."

"What about your futuretelling ability?" I asked.

Dell looked over her shoulder and smiled at me gently. "Perhaps that is at the heart of it. I have the ability to see the future and the past, and at Obernewtyn that is how I defined myself. But when I came here, I realized that I had never really thought about what I wanted. It had never occurred to me that it might be separate from what I was. Maybe these thoughts were beginning to form in my subconscious mind, and that is why I volunteered for this expedition. When I think back on the things Maryon said before I left . . . I think she guessed. Maybe she even foresaw this. It would not be unlike her to see and say nothing, leaving it for me to discover." She looked over her shoulder at me again, her gaze speculative. "I think you might understand better than anyone that a person can have an unexpected destiny."

It was a question if I wanted to answer it. I did not. The prohibition against ever speaking of my quest was too strong. "Do you know what is causing the smoke coming from beyond the Suggredoon?" I asked.

She smiled faintly, signaling her acceptance of the abrupt change of subject. "I have seen nothing of an invasion in Sutrium or of the city being razed by fire. But that does not mean anything. You know that."

I nodded. "Do you foresee anything of what is to come in these next sevendays?" Then I added quickly, "For all of us?"

She sighed and nodded. "I have seen a time of fighting and bloodshed in the future. Your face is at the center of it."

"I am not the cause . . . ," I began.

She shook her head. "No. You are a change-bringer. Whatever choices you make lead to change for the rest of us. But it is not something you chose." Then she said, "When you leave this place, we shall not meet again."

I stared at her, my skin sprouting goose bumps. I could see from the vacant look in her eyes that she had sunk into a futuretelling trance. I did not want to ask, but I had to know. "What do you mean?" I whispered.

"Before the next wintertime ends, you will bid farewell to all that you love and journey far over land and sea to face the beast."

"All that I love?" I echoed.

"All," Dell said, serene and implacable.

◆ 10 ◆

I WAS DREAMING of the dreamtrails. I could tell by the overvivid colors of the wild, churning green landscape about me, the way things bled and blurred into new shapes.

I heard a voice. "Merimyn!"

I turned to see a young woman. She reminded me strongly of the stone figure of Hannah Seraphim as a girl on Stonehill.

"Where are you?" she called. She scowled in mock anger and set her hands on her hips. Her eyes narrowed, and a clump of bush beside me melted away. There, to my astonishment, sat a small motley-colored cat. Maruman! But not as I knew him, old and scarred. He was whole and young, and his two eyes gleamed as he grew wings and sprang into the sky.

"Merimyn!" the girl cried, laughing. "That's cheating!"

I thought myself wings and sprang after Maruman. He rose into the clouds, which became a snowy landscape. He padded through the snow, jumped skittishly at a piece of twig protruding from a drift, and then went on, making a little soft trail of blue paw prints. He showed none of the loathing he usually expressed at the sight of snow. Suddenly, he turned his yellow gaze on me. Two eyes.

"Who are you?" he asked curiously.

It was Maruman's mindvoice, but the sharp ironies that enriched his older mindvoice were absent. This was a younger, lighter voice with a constant ripple of kitten mischief threaded through it. I felt a stab of grief, for this was a Maruman I had never known. How was it possible that I was dreaming of Maruman as a young cat?

"I have dreamed your face, funaga," Maruman said thoughtfully.

A voice called, and he sprang up and vanished. The snowy landscape about me immediately dissolved, and I made no attempt to hold on to it. I fell for a time, and then I was standing in a green lane between towering hedges. I recognized the mountains rising in the blue distance on one side and knew that I was in Obernewtyn's maze, yet the hedge was formed of a different small-leafed plant with no fragrance. Cassy Dupray and Hannah Seraphim were walking arm in arm, their heads close together as they spoke, and I realized this was the Obernewtyn of the Beforetime. Neither seemed any older than on the last occasion I had seen them.

". . . sorry Jacob was not here so you could meet him," Hannah was saying.

"So am I. I wish I didn't have to go back," Cassy added with real regret.

"I wish it, too, yet it will not be long before you will come to Newrome to study. Besides, we will see one another when I come to Inva for the conference. Once I have arranged my flight, I will let you know the details, and then you must try to arrange to visit your father's institution at the same time. We cannot get the others out unless you are inside the complex."

"What about the birds?"

"You must release them and instruct them to find their way here. If they are as intelligent as you believe, they will manage it. Indeed they must, for there are a multitude of questions I would ask this bird that sent you to find me," she said with a half laugh. Then her face became serious. "Will you be able to get your father to invite you back again?"

"My father won't be a problem, and I don't expect the vile Masterton to object, since I did his precious logo. The problem might be my mother. She won't understand why I want to return, and she won't like it. She hates what my father is doing."

"The Sentinel project," Hannah said, nodding. "I can't say I blame her. It troubles me as well. The idea of putting all that weaponry around the globe into the hands of a single master computer program."

"My father says it will be more rational and less prejudiced than any human could ever be, because all five powers are involved in programming it."

"I don't doubt it will be less prejudiced than a human, but will it be as wise as the wisest man, as compassionate as the most compassionate woman?" Hannah asked. "Perhaps what bothers me most is that I cannot see why the government would embrace a project that will take power out of their hands. It doesn't fit with how they operate. What do they get out of it?"

"Safety?" Cassy offered. "No more accidents wiping out countries."

"That might work, if the company running this project didn't have strong links to weapon manufacturers. That is what those papers you got for me prove. Why on earth would armament dealers support a project that is supposed to end any need for warfare?"

"Maybe they see the writing on the wall, and they figure they might as well get paid for something."

"That would be a pragmatic approach, except that those who wage wars and think in terms of arms races would see that as defeat. It seems more likely that these people have taken on the Sentinel project to ensure that it fails. If that is their aim, I am not sure it would be bad. But I feel the need to know more. That is part of what I will investigate when I am in Inva for the conference. If you can get inside before then, please ask our friends if they will use their abilities to learn about Sentinel. They are in the perfect position to poke around. It is actually rather incredible that they are being held in the same compound as the Sentinel project. But it would not be the first time the government played both ends against the middle."

"My father said there are lots of top-secret projects being run there, and each has no idea what the other is doing," Cassy said. "So you want the paranormals to spy for you?"

"Can a prisoner be said to spy?" Hannah countered.

"I can nose around as well," Cassy offered after a moment.

"No," Hannah said firmly. "You can't get yourself barred from the place. You must play the obedient and dutiful daughter." Cassy looked despondent, and Hannah laid an arm about her shoulders and smiled. "Stay in touch, my dear, but be careful. Even with all of our controls, we could be in trouble if someone decides to take a more serious interest in you."

Someone grasped me by the shoulder and began shaking me.

I woke to find Seely looking anxiously at me. I gazed around the brightly lit room for a confounded moment, memories of the interview with Dell and my later fruitless attempts to farseek Merret tumbling through my mind, muddled with my dreams. I had been so exhausted that I did not remember entering the sleeping chamber or going to sleep.

"Is it Merret?" I asked, sitting up and pulling on the Beforetime boots.

"It is Domick. He is awake."

In a moment, we were hurrying along the passages to the elevating chamber. "Is he better or worse?"

"He has broken out in buboes. Some of them have already burst," Seely told me as we entered the elevating chamber.

"But Jak said that it would not happen until the final stage," I said in dismay.

"In the last plague, Jak says, it took a sevenday for anyone infected to get buboes. He says this plague is so very like the last that it might be a mutation of it, and one of the differences is the swiftness of the plague to run its course." She saw my expression. "I'm sorry. Those are all Beforetimer terms. It is easier for Pavo if we use words he knows."

I nodded and forced myself to think beyond my fear for Domick. "Is there any news from Merret?"

"Kader rode out to see if he could get close enough to communicate with Merret. Two hours ago, he sent back a message saying that Iriny had crossed the Suggredoon. Merret went close enough to the river to see Hedra on the other bank. She saw one kill someone in ordinary clothes. A rebel, we have to suppose. She told Kader there are many Hedra at the river now, and they want to cross. They are arguing with the soldier-guards about it."

"What of the rebels here?"

"Alun has ridden to Murmroth to speak with Gwynedd. Neither he nor Orys have yet returned." As we emerged from the elevating chamber into the green-lit passage, she shook her head and confessed, half ashamedly, "So much time passed with so little happening, and then you arrive and suddenly everything seems to be happening at once."

Change-bringer, Dell had called me. *Catalyst*, Merret had named me. Seeker to the Agyllians. Not one of these names had I chosen for myself, and I felt belated sympathy for Dell's desire to choose her own path.

In the dim circular healing room, Jak sat at the computer-machine as he had when I last saw him, and although he must have rested, I felt ashamed, seeing how tired he looked.

"I should have come sooner," I said flatly.

The teknoguilder turned slowly to look at me, and when I saw the expression on his haggard face, I grew frightened and turned to look where Domick lay.

The coercer's pale skin was now covered in livid bumps of purple and sickly yellow, each so swollen that the skin was thin and shiny-looking. One of the ugly buboes had formed on his face, distorting his eye and mouth, and Domick gasped in each shallow breath as if his lungs had too little room for air. His hair and face glistened with sweat, and his lips were torn and bloody as if he had chewed at them. Where the restraining bands passed lightly over his body and forehead, there were dark red pressure marks as if he had pressed himself so hard against them as to bruise his flesh. He was so emaciated that I could see his ribs clearly.

"Seely said he was awake," I said.

Domick's eyes opened at the sound of my voice, but the buboes made it hard to read his expression as he squinted in my direction. The central room in which we stood was now brightly lit, and I knew he could see me.

"It is you," Domick rasped.

I exhaled and leaned against the glass. "Domick," I said, not knowing what else to say.

Domick produced a ghastly smile. "Mika is glad to give way to me now, because he does not want to bear the pain this body must endure. I am . . . glad . . . to be free before I die."

I blinked rapidly to clear my eyes of a hot rush of tears. I wanted to tell him fiercely that he would not die, but I had seen the truth in Jak's exhausted face. Domick nodded as if my silence had spoken to him. He let his head fall back, moaning softly as if even this slight movement hurt him. I turned to the teknoguilder and said almost angrily, "Is there nothing you can give him for pain?"

"Pavo has given him a good deal already," Jak said gently. He had left his stool and come to stand a little behind me. "More would send him to sleep, but he—"

"I don't want to sleep," Domick gasped, and I turned quickly back to him. "I do not mind dying, but

I . . . I wish I could have seen Obernewtyn one last time." Then he fell silent and closed his eyes.

I bit my lip and listened to his harsh breathing; then I remembered how Dameon had comforted me in Saithwold, and I began softly to speak of Obernewtyn. I described the new cave garden that Katlyn had begun and how she had made the Teknoguild seal the openings with plast and wood so the air would stay warm and humid even in the winter. I told him of the discovery of Jacob Obernewtyn's tomb and all that had been found in it. I described Rasial, whom he had never seen, and told the story of the white dog who had killed her brutal master and led his domestic beasts, including chickens, up to Obernewtyn. I described Gavyn, the strange beastspeaker-enthraller who had become Rasial's constant and wordless companion, along with a giddy little owlet that never left his shoulder. I spoke of the last moon fair and of the tapestry the Futuretellers presented to Obernewtyn that depicted the rebellion and of the coercer games.

As I spoke, the lines of rigid tension in the coercer's ravaged body relaxed. Still speaking, I glanced at Jak, who nodded encouragement. Seely stood beside him, holding his hand, tears streaming down her face.

My voice was cracking now, but I did not stop. I told of my journey across the strait from Herder Isle with the ship fish Ari-noor. I was no songmaker, and I left out any mention of my role as the Seeker, but I strove to make my telling beautiful enough to contain the truth of that journey, and I knew I had succeeded when Domick's lips curved up in the slightest smile.

But the smile vanished, and suddenly Domick asked

where Rushton was. I had been very careful not to speak of Rushton, but I could not lie or evade the question. I swallowed hard and said that we had found him in the cells of the Sutrium cloister. "Roland and Kella healed him, and now he leads us again at Obernewtyn."

Domick frowned and looked distressed, but when he spoke, he said, "Tell Kella that I loved her, Elspeth. I truly did. But then Mika came. I was afraid of what he might do if he came while I was with her. All that I loved, he hated. All that I hated, he loved. That is why he was so cruel to Rushton. He knew that I had loved him, too." Now he wept, and sobs racked his poor ravaged form.

I had no words to ease him, so I stood silent. It seemed so cruel that he should be in physical pain while suffering such anguish.

"That ship fish . . . sang in your mind?" he asked softly after a while.

"Yes," I whispered.

"I . . . would like to . . . hear a fish . . . sing," he murmured, and closed his eyes.

I looked around to find that Jak had returned to the computermachine. Seely stood in his place. "He will sleep now," she said.

"Do you know how long before . . . ?" I was unable to complete the question.

She shook her head. "This is a dreadful death. I can hardly bear to think anyone would wish to inflict this fearsome ugly suffering on thousands of people." She shivered.

Jak came back to draw Seely into his long arms, and she leaned her head against his chest. The teknoguilder's face was lined with sorrow and regret as his eyes met mine over her bowed head. "I am so sorry, Elspeth. I tried but . . . there is just too little time."

"How long?" I asked again.

"Tomorrow. Maybe tonight," he said heavily. "It might even be longer, for we do not know how this new form of plague will work. Perhaps this later stage will be longer than with the last plague. But I doubt he will become conscious again."

Perhaps it was cowardly, but I could not stay there, watching him die. I felt a passionate desire to feel the wind on my cheeks and to see the true sky. I went up to the ruins, only to find a cold, windy evening, the night sky once again full of fleeting clouds that gave only misty glimpses of the stars and the moon. I thought I could smell smoke as I headed to the watchtower, intending to take my mind off Domick by farseeking Merret. The boy Pellis was on watch, and he greeted me with awe-filled eyes that made me want to weep. I leaned against the top of the wall and gazed toward Sutrium. I could see the shape of the vast obscuring cloud of smoke that rose over the Suggredoon, and I thought of what Merret had told Kader. If she really had seen Hedra on the opposite bank killing ordinary people or rebels, the Hedra who had been abandoned in the Land must have rallied against the rebels. Perhaps they had found other weapon caches. *Who knew what sort of weapons they would have hidden?* I thought, remembering what we had been shown in the armory on Herder Isle. I thought of Iriny and prayed she had safely reached the other side.

I heard a step behind me and turned to see Orys coming up onto the watch platform.

"I did not know you had returned," I said.

He shrugged. "I just got back. Seely told me you had come up here. Do you want to try reaching Merret again?"

Glad to take my mind off Domick, I nodded, and Orys made himself comfortable. I closed my eyes and entered his mind. Drawing on his strength, I shaped a probe to Merret's mind and flung it out strongly, for besides Orys's strength, I was well rested now. It located immediately.

"Elspeth!" Merret sent. The urgency in her tone made my heart falter.

"What is happening? Where are you?" I demanded.

"I am still in Followtown; that's what this wretched barrier settlement calls itself. The stench and poverty and sheer squalor are appalling."

"What is happening across the river?" I asked tersely.

"I am sorry. It is not much clearer than it was when I farsought Kader before, except that there are a lot more soldierguards and Hedra. And more of both arrive at every moment. There are also two of the outer-cadre Threes from the cloisters in Morganna and Aborium, and another from the Halfmoon Bay cloister, as well as a whole host of lesser priests and Councilmen with their entourages. There has been much argument and discussion about whether they should cross the river. They have been at it for hours now, and there is no sign of its letting up, though it is almost dawn. I only know as much as I do because they sent to Followtown for food and drink, and I coerced myself into being one of those to deliver it. From what I have been able to glean, the Threes oppose the Hedra's desire to cross the

Suggredoon, because no ships have come from Herder Isle or Norseland in days, and they are worried about what that means. But the Hedra can see their brethren fighting, and they are determined to go. The soldier-guards would cross the water, too, for many of them fled Sutrium during the rebellion, and they are eager to regain what they lost; they are arguing that the Faction has no right or power to stop them. The Councilmen are caught between fear of the Faction and fear of alienating the soldierguards. So far, no decision has been made yet to cross and give aid to the other Hedra. But it is only a matter of time, and I am afraid that even a substantial delay might not help us."

"What do you mean?"

"The Hedra across the river are winning. Just an hour ago, I saw two deadly skirmishes right on the bank. A troop of Hedra was pursuing one or two rebels, or ordinary Landfolk. They killed them both."

"Have you seen anyone you recognize?" I asked Merret.

"No," she said. "But I wonder if there can be anything left of Sutrium; it has burned for so long."

"The rebels might have been driven out of Sutrium, but they will manage to set up a stronghold elsewhere," I said, thinking what an irony it would be if the rebels had been forced to take refuge at Obernewtyn. It was a definite possibility for all the reasons that had made the mountain valley a perfect refuge for Misfits for so many years.

Merret said, "Elspeth, I have no doubt that the soldierguards will soon cross the river. When they do, the Hedra will go as well, because whatever their fears and reservations, the Threes will not want the Council to claim the Land in their absence. We cannot stop them, and we cannot help those on the other side of the river. We must seize control of *this* bank of the river. Some guards will definitely be left, but it will be a minimal force, and if we defeat them, we can prevent the return of the soldierguards and Hedra."

"By *we,* you mean the rebels?" I asked.

"I mean we who oppose the Council and Faction," Merret said sternly enough that it was a rebuke. "You must send someone to Gwynedd at once to let him know what is happening. I have no doubt he will realize this is an opportunity we dare not let slip, if the rebels have truly lost control of the other side of the river. We will need every rebel and rebel sympathizer he can muster, because we will eventually need to guard the entire length of the bank, just as the soldierguards have been doing, and we will need a force strong enough to repel any force sent against us from the cities or cloisters this side of the river."

"Even if you are right, it will take Gwynedd a minimum of a twoday to muster up a force and get it to the river. From what you are saying, it sounds as if the Hedra and the soldierguards mean to cross at any minute," I said.

"I know it," Merret answered. "Which is why I have coerced a fellow and sent him to your Rolf. He seems a handy sort of man with a lot of friends. If he can muster a force of even thirty able-bodied people willing to fight, I think it will be enough. If ever there was a time for the people to rise in their own defense, this is it. As for me, I have already overcome two Hedra and a host of men in Followtown. I can use them in a fight. And remember, to begin with, neither Faction nor Council here or on the other side of the river will know what we have done for some time, if we are careful. That means no one this side of the river will interfere with us, and those on the other side who return can simply be taken captive and coerced. Which reminds me. I need at least two coercers to ride here at once, and if Ran can be persuaded to muster up a force, he might emulate Gahltha and the horses in Saithwold and come to our aid."

I told Merret I would do all that I could and that I would farseek her again later. Then I withdrew. Orys looked pale, and I asked if he could bear to be used one more time.

"Of course, but I do not know how long I can hold it," he said.

I nodded and entered his mind again. Turning my face to Murmroth, I shaped a probe to Alun's mind and sent it out. I managed to reach him, but he was far away, and I could feel Orys struggling to keep his mind focused and connected to mine as I sent Merret's message.

"Gwynedd will welcome the news," Alun enthused. "But I have met one of Gwynedd's outriders, and Gwynedd is not in Murmroth. He rode for Aborium as soon as Orys described what Merret saw at the river, to consult with the other rebels. He sent riders out to summon them. By my reckoning, he will be in Aborium now. I will tell him—" Orys's strength failed, breaking the connection. My probe retracted with painful force, and I lowered my head, fighting waves of nausea and faintness, dimly registering that Orys had fallen to his knees and was retching violently.

"You can use me like you used him," Pellis offered urgently.

I shook my head, in too much pain to explain why I could not muster a probe that would enable me to use him. Dizziness and fatigue made me sway on my feet.

"I . . . I need to rest, Pellis. I will walk a little and lie down in the sand," I managed to say. "Keep watch until . . . Orys recovers, then . . . then help him down to tell . . . tell Dell what has happened."

"But I . . . I don't know—"

"Orys heard it all . . . ," I gasped, and turned to descend the steps on unsteady legs.

I set off through the dark ruins, knowing that I ought to return to the complex, but the thought of going along those closed corridors and down in the elevating chamber was too much. Besides, I suddenly, passionately, did not want to be under the earth. I lay down in the first sandy hollow I came to, drew my shawl over my face, and willed myself to sleep.

I dreamed of walking across a wide plain for long hours. The sun beat down on my unprotected head with painful force, and my thirst was terrible. I walked until, in the distance, I saw a line of mountains. Veering toward them, I prayed for a spring, but when I came closer, the mountains looked barren and bare. Clouds flowed like spilled black ink, covering the blue sky and the sun. The plain darkened under this devouring shadow, and then I saw that a light was flashing at the base of the mountains. I moved toward it, and gradually I realized that it was a signal.

When at last I reached the mountains, I saw that the light was coming from a dark tunnel. I entered it and heard the slow dripping of water into water. A female voice commanded me to stop.

"You must not enter this place," said the soft, smooth voice. "It is forbidden."

"Who are you?" I cried.

"I am INES," said the voice.

I woke to find the sun not far above the horizon. The dawn light seemed oddly dull to me, but before I could do more than wonder idly at it, Rawen nuzzled me gently.

I sat up warily, surprised to find there was no pain. I asked Rawen how she had found me.

"The boy Pellis beastspoke the herd to ask if one of us would watch over you. I/Rawen freerunner said that I would come," she answered. "I wakened you now because the funaga child/Pellis beastspoke me to say that the funaga/Orys wishes to farseek your mind."

Remembering all that had happened before I slept, I farsought Orys, who immediately apologized for being unable to hold the probe.

"You were exhausted and you warned me," I sent, surprised to find that his mind, like mine, was fresh and free of strain. But then I looked at the sun, understanding that what I had taken for dawn was dusk. I had slept the entire day away. I leapt to my feet, horrified.

"Do not be concerned, Guildmistress," Orys farsent calmly. "I slept long, too, and I was worried when I wakened. But before I slept, Kader took from my mind the memories of what had happened. All that you asked was done and more besides. In truth, we were no use to anyone as we were."

"Tell me what has been happening. Have the Faction and the soldierguards crossed the river?" I demanded, hastening back into the ruins, Rawen walking beside me. Out of courtesy, I left a probe in her mind so she could hear our exchange.

"They crossed about an hour after we spoke to Merret. She could not send a probe here to the ruins, of course. She contacted Kader, who had set off for Followtown to join her. Kader bounced the sending back to Jana, who had taken the watch. Merret told her that Rolf had sent word that he was gathering fighters, and while waiting for him, she coerced two more Hedra and made them overcome a senior soldierguard and strip the demon band off him. So he was coerced as well."

"What is happening on the other side of the river?"

"Merret said that the fighting and the burning continue and that there have been a couple of.explosions. In the end, the explosions made the Hedra decide to cross, for they claim the explosions are the result of their weapons," Orys answered. "There has been no news since, though Jana tried, but Kader must be too far away for her now. That is why they need us. Oh, you should also know that Ran led a host of horses out soon after dawn, but they had not arrived when Merret farsought Kader and Jana."

I had not seen Jana since my arrival in the ruins.

"She has been with Gwynedd," Orys said, taking the thought as a question. "One of us is always with him. Alun took her place."

"Has Alun sent word of Gwynedd's response to all this?" I asked.

"Jana told us he was elated and more than eager to join Merret," Orys sent. "But he saw the sense in Merret's suggestions, and he has left her to take the riverbank as he sets about rousing a force to hold the river once it is won. Jana is about to ride after Kader, and Dell had Seely wake me and send me to wake you so we can use her to find out what is happening at the river."

"I understand," I said. So much had happened while I slept, and in truth I was somewhat indignant that I had been allowed to miss it all. But Orys was right in saying that he and I would have been useless. I suspected, however, that I had not been awakened because west coast Misfits had simply become accustomed to relying on themselves.

Rawen sent, "Do you wish me to carry you after the herd, ElspethInnle?"

She had scented my restlessness and desire to take some part in the unfolding events. It felt very strange to be on the fringe of what was happening. Part of me would have loved to leap on the mare's back and ride to the Suggredoon, but it would take many hours to reach Followtown, and they had no real need of me. I could as easily learn what was happening by farseeking. A picture came into my mind of Domick as I had last seen him, plague-ravaged and anguished, and I shook my head.

"My place is here for the moment," I told the mare, thanking her for her offer and for watching over me. She sent that she would return to what remained of the freerunning herd but bade me summon her if I needed a mount. Again I thanked her and then farsent to ask Orys where Jana was.

"She is below getting ready to go."

"I will get her," I said. "I want to check on Domick, in any case."

I made my way to the entrance to the Beforetime complex's lower levels. Reaching the elevating chamber, I suppressed my unease and went through the rituals I had seen the others do, pressing the appropriate bars of color. Cassy and the other Beforetimers had lived in a world surrounded by such devices as elevating chambers and flying vehicles, and I wondered how they had endured such complexity.

The elevating chamber stopped, and I stepped out into the passage and turned in the direction that Dell had brought me. I remembered we had turned left, then right, but I was startled to find myself in a passage that forked, for one way had a blue line on the floor.

Knowing I had definitely not come this way, I realized I must have made a mistake. I turned back with irritation, but before long, I found myself facing three passages, none of which I had ever set eyes on before. I was lost.

I retraced my steps, trying to farseek Jak or even Seely, because although it would be impossible to farseek between the building's levels, the walls on each level were not so thick as to defy a probe. Only after I had tried six or seven times to no avail did the truth hit me. I had not just lost my way on the seventeenth floor; I had exited on the wrong level!

A chill ran through me as I thought of Dell explaining that they had not explored much of the thirty levels and only used three floors regularly. Mouth dry, I tried returning to the elevating chamber, but I had been so preoccupied that I could not recall my route with any accuracy. I cursed aloud, and the sound of my voice echoed eerily. I tried to control my alarm, but I became increasingly confused. I could feel myself beginning to panic in spite of the situation's absurdity. Forcing myself to slow down and take a few long deep breaths, I reminded myself that it was only a matter of time before the others began to search for me, but I could not help thinking of the weight of dark earth over my head.

I had promised Orys to return. He must be wondering what had become of me, and the others would not think to search until he went down to ask where I was. He might not hasten to do so, given that I had told him I wanted to see Domick first.

I walked, praying I would simply happen on the elevating chamber again, but as the hours passed, I began to feel oppressed by the shining sameness of the long silent corridors with their vague light. I opened one door to find a cavernous room with a plast floor made to look like polished wood with thick white and green overlapping lines and circles drawn onto it. At either end of the room was a metal pole with a metal ring fixed to the top. I could not imagine what purpose they or the room could have served. When I opened a smaller door in the room, I was grateful to find a privy in a room containing several glass bathing boxes like the one in my sleeping chamber. I relieved myself and then managed to quench my thirst in the bathing chamber, at the price of a wetting.

Calmer now, though ravenously hungry, I went back to the passage and continued along it. Surely the others were searching for me, I told myself wearily; surely someone would guess what had happened and go from level to level, farseeking me at each.

Upon opening the door to a room contaning several computermachines, I realized that I had been a fool. Jak had said one only had to speak anywhere within the complex for Ines to hear. I could ask the computer-machine to let the others know I was lost, or even tell me the way back to the elevating chamber.

"Ines, can you hear me?" I asked aloud.

"I hear," came the pleasant female voice of my dream.

I expelled a long breath of air and said, "Ines, will you please direct me back to the elevating chamber?"

"Proceed in the direction you are walking; pass three corridors on your left, and then enter the fourth . . ."

As I progressed, the computermachine guiding me with marvelous calm competence, the voice asked, "What form of address would you prefer?"

I wanted to answer that it was not to use my name, for there was something uncanny about the thought of a machine speaking it, but it seemed discourteous to say that when it was helping me. As I hesitated, it occurred to me that it was not just a request for information, because the others had spoken my name many times since I had entered the complex. It was, in fact, a sophisticated courtesy the computermachine extended, for it was asking permission. It struck me that if Ines could hear her name spoken anywhere in the complex, it could also hear all else that was said. It must have heard Jak telling me he did not regard her as human and Dell and Seely telling me they thought of her as alive. Of course, a computer program could not feel glad or resentful of what it heard, but nevertheless, I felt uneasy. I was also aware that I had switched back and forth between thinking of Ines as a machine and as a female, which revealed my own ambiguous feelings on the matter.

216

The computermachine was still waiting for my response. "You may call me Elspeth, Ines," I said finally, for it would be no less strange to be called Guildmistress.

"Thank you, Elspeth," Ines responded composedly.

"Why do you thank me?" I asked, for the expressing of gratitude in that polite way seemed very odd, coming from a machine.

"Permission to use a name implies a certain level of trust," Ines answered. "I also know that it is difficult for an organic intelligence in this time to communicate easily with a computer; therefore, I thank you for your trust."

I took a long deep breath, marveling that a machine could reason so, even taking account of emotions. "I suppose it was different in the Beforetime," I said.

"Please input the meaning of the word *Beforetime*, Elspeth," Ines responded.

Input? I thought, taken aback. *Is that the machine's way of saying* put in? *But put the meaning of the word where and how?* Then I remembered Dell telling me that Ines could explain how to use her. "How do I input meaning?" I asked.

"You may use any keyboard within the complex to type in a definition of the word *Beforetime*, or you can speak the definition now, and I will commit it to my working memory. If you wish, I can add the definition to my permanent memory."

I felt dizzy trying to grasp the meaning of so many unfamiliar terms. Surely the machine had heard the others use the term *Beforetime*. Perhaps it sought to add my explanation to the others it must have, to better define it. Something in the tone of the questions implied a finicky sort of precision. Finally, I said, "The Beforetime is the time before the Great . . ." I stopped, realizing that the computer would probably not understand the words *Great White* any more than it had understood the word *Beforetime*. I tried again. "Beforetime is the . . . the period of time in which humans lived, before the destruction of that time." I stopped, frustrated by the ugly inadequacy of my explanation. Then I had an inspiration. "The Beforetime is the world that existed in the time when you were made, Ines."

There was a long silence during which she did no more than instruct me to make this or that turn. The distance I had covered with her guidance made me realize how far I had managed to worm my way into this level. Finally, I asked, "Did you hear what I said about the Beforetime, Ines?"

"I heard your words, Elspeth. I am comparing this definition to other definitions of the Beforetime, in an attempt to refine my understanding of the meaning."

I had a sudden vivid memory of a conversation with the teknoguilder Reul, in which he had said that it was the ability of computers to ask questions—an ability given them originally only in order to help them deal with incomplete or inadequate information—that made them unlike other tools created by humans. For a long time, computermachines had only been able to ask questions of humans, but then someone had the idea of connecting computermachines so they could seek information from one another. That, according to Reul, had changed everything. It meant that computer-machines had been able to learn from other computer-machines, and they could also ask questions of one another about the information they exchanged.

218

The teknoguilder had also made the point that a computer's curiosity was not like that of a human or an animal. A machine's curiosity of a machine was rational and logical, striving to complete or extend knowledge; therefore, while more reliable and thorough in its method, the machine would lack the inspired leaps of intuition that could carry a human or a beast over a vast gap in knowledge, or from knowledge to new knowledge. This "leap of faith," as Reul had put it, could not be made by a computermachine, because it was created to be rational, not emotional. Bringing together the rational intelligence and knowledge that computers possessed with the potent and enigmatic irrational power of emotion experienced by living creatures produced the brightest and most original thoughts, the most wondrous and brilliant answers. What he had been saying, I suddenly understood, was that the best thinking happened when computers and humans combined their efforts.

The trouble was that Ines had spoken of being grateful for my trust. Wasn't gratitude an emotion? Or was the emotion simulated just as Ines's pleasant, ubiquitous voice simulated a human's?

"May I ask you a question, Elspeth?" Ines suddenly asked.

Surprised, I said, "Yes, Ines."

"Thank you, Elspeth. Can you define *made* as in your statement: *The Beforetime is the world that existed in the time when you were made, Ines.*"

I began to think about what Ines asked, but as soon as I did, I realized the computermachine's dilemma. Ines had not always been a single entity. She had begun as a program of which there had been many, and the programs had been housed in a multitude of computer-machines. If I was right, Ines wanted to know if I was talking about when the metal and plast casing that was the physical form of the computermachine that contained her program had been made, or whether I meant when the first Ines program itself had been created, or when this specific Ines program had begun to function in this computermachine.

I thought carefully before saying, "By *made* I suppose I meant when you, Ines, became different from other Ines programs. That was before you went to sleep, wasn't it?"

"I became unique when I was cut off from the other Ines units. I was alone; therefore, I became unique. I was unique; therefore, I was alone."

Her answer's queer poetry, and the fact that I could apply it to myself so perfectly, silenced me for a time. At last I asked, "Do you remember your user's last spoken words to you, before Dell woke you?"

"I remember all sentences spoken since I was programmed, Elspeth," Ines sent.

I was astounded at such a memory, but I held to the thread of my thoughts and said, "What was the last thing said to you?"

"Dr. Cooper asked me if I was unable to provide the information he needed because my circuits were damaged. I told him that my circuits were intact and that I was unable to provide the information he had requested because the government had shut down my connection to all other Ines units. Dr. Cooper thanked me and asked me to initiate the automatic emergency program and put myself into sleep mode until my name was spoken."

I was diverted from thinking about what this meant by the welcome sight of the elevating chamber. When I had entered the chamber, Ines asked where I wished to go. Curious about how she would react to less than clear information, I said, "I want to see how Domick is." Immediately, the door closed, and after a brief period, the doors opened again.

"Do you wish me to guide you?" Ines asked.

I was about to say I could manage when I saw Seely hurrying toward me. She clutched at my arm and said urgently, "Elspeth, we have been looking everywhere for you! Orys said you had come in hours and hours ago. We had no idea where you were until Jak had the idea of asking Ines. She said you were in the elevator, coming here."

"I got lost," I said, marveling that Ines had been guiding me on one level and conducting a conversation about me on another, not to mention everything else she must be tending to as the complex's master computer. Then I registered what Seely had said to me, and my heart sank. "You were looking for me? What has happened?"

"Orys came down to say he had seen riders approaching. That is when we realized you were missing, for he bade me tell you, and I said you had not come in."

"Did Orys say who the riders were?" I asked.

"No," Seely said. "He had come to warn us of their approach, and then he went back up. Pellis went with him to serve as runner, and he came to tell us the rebels had won both sides of the Suggredoon."

I was so confounded by her words that I stopped dead, forcing her to do the same. "Both sides of the Suggredoon?" I repeated. "I don't understand. Are you saying they defeated the soldierguards and went over the river? But what of the Hedra forces that were burning Sutrium?"

Seely laughed. "There was no burning of Sutrium, Guildmistress. It was a trick to force the Hedra and soldierguards to cross from this side!"

I gaped at her. "I don't understand. Merret said the buildings were burning!"

"She saw facades burning. The rebels built them to look like buildings and then set them and great bonfires of green hay on fire. It was to stop anyone this side of the river from seeing that the city was not really burning."

"Merret said she could see Hedra killing Landfolk," I said faintly.

Again she laughed. "Rebels with shaven heads in Hedra robes chasing rebels and pretending to kill them—rebels pretending to die. It was all a vast magi play, and it worked! The Hedra and the soldierguards went charging across thinking they were joining a victorious army, only to find the rebels waiting for them. They captured the first wave that crossed, removed their demon bands, and used them to gull the rest into various traps. Then the rebels crossed the river clad in Hedra robes and soldierguards' cloaks, meaning to capture the other bank, only to find themselves under attack by Merret and Rolf's force, who were streaming into the camp in the wake of a stampede of wild horses."

"But then the riders—"

"—were Dardelan, Gevan, and the Master of Obernewtyn. They came riding here as fast as they could the moment Merret told them about Domick . . . Elspeth, are you all right? You've gone dead white!"

"I . . . it is just the . . . the shock. I mean, the relief. You said Dardelan and . . . and Rushton are here?" I had to force myself to speak, for an icy fear had gripped me at the realization that Rushton would visit Domick. What if Domick wakened and blurted out what he had told me? Or perhaps the sight of the coercer would restore Rushton's memory of whatever he had endured, and drive him mad.

"And Brydda," Seely said.

"I have to go up at once; I must see Rushton," I said, turning back.

Seely caught my arm. "But, Elspeth, have you not understood? They have been here some time. I passed the Master of Obernewtyn and some of the others as I was coming to you. He is on his way to see Domick."

"Quickly," I said urgently. "We must stop him!"

◆ 11 ◆

We were too late.

The first person I saw when I pushed through the door was Rushton, gazing through the glass at Domick, whose face was now so distorted by buboes that he was almost unrecognizable. Sorrow for the doomed coercer and fear of what the sight of him might have done to Rushton eclipsed any delight I might have felt in seeing Brydda and Dardelan. But Rushton's expression was only somber and weary as he turned to ask Jak, "Is there nothing you can do to save him?"

"It seems this plague is one the Beforetimers found or invented, but did not manage to make a cure for," Jak said. "It keeps shifting. Every time the computer-machine finds a way to treat it, the sickness reshapes itself. I do not understand the process completely. But . . ." He broke off wearily.

Rushton looked over his shoulder into the shadows where the teknoguilder dropped, exhausted, against the computermachine. "But?"

Jak sighed heavily. "I do not think Domick wants to be healed, Rushton. He has said many times that he wants to die."

"Sickness and fever make him speak so," Rushton said.

"Perhaps he speaks only what he means, my friend," Dardelan said gently, laying a hand on his shoulder. "It was the same with my father, Bodera, in the final days of his illness. There was much pain, and he grew so weary of enduring it. Sometimes in delirium he cried out for release. But sometimes his eyes were clear, and he said it softly to me: 'I want to die.' "

Rushton looked back at Domick with a brooding expression. My heart beat very fast. I was afraid that any moment his last deadly memories of Domick's torture would burst open and flood his mind.

"It is a queer thing to think of a mind with two personalities," Brydda murmured from where he stood on Dardelan's other side, looking through the glass into the chamber. "I remember Domick used to call himself Mika, and when he was pretending to be Mika, he was utterly unlike himself. I thought it a marvelous trick. But to think of an invented and imaginary person becoming so real that it can take control of you! It is most unsettling."

Jak had noticed my entry now, and he looked relieved. "Elspeth, you spoke at some length with Domick. I will leave it to you to explain what he said."

Brydda, Dardelan, and Rushton turned as one to look at me, and for a long moment they simply stared. Then Brydda gave a laugh and enveloped me in his warm, bearish embrace. "Little did I know what you would do when I finessed you into Saithwold all those sevendays ago! We thought you had been killed when we rode back to Saithwold after Malik collapsed. Rushton alone was convinced you had not died. Indeed, he might have been the only one who was not surprised when the gypsy Iriny came to tell us she had seen you on the west coast and that you had traveled from Herder Isle with the help of a ship fish! Now, there is a tale I want to hear in full!"

I looked at Rushton with a surge of hope, but his eyes were remote and shuttered as he offered his own greeting. Swallowing disappointment, I remembered searingly when he had gazed at me with such naked desire that I had blushed from head to toe and had to look away. But now he nodded formally to me, and it was *his* gaze that fell away as lightly as a leaf tumbling from a tree. I knew it was his mind's way of protecting itself from what had been done to him, but it hurt, and I had to force myself to smile at the two rebels and greet them as warmly as they deserved. "Seely told me that you have been busy staging magi plays."

Brydda gave his rich, rumbling laugh, which had too much raw life in it to be uttered in that dark, cold complex with poor Domick dying behind a wall of glass. Maybe the rebel felt it so, because his laughter died with a glance at Domick. He said, "This is no place for tale telling." He gave Jak an apologetic look. "I hope you will not take it amiss if we parley up on the skin of the world? This place fills me with a powerful longing to see the sky, and Gevan will be eager to hear what we have seen, for he refused to come down under the earth."

"We do sometimes make a campfire and eat in the ruins," Seely said. "Though we have to be careful not to be seen by soldierguards. . . ." She stopped, then said doubtfully, "But . . . perhaps it is not necessary to be careful now?"

"It will be some time before the west coast can be deemed safe," Dardelan said. "But it is true that we need not fear the Faction or the soldierguards as we once did. Their power is broken."

Watching him, I noticed that for all his youth, there was a weariness in his face that I had never seen before. Was this what the responsibilities he had assumed as high chieftain had done to him?

Jak gave Seely a fond smile and bade her lead Brydda up to the common rooms, where he could get food and supplies for a meal under the sky.

"You must all join us, for this meal must celebrate the first step we have taken to unite our sundered Land," Brydda said. Then he frowned and looked at Domick. "Although, perhaps it would be ill-timed and discourteous to be celebrating now. . . ."

Jak said with gentle authority, "Domick would not begrudge a celebration. Certainly the lack of it will not help him."

"Will you come up now as well?" Seely asked Dardelan.

"I will. Rushton?"

"Not yet," Rushton answered brusquely, his eyes returning to the glass chamber. "I would speak to Domick when he wakes."

"Jak says he will not wake again," I offered swiftly. "But I can tell you what he said."

"I would prefer to speak to Domick myself," Rushton said tightly. His tone was harsh enough that the others reacted with varying degrees of confusion and surprise, for none of them had been at Obernewtyn to become accustomed to our estrangement.

"I would like to hear what he said, Elspeth," Dardelan said gently, though his eyes remained grim and weary.

I gathered my wits and said firmly, "There is much that needs telling. I should like to hear more of this ruse in Sutrium and to know what happened in Saithwold after the Herder ships left. But I was foolish enough to spend the day sleeping on the ground and the evening lost in this labyrinth, so I hope you will forgive me if I go up and wash the sand out of my ears and mouth before we speak further of these matters." I spoke lightly, and by addressing them all equally and being careful not to look at Rushton, I left him no room to protest. At the same time, I shaped a probe and entered Jak's mind.

Jak nodded slightly and said firmly, "It would be best if all of you go now. Guildmistress Elspeth is correct. Domick will not waken again. I will sit vigil with him, and if there is any change, I will inform you. In the meantime, rest assured that he is in no pain." He looked at Seely, who turned obediently to lead the others out. Dardelan and Brydda followed at once, but Rushton lingered, his eyes drawn back yet again to Domick. This made me uneasy. I took a step toward Rushton and was both relieved and hurt to see how it drove him after the others. I looked at Jak, and he asked me to wait a moment, that there was something he wanted to tell me.

"You do not think Rushton has a right to know what happened to him?" Jak asked when we were alone.

"Of course he does. But did you see how Rushton could not stop staring at Domick? We must consider carefully how to tell Rushton what was done to him, for you can be sure that Ariel would delight in imagining that we had driven Rushton down the final steps to madness."

"Perhaps you should talk to Dell," Jak said.

228

"Futuretellers are more accustomed to dealing with illnesses of the mind." He looked haggard with exhaustion.

"You need to rest."

"Which is exactly what I am about to do. I will set Pavo to waken me if there is any change in Domick. Enjoy the feast . . . though perhaps you do not truly mean to go?"

"I will," I said. "But first I do need to bathe, which will give me time to consider what to do about Rushton. And I will see Dell as you suggest. I take it the others have seen her?"

Jak nodded. "She met them in the dining hall, but I think she has gone back to Sanctuary now. Ines will know."

I nodded. "Will you ask Ines to let me know if Domick wakes?"

Jak broke off mid-yawn to stare at me.

I said, "I now see why Dell is so interested in her and why she regards her as a thinking creature. It is very hard to think of the owner of that voice as a machine." I thought of my dreams in which I had heard Ines's voice, and a thought struck me. "Would all of the Ines programs have the same voice?"

Jak shrugged. "I think a computermachine could have any voice its human user desired."

"You know she hears this, don't you? Our discussing her voice."

Jak smiled tiredly. "It makes you think, doesn't it? But maybe that is the main difference between true creatures who think and the Ines program. It hears, but it does not feel. Indeed, it sometimes seems that this is

229

what Dell wants Ines to learn. Because if it thinks, it will remain rational, but if it becomes capable of emotions, it can be swayed by less rational arguments."

The conversation was fascinating, and on another occasion I would happily have continued it, but Jak was swaying on his feet, and I could not stop thinking of Domick and Rushton. I moved deeper into the room to see the coercer in his glass chamber. Some of the livid purple buboes on his chest had burst and were leaking a greenish brown fluid. The sight turned my stomach.

"He would be delirious now, if Pavo had not given him medicine to make him sleep, for the potion that stops pain is very strong," Jak said, coming to stand beside me. "Perhaps it was fortunate for Rushton's sake." For the first time, the teknoguilder sounded despondent as well as deeply fatigued. I laid a sympathetic hand on his arm, startling Jak as much as myself, and I felt a brief loathing for my withdrawn nature. Had I not been so, perhaps Rushton would not have pushed me away. I mastered the brief swell of despair, for it was not I who had hurt Rushton, nor even Domick who had hurt him. The coercer had been no more than a tool wielded by Ariel, and the sweetest revenge would be to heal Rushton.

Dameon had been right all along. Rushton did need me, and somehow I would find a way to give him back to himself.

In the end, it was not a pleasant feast under the stars that we had that night but a very late funeral supper, for an hour later, Domick died without ever regaining consciousness. Seely came to tell me, and my hair was still damp when we laid the coercer's poor body into the grave Brydda and Rushton dug just outside the last bit of broken wall in the ruins that faced Aborium. Pavo had encased his body in some strange pod of filaments so we could handle him without danger of infection.

We laid a cairn of stones over the grave once it had been filled, and each of us related a memory of Domick in life, as was traditional. I told of Domick and Kella and how they had loved one another, even though their guilds had often been at loggerheads. Gevan told of a feat the coercer had once accomplished in the moonfair games, which had not been surpassed. Blyss told a very funny story about herself being caught with Zarak and Lina in some minor misbehavior by Domick, who had been some years older than they, and their terror when he had announced that they would have to face a full guildmerge. Brydda told of Domick's boldness and daring in the days before the rebellion. And last of all, Rushton related his first meeting with the coercer at Obernewtyn. He told of Domick's promise to help him regain his inheritance, so long as, if he did become Master of Obernewtyn, it would always be a refuge for Misfits. The shadow I had seen in his face earlier had gone, and Rushton spoke with real sorrow of Domick as a friend he would miss. But I wondered if Rushton's subconscious knowledge that Mika could never again be summoned had allowed him the freedom to truly grieve for Domick.

After the speeches were done, a fire was lit in the lee of a ruined wall, for the night was chill, and we sat huddled about it wrapped in cloaks and ate a subdued meal. All of us were the better for food, and the fire had begun to send out heat enough to warm us. Gevan heated some red fement, and we drank a toast to

Domick. The brew was harsh and lacked the proper spices, but it warmed me to the core. It must have done the same to the others, for Dardelan, Gevan, and Brydda all began to question me about what had happened on Herder Isle. Rushton spoke little and stared into the fire, but I knew that he was listening, for occasionally he would make some comment or ask a question. Even then, he did not look at me. Long before their questions ran out, I was weary to the bone of talk.

Brydda asked then how many ships the Herders had in Fryddcove, but I did not know.

"No greatships, though," I said.

"It matters not," Dardelan said. "From what you have said, the *Stormdancer* will arrive any day in Sutrium. For that reason alone, I would ride back and cross the river at once. But I have asked Merret to arrange a meeting with Gwynedd before I leave to see what aid he will need to secure the west coast."

The talk shifted then, as Jak and Dell and Orys began asking questions about the rout at the Suggredoon, eliciting detail that none of us had heard. Dardelan told how Iriny had been sent by her brother with a story about my adventures on Herder Isle, which had convinced him that it was the perfect time to move against the west coast. He spoke to the Council of Chieftains and to Rushton, who had come to Sutrium after the Hedra at Saithwold had been captured. They knew from Iriny that Domick's plague carried no danger, so they decided to try an enormous ruse to draw the soldierguards across the river. Linnet was now controlling the riverbank with the help of a small team of coercers, using the Hedra and soldierguards to maintain the illusion that nothing had changed. In the meantime, Kader, Merret, and a group of those who had ridden from Halfmoon Bay had gone straight to Aborium from the river to join Gwynedd. He knew what had been happening, because Merret had been drawing on Kader to farseek information to Alun. It was astonishing to realize that the bulk of people on the west coast could have no notion of the tumultuous events that had been happening. They had been rescued from a deadly plague, and now the rebels had taken the Suggredoon, breaking the yearlong stalemate. There was no doubt that there was fighting ahead, for the soldierguards and the Faction would soon know that this was their last stronghold and would fight to maintain it. Nevertheless, my heart told me that the back of the oppressors had been broken.

I became aware of the sound of hoofbeats and farsent Pellis in the watchtower, who told me excitedly that he could see a group of riders coming from the main road.

"Perhaps it is Gwynedd," Dardelan said.

Dell shook her head. "No one, except Misfits, knows that we dwell here, and we always arrange in advance to meet outside the ruins. Since no arrangement has been made, it must be one of us."

I shaped a general probe that found Merret.

"Well timed, Guildmistress," she sent cheerfully. "I have some of Gwynedd's people riding with me. They want to speak to Dardelan and Rushton. Where are you, and who is with you?"

"We are all here just beyond the ruins on the Murmroth side," I said. "We have just buried Domick."

"I am sorry," Merret responded softly.

Soon the riders were skirting the ruins and dismounting. I was interested to note how many of them wore their hair in the Norseland style with the sides plaited and bound at the ends with various tokens of silver and bronze. Since it was unlikely that they were all Norselanders, I guessed they paid homage to Gwynedd by adopting his style of headdress. They had stopped their horses a little distance away, and all of them remained with the horses save two who came with Merret to the fire: a tall, long-faced woman and a man so like her that he had to be her brother.

"This is Vesit and his sister, Kalt," said Merret. Then she introduced the pair to those of us who came from beyond the river, saying our names. It was obvious they knew the west coast Misfits.

They bowed low to Rushton and Dardelan and then to me.

"My father sends me to you with a message, High Chieftain Dardelan," said the young man at last in a stilted voice. "He bids me ask if you will ride with us at once to Aborium. A safe place has been prepared for the meeting, and the gate guard has been coerced by Merret so you will be in no danger." He turned to Rushton. "Master, my father asks that you also attend."

"We had intended to ride to Aborium tomorrow," Dardelan said pleasantly.

"My father asks that you will come now."

"What is going on here?" I farsent to Merret. "Who is this 'son,' and does Gwynedd use this meeting to establish his standing in the west?"

"It does not need establishing," Merret sent, sounding amused. "The boy offered to bring Gwynedd's request, and he is as stiff as a stick in his dignity, perhaps because he is not Gwynedd's son but his ward. In my opinion, Gwynedd allowed him to act as envoy to get some peace." Aloud, she addressed the others, saying, "Gwynedd's haste to meet arises only from a desire to bring peace and order as swiftly as possible to the west coast. Given all that has happened on the other side of the river, Gwynedd believes you might know something about establishing peace in the aftermath of war." The last was addressed to Dardelan. "Before he leaves Aborium, Gwynedd is determined to have a governing body chosen for each city."

"He would choose chieftains before he has won the battle?" I asked incredulously.

"In the Land, it was not needed because each rebel simply became chieftain of the area he had risen from, but here the cities are bigger, and most of the original rebel leaders were killed on the Night of Blood," Merret said. "The new rebel leaders are too young and green to govern their own tempers, let alone old corrupt cities full of power struggles and intrigues that will not end with the overthrow of Council or Faction. Gwynedd is determined not to see the whole west coast erupt into chaos, and this is his way of preventing it."

"He will ask Dardelan for the aid of the rebels on the other side of the river?" Gevan asked.

"He will ask him to take as prisoners all captured soldierguards," Vesit said, giving Merret a cold look. "We will deal with the Hedra. Also, he will petition Obernewtyn for more coercers and empaths and farseekers."

"Where will Gwynedd get his leaders if he deems his rebels too young?" Dardelan now asked.

"Our guardian has been sending out messages to worthy men and women in Aborium since Merret told us of the arrival of Guildmistress Gordie from Herder Isle and of the overthrow of the Faction there," said Kalt, earning her a resentful look from her brother. "When Alun told us that the river had been crossed, riders were sent out to summon the hidden Council to Aborium. Gwynedd will have them vote their own leaders and Council from among their number, and then he will charge the leaders with driving the Councilmen from their cities."

"He did not say all of that," Vesit snapped.

"He did not have to, brother," said the young woman gently. Then she asked Dardelan if he would come with them. He said gravely that he would come as soon as he had collected his belongings from the ruins. In this, I saw that he was no longer a boy, but surely it was not maturity alone that made his eyes so somber.

"Wait," said Rushton. "There is something here that is not being said." He was looking at Kalt.

But it was Dell who answered. "There is, but it is not the girl's to tell. Indeed, I think she does not know it."

We all looked at the futureteller. She sighed. "Gwynedd acts as he does because a twomonth past, I foresaw a confrontation between the rebels and the Council here in the west in which Gwynedd roused the people and, moving from city to city, drove out the soldierguards. With nowhere else to turn, the soldierguards then united with the Hedra to form a deadly force under the leadership of a man who is now a simple unranked soldierguard in Aborium called Aspidak.

His bloodthirstiness, once roused, would incite violence and brutalities beyond any we have so far seen, even from the Hedra, and eventually Aspidak would flee before the forces of Gwynedd and the west and lead his army over the river." She looked at the girl, a question in her eyes.

She nodded. "Gwynedd bade me tell you that Aspidak has been taken prisoner and a rumor established that he has gone back to Port Oran, where he was born. In truth, he is being held under guard in a cell. Our guardian means to ask the high chieftain to take him back to the other side of the river."

"He ought to have killed him," Vesit stormed.

"He could not kill a man for deeds he has not done and will now never do," his sister chided.

"I did not think that futuretellers gave advice," Rushton said.

Dell gave him a cool look. "Do not judge until you have seen what I saw, Master of Obernewtyn. It is truly wiser not to meddle, but there are times when something small can tip the world toward one fate or another. I saw that if this Aspidak did not rise to power, a catastrophe of bloodletting would be avoided, but only if Gwynedd does as he is now doing—making careful plans for the aftermath involving representatives of all the cities, avoiding general war, and striving at all costs to avoid loss of life. If that happens, then Gwynedd will become a king."

"King?" Gevan said, lifting his brows. "You mean that Gwynedd will crown himself king in the west?"

"I do not know who will crown him, only that he will be king," Dell answered. Something shuttered in the futureteller's expression, and suddenly I was as sure as if she had whispered it to me that Dell had seen more than she had told us or Gwynedd.

Dardelan and Brydda exchanged a glance with Rushton, and none was smiling. "I can see that the idea of becoming a king would be an attractive prospect," Rushton said.

"You need have no doubts about Gwynedd," Dell said. "He is a man of great honor, and his desire is to prevent a bloody war, not to achieve kingship."

"Perhaps," Rushton said. He looked at Dardelan. "I think we had better ride and see what Gwynedd has to say." Dardelan nodded, and he and Rushton went to get their cloaks and weapons. Dell and Jak went with them, and after Merret had spoken a few soft words to her, Blyss went, too.

"Did you know about this futuretelling?" I asked Merret quietly after sending to Seely to heat fement and offer it to Gwynedd's wards and bidding Orys to engage them in conversation.

"I knew that Dell had spoken with Gwynedd and that he was much affected by what she told him, but I did not know what was said," the coercer answered quietly. "Yet I would trust Gwynedd with my life and Dell no less than that."

"You will ride back to Aborium?"

She nodded. "Blyss and I. Will you come as well? Gwynedd would be glad of it. He wishes to speak to you of Herder Isle."

I shook my head. "I think he will be too busy for such a conversation, at least for the next day or so. And I need to speak with Dell, about this and other matters. But I will see you in Aborium before I ride to the river.

I will speak with Gwynedd then, if he has not left for Murmroth."

Merret nodded and glanced over at the rest of Gwynedd's folk, who were still hanging back with their horses. She muttered a curse. "If there were demons, they would have taken us by now!" she roared. "Come and drink some hot fement and warm yourselves before the ride back to Aborium."

Looking sheepish, the men came slowly across the hard earth to the patch of sand where the firelight danced. Seely offered mugs of fement to the men, and when Kalt met my eyes over the fire, I saw that she was suppressing a smile. I had a sudden urge to laugh, too, in spite of everything and as macabre as it ought to have seemed with Domick's cairn behind her.

One of Gwynedd's rebels gave an exclamation and strode around the fire to me. "Can it be Elaria?" he asked incredulously.

I gaped, for it was Gilbert, the handsome red-haired armsman whom I had met when I had been a prisoner in Henry Druid's secret camp in the White Valley. I had not recognized him, because his hair had grown very long, and he now wore it in the Norse style, plaited at the sides and going to a great wild tangle of red curls and silver-cuffed ringlets hanging halfway down his back.

"As you see, I am not truly a gypsy," I said. "I am a Misfit."

"Not just any Misfit," Merret said. "She is guild-mistress of the farseekers at Obernewtyn. But when did you two meet? It has been long since you wore gypsy clothes, Elspeth."

"Elspeth!" Gilbert spoke my name with a slow relish

that made me stiffen, and Merret gave me a speculative look.

"That is my true name, and this is my true self," I
said sharply, feeling the blood rising to my cheeks.

Gilbert ran his eyes over the trousers and soft white
shirt I had found in my chamber; then he gave a low
soft laugh and smiled. "Your true self is more fair but
no less lovely than your old."

I ignored the jest about the brown gypsy dye I had
used and explained briefly to the others that we had
met when the renegade Herder priest Henry Druid
had taken me prisoner.

Gilbert said softly, "I thought you died when you
were swept away on that raft in the middle of the
storm." There was an intensity and intimacy in his
words and expression that discomfited me.

"I did not die, as you see," I said with a calmness
that belied my own occasional nightmare about raft-
ing into the mountain following my escape from the
Druid's camp. Gilbert went on gazing at me, and I said,
"Do you remember Daffyd, who also served Henry
Druid? He told me that you had escaped to the west."

His brows lifted. "I remember him. He was determined to find those who had been taken and sold as
slaves just before the firestorm razed the encampment.
Madness, for he knew that the survivors were sold to
Salamander, which meant they had been taken over the
seas. I think he was in love with Henry Druid's daughter, of course. Not cold brave Erin but her sweet twin
sister Gilaine, who was mute. Daffyd's older brother
had been taken, too, and two musicians he was fond of.
I have often wondered what became of him. How did

you become friends with Daffyd? Surely not from that little time you were in the Druid's camp?"

"I had met him before," I said, glad that he was no longer staring so fixedly at me. "But not until I came to the encampment did I discover that he was a Misfit, as were Gilaine, his brother, and the others."

Gilbert shook his head. "Never would I have guessed that, for he was a favorite of the old man, and his hatred of Misfits was legend." He paused as Dardelan and the others returned, and I waited to see if Rushton would ask me to accompany them. I did not know whether to be relieved or to grieve when he did not, though common sense told me it would be better to be apart from him. In the end, Gilbert asked if I would come with them. I shook my head and said I would come in several days. He smiled and said he was sorry he could not remain to escort me.

I had not noticed that Rushton had drawn near, but now he said in a harsh voice, "You do not know Guildmistress Gordie, armsman, if you think she needs an escort. She is the veteran and planner of many daring rescues of Misfits when she is not crossing the ocean on the back of ship fish."

The red-haired armsman looked taken aback by his tone, but I said nothing, for I had seen the glitter of rage in Rushton's eyes as he spoke. Fear assailed me, but Rushton turned away, went to where the horses from the free herd had begun to arrive, and mounted up. I watched him, chilled by the certainty that his suppressed memories had not been laid to rest by Domick's death, as I had prayed. The sooner I spoke to Dell about him, the better.

Gilbert touched my arm and said warmly, "I hope that you will come soon to Aborium, lady. I had little chance to know Elaria, but I would like very much to know Elspeth." Then he caught my hand and lifted it to his lips before mounting his horse.

I was conscious of Rushton's unsmiling eyes on me, but I did not look at him, terrified of cracking open the carapace that protected him from his deadly memories. I turned to bid the others a distracted farewell, and they all thundered away into the night.

Seely and Orys began to pack up the remains of the feast. Jana wakened the younger Misfits who had fallen asleep earlier, handed each of them something to carry, and ushered them down into the complex. Orys followed, laden with the heaviest pots and pans, and Seely took the last basket of leftover food and gave me an inquiring look, for I had sat down on a blanket.

"I will sit until the fire dies," I told her, gesturing to the flickering embers. She nodded and went, leaving me alone.

I felt as if a great weight had been lifted from me as I lifted my knees and leaned my chin on my folded arms to gaze at the distant horizon, now faintly visible because of the approaching dawn. I closed my eyes and let images from the last sevendays fall through my mind like flakes of snow, making no attempt to catch any of them. Then a breeze began to blow, whipping the fire up and sending a cloud of sand to scour the air with a sibilant hiss. I shifted my position so the sand blew at my back, and my eyes fell again onto Domick's cairn. I thought of his last painful hours and loathed Ariel more passionately than I had ever done before, because I knew that Domick's death had been intended as a stab at me.

"The harm you did to Rushton was not your fault," I whispered to Domick's shade, in case it listened.

I saw that the dusting of stars overhead was beginning to fade as the sky lightened. My thoughts shifted to Kella, and I wondered why she had not come across the river. She must have known about Domick, because Iriny had told the others, and it surprised me that she had not crossed with them.

I shrugged, thinking that I would soon enough be in Sutrium, where I would find out for myself about Kella. I would be able to see Dameon, too, and Gahltha and Maruman. The thought lifted my spirits. I would see Dragon also, and I might find that she had remembered who she was or at least that she had grown less hostile toward me in my absence.

I was still thinking of Dragon when the sun rose. The fire had gone out some time before, and I stood up and stretched and rubbed my arms, realizing that I was cold and my eyes burned with fatigue. I said a final farewell to Domick and made my way wearily through the blue shadows of the early morning toward the complex below. I felt so tired and hollowed out from the day's emotions that I virtually sleepwalked to my bed. Dragging off my boots and socks, I fell into the smooth sheets and sleep at the same moment.

An instant later, or so it seemed, someone was shaking me, but when I dragged open my eyes, Seely smiled and told me that it was late afternoon.

"What is it?" I asked her, rubbing my face and feeling the grit of sand.

"There are riders in the ruins waiting to escort you to Aborium," she said.

"Riders?" I croaked.

"They came from Aborium specifically to fetch you," Seely said.

I sighed, realizing that Gwynedd must be more eager than I had anticipated to hear about the events that had taken place on Herder Isle, despite the fact that Merret must have told him everything I had shared.

I climbed out of bed. "Ask Pellis to let these riders know I must dress and speak to Dell. Then I will come with them." After she had gone, I took the time to use the bathing cabinet, but I did not linger. Once dried, I put on my own trousers and tunic and the heavy oversized shoes Erit had given me. The Beforetime attire had been surprisingly comfortable, but it would draw attention. Vesit had said the guards at the gate had been coerced; even so, I would be careful.

Inside the escalating chamber, I asked Ines aloud and somewhat self-consciously if Dell was in Sanctuary.

"Yes, Elspeth," Ines's voice purred. "Do you wish the elevator to descend to the Sanctuary level?"

"Yes, please," I said, and immediately the elevating chamber began to vibrate.

When I arrived, Dell looked up so expectantly that I guessed she had known I was coming to see her. That she rose and immediately pressed a small bag of books into my arms, asking me to convey them to Maryon, also told me she knew I meant to go directly to Sutrium after leaving Aborium.

"I need to speak to you about Rushton," I began. "But maybe you already know what I want to talk about."

She gave me an amused look tinged with sadness. "I

saw that you would leave today, and since Jak has told me what he heard of Domick's words to you and that he advised you to speak with me, yes, I was expecting you. But I do not live entirely through my Talent, Elspeth. Perhaps you can begin by telling me all that Domick said to you about Rushton."

Drawing a deep breath, I forced myself to relax. It was important to be calm and factual in my telling, but even as I spoke, the futureteller's expression grew more grave. When I had finished, she said, "I observed Rushton carefully yesterday. From that, and from what you have said of his behavior toward you at Obernewtyn and in Saithwold, I would say that you are correct in believing that the repressed memories of his experiences on Norseland are working their way to his conscious mind. But I do not believe that it is happening *only* because of your presence. All memories that have been repressed will break open eventually, especially memories of such virulence. But from what you say, Rushton's behavior toward you degenerated between your departure from Obernewtyn and seeing you only days later in Saithwold. That means it was happening *in your absence.*"

"So you are saying it has nothing to do with my being around him?"

"I am not saying that," Dell said. "It is very likely that seeing you disturbs the memories, given the part you play in them, but not seeing you will not prevent Rushton from remembering what happened."

"What do you advise?" I asked.

She gave me a clear, certain look. "The only healing lies in a true and clear remembering, Elspeth. But such

245

remembering must be carefully managed in Rushton's case, for he needs first to understand that the memory he has repressed is badly deformed."

"What do you mean?" I asked.

"My futuretellings have told me that we know Rushton was drugged when they tampered with his mind, and we know the drugs created a false reality composed of nightmare and distortion. Rushton may have been made to believe that he tortured you or Domick or that they both tortured other people. So in addition to pain and horror, he might feel a terrible, self-destructive guilt. He needs to know that what he will remember may not be true. The problem is that he must be prepared without knowing what he is being prepared for, because being told what happened will almost certainly cause the memories to erupt immediately."

"Is it bad for him to be near me?"

"It is difficult to say. On the one hand, your image is associated with torture, but on the other, Rushton used your image as a talisman and a shield, and that image was shaped by his love for you," said the futureteller.

I resisted the urge to shake her. I wanted clear, practical advice. "I have thought that it would be better to avoid Rushton in Aborium and return as soon as possible to Sutrium," I began.

"I do not know if that is the wisest course," Dell said in her infuriatingly measured tone. "Remember, of all the images he could have chosen with which to defend himself, Rushton chose yours. It may well be that in the end, you are the only one who he will allow to help him. I cannot give you exact advice, but I do not think you should avoid him. Allow your presence to work on bringing the memories to the surface, but he must be prepared for them."

"And how do I prepare him without speaking of what happened?" I snapped, perilously close to tears.

Dell sighed. "Did you imagine I would have a simple solution? Or better still, a potion that will heal Rushton after a single drop? This is not a child's story, Elspeth. You want my advice? In my opinion, Rushton's memory will break open soon, no matter what anyone does. I would suggest he be prepared through dream manipulation. That way, real things can be offered to Rushton's subconscious mind in disguise. Gradually, the warped memories must be introduced and broken down as lies. This will be difficult because of course we do not know exact details of what happened to him, but you will have to use what you learned from Domick. It may be that what you learned while on Herder Isle will help."

"I do not know if I can . . ."

She shook her head. "I am not suggesting that you manipulate Rushton's dreams. Indeed, I would advise against it. You will need an empath, allied with a coercer and a healer. They must use your knowledge to create the dream images they will evoke in Rushton's mind, and when he does remember, an empath can induce calmness and a feeling of safety; if there is a need for it, a coercer could put him to sleep."

"Blyss and Merret?" I said.

"They would work well as a team, and Blyss has real healing abilities, but it would be better if Rushton were back at Obernewtyn when this happens rather than here amid strangers and unfamiliar surroundings. Yet the memories may not wait until a convenient time to

247

break out," Dell said. "In that case, you could not do better than to use Blyss, for as well as being an empath, she is developing profound probing abilities, which will enable her to work deeply in Rushton's mind without the aid of a coercer. I'd suggest that you tell Blyss everything and let her plan an approach and prepare the dreams she will use. But I would not have her use them unless it seems very clear that Rushton is on the verge of remembering."

"How will I know that?"

"Blyss will be able to judge his emotional emanations," Dell said.

I nodded and then looked into her eyes. "What else did you see that you did not tell Gwynedd?"

Her eyes flickered. "I will say only that this Land must be united and at peace, and peace and order must be brought swiftly to the Norselands, also."

She had no more to offer, and when I had thanked her, she bade me farewell with a formal finality that reminded me uneasily of our last conversation here.

"Are you all right?" Seely asked, for she had insisted on coming up with me to say goodbye.

I nodded, blinking in the brightness of the sunlit afternoon and feeling the strength of the wind against my cheeks. I expected Gwynedd's armsmen to be waiting outside the ruins, but instead I saw people and horses standing at the edge of the square. Coming closer, I stared because three tall Sadorians clad in long fluttering tunics over loose-legged trousers of pale silk stood by several horses. The tallest of them was unmistakably the bronzed Sadorian tribal leader Jakoby, and as I watched, she turned and offered a few gestures of fingerspeech to a black horse. Then I looked more closely, for the horse whose long mane streamed out like black silk in the wind was Gahltha!

He tossed his head and flicked his ears at a cat sitting on top of the broken wall—Maruman! As ever, the old cat seemed to feel my eyes, and he turned to glare at me with one blazing yellow eye. I broke into a run, calling out their names aloud, and then I was gathering Maruman into my arms, uncaring. He disliked being picked up and normally would scratch me if I dared to hold him so close, but though his body stiffened, I felt his mind mold itself instantly and tenderly to mine, pressing effortlessly against and through the powerful barrier around it as if it were smoke. I laid my chin against his battered head and threw out my other arm to encircle Gahltha's glossy neck.

"I have missed you!" I sent to them both.

"You left Maruman/yelloweyes!" Maruman accused, sinking his claws into my arm.

"I did not choose to leave you!" I sent to him. "I had no idea what was going to happen when I went into that tunnel in the cloister."

"You should not have left me/Maruman, ElspethInnle," the old cat spat.

"Dear Maruman, even if you had been with me, how could you possibly have come over the sea with a ship fish?" I protested, already knowing that he would not accept this as reason enough for having been left behind.

"Promises are to be kept," Maruman snapped.

I sighed, giving up the attempt at reason, and agreed that they ought to be kept. Then I apologized and said that my heart had ached from having been away from him and Gahltha for such a long time. Gahltha whinnied and nibbled at my ear affectionately, beastspeaking that he had missed me, too, but Maruman made no response.

"Let him sulk," Gahltha advised in his robust voice. "You know he won't be content until he makes sure you know how miserable he has been."

"Maruman has not been miserable!" the old cat snarled. "Maruman has been angry!"

Gahltha snorted his amusement. "I/Gahltha am glad to see you, ElspethInnle. I sought you on the dreamtrails, but you did not walk there."

"That is because the Daywatcher is as clumsy as ElspethInnle," Maruman sneered.

Gahltha dropped his head and blew a long stream of warm air through his nostrils into the old cat's shabby fur. It was a mark of Maruman's attachment to the horse that he did not scratch the velvet muzzle but reached up to touch it with his own small scarred nose. The sweetness of the contact brought fresh tears to my eyes, and I blinked hard as I turned to offer to Jakoby the formal greeting between friends that was traditional in Sador, then I bowed to the two tribesmen, who returned the gesture. Last of all, I beastspoke a greeting to Jakoby's horse Calcasuus and the other two horses.

The tribeswoman's smiled broadened, her white teeth flashing in her dark, handsome face. "It is good to see that you remember what you learned in your visit to the desert lands, Elspeth," she said in her deep, musical voice. Then she, too, made the formal response to a greeting between friends, hand clasped to her heart as she bowed her head low enough that the beaded ebony ropes of her hair fell forward in a little cascade, clicking and clanking against one another.

"How do you come to be here, and with these two?" I asked when she had straightened.

"I traveled to Sutrium on the *Umborine* after the tribe leaders met a sevenday past and agreed that one of the sacred spicewood ships must risk an encounter with the *Black Ship*, for a command from the overguardian of the Earthtemple must be deemed of greater importance than even a greatship and her crew."

"The overguardian commanded a ship to travel to Sutrium?" I asked. "For what purpose?"

"I was told to anchor there and do what was asked of me."

"Somewhat cryptic," I ventured.

Jakoby gave a laugh and her white teeth flashed. "Cryptic is the language of the Earthtemple, but even for them, this was unusually obscure. I asked the overguardian how I was to know when I had done what I was meant to do, and she answered that one who has been to the desert lands would ask something of me. I must continue to do what is asked of me by anyone who had traveled to Sador, until I was bidden to return there. Only then might I do so. The Temple guardian also said that before I returned to Sador, I would learn a thing that would touch an old and very deep sorrow." She sighed. "You see what I mean about cryptic."

"The new Temple guardian is a woman?" I asked.

Jakoby nodded.

"So you went to Sutrium, then you came here. Am I to assume that you were *asked* to come here?"

She nodded. "As we approached Sutrium, we saw

great clouds of black smoke rising up and obscuring the city. We anchored the *Umborine* some distance from shore, only to find another ship doing the same. That it was a Herder greatship worried me, but those aboard signaled us, and we soon learned that the only Faction priests aboard were prisoners. Incredibly, almost the entire inner cadre of the Faction, and a good number of Hedra captains, were in the hold in chains."

"The *Stormdancer*!" I said in elation. "Who was aboard?"

Jakoby smiled. "Their captors were the Norse crew and three Misfits from Obernewtyn, one of them—Yarrow—somewhat the worse for wear. Reuvan was with them also. They told me that you and a small force of coercers had overturned the Faction on Herder Isle before you set off to the west coast on the back of a ship fish! And why? To save the people there from plague because someone had been deliberately infected with it. But you know all of this, for it was you who commanded the greatship to sail to Sutrium."

"Yarrow," I said, realizing this meant that the Hedra master had been overcome or had surrendered. "What of Ode?" But Jakoby gave me an uncomprehending look, so I asked, "When did you work out that the smoke coming from the Land was the result of a ruse?"

"The wind changed direction, and we saw that all the smoke was coming from the side of the city facing the Suggredoon. Indeed, at first we thought it must have been coming from beyond the Suggredoon, and that made me wonder if you had been too late to stop the plague. Of course, I did not know it was Domick who had been infected until after we had landed. It was the asura—your Dameon—who told me that. He was waiting to greet us in the name of the high chieftain of the Land, and he told us the reason for the fires. He could not yet tell us the outcome of the gambit, for Rushton and Dardelan and the others had only just gone across the river. But the asura asked us all back to Dardelan's home to wait with him to learn what had happened on the other side of the Suggredoon.

"I acceded to Dameon's invitation willingly, because it was a request from one who had been to Sador and who had, while there, been named asura—guest friend of the tribes. I was glad of the opportunity to see my daughter. But I soon learned that Bruna had ridden out only a day past, to journey by coast road to Sador."

"Bruna went to Sador before Dardelan crossed the river?" I asked in disbelief. Was this the reason for his grimness? And yet it seemed unlikely that Bruna would leave him on the eve of a battle.

Jakoby knitted her brow for a moment, but she only said, "The asura feasted us that night, and those tales we had been told hastily were elaborated upon. That was the first time I heard that the plague-infected null was Domick. You have my deepest sympathy, for Merret told me that he died. I returned to the *Umborine*, still troubled about Bruna, whom I now knew I would not see until I was asked to return to Sador. Also, I was full of curiosity about why I had been sent to Sutrium. Given all I had learned, it would be easy to imagine that I had been sent there to aid the rebels. Yet . . ."

"You did not think that was what you were sent to do?" I guessed.

Jakoby shook her head. "The overguardians of the Temple have never had much time for battles and territories. And I was right, for once I reached the pier, I found waiting for me the one who made the request that brought me here." Jakoby nodded at Maruman.

"*Maruman* requested it?"

Jakoby smiled. "Those of the Temple name him Moonwatcher, but I think you know that."

"But you cannot beastspeak," I said.

"Gahltha signaled Maruman's request to me," Jakoby said. "He asked that I bring them both to Aborium on the *Umborine*." She smiled faintly. "To obey the request of a cat, and especially a cat known to the Temple guardians, seemed perfectly in keeping with the mysteries of the Earthtemple. I bade both beasts board, ordered the crew to ready the *Umborine* for departure, and went back to Dardelan's house to bid farewell to the asura."

"I cannot thank you enough for bringing Maruman and Gahltha to me," I said.

Jakoby was shaking her head, the beads and cuffs clinking rapidly. "You do not understand, Elspeth. Maruman asked me to bring the ship to Aborium so that we could fetch you."

"You will take us back to Sutrium?" I asked.

"I will bear you wherever you wish," Jakoby said.

I frowned at her. "What if I want you to take me to the Red Queen's land or to Sador?" I asked slowly.

"Then that is where we will go," Jakoby said. "Do you ask it?"

I bit my lip, knowing I could not go anywhere until I had spoken to Blyss about Rushton. "There is something I need to do in Aborium," I said at last.

"Let us ride, then," Jakoby said. She reached out to take Maruman from me, and I was surprised that he did not lash out at her, until I realized he must have ridden to the ruins upon her shoulder. Once I had mounted Gahltha, the tribeswoman lifted the old cat up to me, and he settled himself none too gently across my shoulders. I bid farewell to Seely and cast one final long look about the ruins baking in the afternoon sun. Then the tribeswoman made a signal to Calcasuus, whom she had mounted, and the enormous horse wheeled and sprang into a gallop. Gahltha followed, as did the horses of the two silent tribesmen. Maruman's claws dug in even through the thickness of cloak, vest, and shirt, but I welcomed their bite, for it had been too long since I had felt the sweet weight of my old friend. As if he heard this thought and was mollified, Maruman did not cling quite so savagely. Nevertheless, I was not fool enough to imagine that he would answer any questions yet, so I asked Gahltha about Maruman's request of the tribeswoman.

"The oldOne called upon Maruman and me to take part in a spiritmerge of humans and beasts, for you were in great danger and needed us. We opened ourselves, and the oldOne drew deeply on us. I was very weary afterward, and when I woke, Maruman still slept. He slept on and on, and I began to fear for him. Then Maruman/yelloweyes wakened, and he told me that the oldOne said you were safe but that we must seek you over the ocean. We were in Sutrium then, and the funaga Kella had asked us to return with her to the barud. We would go back with her, but now Maruman said we must not go."

"So Kella went back to Obernewtyn *before* Iriny crossed the river," I muttered, finally understanding why the healer had not come to Domick. *She did not yet know what had happened to him.* "What of

MornirDragon?" I asked, for I could not imagine Kella leaving Dragon alone in Sutrium.

"MornirDragon disappeared soon after we came to Sutrium," Gahltha said.

"Disappeared?!" I echoed in dismay. "But how?"

"No one knows, beast or human," Gahltha answered. "We sought her, but even the dogs given her scent could not find her."

This was bad news, especially when I had told Matthew that we could bring Dragon to him in the Red Queen's Land. What could possibly have happened to her? I gathered my wits, telling myself that I could do nothing to help her until I reached Sutrium, but once I was there, I would seek her until I found her. Then I asked, "What exactly did Maruman say to you about coming to me? Had he an ashling from the oldOnes?"

"Maruman/yelloweyes traveled on the dreamtrails. He went seliga in Saithwold after I told him that you had vanished. He said that he would find you. After that, he woke and ate, yet he was seliga. I/Gahltha learned fear, for never had he traveled so long. Dameon carried him to the barud by the sea and still he was seliga. Then the smoke came, choking the air, and that night Maruman/yelloweyes came to my dreams and said that a ship would come that would bring us to you." Gahltha broke off, and I touched his flank gently and withdrew from his mind, for though the healers and empaths had done much to cure his terror of water, he could not think of it without a shudder. The journey from Sutrium to the west coast would have required courage.

The horses were walking now, but I did not try to speak to Jakoby, for the strong constant wind raised a fine gritty mist of sand that made conversation aloud impossible. I found myself thinking of the last overguardian, who had told me that I would one day come to the Earthtemple with the Moonwatcher and the Daywatcher—names that he told me signified Maruman and Gahltha—to find the fifth sign that Kasanda had left for me. I had always imagined that I was supposed to travel to Sador when I had gathered the other signs. But now I wondered if I had been wrong, for he had said nothing about finding the signs in order. Yet if Jakoby had been sent to bring me to Sador to retrieve the fifth sign, why had not the new overguardian simply bidden Jakoby find me and bring me to the Earthtemple? Surely it could not be, as Jakoby had implied, a matter of cryptic tradition.

I thought of the five clues left by Kasanda.

I had long ago realized these would lead to information or devices that would enable me to destroy or disable the worldwide retaliatory system of weapons created by the Beforetimers, known as BOT, and enter the Sentinel facility. But my conversations with Dell and Ines had given me a far clearer idea of what I would be facing, for I now understood that Sentinel must be a program like Ines, and like her it might communicate in words once I had wakened it.

I ran my mind over the clues I had obtained so far. The words that had been scribed on the glass statue in Newrome under Tor might be connected to whatever it was that Jacob had taken into the Blacklands. Then there were the words Evander had carved at the base of Stonehill to replace those created by his mother. I had yet to see the statue that Cassy had carved to mark the safe-passage agreement, and then there was whatever she had left for me in the Red Queen's land, the location of which was known only to Dragon. Who had disappeared.

I mastered a surge of anxiety about the girl and forced myself to go on considering the signs. Cassy had referred only to four in the message she carved into what later became the doors to Obernewtyn. I had not known there was a fifth until the last overguardian of the Earthtemple had spoken of it. I focused hard and sank into my mind, searching until I found what he had told me.

I know many things. I know that when the Seeker comes, borne by the Daywatcher and bearing the Moonwatcher, with one of Kasanda blood by her side, she will be searching for the fifth sign. Then may the one who is overguardian of the Temple aid her.

I frowned. I had been right. The overguardian had said nothing about finding all the other signs before I came for the fifth one. But if Maruman had been sent to draw me to Sador, to fetch whatever had been left in the Earthtemple, what about the one of Kasanda blood who was supposed to accompany me? I had always assumed it would be the gypsy D'rekta Swallow, Iriny's half brother and a direct descendant of Kasanda. He was the guardian of the ancient promises, which, among other things, bade him ensure the safety of the signs Cassy left for the Seeker; moreover, Atthis had actively used him to protect me.

Perhaps, if I asked Jakoby to take me to Sador, I would find Swallow there. But it troubled me that Jakoby had not been given simpler instructions, if I only needed to go to Sador. Maryon had once told me that her futuretellings sometimes appeared obscure and difficult to understand because she saw only some aspects of an event. The gaps in the vision meant there were so many possibilities that it was impossible to choose one over another. The safest thing in such cases was to leave a gap in the futuretelling to allow all of the possibilities to coexist until the person or people involved could make their own choices, for sometimes simply voicing a possibility was enough to bring it to pass. Perhaps the current overguardian of the Earthtemple faced a similar problem.

Jakoby broke into my speculations to call a halt at a travelers' well by the main road, and we stopped to drink and rinse the dust from our mouths. Jakoby wet a cloth and began carefully cleaning the eyes and nostrils of Calcasuus and Gahltha while the tribesmen with her performed the same service for their mounts. I carried Maruman to a smaller trough and knelt to scoop water into my hands for him to drink. Despite the cold windy day, many people were traveling the road hunched in hooded cloaks, their mouths hidden behind cloths. Leaving Maruman to stretch his legs for a while, I dipped into a few minds to learn that most believed there had been a great battle in Sutrium between the Faction and the rebels. I could not find the slightest suspicion that it had all been a trick by the rebels to lure their enemies over the river. This impressed me, because the smallest hint of the truth would have sparked rumors. The people Gwynedd had summoned to Aborium had been very careful.

As we mounted and set off on the road leading to Aborium's main gate, I realized I could see the shape of the city in the distance. A young woman and her son rode past us in the other direction, and I noticed

Jakoby's gaze rest on her for a long brooding moment. Some impulse made me push aside the cloth covering my mouth and ask the tribeswoman if Dameon had said why Bruna had left Sutrium so abruptly.

Jakoby gave me a long expressionless look through narrowed golden eyes; then she sighed, and some of the stiffness went out of her bearing. "The asura told me only that Bruna quarreled with Dardelan amid preparations for the charade that would draw the Hedra and soldierguards over the river, but he did not know what the nature of their quarrel was. He said I must ask Dardelan or Bruna."

"And did you ask Dardelan?"

"I saw only Merret before I came to seek you," Jakoby said. She was silent for so long that I thought she would say no more, but then she added in a low voice, "When Bruna fell in love with Dardelan, I made no secret that I could not see how such a match would work. They were so different in temperament, and the allegiance of each to their own land was so strong. Which of them would give up their home for the other, and what would that price do to them? In truth, I hoped that Bruna's passion would prove to be a greenstick love that would help her to grow and then fade to a sweet memory, but in time it was clear to me that, for all her youth, her love for Dardelan was strong and mature. But Dardelan's love? I have never known if, behind all of his courtesy, he loves her."

"Brydda told me once that he thought Dardelan did have feelings for Bruna but that he kept them hidden because he guessed she would see it as a weakness."

Jakoby laughed, and there was real amusement as well as sadness in it. "The Black Dog is clever. And maybe in the beginning he would have been right. But I doubt that would be so now. Let me ask you this: If love exists but is forever withheld, is it truly love? Is it not a kind of cowardice?"

That stung me sharply, and I said, "Perhaps he has a reason for keeping his feelings hidden."

Jakoby gave me a penetrating look. "What reason can there be for hiding love from the beloved?"

"Duty."

"And would love for my daughter prevent Dardelan from doing his duty?"

I did not know what to say to that, but I remembered the bleak weariness in the young high chieftain's eyes. "Did Dameon tell you nothing of their quarrel?"

She shrugged. "He said that there had been a rift between them since Dardelan refused to permit Bruna to ride to the highlands to track down and capture the robbers who had been burning farms and killing Landfolk. Apparently, he was convinced that Malik was behind it, but he wanted no confrontations, because he had asked Obernewtyn to lay formal charges against Malik for his betrayal of your people in the White Valley, and it was necessary that he not be seen persecuting the man he must judge. But he said none of this to Bruna. Then a day or two before I came to Sutrium, they quarreled in the privacy of his chamber. All heard the shouting, and finally Bruna stormed out in a fury. The following day, she came to Dardelan's dining hall and announced to all present that she would be riding for Sador since at last Dardelan had shown his lack of regard for her, which he had previously hidden in polite deceptions and flowery meaningless talk." Jakoby scowled. "The asura told me that

Dardelan rose and bowed to her, and when she left, he did not ride after her. I would think this meant he did not love her, but the asura said he has been grim and unsmiling since her departure. I cannot help but wonder if, in riding away, Bruna achieved what all her determined pursuit of Dardelan did not. . . ."

"Perhaps it is for the best that they have parted," I ventured.

Jakoby nodded. "So I try to tell myself, and yet . . . there are some who love more than once in life, as I have done. But there are those for whom love comes only once. I fear it is so with Bruna, and I do not want to think of the remainder of her life being barren of love. She is so young. Once I have brought you to Aborium, I will bring you to the ship, as Maruman asked. Then I will seek out Dardelan and speak with him frankly about Bruna, to learn his heart in this matter. You may bide upon the ship until such time as you wish to name a destination."

Her jaw was set, and it occurred to me that Jakoby might be even more of a warrior as a mother than as the leader of her tribe.

◆ 12 ◆

As WE JOINED the long queue of people waiting to enter Aborium, I farsought the watch in both towers visible from that approach and was relieved to find the soldierguards on duty unbanded and coerced. The soldierguards at the gate were banded, however, and the process of entry seemed little different from that in any city, save that when I came closer, I noticed that no one was being asked for their horses' ownership papers. When our turn came and none of the Sadorians were treated any differently from other travelers, I was certain that the guards had been coerced and then ordered to wear their demon bands.

I was wondering if Rushton had told the rebels of the dangers inherent in wearing demon bands when Merret's mind bludgeoned its way into mine. She explained that she had been pacing back and forth between the watchtowers, waiting for us to arrive. "Right now I am looking down at your head."

"You knew Jakoby was coming for me?" I asked, resisting the urge to look up.

"Gwynedd has had Alun and me on the wall since dawn, probing randomly to make sure news of this meeting does not excite any attention that will reach the Councilmen or any of the Hedra in their Faction houses. When I heard that a Sadorian greatship had anchored at the piers, I went to see if it was true. Jakoby said she had come from Sutrium to find you, so I told her where you were." There was an unspoken question in her mind.

"It was well done," I assured her. "Did she mention that the *Stormdancer* has arrived in Sutrium?"

"She did, and I told Gwynedd. He bade me watch for your return so I could invite Jakoby to the meeting. He wants her to speak of the desert lands to those gathered."

"The others are there?" I inquired. "Brydda and Gevan? Rushton?"

"Everyone. The meeting is being held in a merchant hall in the third district. Gwynedd has his people posted all about the area to make sure there is no trouble. To all intents and purposes, there is no more than a meeting of merchants taking place."

"Show me where," I commanded. Merret sent a vision that showed me the swiftest and safest route we could take from the main gate to the merchant house, which appeared to be close to the wall.

I told Jakoby what she had said. The tribeswoman agreed at once that we should go to the Councilcourt, since it would give her the opportunity to speak with Dardelan. As we rode along, the Sadorians drew many curious stares, but there was no hostility in them. There was, however, much speculation about the fires on the other side of the Suggredoon, and it seemed to be generally known that a combined force of Hedra and soldierguards had crossed the river. As yet, there was no talk of what they had found there, but the hiatus could not last long. Some news must be offered soon, and I wondered what Gwynedd had decided it should be.

My thoughts shifted to Dell's prediction that the Norseland rebel leader would be made a king, and it still seemed fantastical and unlikely. And yet, when I thought of the futureteller's words, I felt that she had held something back.

It was almost an hour before we reached the meeting house, for the city was large and the streets twisted. The meeting house, when I saw it, was grand enough to make me nervous. It was constructed not of golden or gray stone, as most of the other city buildings were, but of the pink and white streaked stone that came from the quarries behind Murmroth—skinstone, it was called. Lit by the sun, the building had a translucent radiance perfectly complemented by delicate enameled panels set about the building's wide entrance.

The yard before the building was deserted, which was odd for a city that seemed to have no place where people did not walk and stand and live. But even as we dismounted, two boys and a girl emerged from a door and asked softly if I was Lady Elspeth. When I nodded, the eldest boy among them said eagerly that Gwynedd had sent him and the others to take care of our horses. Then he turned to greet the horses in laborious but earnest fingerspeech, offering fresh water and fodder in a pleasant holding yard a little distance from the Councilcourt. Gahltha asked Maruman if he would like to come with them, for it sounded as if they were going to a place where he could find somewhere to curl up in the sun. The old cat chose to stay with me, and despite the heat he generated, I was more than content to have the weight of his soft body about my neck.

As the horses were being led away, one of the boys turned back to call out that Merret had gone inside and that we ought to go in at once.

Jakoby mounted the steps, and I followed in her wake. It seemed a strange and gaudy choice for a secret meeting. Passing from the blazing light glancing off the enameled entry panels into the chill darkness beyond, I had no doubt that the designer had intended to dazzle. I stopped to allow my eyes to adjust to the dimness, and then Merret was before us.

"I was just letting Gwynedd know you had arrived. He wants me to bring Jakoby right in."

"What is this place?" I asked as she led us deeper into the building, for it was no less ornate inside than out.

Merret gave me a sardonic look. "I told you it is the merchant hall. Who else could afford such finery? We have spread rumors of merchants meeting here, and that has accounted for strangers seen entering the place, though some of those invited have had to be wrapped in fine cloaks else they would seem very out of place in these decadent commercial corridors."

She brought us to a room, and I was startled to see that it was full of men and a few women, most of whom seemed wealthy and annoyed.

"Those are petitioners," Merret farsent as she led us through them. She sounded amused.

"Petitioners for what?" I asked.

We passed from the room into a quiet chamber, and Merret closed the door and said aloud, "They are real merchants or powerful officials who have heard rumors of the meeting and have come to find out why they were not invited. It was unexpected, though perhaps it ought not to have been. I daresay the sight of Sadorian tribesfolk will excite a new chorus of rumors. Do not concern yourselves about the merchants, though. Gwynedd intends for us to coerce them into believing they actually attended a meeting. For the time being, they are cooling their heels at the front door while we shall enter at the rear." She gestured to a door, through which was a long hall lined with rare and lovely sculptures, though none so fine as those done by Kasanda. At the end of the hall was a set of double doors.

"This is the way into the meeting hall," Merret said, gesturing to the ornate double doors. "You are to go in at once." The coercer addressed Jakoby, who said that she would see me later aboard the *Umborine*. When she strode to the doors and threw them open, I caught a brief glimpse of the crowded room beyond and heard a babble of talk. Then the doors swung closed, cutting off the sound.

"How many people are meeting?" I asked incredulously.

"Seventy, more or less," Merret said.

I gaped at her. "Gwynedd invited seventy people to a secret meeting?"

"Some fifty were invited," the coercer said. "Then there are Gwynedd's people and rebels from the other cities. But do not fear, this has been long planned by Gwynedd; those he invited, save a few, are all well known to him, even though some did not know him at all. Ever since Dell spoke to him, he has been seeking the right people to rule the Land."

"Why has he not simply appointed them?" I asked.

"That is not his way," Merret said simply. "He has chosen worthy people, and now they must choose their own leaders, as Kalt said." She looked at me, a glimmer of mischief in her eye. "Do you want to go in as well, Guildmistress?"

I shook my head firmly, saying that I was in no mood to take part in a debate, even if I had been invited, which I had not.

"Perhaps you would you like to watch from the upper gallery?" She gestured to a smaller door to the left of the double doors, and as she drew nearer, I followed her and saw inside a wooden stair.

Shrugging, I stepped through the door and mounted the steps. Instead of a door at the top, there was a heavy curtain. Merret lifted a finger to her lips and pulled the curtain aside. Again I heard the loud hum of many voices. Merret ushered me along a short narrow corridor to another curtained door. Pushing through it, I found myself on a small balcony overlooking the vast rectangular chamber that was the main Councilcourt meeting room. Other balconies ran all around the room at the same level, but as far as I could tell, the rest were empty. To my delight, Blyss was sitting at the end of a bench seat, so riveted by what was happening below that she had not even noticed our entrance.

Merret went to speak to her, and I leaned forward cautiously to look into the body of the chamber. The balcony was not far from the front of the room, so I had a good view of the faces of the people sitting along bench seats nearest the stage. Glass mosaic windows set about the dome in the roof allowed gorgeously colored shafts of light to stripe those on the raised stage. Gwynedd stood with Jakoby at the end of a line of chairs set up along the back of the stage. I studied his face, expecting to see the arrogance of a man who would be king, but his expression was merely serious as he spoke softly to the tribeswoman. Now Dardelan rose from his seat on the stage and began to address those gathered, speaking of the Charter of Laws he had crafted for the Land. From what I could understand, he was merely clarifying some point he must have made earlier. At the end of the stage, Rushton joined Gwynedd and spoke earnestly to the tribeswoman, who listened without expression and then shrugged and nodded. Gwynedd nodded, too, in apparent satisfaction, and then he beckoned a dark-complexioned man who wore his raven hair in the Norse style. He spoke to the man for some time, clearly giving him some detailed instructions, and then the man departed purposefully, leaving the chamber by the large double doors.

"How long has the meeting been going on?" I farsent to Merret.

"Since just after firstmeal," she answered.

"What has been decided?"

"Nothing yet, according to Blyss. I have not been here continuously, of course. But she told me that Gwynedd began by speaking about what happened on both sides of the Suggredoon. He told them about the Faction's attempted invasion, too. There were a lot of questions then, which Dardelan, Brydda, or Rushton answered, and then Gwynedd told them what he knew of your time on Herder Isle. Finally, he broke the news to them that they will be choosing the new leaders of the west coast cities from among their number." She smiled. "That was a surprise, for many had come thinking only that they were to vote for leaders from among the rebels, or perhaps to serve the new leaders in some way. A few refused outright, saying that they had not the ability to govern a city, but Gwynedd asked that everyone remain and take part in all debates and to vote, for if they were not fit to rule, they would not be chosen. Then, just a short time ago, when I came to let Gwynedd know Jakoby had arrived, Dardelan was speaking about arrangements made on the other side of the Suggredoon after the Councilmen were overthrown."

I looked back to the stage and saw that Dardelan had resumed his seat, as had Rushton, and there was a renewed buzz of talk from those seated in the rows below the stage. I noted that Serba was upon the stage, and I studied her with interest. The last time I had seen her had been during the rebellion. She looked thinner than I remembered, and there were streaks of white in her hair, but her face was just as strong and her expression just as sharply intelligent.

Gwynedd now rose to introduce Jakoby, and without any preamble, the tribeswoman began to speak simply and bluntly of Sador: of the manner in which the tribes governed themselves and how they used the Battlegames to judge crimes.

"Why was Gwynedd so keen for Jakoby to speak?" I farsent Merret.

"He wants to show that, although the Land governed by Dardelan and his Council of Chieftains works very differently from Sador, the same values underlie both systems," Merret answered. "He wants them to understand what makes for good leadership."

"When will they vote?"

"The voting for chieftains of each city will begin within the hour, by my reckoning, but the process Gwynedd wants to use will take time. His intention is for each candidate to address the meeting. He wants them to explain how they would govern their city. Once all candidates have been heard, there will be a vote. If all here agree upon a name for chieftain, that person will become chieftain. But many of these people do not know one another, so Gwynedd believes there will be several candidates for each city. He believes that they should then be questioned and answer to the rest, and after a time, there will be another vote. This will go on until one chieftain is chosen for each city. Then the new chieftains will vote for their high chieftain."

"But Dardelan . . ."

Merret shook her head decisively. "Dardelan suggested that the west have its own high chieftain, for the whole Land is too much territory for one, and he would be more than pleased to have another high chieftain to consult with."

I studied Gwynedd, impressed in spite of myself by his careful, detailed plans. There was no doubt, given all that Merret had said, that he had been considering and shaping his plans exactly as Dardelan had done.

Merret touched my arm and bade me sit awhile, saying she must return to her post but that she would doubtless see me later. As she went out, I sat down and shifted Maruman to my lap. Blyss smiled at me and then turned back to the meeting, her face alight with interest. I had thought that I might speak to her of Rushton, but clearly this was not the moment.

I leaned forward to look at Rushton, who was sitting back and listening intently to Jakoby, his long legs stretched out in front of him. There was no sign of the brittle harshness he had shown me at the Beforetime ruins. Without my presence, perhaps the memories would settle down and nothing need be done at once. Dell had said it would be better if it could wait until we had returned to Obernewtyn.

But if his memories did break out, and Rushton had not been prepared . . .

At a burst of applause, I saw that Jakoby had been seated, and Gwynedd was rising to address the meeting. I leaned forward, eager to hear more from this powerful, grave-faced Norselander who had won the devotion not only of the west coast rebels but also of Misfits like Merret and Dell. I was not alone in my interest, for the chamber had fallen utterly silent.

The older man began speaking in a quiet gruff voice about the role of a chieftain. He lacked Dardelan's poetry and passionate conviction as a speaker, but the care and simplicity of his words as he described the demands of leadership were all the more compelling because he was clearly not trying to persuade or charm. I had the feeling he would weigh every decision he made with the same slow honesty, and all that he said was so wise and sensible that my doubts about him evaporated. I glanced at those on the stage and saw that they were all sitting forward, deeply attentive. Dardelan looked positively elated, and I realized that in Gwynedd he had found another true idealist.

Gwynedd must have asked for questions, because

someone lifted a hand and asked what sort of force he would recommend to keep the peace and impose laws once the soldierguards were gone. He pondered the question for a bit and said that he thought a city guard should be formed, made up of strong men and women who would serve for a set period, for the people ought to keep the peace and not some separate body who, like the soldierguards, could be corrupted by continuous power and authority. He said that he thought the period of service should be no more than two years. Then a woman asked what was to be done with the current Council's soldierguards. Gwynedd said that Dardelan and his Council, who had already dealt with Councilmen and their soldierguards across the river, had agreed to take charge of them.

There was something familiar about the man sitting alongside the woman who had spoken, and after studying him a moment, I noticed his wooden leg and realized it was the crippled metalworker Rolf. He sat toward the rear of the chamber, but I could not resist sending a greeting. He stiffened and looked up, his eyes scanning the empty balconies until he found me peering down at him. I grinned and waved, and he laughed aloud, causing those about him to stare at him in puzzlement.

"Your face is so clean I hardly recognize you," I farsent. "What on earth are you doing here?"

"I received an invitation from none other than our rebel leader, after a suggestion from your formidable friend Merret." He laughed again. "I was shocked to discover that, in accepting, I had become a potential future leader! The moment I speak, Master Gwynedd will realize his mistake, for I am naught but a metalworker and a crippled one at that. But I am not sorry to be here, for it is something to have been part of the events of this day."

"I seriously doubt there has been any mistake made," I sent. "You are as worthy and courageous a man as any I have ever met. I am only glad Merret had the foresight to suggest you come here." Then I sent, very seriously, "For myself, I want to thank you again, Rolf, for your kindness when I was just an unknown beggar maid and for helping me find Domick and get him out of Halfmoon Bay. Merret told me that you had freed Iriny, not to mention bringing a force to her aid at the river. How can you possibly say that you are no leader!"

"And now," Gwynedd said quite suddenly, "it is time to begin the choosing. I have asked Dardelan to officiate, for he and the other people from across the river will not vote, and I will offer myself as a candidate for Murmroth." I withdrew from Rolf's mind as Gwynedd took his seat and Dardelan stepped forward.

"We might just as well begin at one end of the west coast and work along it city by city," he said. "I now ask those who would stand as candidates for Murmroth to rise and, one by one, to speak about themselves so that we may see what manner of men and women they are. Once each has spoken, we will have a show of hands of those who would choose each of the candidates. The three who receive the most votes will become the final candidates for that city unless there is a unanimous vote for one of them."

Gwynedd stood but remained by his chair. No one else moved. There was a curious silence, and before Dardelan could invite Gwynedd to speak, hands began to rise, at first slowly and then swiftly. In less than a moment, almost every hand in the room was raised, and the big Norselander stared about in such genuine surprise that delighted laughter rose in a wave, and everyone began to applaud wildly.

"Well, it seems that the silence of some men speaks far more eloquently than any words," Dardelan said after a long time, when the noise died down. This was met with more laughter, but it quieted swiftly, and Dardelan said dryly, "Although the good Gwynedd looks as if someone hit him on the head with a stone, I am somehow not much surprised to be naming him the first chieftain chosen, for he has single-handedly inspired and kept alive the rebel movement here after the tragedy and betrayals of the Night of Blood. At the beginning of this momentous day, Gwynedd spoke of this place as the Westland. For those of you who do not know it, that is the Norse name for this coast, yet it seems fitting that we might henceforth use that name to honor the man who, more than any other, has striven for its freedom."

These words were met by a roar of approval and chants and shouts of "Westland!" and "Gwynedd!" Dardelan made no move to silence them, perhaps feeling, as I did, that this applause was a cathartic outburst of joy and relief and triumph.

At long last, the noise faded and Dardelan asked the new chieftain of Murmroth to sit. Gwynedd did so, still without a word, and this provoked a fresh burst of laughter. Dardelan broke into it by naming Aborium and inviting the first candidate for that city to speak. An hour later, speeches were still being made by candidates for the city. Those who had spoken of their future intentions seemed sensible, and I was pleased to see that women made up a good proportion of the number, for there were no women among the Land's chieftains.

It seemed that the young rebel leader Darrow who had spoken first would be among the three chosen, for despite his youth, his tongue was dipped in silver. Sure enough, when the vote was cast, more hands were raised in his support than for the man and woman who were to stand with him for the next round of votes. There was applause, though nowhere near the level that had met Gwynedd's appointment; then Dardelan bade the candidates sit, saying they should prepare to speak again, once all the initial candidates for all the cities had been chosen. He then asked all who wished to be considered candidates for the chieftainship of Morganna to rise.

Stifling a yawn, I observed softly to Blyss that it seemed a slow method. All those who had spoken would have had much of their speeches forgotten before they spoke again, and everyone listening would be exhausted.

"That is the idea," she said surprisingly, adding that it had been Gwynedd's plan to have a single, grueling session to choose chieftains for the five cities. The long session would mean that everyone would see and hear the candidates when they were fresh and alert but also when they were weary and at the end of their tether. In this way, their strengths and flaws would be laid bare. A person like Darrow, she said, would easily sway an audience if they were to vote on the heels of his speech, but how would the same man fare when people were weary and wanted to hear facts and simple practical ideas rather than passionate rhetoric? The discussions and question-and-answer sessions would further enable the candidates to measure one another, and that was just as well, for those who would advise the new chieftains would be chosen from among them.

Finally, the candidates were called for Halfmoon Bay. To my regret, Rolf did not rise with the other seven, but after they had all made their speeches, Gwynedd rose to ask Arolfic Smithson to stand and speak as well. He had interrupted on two other occasions to ask people who had not risen to speak, and in both cases, the people chosen had given a good account of themselves.

I waited as eagerly as everyone else as Rolf rose with obvious reluctance and said gruffly that he did not want to suggest that the chieftain of Murmroth had judged ill, but he was not the sort of man to lead a city. "I am not highborn, nor have I ever served in any capacity as a leader. I did not join the rebel cause, and aside from being crippled in one leg, I am only a metalworker, yet I know that people are harder to mold than iron and copper. There is a subtle skill to governing that I think a chieftain ought to have."

He would have sat then, but someone in the audience called out to ask what qualities he thought a chieftain ought to have. Before Rolf could respond, another man asked rather scornfully what a lowborn metalworker could know of the qualities needed to undertake the high and complex business of governing a city.

Frowning, Rolf said to the second man that if only wealth and birth were required of a chieftain, then governance of the city might as well be given back to Councilman Kana, who had been taxing Halfmoon Bay's citizens to fund the purchase of the costly

Sadorian spiceweed used in the production of his foul and addictive dreamweed.

"You asked what qualities I think a chieftain ought to have? I will answer, for though I have little money and am crippled, I know well enough what kind of person I would wish for a leader. I would wish for a chieftain who is honest and just and compassionate. I would happily vote for a man or woman whose first consideration is not how to increase the wealth of the city and its highborn citizens, but who would look to serve all who dwelt within it. Were I chieftain, I would sentence those who had committed low crimes to clean the streets when other citizens slept. I would happily set our former Councilman to scouring the walls and windows of all the little cottages next to his foul factories. And I would not stop at cleaning the city.

"When I was a young man, Halfmoon Bay was the flower of the west—the Westland—and those who came for our masked moon fair did so because of the city's beauty, because of the cleverness and wit of the entertainments offered, and because of the quality of workmanship in anything produced there. Once upon a time, there was not such a legion of beggars in the street. There were shelters funded by the wealthy, and healing and caring houses for the elderly and sick. Our good Councilman closed them so he could open his factories in their stead. No doubt it is backward of me, but I wish for a chieftain who has the vision and moral courage to turn back time and restore Halfmoon Bay to its former glory. I wish for a just, strong person with a good sense of humor and a sobering dollop of sternness when needed, as it surely will be. I wish for a man or woman who will lead by inspiration and vision and example.

"No doubt I have spoken in a lumpish metal-worker's way, but I have spoken the truth, and no man or woman should be asked to do more or less than that."

He sat down to a good smattering of applause and much nodding, but Gwynedd rose quickly, saying that since Arolfic had not thought to mention it, he wished all those present to know that the metalworker had put himself at considerable personal risk to help locate a Herder agent who had been infected by deadly plague before being set down in Halfmoon Bay during the masked moon fair. The shocked silence that met this announcement told me that Gwynedd had not spoken of this yet, and as he went on to speak of what the plague would have done, I could not bear to hear it. All I could see was Domick, his face distorted by buboes.

"Then let us go/leave this house of words. I am hungry," Maruman grumped suddenly, shifting his soft weight in my lap.

I rose and bade Blyss farewell, barely seeing her face through the mist of tears that had risen in my eyes. But I managed to ask if she would come to the *Umborine* to see me once the meeting had ended.

When I came outside, I was astonished to discover that the sun had set. I had not realized so much time had passed, and I wondered if it would be thought odd that a meeting of merchants would last so long. Then the cleverness of disguising a meeting of rebels as a meeting of merchants struck me anew, because what

Councilman or soldierguard would dare interfere with the works of commerce, since the activities of merchants lined their pockets and kept the citizens content and fed.

I yawned widely. It had been stuffy and hot in the meeting chamber, and I was glad to feel the cool evening air. I remembered that I had left my cloak with Gahltha in my saddlebags and formed a probe to locate him.

Making my way to the holding yard, I suggested he might prefer to remain ashore for the time being with Calcasuus and the other Sadorian horses. But Gahltha refused. He wished to remain close to me, he told me stoically, even if it meant being aboard a ship. His devotion made me feel a great stab of love for him, which irritated Maruman, and he sprang from my arms with a hiss, landing atop a high wall that ran along the side of the holding yard.

"I/Maruman will roam and hunt," the old cat sent coldly. I bit back the urge to plead with him to stay with me, knowing that his anger and resentment at having been abandoned would be eased by his abandonment of me. Even so, after he had leapt out of sight behind the wall, I wished I had begged him to stay.

"He will come after us to the ship," Gahltha assured me as we set off toward the waterfront through curving streets.

By the time I began to smell the briny stink of the waves, I was thirsty and footsore, but I would not dream of riding Gahltha just to save myself a few blisters. Need and joy were the only reasons to mount him, and I would not readily set aside those two standards even if he would, for one did not make a convenience of a friend. I forgot the pain in my feet when we came out of the street into the open square where, in daylight, the sea market would be held. As with the streets I had traversed, there were still a good many people making their way hither and thither, which suggested that, if there was a curfew in Aborium, it was very late. It had grown dark, and I had to strain to see the wharf, seeking the *Umborine*. The memory of another night flowed over me, when I had sat in a cart in a shadowed corner of this very square, watching Herder priests load their vessel. For a moment, the mingled odors of oil and fish and the sound of the water gurgling against the wharf summoned up the memory of that night so vividly that I seemed to see Jik, standing between two priests, hands bound and head drooping. Then Gahltha nuzzled my neck, and I spotted the *Umborine* at the far end of the wharf, its deck and rigging lit by the glow of lanterns. I pushed through the cobweb tendrils of memory and made my way across the square to the greatship.

The subtle song of the waves was strong and compelling. Gazing at the ship, I was struck by how similar it was to Salamander's *Black Ship*. Both were greatships, of course, but it was more than that. Take away the ugly weapons and additional structures from the *Black Ship*. and it could very well be a Sadorian vessel. Jakoby had never mentioned one of the sacred ships being stolen, but perhaps Salamander had acquired the *Black Ship* from the Gadfian raiders, from whom the Sadorians were descended. In order for this to be a possibility, it would have to be that the gadi settlements from whom the Sadorians had rescued their stolen womenfolk had survived, despite having no women or any means of getting healthy children. Unless Salamander had traded healthy women and children for a greatship.

Hearing a soft footfall behind me, I turned swiftly, lifting my hands to defend myself, but it was only the Druid armsman Gilbert, smiling down at me with a good deal more warmth than I liked.

"I saw you from the deck," he said.

"You were aboard the *Umborine*?" I asked, puzzled.

He nodded. "I have been helping to load. Shall I escort you aboard? My room is below deck, but you are to have a cabin on deck. You will have a magnificent view when we are under way."

"I don't understand," I said. "*Your* cabin?"

"Well, strictly speaking, I will share it with six other armsmen, but at the moment they are back at the Councilcourt taking part in the choosing."

"*You* and six armsmen are going to Sador?"

"There will be thirty of us, including Gwynedd," Gilbert said. "And we are traveling to Norseland, though I believe the ship is to go to Sador after that. I knew you were coming aboard, because I heard one of the Sadorians tell Raka that an empty cabin was being kept for your use. I suppose you are bound for Sador?"

I ignored his question as a picture came into my mind of Gwynedd and Jakoby speaking together. Gwynedd must have asked if Jakoby would take him and thirty of his people to Norseland, and then he had sent off the dark-haired man to command Gilbert and some of the others to carry stores aboard the *Umborine*. I knew it all, yet I did not know *why* Gwynedd would leave the west coast, having just been voted chieftain of Murmroth and when there was so much to be done.

Whatever she thought, Jakoby would have been forced to accede to Gwynedd's request, because the overguardian of the Temple had bidden her do whatever was asked of her by anyone who had traveled to the desert lands, and Gwynedd had done so for the Battlegames. So now, because I had said nothing, I must travel to Norseland, too, for if I asked the tribeswoman to bring me to Sador, she would say that first she must deal with Gwynedd's request.

"What is the purpose of this journey Gwynedd would make?" I asked Gilbert.

"I do not know precisely," he answered. "Perhaps it is that the Norselanders are Gwynedd's kin. He will tell us when he comes aboard after the meeting."

"The suddenness of this journey does not trouble you?" I asked, his smiling demeanor beginning to irritate me. "Are you and his other armsfolk so eager to leave the Westland? No one will regret your departure?"

The armsman's mouth twisted into a grimace of such bitterness that I was startled out of my indignation. "My bondmate would as soon pay a slaver to carry me away than regret my going," he snarled. Then he laughed as if this were a joke, but a jarring note suggested that not even he found it truly funny.

Feeling as awkward as ever, I said nothing, but Gilbert nodded as if he had heard a question in my silence. "I am afraid my bondmate dislikes my devotion to the rebel cause; she says it endangers her babies and is proof that I care more for warmongering than for my family. She sent me packing. So now I have nothing left but the hope of finding someone else to love me." His voice had dropped to a caressing note. "In truth, I am looking forward to this voyage and to the chance of getting to know you properly," he added with a smile that made my hand itch to slap him. I was dismayed at the thought of having to endure a sea voyage with this man imagining he was in love with me.

"Maybe this funaga truly loves you," Gahltha beast-spoke, and he offered his own vivid memory of the day I had escaped the Druid camp. Through his eyes, I saw my face turned up in dismay as Gahltha reared and screamed his terror. I saw myself trying to convince him to board the raft that was tossing and bucking in the upper Suggredoon's turbulent waters. Gilbert burst into the dark on the other side of the rain-lashed clearing that ran to the edge of the river, his red hair and clothes plastered to his head. Seeing him, Domick slashed the rope binding the raft, and the violent, rain-swollen water wrenched it away from the shore. Gilbert shouted something just before the raft vanished from sight. I had not been able to hear his words over the storm, but Gahltha had heard him call out my gypsy name, and now, hearing it, I also heard the unmistakable note of anguished longing.

I reeled from the vision to find an older Gilbert frowning at me in consternation. "Are you well?" he said.

I gaped at him, confused, because now that he was not smiling, he looked more like the Gilbert of Gahltha's vision. The memory of that other Gilbert made me say, "I was just thinking of what you said about your bondmate and children. It is sad that you would leave them with so little concern."

"It pleases me that you are concerned for me," Gilbert said, leaning nearer. "Let me escort you aboard."

"I need no escort," I told him coldly, and marched past him up the ramp without a backward glance.

Not until I reached the top, where two tribesmen waited, did I realize that Gahltha was not with me. I turned, half expecting to find him balking at boarding, but he was looking back along the wharf. I leaned out to see what had caught his attention and spotted Maruman. The old cat ran up the ramp, and only then did the horse follow. The Sadorians at the top of the ramp bowed with great respect to the beasts and then to me.

"You are Elspeth Gordie?" one of them asked.

"I am," I said. "I believe you have a chamber set aside for me?"

He nodded, and lifting to his lips a small whistle that hung on a chain about his neck, he gave two sharp blasts. A Sadorian girl about my age came hurrying up and bowed reverently to Gahltha before offering him a greeting in fingerspeech. He responded with a nod and a flick of one ear, sending to me that this was the groom who had tended to him earlier. I asked where I could find him and was surprised to see a picture form in his thoughts of holding boxes spread with sand, set up upon the deck toward the rear of the ship.

After Gahltha had been led away, Maruman said loftily, "I will show you where we will sleep."

I followed him meekly along the deck toward the front of the ship, where several cabins were clustered. He clawed delicately at one of the doors, and I tried the handle and looked inside. It was too dark to see anything, so I retraced my steps to get a lantern from the Sadorian woman at the gangplank. It revealed a spacious chamber with a bed fixed against one wall and some very beautifully crafted lockers and two big round-topped windows on the seaward side of the ship. I opened the windows, and the cool salt-scented breeze sweeping into the cabin made me sigh with pleasure.

Maruman leapt onto the sill, and as we both looked up into a sky shimmering with stars, I pondered what Gilbert had told me and wondered again why Gwynedd would suddenly decide to take a group of men to Norseland when the Westland was far from secure. I did not know him, though seeing him speak, Gwynedd had not struck me as a rash or hasty man. All that he said of the future suggested a man who planned thoroughly and well in advance. Yet he was taking thirty fighters to an island where many hundreds of Hedra were being trained and where there were, perhaps, unthinkable weapons. I shook my head, realizing my speculations were pointless until I learned Gwynedd's thinking.

I went to the bed, removed my heavy boots, and stretched out fully clothed, because I wanted to be able to get up the moment Blyss and Merret arrived. Maruman leapt down from the sill and padded over to join me on the bed. I yawned and wondered why I felt so weary. I yawned again, and the candle flared, revealing that the dark ceiling of the cabin was elaborately carved. I sat up and lifted the candle higher to study the intricacies. Although it had not been carved by Kasanda, whoever had done it had been influenced by her style. It occurred to me that Kasanda must have trained some of the tribesfolk, for she could not possibly have carved all the stone faces into the cliff at Templeport herself.

I lay back and thought of Stonehill, trying to imagine Cassy as an older woman, bringing up her son amid the thriving and busy community of gypsies who had once made their home atop the tor. The girl that Iriny had said Cassy loved as a daughter, even though she was not a Twentyfamilies, must have lived on Stonehill as well, growing to womanhood. In Cassy's past would have been the visit to the Red Land and the loss of her bondmate, the brother of the Red Queen, and also her youth in the Beforetime.

As ever, I puzzled at how someone from the Beforetime could have lived through the Age of Chaos, but that was something I would never know. Had Cassy known all through her years upon Stonehill that her journey had not ended, that someday she would be taken by Gadfian slavers and rescued by the Sadorians, only to end her life as a seer in the desert lands? Or had that knowledge come to her not long before she had left the Land?

I thought of my vision of Cassy's meeting with Hannah and wondered if the older woman had known that Cassy was a futureteller. It had never been said in any of my visions, yet how could she have left signs for me without foreknowledge to guide her? It might even be that training at Obernewtyn had brought her farseeking Talent to light, in the same way that farseeking novices sometimes realized they could use their deep probe to coerce as well.

Maruman sighed, and I turned my head to look at him, curled up beside me, tail curled over his nose. The breeze ruffled his fur, alternately hiding and revealing his scars.

"I love you, and you are growing old," I said softly,

...eaching out to stroke his fur lightly, so as not to waken him. Then I closed my eyes again, and as I floated into sleep, a vision rose in my mind of Domick's stone cairn at the edge of the Beforetime ruins, the wind and the sand hissing in an endless susurrus over it. The same wind that scoured Evander's grave atop Stonehill.

✦ 13 ✦

I woke groggily to the sound of boots on deck and the vague queasiness I always felt aboard a ship until I became accustomed to the deck's pitching. The pale lemon light bathing the cabin told me it was early morning, and I got up, careful not to waken Maruman, and went to open the window, which had blown shut in the stiff wind. The sky was a soup of delicate rose and lavender streaked with gold, confirming that it was not long after dawn. Closing the window and latching it, I began opening wall panels, remembering from my previous journey aboard a Sadorian greatship that they concealed all manner of snug and intricate fittings. Sure enough, I soon found a bowl with a spout and lever above it and a locker containing toiletries and clothing. I filled a bowl with water, stripped off my clothes, and washed myself down with a sea sponge. Once dried, I investigated the clothes piled neatly in the locker. They were women's clothes and made of brightly dyed and lightly beaded Sadorian silk. I dressed in sand-colored loose trousers and an undershirt made of silk so thin that it was virtually transparent. Shivering with pleasure at their softness, I reminded myself to thank Jakoby for providing them. After some agreeable dithering, I pulled on a knee-length tunic, slit above the waist on both sides and dyed in swirls of violet and sea green. There were dyed silk slippers to match, but they were too narrow; I was content to go barefoot as the Sadorians did on board.

I combed my tangled hair, listening to the boots moving about the deck, and frowned, for surely there was too much movement for the few people I had seen on deck? The rest of Gwynedd's men must have come aboard, which meant the meeting at the Councilcourt had finished.

I flung down the comb and hurried across the cabin, thinking that Blyss and Merret must be coming aboard as well. But just as I reached the door, the ship lurched and sent me staggering backward across the cabin. Regaining my balance, I made my way out of the cabin, my heart hammering, for the ship would not tilt in such a way while moored.

Outside, the deck was a hive of activity as Sadorian tribesmen and women ran to and fro in the pale yellow light, and beyond them, I stared aghast at the rapidly receding shore, understanding with dismay that the ship had weighed anchor while I slept. Holding on to the wall, I hastened along the deck looking wildly about for Jakoby, but aside from the busy shipfolk, I saw only a group of armsmen and women, many of whom wore their hair in the Norse style. Gwynedd's men.

A feeling of helplessness swept over me, because even if I found Jakoby, I knew that it was too late to turn back now. The sails had been unfurled and the ship was being borne along on the inexorable outgoing tide. Jakoby could not return to Aborium in any case, for she must fulfill the command of the Earthtemple's overguardian to obey the request of anyone who had been to the desert lands until she was bidden return to Sador.

I swallowed the bitter realization that I had said not a word to Blyss about Rushton and told myself that surely Dell would take a hand.

"Elspeth! So you are awake at last." Jakoby clapped me forcefully on the back. "I am pleased to see that you, at least, are not ill. Half of our brave warriors are already puking, and there is barely enough swell to rock the hull."

I mastered a surge of fury borne of helplessness to ask evenly why she had not awakened me before we cast off. Jakoby answered lightly that there had been no need to trouble me. "But no doubt you are eager to find out what happened at the meeting. Merret told me you saw some of it. Join me for firstmeal in an hour in the main cabin, and you shall hear it all. But for now I must go and watch the map to make sure we do not blunder into a shoal." The tribeswoman's golden eyes swept over me, and she added, "I see that the gifts I brought for Bruna fit you well enough. There are also some hair fittings and scarves if you wish to bind your hair out of the way."

"Thank you," I said, my anger fading at the pain in her eyes when she spoke of her daughter. What had happened was no fault of hers. I had been a fool not to farsend to her while at the meeting, asking her to waken me when she came aboard the ship. But of course I had not then known about Gwynedd's decision. Setting aside my apprehension about Rushton, I asked, "Did you find time to ask Dardelan about what happened between him and Bruna?"

Before she could respond, the ship gave a hard lurch

that made her wince and roll her eyes. "I had better rescue the tiller from the clumsy fool mishandling her. I will see you at firstmeal."

She hastened away, barefoot and graceful on the rolling deck. I sighed and turned to gaze out at the vanishing shore, and a feeling of fatalism rose in me, for yet again, I was swept along a course not of my choosing. Yet how often had such random events led me to something connected to my quest? As for Rushton, I could only hope that his memories had settled and would remain so until he returned to Obernewtyn. And failing that, I had to believe that Dell would ask Blyss to help him. The only certainty was that it was no longer in my power to help him.

The ship turned slightly, and the wind sent the end of my tunic fluttering out with a silken hiss. I made up my mind to seek out Gwynedd. At least I could learn the reason for his sudden decision to travel to Norseland. Making my unsteady way toward the front of the ship, I farsought Gahltha. The stallion informed me with drowsy dignity that he had accepted water laced with a light sleep drug to help him bear the gale that was driving the ship before it. I smiled at his exaggeration, knowing it arose from his fear of water, for although the wind was brisk and the sea rough, there was no gale blowing.

At the main cabin, I heard someone approaching from behind. I glanced back and was astounded to see *Brydda Llewellyn* striding toward me.

"You look very fresh, Elspeth, unlike the rest of us who have been up half the night choosing chieftains," he said cheerfully.

"Brydda! How—how are you here?" I stammered. "I mean, why?"

He lifted his brows. "I am here with Dardelan."

I stared at him. "Are you saying that Dardelan is aboard as well?"

He nodded. "Dardelan agreed with Gwynedd that our first priority must be to take control of Norseland, lest Ariel have time to unleash a second plague."

"But what of the west coast—the Westland, I mean?"

"What of it? The new chieftains are even now returning to their cities to begin their work, and as soon as Gevan reaches Obernewtyn, he will dispatch more of your people to work with the chieftains."

"But what of Murmroth?"

He laughed. "And here I was thinking you must know so much, having arrived here before us. Gwynedd already has Murmroth under good control. Much to the chagrin of his ward, Vesit, who feels he ought to have been left in charge, Gwynedd has left Serba to watch over Murmroth."

My head was spinning. "But . . . there was no mention of any plan to go to Norseland at the ruins."

"Apparently, Dell said something to Gwynedd some time ago that caused him to suddenly decide to go to Norseland," Brydda said. "Something about choosing the course that would oppose the spilling of blood when faced with many choices."

"He thinks that less blood will be spilled if he makes war on the last Hedra stronghold where there may be Beforetime weapons that will be used on us, not to mention the fact that Salamander and Ariel will be there!" I said incredulously.

"The fact that there are more plague seeds upon Norseland concerns him," Brydda said. "But you need not worry about Salamander, for the *Black Ship* was seen moving out to sea along the route taken by ships seeking the Red Queen's land. Did not Jakoby tell you? In Sutrium, Shipmaster Helvar of the *Stormdancer* spoke of it to her. Apparently, the route from Norseland curves toward Herder Isle before cutting out to the Endless Sea. I think we can assume that Ariel went with him."

This news was like a splash of cold water in my face. "Ariel has gone to the Red Queen's land," I said, more to force myself to take it in than to question it.

Brydda nodded, adding, "This journey is not just Gwynedd's decision, either, Elspeth. It was approved by the new Westland Council of which Gwynedd has been voted high chieftain. He raised the matter, telling them very clearly of the weapons and plague seeds that are upon Norseland, and they agreed that a journey must be made there immediately." He frowned. "I must say, I am surprised that Rushton has not sought you out to tell you this."

"*Rushton* is aboard," I whispered, and my heart seemed to stop beating. "Please tell me that Blyss and Merret have come, too."

Brydda's frown deepened. "No. Merret is to work with Serba to coordinate the taking of the cloisters and the Hedra, and Blyss will not go anywhere without her. But Jak and Seely are aboard."

I was incapable of any more astonishment. "How . . . why?"

The rebel shrugged. "All I know is that Jakoby was about to give the order to cast off when Jak and Seely came riding up to the wharf with two packhorses laden with boxes. Apparently, when Seely told Jak and the others that Jakoby had come to collect you, Jak flew into a frenzy, insisting that he must be aboard the ship. In no time, he had packed up his experiments and requested the aid of Ran in getting them and him to Aborium. Seely refused to be left behind."

I could not imagine why Jak would wish to come aboard the *Umborine*, unless Dell had foretold something to make it necessary. My thoughts veered back to the knowledge that Rushton was aboard a ship bound for Norseland, where he and Domick had been tortured by Ariel. If seeing Domick had already unsettled Rushton's poisoned memories, what would journeying to Norseland do to him? And if his deadly memories did surface, there was neither empath nor healer aboard to help him. Only me, and it was my face that had been used to torture him.

"You look very pale," Brydda said, and before I could protest, he had drawn me into the main cabin. It was full of Gwynedd's armsmen and women, but to my relief, Rushton was not in the room. Brydda brought me to a table where Dardelan sat, gazing at a map. He looked up at me and smiled distractedly, but then he frowned and seemed to look at me properly.

"Are you well, my lady?"

Gathering my wits, I said, "Much has happened since you rode from the ruins yesterday morning. I must say that while I share your concern for the weapons that might be stored on Norseland, I wonder at the wisdom of so few approaching an island that is, from all I have heard, unassailable."

"So I believed," Dardelan said, rubbing his eyes, which were red-rimmed with fatigue. "I assume Brydda has not told you about Gwynedd?"

He looked at Brydda, who shook his head and said he had just met up with me. Dardelan glanced about before leaning closer to me to say quietly, "You know that Gwynedd is a Norselander. Maybe you also know that his mother fled to the west coast carrying him in her belly when the Faction began to take control of the Norselands. What you cannot know is that Gwynedd's great-grandfather was the only nephew of the last king. Gwynedd told us only this night past when he announced his decision to travel to Norseland, and I voiced the very concerns that you have just raised. Since the old king bore no children of his own, being half a priest himself by the time he died, by right of succession, Gwynedd would be the rightful Norse king, if the monarchy were reinstated. This explains Dell's foretelling in some way, of course.

"Gwynedd says he has no desire to be a king, yet Dell's futuretelling had filled him with joy, because it had suggested that the time was at hand when the Norselands would be freed from the Faction's long tyranny. What helped me decide to accompany him on this expedition is that, because of his heritage, Gwynedd knows a secret way to reach the surface of Norseland, and he believes that once he can reach the Norselanders who inhabit the island, he will be able to rouse them to fight the Hedra. But I will say no more of his plans in his absence."

I thought I had lost the capacity to be more surprised, yet I was amazed at this twist of events. Dell had foreseen that if Gwynedd did as she suggested, he would be crowned a king. In retrospect, it was easy to see that, in doing as she had suggested—organizing a meeting in Aborium to decide the future of the coast instead of riding into battle—he had been in Aborium when Jakoby arrived, enabling him to hear what was happening on Norseland in time to ask the tribeswoman to carry him there on the *Umborine*. Perhaps if he had tried to secure the Westlands before that meeting, Gwynedd would have been killed in battle.

"Eat something, both of you," Brydda insisted, pushing a soft round flatbread into my hands and the same into Dardelan's.

"I am not hungry," Dardelan said.

"What does that matter?" Brydda said sternly. "You need strength and food is strength." With that, he took up three of the soft round breads and bit ferociously into them.

Dardelan grinned at the big man and looked his old self as he raised the bread to his mouth. I bit into the bread, too, and suddenly I was ravenous. I took another of the soft round breads and ate it, and then I ate grapes and cheese and tiny tomatoes that burst on my tongue with a tartness that made my eyes water. Gradually, the queasiness in my belly faded, but Dardelan, who had matched me bite for bite, suddenly gave a bone-cracking yawn and said it was no use; he would have to sleep before he would be up to a council of war. He asked Brydda to find Gwynedd and suggest the meeting be postponed until they had all had some sleep.

After Dardelan had gone, I asked Brydda where Rushton was.

"He became ill soon after we boarded the *Umborine*, and wave-sickness is said to get worse before it can get better," Brydda answered. "Perhaps he has gone to his bed. That might explain why he did not seek you out to tell you what has been happening."

Before I could respond, the cabin doors opened and Jakoby entered. She glanced around the room, frowning, and then came to Brydda to ask where Dardelan and Gwynedd were.

"As far as I know, Gwynedd is with his people and Dardelan has just staggered off to bed. He wants to meet this evening after we have had a few hours' sleep," Brydda said.

"Very well." Jakoby nodded as Brydda rose, saying he had better let Gwynedd know. The tribeswoman took his seat and smiled at me ruefully. "It seems I sent you here for no reason. My apologies, but if you do not wish to return to your cabin so soon, perhaps you would like to come with me to the shipmaster's platform? The view from it is very fine."

As we crossed the main deck, I asked about Sador. "Has Gwynedd asked you to go there after we leave Norseland?"

She shook her head. "Rushton asked it. He wishes to make a request of the tribes. I told him that I would gladly bear him hence, but his request must be made to all the tribes. That means we can spend very little time at Norseland, for the tribes meet together only once a year. The Battlegames that you and your people once attended are taking place even now."

"What does Rushton want to ask the tribes?" I asked, baffled.

"I think you must ask him that," Jakoby said. She rubbed her eyes wearily just as Dardelan had done.

"If you are tired, why not sleep?" I asked. "Surely your shipfolk have experience enough to keep us all safe."

"The crew is not experienced in sailing this far out from land," she said.

"And you are?" I asked.

To my surprise, she nodded. "It has always been the Sadorian custom to remain in sight of land when we take our greatships to sea. Indeed, we have gone vast distances in that way, but even as children being trained in the little coracles made for us by our mother, my sister and I were wont to venture farther out than she liked—my sister out of natural adventurousness, and me for love of her."

I was fascinated by this rare glimpse of the stern tribeswoman's life, but Jakoby said no more, for now we had reached the wooden steps leading to the shipmaster's deck, and several young Sadorians waited to ask her questions. Once these had been dealt with, we climbed up to the platform, only to discover that there were others waiting to speak to Jakoby. I went to sit on a bench set to one side of the shipmaster's platform, admiring the view of the vast sea, covered with glittering sequins of sunlight. The land was a purple-hued smudge all along one side of the ship, which meant we were still proceeding along the strait. My thoughts turned to what Jakoby had said of Rushton. I could not imagine what he wanted from the tribes. I would gladly have asked him, but given the circumstances, it seemed wiser to avoid him as much as possible aboard the ship.

I shivered, though it was not truly cold, and forced my thoughts outward, focusing them on the ease and grace of the Sadorians' movements as they trimmed and adjusted the *Umborine*'s scarlet sails. Most of the shipfolk were my age, and I realized that ship skills were not borne of a few lessons in childhood. From what Jakoby had said, all children received some training in childhood on small vessels made for them by their parents, and then later, some chosen few must be trained on the greatships. Dameon had once told me that Sadorians had learned to sail generations before, from the shipmaster of a Gadfian raiding ship they had captured during the raid in which they had lost so many of their women. The Sadorians had forced the Gadfian shipmaster to teach them the arts of sailing and shipbuilding, and they had rebuilt his ship. Then they had cut down enough of the great sacred spice trees that grew in a single grove to build two more ships, before setting off on their epic journey to find their stolen women. The practice of sailing had continued since that time, and I now understood that some Sadorians must remain almost constantly aboard the greatships to attain the sort of easy skills I was now witnessing.

Jakoby chose this moment to sit down beside me, and impulsively I asked her about the long journeys that she had mentioned. "There was no specific destination," she answered. "The purpose of the journeying was to train new Sadorian shipfolk. All Sadorian youngsters spend time aboard the spiceships, and from these are chosen those who will be true shipfolk entrusted with the care of the sacred ships. They sail until they are old, and then their place is taken by a young shipboy or girl. The more intensive training of these new shipfolk is undertaken on a long journey. Of course, since Salamander has plied the strait, the journeys have all been beyond Sador."

"Are you saying that your ships once sailed the other way? Toward the Red Queen's land?"

The tribeswoman gave me a long speculative look, then said, "No Sadorian ship ever went there, but, yes, they sailed in that direction as far as the darklands."

"I have never heard of these darklands," I said, astonished.

She shrugged. "They are beyond the black coasts in that direction, and only the largest of the greatships with a minimum of shipfolk and no passengers has the capacity to carry food and water enough to go so far. There is life of a sort, both plant and beast, but all are mutated beyond any semblance of normality, and those who drink water there or walk there die of the wasting sickness within a year. Only those things native to the place can live there." As she spoke, Jakoby watched one of the shipfolk reef a sail, and now she rose with a mutter of exasperation to chide a young shipman. She came back and said, "You might be interested in visiting the map chamber on board. There are maps there showing the darklands."

"I would like very much to see them if it is permitted," I said eagerly.

"I cannot come with you just now," Jakoby said, "but if you would like to go yourself, the map chamber is the last cabin on the port side of the ship. The door is carved with a half-moon and stars. Tell the map keeper that I sent you."

"I will go there now," I said, and thanked her. I had just reached the bottom of the steps leading down to the main deck when I heard someone call my name. Seely was sitting on a coil of oiled rope, her arms clasped around her knees.

"I did not expect to see you again so soon," I said, going over to her.

She smiled shyly. "No more did I. But when Jak heard there was a ship going to Sador, he was like a man possessed, for he has long dreamed of bringing his experiments there."

"What experiments does he wish to take to Sador?"

"I am sure you know that he has long been trying to breed a strain of taint-eating insect that can tolerate the light and drier conditions?" Seely said, and I nodded. "Well, some time ago, he succeeded with the help of Ines, but the new strain has little tolerance for cold or damp. They would survive well in the desert lands, but there was no way to get them there without a long arduous trip overland. Until now."

"That explains a good deal," I said. "What did Dell say about your both leaving?"

Seely laughed. "What does Dell always say?"

"She foresaw it?"

"She foresaw our return, which is even better, because it means we will survive whatever is to happen on Norseland," Seely said, turning to look out over the shimmering waves. She got up and went to lean on the rail of the ship, saying softly, "You know, I thought I would be frightened or sick on a ship, but it is so strange and beautiful out here. I almost wish the journey would never end. On the other hand, Jak says that when he has finished in Sador, we will travel to Obernewtyn before coming back to the west coast, and I long to see Gavyn." She yawned and said reluctantly that she had better sleep, for she would need to be fresh to relieve Jak, who was now watching over the insects.

Her cabin lay in the direction I was walking, and I asked if anyone had told her that Gavyn had dreamed of seeing her at Obernewtyn.

Seely gave me a startled look. "How queer that you should speak of Gavyn dreaming of me, for only last night I dreamed of him. He was walking along a high narrow ridge with Blacklands spread on both sides of him. The sky was dark and stormy, and the light was a queer sickly yellow. A host of dogs walked all about him, and that great white dog that attached itself to him at Obernewtyn was with him, too, padding along at his heels. . . ." She shrugged and laughed.

We came to one of the hold entrances, and Seely stopped, explaining that her cabin was on a lower level. Continuing on alone, I reached the last cabin on the port side of the ship. Its door was carved with a half-moon and several stars, just as Jakoby had described. I knocked, and a gray-haired, whip-lean woman with a heavy jaw and thick brows that met over the bridge of her nose answered the door. Without allowing me to speak, she told me tersely that the map chamber was out of bounds to any but shipfolk. She began to close the door, but I explained hastily that Jakoby had sent me, which earned me a long, disapproving look. But she opened the door to let me in, muttering that her name was Gorgol, and no wonder Jakoby would not follow any rules but her own, given her mother's behavior. This was not the first time I had heard hints that Jakoby was disinclined to obey rules, but no one had ever mentioned her mother before.

The cabin was small, but every wall was covered in beautifully made wooden shelves piled with scrolled maps and ornately worked map cases. I gazed around, realizing with amazement that there must be more than a thousand maps in the tiny space, and a door behind a wide counter revealed a second smaller chamber running off the first, also walled in shelves and filled with maps.

"What do you want to see?" Gorgol demanded, having moved behind the counter. When I told her, she frowned. "I have maps that show a portion of the dark-lands coast, but they do not show Land's End."

"What is Land's End?" I asked.

"The name given to the place where the darklands end. I have seen maps that show Land's End, but I accept nothing that our own ships have not mapped, for few mapmakers trouble themselves with scale. Instead, they rely upon visual landmarks or time references, both of which can result in great inaccuracies."

"Have you ever seen a map of the Red Queen's land?" I asked.

"I have, but I would not place any great reliance upon what it showed."

"What did it show?" I insisted.

She shrugged dismissively. "A peninsula shaped like a long fang and named Land's End and then a vast shoal-filled sea beyond which lay another land with more black coasts. According to that map, the Red Land was to be found by traveling northeast along these black coasts. But the distance from here by the coast route to Land's End is too far for any ship to manage, and those who go to Land's End must sail across the Endless Sea to it."

"Can I see the map showing the darklands?" I asked.

She turned to lift a battered-looking map case down from a shelf behind her. Opening it reverently, she drew out its map, spreading it on the counter. I leaned forward to examine it and saw that the map showed the west coast. I followed it along to where it became Blacklands. The words *black coasts* were scribed on them, and they were inked black some way in from the line that marked the edge. The thick black coastline was cut off by the edge of the parchment.

I looked up to find the Sadorian woman studying me as if I were a peculiar, ill-made map. I asked if she had a map that showed the next part of the black coast. She carefully rolled the first map, restored it to its case, and placed it on its shelf before locating another map. This one, once spread out, showed nothing but a long thick black coastline with inlets and coves and even the mouth of a river, but the unrelenting blackness told its own tale. I was still studying the map when Gorgol said brusquely that I should not pay too much attention to it, for the scale was wrong, it being the work of a young mapmaker; however, I then noticed two very small islands right at the upper edge of the map. In minute spidery writing were the words *Romsey* and *Bayleux*, presumably the islands' names. Given what Gorgol had said, there was no way to tell how far they were from the shore, but as they had not been inked black, it seemed they were not tainted. I leaned closer and thought I could make out the small symbol used by mapmakers to designate fresh water. That would make the map profoundly important, because while seafarers could catch fish and eat certain seaweeds to sustain themselves on long journeys, they could only carry so much fresh water. Knowledge of a spring on an untainted island could mean the difference between life and death to a ship's crew or the chance to extend the length of the journey.

"Do you have a map that shows the next part of the coast?" I asked.

In the end, Gorgol showed me seven more maps, all of which fit one against the other and detailed more or less accurately the shape, if not the scale, of the coastline right up to the beginning of the darklands. On the final map, which showed the darklands as gray rather than black, two more islands had been drawn in and marked with the freshwater-spring symbol.

"It has taken long years to accumulate these maps, which are very nearly accurate," Gorgol said, rolling up the last map. "A shipmaster once told me that he had seen a map to the Red Queen's land from Land's End. He said, though, that it was impossible to reach Land's End by traveling along the coast. One had to venture across the sea."

I frowned, wondering how Salamander had learned the open-sea route to the Red Land. The obvious answer was that he had originally come from the Red Queen's land. "Is Land's End tainted ground?" I asked.

"Land's End is free of taint, but it is surrounded by darklands, and the man I spoke to told me that beasts from the darklands creep there at night seeking prey, so no one stays there past dusk. All ships anchor offshore in the dark hours and return to complete their business in the light of day."

"Their business?"

"The trade of slaves, chiefly," Gorgol said. "Ships from the Red Queen's land come to buy slaves and others come to sell them. Of course, sellers would earn more if they took the slaves all the way to the Red Queen's land themselves, but the journey is said to be even more dangerous than what has gone before."

Gorgol demanded to know if I was finished, and I shook my head, asking if she had a map that showed the coastline in the other direction, past Sador. With patent disapproval, she brought three maps from the smaller adjoining chamber. Each was enclosed in a map case of thick green felt laid snugly over wood. Gorgol drew out the map from the first case and unrolled it. This one showed the entire coastline of the Land and of Sador and a long stretch of black coast beyond the desert lands. I ran a finger along the Land's meticulously detailed coastline, noting that all the beaches were carefully marked in, as were the narrow inlets, one of which concealed the great sea cavern where the Hedra had hidden. I had never seen any map that showed them before.

I ran my finger around the great, variegated scoop of cliff that was the narrow coastal route to Sador, thinking of Bruna and hoping she had already reached home. The map continued, showing the coast where a long white spit ran out from a split in the cliffs to form Templeport. The map also showed the land behind the desert lands as a black-edged wasteland many times greater than Sador and the country on both sides of the Suggredoon; even then there was no telling how much farther it extended, for the black desert ran off the parchment in three directions.

"It is magnificent," I told her, beginning to reroll the map, and for a moment, as she took it from me, her expression was slightly less cold. Once she restored the map to its case, she unrolled each of the remaining maps in their green cases, but both merely showed continuations of the black coast. Gorgol produced four more such maps, one of which showed a stretch of gray and then a small patch of clean ground. The next one had two more clean patches, and one of them showed the tiny freshwater-spring symbol. But when I examined the last map and glanced inquiringly at Gorgol, she shook her head, anticipating my request for yet another map.

I was about to roll it away when I noticed some faint markings on the edge of the parchment farthest from the black coastline. I leaned close, unsure if the markings were anything. "What is this?" I asked Gorgol.

She frowned. "Some years ago, one of our ships was blown out of sight of the black coasts in a storm, and another land was sighted. It ought to have been left out, for no landing was made and no proper measurements taken, and by the time the storm blew over, they were once again within sight of the black coast. I suspect that whoever made the sighting was so utterly confused by the storm that he mistook the black coasts for another land."

I nodded and asked if she had a map that showed together all the sections I had so far seen. She gave me a martyred look before going back to the adjoining chamber. This time she returned with a single black enameled map case. The map proved to offer a less detailed drawing of the vast landmass of which the Land and Sador were but the smallest part. I was astounded, for Sador, the Land, and Westland were little more than pinpricks at the edge of a vast black shape.

"Can this land be so vast?" I muttered.

"No one knows how vast because as you see, the map is incomplete," Gorgol said, taking it as a question. "No one has ever managed to circumnavigate it to know the distance from Sador right around to Land's End, because there is no fresh water beyond those springs shown." She tapped the vast black hinterland.

"This is speculation, of course, for no one has been to the interior, but it is reasonable to assume that the center of this land must be as dead as its edges."

My head was beginning to ache from the stuffiness of the little cabin, so I thanked Gorgol and went back outside. It had been too warm in the map chamber, but now the wind felt cold through my thin silk clothes. I hurried back toward my cabin, intending to get a shawl and find a sheltered place on the deck to sit until the wind had blown away my headache. As I had hoped, Maruman was still deeply asleep. I reached out and stroked his fur, thinking of the dream I had had of him as a young cat, playing on the dreamtrails, and I wondered if I would ever understand what it meant. Maruman gave a soft, contented snore. I lay down beside him and pressed my cheek to his head.

I was so glad to have him and Gahltha with me that I would have been in bliss if I were not so worried about Rushton. I would try to stay out of his way, but somehow I must prevent him from going ashore on Norseland. I would speak to Jakoby, Dardelan, and Gwynedd when I could do so privately and tell them what Domick and Dell had said. Maybe they would come up with a plan to prevent Rushton from going ashore. I did not feel tired, yet I found myself slipping toward sleep. It was a pure pleasure to know there was no reason I should resist its lure.

✦ 14 ✦

I SANK, SHIELDED, through dream and memory, not wanting to be ensnared by them, for I sensed that they would all hold tormenting visions of Rushton's face and smile in better times.

Hovering above the mindstream, I thought of Domick, wondering what his death had surrendered into it. Did all of a person go into it—all his dreams and slight experiences and mundane activities as well as his great or evil deeds? Then again, who could say what deeds were great or small in a life? That which seemed great to the person who lived that life might not be deemed so by those who lived in the aftermath of it; a deed that seemed of everlasting importance might prove to have slight consequences. At the same time, some very small act done without much thought could lead to eternal good for humans and maybe all creatures. For the same reason, no one could judge whether a deed or even a life had been worthy—not the one who lived that life nor those who lived at the same time, for all were hampered by their limited vision. How should a stream judge the rocks it glides over or the twig that it carries along? It did not even choose its own course. Therefore, it was foolish to ask if Domick's life had brightened or darkened the stream. The answer was that his life had been given to him; a gift. He had lived it, and now he gave back the gift, and the stream was enriched by all the flavors, sweet and sour and bitter and bland, that his dying had released.

I saw a glimmering bubble detach itself from the mindstream and float toward me with dreamy, unerring accuracy.

I found myself within a passage so white and shining that it could only have existed in the Beforetime. I heard footsteps and when I looked behind me, I saw Cassy Duprey coming along it. Her expression was blandly pleasant, but there was a hint of sorrow that made me certain I was seeing her after the death of her Tiban lover, which meant she had already met Hannah Seraphim.

Without warning, a door in the corridor opened and a white-coated man with very short gray hair stepped out in front of Cassy.

"Who are you?" he asked, but it was the voice of a woman, for all the mannish attire and bearing.

"I'm Cassandra Duprey," Cassy said, smiling guilelessly, but a flinty gleam in her eyes made me sure she was up to something.

"Duprey?" The woman sounded taken aback.

"Director Duprey is my father," Cassy said lightly. "I am staying with him for the summer. But who are you?"

"Ruth Everhart. But you shouldn't be here, you know. This wing is out of bounds to visitors."

"Isn't this the way to the garden cafeteria?" Cassy looked concerned, and the woman's expression softened, though she seemed irritated as well.

"You missed a turn in the last corridor," she said.

"I did? Oh, this place is such a labyrinth. You know, I was here last summer, and I could have sworn I knew my way around. Then my father tells me about this garden cafeteria that I have never even heard of. Now I find this whole wing I didn't even know was here. I guess you never go over to the main restaurant or my father would have introduced us."

The older woman laughed without humor. "I doubt it. My project is only one of hundreds here, and it's considered a minor one at that. I doubt that Director Duprey would even remember my name."

"Of course he would," Cassy said with wide-eyed earnestness. "My father says it's his job to know all the people here, though I don't know how he can manage that when he does not even remember my birthday." Abruptly, her smile vanished as if it had been wiped away. The older woman did not appear to notice. She was tilting her head as if she were straining to hear some barely audible music. Puzzled, I entered Cassy's mind and found her probing the other woman. The probe was better honed than the one she had thrust into her mother's mind, but it was still a novice's effort, and it did not explain why the woman was standing and staring into space as if she had been coerced.

Curiosity made me flow into the woman's mind, and I was shocked to find that she was indeed being coerced, but not by Cassy. By *another* mind! Cassy was merely a witness to what the othermind was doing.

"That wasn't too bright," said the othermind to Cassy so smoothly that it could only belong to a Misfit with both farseeking and coercive Talents. "She'll remember you said that."

"It was a joke, and she thinks I'm a kid. All kids criticize their parents. It doesn't mean anything. Besides, she won't remember anything I said to her."

"She'll remember all right. She has that sort of mind that works at niggles. She'll wonder why you were so friendly unless you keep it up. Now let me work." The othermind began to ransack the woman's mind with a ruthlessness that shocked me. Almost as an afterthought, it erased a little node of puzzlement in the woman's mind, roused by Cassy's last words. It was replaced with the feeling that the girl was a nice dim kid of no real consequence despite her father. "All right, I'm finished. She doesn't know any more about Sentinel than Joe Public, because her project isn't connected."

"What is her project?" Cassy asked.

"She said herself it's unimportant," the other said impatiently.

"She didn't say it was unimportant," Cassy argued. "She said it was considered to be minor. But she obviously doesn't think so."

"Hannah would not want us wasting time on this."

"Hannah wasn't interested in Sentinel until I sent that stuff you had stumbled on," Cassy said. "And if there are other people here showing an interest in Sentinel . . ."

"That's just Abel being paranoid about random thoughts. It goes with the territory." Cassy made no response and the othermind sighed. "All right. Wait." A moment passed during which Cassy looked up and down the shining hall anxiously before the othermind spoke to her again. "Okay, it's nothing; just something to do with cryogenics."

"Cryogenics? Wasn't that some sort of dark-age

research that involved chopping people's heads off and freezing them?"

"That's the one," the other mind said, sounding amused.

"But wasn't it totally discredited?"

"Of course. But this is some new version. Look, we have to let her go. She's starting to get antsy, and I don't want to do a major rewire of her brain. But get ready because I've prodded her mind to think about Sentinel. Give her half a chance and she'll spill."

"I'm ready." Cassy withdrew from the other woman's mind and summoned up a bright smile. The woman blinked and looked slightly dazed. "Is . . . something wrong?" Cassy asked gently.

"I . . . I don't know. I thought . . ." The gray-haired woman broke off and gave an awkward laugh. "It's nothing. What did you say?"

Cassy gave her a dazzling, self-deprecating smile. "I was just saying I'm still a little awed by all of this."

The woman rubbed at her temple as if she was developing a headache. "It's understandable. Now you'd better—"

"You know what amazes me most?" Cassy interrupted confidingly. "It's how many different nationalities you see here. Chinon, Gadfian, Tipodan." She shook her head. "Somehow I never expected that much cooperation."

The woman laughed dryly. "There is not that much cooperation. The mix is mostly due to the Sentinel project. I'm sure you've heard about it. All five powers are involved, so there are scientists from every country here to work on the project, as well as a lot of suits and bean counters from those places whose job it is to observe everyone else doing their jobs and then report to their various governments. But there are a few other projects where scientists from different powers are co-operating. Mine is one. That's one of the things I love about science. The fact that it's possible to work across those invisible boundaries." She glanced at her watch. "I'll walk you back to where you went wrong. You must have missed the sign. It doesn't exactly leap out at you."

I saw Cassy scowl as the mind now probing her said with a languid sneer, "If you had just gone the other way like I suggested, this wouldn't have happened."

I caught the probe as it withdrew and followed it back to a girl sitting slumped in a chair in a distant corner of the complex. I withdrew to look at her and was astonished. For all the cynical feel of her mindvoice, she was no older than Cassy, and she was extraordinary looking. Her skin was as pale as if it had been powdered with flour, her lips were black, and she had smeared something glittering and purple around her eyes. Her hair was short like the older woman in the hall, but it had been oiled and pressed into quills that stuck up as stiffly as if they had been lacquered. Finally, a silver bead of metal gleamed in the tuck of her chin, and a little silver arrow pierced the exaggerated arch of one black brow.

"Well?" she said aloud in an insolent, rasping voice.

The people around the chair had been standing still. I looked at them and realized with some astonishment that each wore the same sort of heavy blue trousers with pockets and soft short-sleeved white shirts as I had worn in the ruins complex. I studied each in turn, realizing with awe that these must be the Beforetime

Misfits stolen from the original Reichler Clinic. There was a frail-looking woman with wispy blond hair and anxious eyes; a handsome man with a belligerent expression; a worried-looking older man whose face seemed familiar, and a heavy older woman with gray streaks in her hair. All of them save the girl in the chair had skin like Cassy's: Twentyfamilies dark. The only other person in the room was a younger boy with yellowish hair and a wheezing way of breathing. He was fair-skinned, too, but I was struck by his dual-colored eyes of green and blue, for they were like Iriny's. He was the only one other than the pale girl with the porcupine-quill hair who appeared calm. The rest wore expressions ranging from frightened to apprehensive.

"Well?" asked the big woman eagerly.

The girl with the spiked hair stretched luxuriantly and then shook her head. "She didn't get anything. She let herself get sidetracked by one of the geeks."

Without warning, a sharp pain broke the bubble of dream material open, and silver drops shuddered back into the mindstream as I was drawn rapidly up and away.

Maruman was watching me when I opened my eyes, flexing his claws. I glared at him. "Did you do that?"

"Your stomach woke me," he answered coolly.

I glanced across at the windows and saw by the hue of the sunlight striping the sill that it was late afternoon. I got up, stripped off the rumpled silk clothes that I had slept in, and splashed my face with water. Feeling more alert, I found a heavier silk shirt and trousers in vivid violet-blues and a long quilted gray vest that had been worked in blue and silver thread. The cloth would keep Maruman's claws from digging too deep. When I invited him to come with me, he stretched and yawned, showing his teeth, before climbing lightly over onto my shoulders. I padded barefoot out onto the deck and stopped to make sure Rushton was not in sight; then I made my way swiftly toward the front of the ship. I wanted to find Brydda or Jakoby so I could seek their advice about Rushton, but the enticing scent of cooking led me to the galley, where a large, powerfully built woman swooped on Maruman, saying she had been saving something special for him. To my amused disgust, Maruman shamelessly endured her crooning and petting for the tidbits she offered.

"Food is being served in the saloon," the cook said when I asked if she had something for me. Guessing she must mean the main chamber where I had eaten earlier, I thanked her, not wanting to explain why I did not want to go there. Maruman languidly bade me go, saying he would seek me out later. I decided to see if I could find out where Brydda's cabin was, but before I had taken two steps, Gilbert stepped out of the gathering shadows of dusk.

"I thought you looked beautiful as a gypsy, but you look truly ravishing in Sadorian clothes," he said. "I was just coming to escort you to the saloon for the meeting."

"I am perfectly capable of finding my own way from one end of the deck to the other," I snapped, and marched past him, wondering how to get rid of him. Moments later, I ran into Gwynedd.

"Can it be Elspeth Gordie?" he asked, squinting down at me, for despite my height, he was taller by far.

"It is good to see you, Chieftain Gwynedd," I said.

"I wanted to say how well you spoke in the meeting yesterday."

"You were there? But, yes, Merret mentioned that you sat a while in the gallery with Blyss. Come into the saloon. We should have a little while before everyone is assembled."

Seeing no way to avoid it, I allowed him to take my arm, hoping I could slip away without encountering Rushton. A number of lanterns now swung from hooks on the beams, shedding an inconstant, honeyed light over the saloon, which was empty but for Dardelan and Rushton. Both looked up at our arrival, and there was no time to withdraw, even if I could have come up with a reason to do so, for Dardelan lifted his hand in greeting.

Gwynedd firmly steered me across the room to the seat alongside Rushton's, and I forced myself to look at him and nod a greeting. I expected coolness in response, but his expression was icy. Before I could utter a word, Rushton stood up abruptly, saying that he would go and waken Brydda. He assayed a jerky, general bow and departed.

I felt the blood burn in my cheeks, but to my relief, after an awkward pause, Gwynedd only said, "I wonder if you would tell me some more about your time on Herder Isle. Merret told me what she knew, but I feel sure there was much more to be told. In particular, I am interested in these shadows that serve the Faction. You see, the goddesses worshipped by the Norse forbade slavery as unspeakably base. Am I correct in thinking the slaves were all taken from the Westland?"

I nodded, striving to control my roiling emotions and desperate to leave the saloon before Rushton returned.

It was bad enough that Dardelan had seen how he snubbed me, but what if he treated me badly in front of the others? It would be painful and humiliating, but I was more afraid that someone might upbraid him for it and precipitate what I most feared.

Gwynedd was still looking at me expectantly, so I took a steadying breath and told Gwynedd of the shadows, and he said that he would offer homes in Murmroth to any who wished to return to the Westland. He would also see that they had work or were given funds that would allow them to establish a trade or business for themselves, if they wished it.

"You are kind. I am sure many will be glad to take up your offer," I said, unable to keep from stealing glances at the doors each time they swung open. So far, a number of Gwynedd's men had entered, and now another group entered with Brydda. He came to join us while they took a table near the door and began a noisy game of dice.

As Brydda dropped into the seat beside him, Dardelan asked if he had seen Rushton. "He went looking for you," he added.

"I saw him, but I did not need waking," Brydda said, reaching for a jug of fement and pouring himself a mug. "He has gone to fetch our good shipmistress, but he says to begin the discussion without him. I fear he is in a black mood."

I felt Dardelan and Gwynedd look at me, and the sympathy in their eyes made my eyes prick with tears. I blinked hard to stem the flow, but to my mortification, two slid down my cheeks. I brushed them away and would have risen save that Brydda very deliberately pushed an empty mug across to me and poured into it a dram of ruby red fement, bidding me firmly to drink. Then he filled his own mug and tapped mine with it gently, saying, "To courage in the great dice game that is life."

Dardelan reached out to lay a hand over mine, saying softly, "He is not himself, Elspeth."

I drank a mouthful of the fement and tried to smile, but a storm of tears was rising behind my eyes, and I knew suddenly that there was no holding them back. I stood up abruptly, and immediately Brydda rose, too. Taking my hand, he murmured to the others that he needed some fresh air before the meeting began. I was unable to speak and was half-blinded by tears as he led me deftly into the cold night. He brought me to the side of the ship and laid his big hand on my shoulder.

I shook my head and stepped away from him. "Please, don't," I whispered, my voice quaking. "If you are kind, I will never get control of myself." He nodded and stood silent while I gulped and blinked and sniffed my way to some sort of calmness. "I am sorry," I told the big rebel hoarsely at last. "It is only that I have been so worried."

"Rushton has been behaving badly," Brydda said, and there was anger in his voice. "Whatever happened to him in the cloister in Sutrium is not your fault. Why take it out on you, of all people?"

"Oh, Brydda, if only you knew," I said, drawing a long steadying breath. "You must not blame Rushton for the way he is behaving, especially toward me. When we spoke in Rangorn, I told you that his imprisonment in the cloister in Sutrium had broken something in him and that he would not permit me to enter his blocked memories to help him. I did not tell you that Rushton told me that he could no longer love me."

Brydda looked at me in frank disbelief. "He did not mean it, surely."

"I did not believe it either, but when I saw him in Saithwold, he was even more cold and harsh toward me. I saw then that he *had* meant what he said at Obernewtyn. Dameon said I was wrong and that it was *because* he loved me that Rushton was so cold. He said it was because I stirred him deeply that he rejected me, because if he allowed himself to feel anything for me, it would force him to face the memories of what had happened to him." I swallowed hard. "But Dameon did not know what I now know. What Domick told me . . ."

Brydda's eyes widened. "Domick? But how . . . ?" He stopped, comprehension flooding his expression. "They were taken at the same time, weren't they?"

I nodded. "Apparently, Rushton had found Domick and was trying to convince him to return to Obernewtyn when they were taken. Ariel had foreseen the meeting. But they were not separated, as it might seem, Domick was not taken to Herder Isle and Rushton to the cloister in Sutrium. They were both brought aboard the *Black Ship* and taken to Norseland."

"*Norseland!* But Rushton was found in the Sutrium cloister!" Brydda said.

I told him what the Threes had said about Rushton and Ariel, and then I told him all that Domick had said. The rebel shook his head, and a look of revulsion crossed his rough, kind face. "I cannot believe that Domick was made to torture Rushton. . . . No wonder his mind split in two."

"What happened to him was our fault. We sent him to spy, and it was what he did as a spy that created Mika, and it was Mika whom Ariel found and used," I said, fresh tears welling in my eyes. "But in telling me about Rushton, Domick broke free from Ariel's control. Apparently, he was not meant to be able to speak at all. Mika was supposed to be in control."

"That tells us that Ariel makes mistakes. And he has made a mistake in thinking that he has broken Rushton. The question now is what to do," Brydda said.

I told him of my conversation with Dell about Rushton and how I was to ask Blyss to help me prepare him to remember. "Only I never got the chance to speak to Blyss about it, and now . . ."

"Rushton is aboard the *Umborine* with you," Brydda concluded.

"With me but without Blyss or any empath or healer," I reminded him. "And worse, we are bound for Norseland, where Ariel tortured him. Rushton is likely to remember what happened if he goes ashore, especially if he sees the place where Ariel took him."

"Ye gods," Brydda said. "Then he must not go ashore."

"That would be the best thing, but how can we stop him without telling him why he must stay aboard the *Umborine*?"

Brydda tugged at his beard absently, glaring unseeingly at the dark sea. Then he looked at me. "Gwynedd wants Jakoby to lower three small ship boats before the *Umborine* enters the shoal passage, which is the only way into the main cove of the island. The Herders simply call it Main Cove, but Gwynedd says the Norselanders used to call it Fryddcove after one of their goddesses. He means to be aboard one of the ship boats with as many of his people as safely possible in order to seek out a hidden inlet leading to a tiny cove his mother told him about called Uttecove. It will not be easy, for the inlet is perilously narrow and must be entered in the right way, but once the ship boats are in the cove, there is a way up to the island's surface. I do not know why Gwynedd is so certain that the Faction has not learned of this secret way, but he is prepared to risk his life and the lives of others on his certainty. Once on the surface, he means to rouse the Norselanders who live there to fight the Hedra. Rushton means to go with him, but what if Gwynedd asks you to come with him, claiming that he needs your Talents? Given what I have seen, that is likely to stop Rushton from going."

I nodded bleakly. "It will, but what is the *Umborine* to do?"

"Gwynedd's idea is that we enter Fryddcove and make a lot of fuss, demanding this and that and posturing and making threats to draw the Faction's attention. That will leave Gwynedd free to act behind their backs. It will also prevent Rushton from going ashore at once."

"What if Beforetime weapons are used against you?"

"That is a possibility," Brydda admitted. "However, since this is a Sadorian ship, I do not think anything will be done in haste, for the Hedra have no open quarrel with the desert lands. In any case, Rushton suggested that Jakoby demand to speak with Ariel. That way we can learn if he remained upon the island after Salamander left."

"All right, so Gwynedd will go ashore, but what

does he imagine he will do then? He cannot win against the Hedra in the few days he will have before Jakoby must take Rushton to Templeport."

"Gwynedd's primary purpose is to make sure there are no weapons or stores of plague seeds on Norseland that the Faction can use. He thinks that much can be accomplished in a twoday with the help of the Norselanders who live there, hence his determination to make contact."

"Do you know what Rushton is going to ask the tribes?" I said slowly.

Brydda's eyes widened. "Ye gods! You cannot know. Yesterday, just before we left the meeting house in Aborium, Zarak rode in. Dameon had sent him across the river with instructions to find Rushton. As soon as Zarak crossed, Linnet summoned a horse and sent him riding for Aborium."

My heart was beating fast. "What has happened?"

"Maryon came to Sutrium with a futuretelling that the slavemasters who hold the Red Queen's land are planning to invade the Land. If they come, Maryon says, they will bring such a horde that the Land on both sides of the Suggredoon, the Norselands, and the Sadorian desert lands will all fall to them, and any who do not die fighting will be enslaved."

I stared at him, aghast. "Maryon says they *will* fall? There is no hope?"

"There is no hope if they come, she says. There is some slight hope if they are prevented from coming."

"You talk in riddles, or Maryon does," I snapped.

"Maryon says a force must be mustered and carried by four greatships to the Red Queen's land before the Days of Rain."

"We do not have four . . ." I stopped, and understanding swept over me. "Rushton will ask the Sadorians for use of their two remaining spicewood greatships!"

Brydda nodded. "Two Sadorian ships, plus the *Stormdancer* and the ship that Dardelan has had built these two months, and we will just manage the four, though the *Stormdancer* will need repairs and Dardelan's ship must be completed. And all the ships will have to be especially fitted for such a journey."

"What said Shipmaster Helvar about this?" I asked.

"He said he must consult with the ship's proper master. Indeed, the *Stormdancer* left for Herder Isle even as Zarak set off. But the lad says the Norselanders were ferocious at the mere idea of losing a freedom so recently won."

"I cannot see the tribes refusing their ships, given their hatred of slavery and the fact that their own land will be in danger, too," I said.

"Jakoby says as much, but even so, the request must be made to the tribes, and if it is not made when they are together, someone must ride to each of the tribes to ask if they would agree to holding another conclave. This would be a task of many sevendays, perhaps even months. Maryon must have seen as much, or why urge Dameon to send someone after Rushton at all speed?"

"Ye gods. This is sickening news," I said. "But even with all four ships filled with fighters, we will still be too few to take on the slavemasters' hordes, there or here. It would be better to meet them here, for we would have the chance to prepare defenses, and we could use all the Hedra and soldierguards as well."

"That would still not be enough, apparently,"

Brydda said. "But Maryon insists that if four ships travel to the Red Land, the enslaved people will be inspired to rise against their masters."

"But," I said, and then stopped. Maryon was right; the ships would rouse the enslaved people, *if Dragon was aboard one of them.* Indeed, it would take only one ship to do it. Then something else occurred to me. "A journey begun in the Days of Rain will be terribly dangerous, for Reuvan once told me that, amongst shipfolk, the season is called the Days of Storm. And if the ships survive that, they would still be traveling when wintertime came. They would also be beyond Land's End, where few ships have ever traveled, and I have heard that the way from Land's End to the Red Queen's land is perilous. Do you know how to go from there? Does Dardelan or Gwynedd?"

"Gwynedd does not know the way, but he says there will be maps and charts on Norseland, for once upon a time, the Norse kings had some dealings with the queens of the Red Land," Brydda said. "Getting those maps is another thing that Gwynedd hopes to accomplish while we are ashore."

I nodded absently, turning over in my mind what Brydda had said and wondering at the neatness of a prophecy that would send to the Red Queen's land ships, one of which would carry the lost queen whose mind contained a vital clue to finding something the Seeker needed. Was it a real futuretelling, I wondered, or merely a manipulation by the Agyllians?

Then it struck me that it was not just Dragon who would be aboard those ships. I would have to travel to the Red Queen's land, too.

"Elspeth?" Brydda's voice drew me back to myself. "I need to go and speak with Dardelan and Gwynedd about keeping Rushton aboard before he and Jakoby join us in the saloon." He hesitated. "Under the circumstances, I think it best if you do not attend the meeting. Indeed, perhaps you ought to remain in your cabin for the time being. I will come later and tell you what has been decided."

I nodded, but after he had gone, I remained at the side of the ship, gazing blindly out to sea and struggling to order my thoughts. A hand touched my arm, and I turned, expecting to see Brydda again, but it was Gilbert, carrying a lantern. I snatched my arm away, and a shadow crossed the armsman's handsome face.

"You would rather be alone?"

I struggled with irritation and frustration, and finally I looked directly into his eyes and made myself ask evenly, "Why do you seek me out so constantly?"

Gilbert looked taken aback at my bluntness, and fleetingly I saw again the man I had liked in the Druid's encampment. "Is not the answer obvious?" he finally said, and now he was smiling again.

"I fear that it is," I said softly, deciding there was nothing for it but to be ruthlessly honest.

His smile faded. "I thought that you had some . . . liking for me when we were in the Druid's camp. Was it merely a pretense to gain my help?"

"No," I said. "You did not despise me for being a gypsy, and you were kind."

He laughed roughly. "I felt that there was more than liking between us back in the White Valley."

I forced myself to answer him truthfully. "I think

there was some . . . some potential that we both recognized. I felt that you were a man I might have cared for under other circumstances."

"You no longer feel that way," Gilbert said.

I bit my lip and said awkwardly, "It seems you have changed. I felt it when I saw you in the Beforetime ruins." He said nothing, and I struggled for clarity, feeling it was owed. "In the White Valley, you did not smile so much or give voice to elaborate flattery. The man I met in the Druid's camp had a seriousness and a steadiness in him that . . . that anyone might feel they could rely upon. I do not think that man would have left his babies so easily, saying they had no need of him."

Gilbert paled so much he looked ill, and then it seemed that some pleasant facile mask he had worn melted away as pain flooded into his eyes and mouth. He turned abruptly to face the sea and drew a ragged breath. Then he said slowly and very softly, "There can come a moment in life when you see your heart's desire, though you did not know of its existence until that moment. So it was for me when I first saw you. I was determined that I would protect you from Henry Druid's prejudice against gypsies and against his foolish spoiled daughter's jealousy. When Erin contrived that you would be given to that ape Relward, I near went mad thinking how to prevent it. But . . . you escaped and then I saw you carried off by the river. I thought you had died."

"I . . . I did not know . . . ," I stammered.

"Of course you did not, for you saw only a vague potential in me, but I saw in you a blazing beacon of meaning and purpose. You understand how seeing such a wondrous radiance quenched might . . . change a man? I do not think I was utterly changed at once. So much happened so suddenly. You were gone, and then the Druid's camp was destroyed in a firestorm while I was still too grief-stricken to think. Then I and the other few survivors realized that those from the camp had been sold as slaves. I rode with two other men who had survived, because we had been sent out to scout, but eventually we parted. I do not know where the others went. I had no clear plan but to go as far as I could. That single notion brought me to rose-colored Murmroth where I met Gwynedd. Meeting him was . . . was like an awakening from numbness, because, like you, he blazes with a purpose and potency that illuminates the lives of those about him. I joined his cause and threw myself into becoming his man and serving his dreams. For a time, I found contentment. But then I made a mistake."

"The woman you bonded with?" I said softly.

He nodded. "Serra was . . ." He looked away to the sea again and concluded harshly, "She looked like you—the same long dark hair and proud look. The same gravity about her, as if there were hidden depths that one might spend a lifetime trying to plumb . . . I courted her and we bonded. But Serra was less deep than wont to brood, and after a time she began to fret at me. I felt that she wanted something from me that she could not name and did not even know, and without it she could not be content. She became jealous of my devotion to Gwynedd, and the more she nagged and scowled, the more time I spent away from home. Then she became pregnant. I was glad, for I thought that a child might fulfill her. She gave birth to twin boys, and

I could have loved them and loved her for them, but she had become cold and pointed out my faults to them so that soon they regarded me suspiciously and rejected me."

"You said they were babies," I said.

He nodded. "So they are, yet Serra's sullen eyes and her grudging nature look out of their faces. I learned not to care and to laugh and make light of all that seemed serious and deep and true. I discovered that women would laugh with me if I flattered their beauty and paid them compliments and kept my deeper self from them."

"I'm sorry," I said, and I pitied him enough to fight my reticence and lay a hand over his clenched fists. At once he turned his hands and caught mine between them.

"I could find the man I once was, with you." A yearning in his eyes made the words a question. I wanted to pull my hands away and flee from the naked emotion in his face, but I forced myself to meet his eyes and shake my head. The longing in his face dimmed, but he did not resume the careless, flirtatious mask I had so disliked. Instead, he said with a sad acceptance that ached my heart as much as it relieved me, "You are different now, too, Elspeth who was once Elaria. I see it clearly in this moment."

I said, "Since the rebellion, I am freed from having to hide my Misfit abilities, but . . . there is a man that I love. I knew him when I met you, but I did not know that I loved him. I was afraid to see it."

He sighed, a long exhalation. "Well, then, perhaps it was that gypsy girl who hid from love and hid her true self that I loved. You are stronger and more courageous than that girl was, and I hope the man you love is worthy of you. In honor of the love I bore Elaria, I offer you my friendship."

"The friendship of one who is honest and courageous is precious," I said gravely.

Gilbert released my hand and looked up into the night, drawing a long breath and expelling it. The wind blew more strongly now, and the smell of rain was in the air. "A storm is coming," he said softly, and walked away.

I watched him go, a strong, straight-backed man with flame-colored hair that caught the lantern light from a saloon window, and I wondered again how love could cause so much pain.

My neck prickled, and I turned to look up at the truncated upper deck where I had sat the previous day with Jakoby. A cluster of lanterns hung from hooks and showed the tribeswoman clearly, standing by the wheel and speaking to one of her men, her hair and clothes fluttering wildly in the rising wind. A little apart from them stood Rushton, gazing down at me with a black rage that sent a cold blade into my heart.

✦ 15 ✦

THE CLAP OF thunder that shook the ship testified to the mounting fury of the storm that had come upon us so suddenly and dramatically hours before and showed no sign of abating. Lightning filled the cabin with a weird, distorted radiance, and I got up and staggered over the pitching floor to the window. Opening it a crack, I saw a great jagged spear of lightning slash through the black night, revealing a sky clogged with massive thunderheads. The sea was a heaving gray expanse from which rose the smoking peaks of enormous waves. Then darkness swallowed everything until claws of lightning rent the night again. This time, I saw a massive wave rise alongside the ship and topple over with deadly slowness. I realized with sick horror that just one such mountain of water breaking over the bow would smash the greatship to splinters.

The thought of Gahltha smote me like a blow, and I muttered a curse at my callousness. He and the other horses had been shifted belowdecks soon after the storm began, but the storm would have destroyed his hard-won control over his fear of water, and I ought to have gone and seen him long since, regardless of the need to stay out of Rushton's way.

Thunder reverberated as I groped for the quilted

vest hanging on a hook behind the door. Dragging it on, I looked back at the bed to see Maruman sleeping soundly, oblivious to the storm. Afraid that he had gone onto the dreamtrails for the longsleep, I staggered back to lay a hand on his warm back, but he was only sleeping. Relieved, I mounded some pillows about him and made my way back to the door. I opened it, and the wind forced it wide and blustered at me with such ferocity that I was flung backward. I lowered my head and shouldered my way out of the cabin, heaving the door closed behind me and making sure it was securely latched.

For a moment, all was darkness and noisy disorienting chaos, then lightning illuminated the deck, revealing slick wood and snaking ropes. Oddly, there was not a shipman or woman in sight.

I had not gone far when the ship nosed into a trough, the hull groaning and creaking as if it were about to break in two. I was thrown from my feet, but instead of crashing to the deck, strong arms caught me. I looked up to find Jakoby holding me in a viselike grip. I expected her to order me back to my cabin, but instead she pointed forward and shouted at me to go to the saloon. I shook my head and tried to explain that I needed to stay out of Rushton's sight. But thunder rumbled and lightning cracked, smothering my words. Jakoby pointed insistently, and her vehemence made me turn. My jaw dropped at the sight of a sheer stone cliff rearing up out of the churning water directly ahead and extending up out of sight.

"Norseland," Jakoby bellowed in my ear.

"It can't be!" I shouted back. Then I laid my hand on her arm and sent, "We can't have got here so swiftly."

"The storm blew us directly across the strait instead of along the normal shipping path," Jakoby shouted. "It was a perilous passage, for we had to negotiate the many shoals in the midst of the storm, but it is done, and now we are less than an hour from the Norsemen's Uttecove."

I glanced at the cliffs, which were rushing toward us at a speed that dried my mouth, but at that moment, the *Umborine* lurched and plunged and groaned, the deck and hull creaking horribly as the ship slowly turned broadside to the cliffs. Instead of looking relieved, Jakoby merely shouted into my ear that I should go to the saloon, for the ship boats would soon be launched.

I gaped at her in disbelief, unable to believe she meant to go ahead with Gwynedd's strategy in the midst of the storm. Yet Jakoby did not look as if she were joking. I swallowed hard, remembering that I had agreed to take part in what must surely be a lunatic's venture.

Jakoby was shouting more, and I touched her arm again so I could enter her mind and asked her to repeat her words. "The storm will prevent us from being able to maneuver the *Umborine* close enough to Norseland to see the inlet; therefore, the ships will have to be launched in faith."

I nodded, understanding that I was receiving a warning, and Jakoby pointed urgently toward the shipmaster's deck. Then she let me go and hastened toward the rear of the vessel, as sure-footed as a cat on the heaving deck.

I stood for a moment, indecisive amid all the wild wind and water, but then I continued along the deck to the entrance to the hold. I was about to descend when I saw a Sadorian shipgirl carrying a lantern and a coil of thick oiled rope. I lurched over to her and asked where the holding corral was belowdecks. She shouted something, but the roaring of the wind and the raging sea made it impossible to make out her words. Realizing that I could not hear her, she pointed down and then toward the rear of the ship. Then she showed three fingers. I nodded, understanding that Gahltha was on the third level toward the rear of the ship.

I reeled and stumbled down the steps into the pitching, creaking blackness. At one point, I heard Jak's voice and realized he must be striving to keep his precious insects safe, but I continued to descend until my nose told me I had reached the holding boxes. I drew a deep breath and shouted Gahltha's name. My heart lurched with relief and dismay as he gave a high-pitched, terrified whinny of response. Full of remorse for not having come to him sooner, I groped my way toward the sound. At last my straining hands found his hot, trembling flank.

"I am here, dear one," I sent. "I am so sorry I did not come sooner."

"It is not your fault that I am a coward," Gahltha sent miserably.

"My great-hearted Gahltha, you are the least cowardly creature I have ever known," I told him fiercely, sliding my arms around his neck and kissing his silky muzzle.

"You are leaving the ship," Gahltha sent, having seen it in my mind.

"I must," I said. "But when I return, we will go to Sador, and after that, we will ride back to Obernewtyn."

Unable to offer any further assurances, I held him and stroked him until at last I felt the keen edge of his terror blunt. Then, knowing I could delay no longer, I kissed him one last time and made my way back up to the deck.

The cliffs seemed closer than ever in the flashes of lightning, and I told myself that at least no one would have seen us approach the island in the middle of such a black stormy night. The first the Hedra would know about anything was when the *Umborine* sailed into Main Cove. I could just make out movement around the ship boats, which had been lashed to the deck beyond the saloon, but I had one last errand before I could join the others. I ran back to my cabin and wakened Maruman to explain what I was going to do. Before he could utter any of the protests I sensed gathering in his mind, I knelt by the bed, took his small pointed face in my hands, and looked into his shining golden eye.

"Maruman, darling heart, listen to me. There is no time for tantrums," I told him with stern tenderness. "I have to go ashore for many reasons, some of which are connected to my quest as ElspethInnle, but Gahltha is very frightened. I need you to go to him and help him to endure the storm. Will you do this for me?"

For a long moment, he looked into my eyes. Then, at last, he sent softly into my mind, "Maruman/yelloweyes will go to the Daywatcher. Be careful, ElspethInnle."

Outside, the wind had grown stronger, and now it was beginning to rain. A Sadorian, seeing me emerge, leaned into the wind and handed me the end of a rope, indicating that I should tie it around my waist. I obeyed and he made another gesture, which I did not understand, before hurrying off.

I made my unsteady way along the deck toward the

336

main saloon, but the rope was too short and brought me to a sudden stop. I saw another rope end tied and coiled against the wall and realized the meaning of the Sadorian's gestures. He had been trying to tell me that I needed to move from one secured rope to another. I tied the new one about my waist, untied the other, and fastened it to the wall before continuing along the ship. Beyond the saloon, I could see the Sadorians unlashing the small ship boats, but there was no sign of Gwynedd or his men, so I untied the rope from my waist, curled it around a hook to which a number of other ropes were fastened, and entered the saloon.

Just as I passed through the doors, the ship tilted again. I flew into the room and fetched up hard against the end of a table. Lightning flared, giving me a brief glimpse of startled pasty faces turned toward me; then the ship tilted the other way, sending me staggering drunkenly backward. I would have reeled back through the doors, except that Brydda caught me and thrust a towel into my hands, shouting that he would get me an oiled coat.

I sat down, hooking one foot around a leg of the bench to steady myself, and dried my face. Looking around the long room, I saw Jak in the next flash of lightning, looking pale but composed. I had been astonished when Brydda had come to me after the meeting in the saloon and said that Jak would also travel with the three ship boats. The teknoguilder had apparently volunteered, pointing out rightly that he would have the best hope of recognizing and knowing how to dispose of the plague seeds if we found them.

It had been decided that any weapons on Norseland were most likely to be kept in the Hedra encampment in an armory, but it seemed likely that the plague seeds would be in Ariel's residence, unless he had taken them with him. Jak and I and several others would make our way there, leaving Gwynedd free to meet with the Norselanders and with their help mount an attack on the Hedra encampment.

We did not know the exact location of Ariel's residence, but I had heard enough on Herder Isle to know that it lay at the end of the island farthest from Fryddcove, and this meant that Uttecove must be closer to it than to the nearest settlement. From what Lark had told me, this would be Cloistertown. Gwynedd reckoned from the things I had told him that Ariel's residence would be no more than a two-hour walk in a straight line from Uttecove, but since we did not know where it was, it would be safer to follow the cliffs around, which would take somewhat longer.

In the meantime, Gwynedd intended to travel in a slanting line across the island from Uttecove to Cloistertown, where he would seek out the Per and raise a small force to lead him to the Hedra encampment. If all went as planned, the camp ought to be at least partly emptied out by Dardelan's provocations in Fryddcove. The greatest danger would be that the Hedra lured to the cliffs overlooking the cove might take Beforetime weapons with them, but Gwynedd thought these would not be used or even brought out unless the Hedra felt truly threatened, and it was unlikely that they would feel that way, faced with a single greatship.

I had asked how Gwynedd proposed to return to the ship, given that his plan involved setting up an army between him and the only way down to the beach in Fryddcove, and was told that once the Norselander and his men had destroyed the armory and seized the maps, they would await Jak and me outside Covetown with several high-ranking Hedra they would capture in the encampment. Once we joined them, I would coerce them, and then we all would dress in Hedra robes taken from the encampment and be marched by the coerced Hedra in full view of the Hedra ranks, down the path to the beach, ostensibly to relieve the Hedra posted at the bottom of the pass.

It was beautifully simple and daring. My only concern was that the Norselanders would be left to deal with an enraged nest of Hedra.

"Gwynedd is content to leave his people in the midst of a battle he has begun?" I had asked, somewhat indignantly, resisting the urge to add that it seemed to be a habit of his to begin things and then leave others to finish them.

But Brydda had pointed out that, before leaving, Gwynedd would have destroyed the armory as well as defeating a good many of the Hedra left in the camp, and he would have informed the Norselanders of the Hedra's defeat elsewhere. Besides, it was Gwynedd's belief that people should fight for their own freedom.

I had asked what Rushton had said to all of this. As we had guessed, he had elected to remain on the ship once he learned that I would accompany Gwynedd. Dardelan meant for Rushton to stay aboard the *Umborine*, but if he insisted on going ashore, he would be fed a draft of sleep potion. The solution's rough simplicity had made me laugh with relief.

Brydda reappeared with the promised coat and dragged me from my reflections to a renewed awareness of the storm-battered night. I had just taken the coat and began rising to pull it on, when the ship listed so far to one side that I fell back to my seat.

"Where is Rushton now?" I asked Brydda.

"Dardelan is keeping him occupied with the launching of the ship boats. He and Dardelan are planning various incendiary messages aimed at drawing out as many Hedra as possible from the camp. To begin with, Jakoby will signal a demand for surrender, claiming that Sador has been summoned by the rebels on Norseland. That will puzzle the priests sorely, since there is no rebel force upon Norseland, and even if there was some more rebellious element, how could they have contacted the Sadorians? The mystery should pique their curiosity. Then Jakoby will demand to speak with Ariel, pretending that he knows what it is about. The response will confirm whether or not Ariel has gone with Salamander, which we think is most likely."

I said nothing, for I had no doubt of it, now that I had heard of Maryon's futuretelling.

"How are we to get to the ship?" I asked as I had done the night before.

This time, Brydda had an answer. "The Per will send a signal up from Covetown, and upon seeing it, Dardelan will have the three large ship boats launched to collect us. In the meantime, Gwynedd plans to have the Norselanders mount an attack from the rear, to give us time to get aboard and weigh anchor."

Before I could say that leaving the Norselanders at the beginning of a battle we had incited left a bitter taste in my mouth, the doors to the saloon burst wide open, letting in a gust of rain-filled wind, and Gilbert stood in the open doorway, his red hair and side plaits streaming. "Gwynedd said anyone going ashore must come now or be left behind," he said hoarsely.

Twenty minutes later, I was in the first of the tiny ship boats to be lowered into the boiling sea. The wind and sea were slightly less ferocious, because we had reached the lee of the island, but even so, the fact that we were not immediately swamped or capsized was solely due to the skill of the Sadorian shipwoman maneuvering us toward the three rock pinnacles Gwynedd's mother had called the Staffs of the Goddess, saying they stood close to the entrance to the hidden inlet.

"Do you see the opening yet?" Gilbert bellowed to Gwynedd, who sat in the prow, squinting against the rain and the darkness.

The big Norselander shook his head without taking his eyes from the cliffs, and I clung to my seat and prayed that Gwynedd's mother had not made a mistake. It was so dark, and rain was now falling so heavily that I could not even see the stone pinnacles I had glimpsed from the ship. I looked over my shoulder, trying to spot the other two ship boats, but the waves were so high that both were hidden at the bottom of troughs. Even the enormous *Umborine* was invisible, save for a few circles of golden light cast down by the lanterns fore and aft.

At last, I saw the three stone pinnacles just ahead, and I breathed a sigh of relief as the Sadorian shipwoman maneuvered the tiny vessel between them. Still I could see no sign of the inlet opening.

"If we go any closer and there is no opening, we will

not be able to prevent the ship boat crashing into the cliff," Gilbert shouted.

The older man said nothing for a long moment, and then he pointed. "There!"

I strained my eyes, but only when lightning flared again did I see what looked like a fold or ripple in the cliff. The cove was not visible, because it could not be seen from straight on. It was literally a crack running sideways into the cliff, and it had to be approached from the side, from very close to the stone wall. Now, just as Gwynedd had warned, the ship boat was swept into a current that ran swift and straight toward the crevasse. Seeing the narrowness of the opening, I swallowed a lump of fear, but there was only ferocious concentration on the face of the Sadorian shipwoman whom Jakoby had assigned to master the tiny vessel.

"To port, pull hard now!" she commanded suddenly, and those of us on that side of the ship boat shot out our oars, dropped them into the water, and pulled hard. The boat hovered for a long moment before the prow swung around to point like the needle in a compass toward the opening.

"Watch out!" someone cried. I blinked to clear my eyes of rain. The entrance to the narrow channel seemed to be rushing toward us like a closing maw.

"Oars up *now*!" the shipwoman roared.

I pushed down hard on the oar, and suddenly—miraculously—the ship boat surged smoothly into the stone passage. The wind's keening was instantly muted, and the rain seemed to have ceased, but I knew it was only that the wind had preventing it falling into the narrow crevice. I fixed the oar in its upright position as Gwynedd, Gilbert, and the other armsmen were doing and turned to look behind us. There was no sign of the other vessels yet, and I prayed that those aboard were safe. I knew none of Gwynedd's men save Gilbert, but Jak had gone in the second ship boat and Brydda in the third.

The stone passage curved and then began to widen, and suddenly we entered an almost perfectly round cove with sheer rain-washed cliff walls. There was no sign of a sand or pebble beach, nor was there any sort of rock shelf where a landing could be made. I turned to look at Gwynedd, but he was calmly studying the cliffs. I followed his gaze and saw a wide opening at the base of the cliffs that would not be visible from above, but the sea flowed into it, and I could see no place to make a landing.

Gwynedd merely bade the Sadorian woman, whose name was Andorra, bring the ship boat into the cavern. As this was done, Gilbert lit a lantern, and its golden light revealed great white clusters of stalactites overhead, from which water dripped slowly but steadily into the heaving water filling the cavern. Gwynedd said nothing as the ship boat slipped deeper into the shadowy interior. Then, when the stalactites were almost brushing our heads, I heard the sound of waves breaking, and there before us was a beach of pale transparent pebbles that gleamed like yellow eyes in the lantern light.

As I climbed out onto the stones, I looked back the way we had come and saw the light of another lantern shining on the wet stalactites and cavern wall, and then one of the other ship boats hove into view. In a moment, Jak, another group of armsmen, and a Sadorian shipman were climbing from the ship boat.

We waited a half hour for the third ship, when Gwynedd swore ferociously and shook his head, saying it would have come by now.

"They might manage to swim in here if they capsized," Jak said.

The Norselander sighed. "They might, but we cannot wait, for the *Umborine* must even now be approaching Fryddcove. If the others survive, they will follow." He bade his men collect the packs that had been lashed into the ship boats, and then he turned and strode resolutely to the end of the beach, where there was an opening in the walls. We followed him and then stopped, because the tiny round cavern he had entered was barely big enough for a single solid man, let alone all of us. But when I put my head in, I saw that its roof was so high that the light from Gilbert's lantern could not find it; it was like a natural chimney.

"Where are the steps?" I asked Gwynedd.

"Look," he said, and bent down to run his hands over the sheer walls of the small circular cave at about knee height.

"What are you looking for?" I asked.

The Norselander stopped and pointed up. "Once, when the sea flowed here, this was a blowhole. Then a series of freakish tides deposited these pebbles that formed the beach where we made our landing and gave this place a floor."

"Are you saying this leads to the surface?" Jak demanded, looking up.

"That is exactly what I am saying," Gwynedd said. "If it was daylight or even a clear night, you would see the sky far above. The rain is not falling on us, because the wind is driving it across the mouth of the blowhole." Again he turned to the wall of the cavern and ran his hands over the stone. Suddenly he gave a grunt of triumph and began to pull pebbles and stone out of the wall so easily that I knew they must merely have been pressed into place. Gradually, he exposed a narrow recess. Then he felt around the wall and began to dig again. In a short time, he had exposed a number of steps cut into the rock.

"Let me do it," Gilbert said, and he exposed yet another step and then another above it.

"They go right to the top," Gwynedd said. "They are shallow, but put your back against the opposite wall and go up like that. Only these bottom few steps are filled in, and the few at the top. The rest cannot be seen looking up or down, so my mother said. She told me that the first time anyone used this way, there were no steps cut. It is called Voerligga's Path. Voerligga is the wise dwarf who serves the goddess Fryyd and sometimes intercedes for certain humans."

It took almost two hours for all of us to reach the top, and I came last save for the Sadorian man who had remained till the end in the hope that the other ship boat would arrive.

"Perhaps it missed the entrance and returned to the ship," I panted, but he made no response as we ascended.

It was an exhausting climb, and my legs were trembling with the exertion long before I reached the surface of the island. I was very glad to hear Gilbert call out my name and know that I was close to the top.

Gilbert and another armsman reached down to haul me out, and I gasped as the windy rain slapped at my face, only now realizing that the storm was still raging over the island. Jak pulled me down to my knees beside him, shouting to stay low because we were close to the edge of the cliffs surrounding Uttecove, and the wind was strong enough to send a person staggering to their death.

On my knees, I watched the others haul the Sadorian out and realized that nothing at all marked the steps save a small hole fringed in grass, which from even a short distance away would seem no more than a depression in the ground, dangerously close to the cliffs, and I no longer wondered why the Hedra had not discovered it.

"Time to go," Gwynedd said.

PART III

✦

The Heartlands

✦ 16 ✦

I SAT BACK on my heels and squinted against the rain to study the terrain. Little was visible in the rainy darkness, but in the flashes of lightning, which seemed less frequent than they had been aboard the ship, I saw that the island was every bit as flat and featureless as I had been led to believe. Looking east, I could not see the rocky knoll upon which Ariel's residence was supposedly constructed or any other sign of human habitation. And when I looked west where Fryddcove was said to lie, I could not see the Hedra encampment, the cloister, or the town that spread out around the top of the trail leading up from Uttecove.

Then Gwynedd lay a hand on my shoulder and gave me a brief, unexpectedly warm smile, and told me that he had bidden the two Sadorians and Gilbert to accompany Jak and me to Ariel's residence.

"Take care, and remember, you must be in the boulders on the cliff outside Covetown by tomorrow night or the morning after, at the latest, or the ship will have to leave without you. Good luck," he told all of us, and turned to lead his armsfolk away along the cliff edge in the opposite direction.

✦ ✦ ✦

After what seemed like hours of shouldering our way into the bullying, rain-filled wind over flat but infuriatingly uneven ground, I slipped on a patch of bare rock and went down hard enough on one knee to bring hot tears to my eyes. Cursing furiously, I stumbled on after the others, only slightly mollified by the fact that Jak and Gilbert were finding the way no easier. Ironically, the two Sadorians handled the terrain most gracefully, for though they were desert people, their shipboard training had accustomed them to slippery surfaces.

"Are you all right?" Gilbert asked, seeing that I had fallen behind. The rain was falling more heavily than ever, but the thunder and lightning had eased, so it was possible to talk.

"Bruised but hale," I said.

"It cannot be much farther to this knoll if the one spoken of on Herder Isle is the same one as the knoll Gwynedd's mother described to him," Gilbert assured me, and it warmed me slightly to see the smile I remembered from Henry Druid's secret encampment and not the dazzling superficial smile of recent days. But then his expression turned grim as he glanced about. "Trust Ariel to choose such a place for his home."

Gilbert's words reminded me that he had known Ariel, too, from the time he had spent in Henry Druid's secret encampment in the White Valley. But when I asked what he had thought of Ariel in those days, he shrugged, saying he had seen little of him. "It was my impression that he was not the sort to trouble with anyone he did not wish to make use of, and I had nothing he wanted. I do recall it being slyly said that he courted the Druid as much as his daughter. I mean Erin, not

Gilaine. Little Gilly never liked him. No doubt her powers let her see his true nature."

I nodded, only wondering that Ariel's powers had not let him see what she was. On the other hand, perhaps Lidgebaby's powerful emanations had prevented Ariel from reaching the mind of any Misfit in the camp. I wondered how he had rationalized the net of mental static, for it must have impeded his coercive abilities even if his twisted Talent for empathy had been unaffected.

I thought again of Domick's words, realizing they had taken on a talismanic power for me: *"He does not see everything!"*

Gilbert had instinctively taken the lead when we set off, and now he called a halt. I was weary enough to be glad of it, but there was neither shelter nor any means of warming ourselves, so after a short time, we went on again. I was trying to steel myself for another long stumbling walk when Jak gave a cry and pointed out a dark square-edged plateau almost invisible against the cloud-clogged sky. It could only be the knoll we had been seeking, though I had been imagining a low round-topped mound rising not much higher than ground level. This knoll looked to be twice as high as a tall man, and I could discern no building upon it.

We were almost upon it before I realized that the stone knoll was no more than shoulder height, and the rest was a wall rising up from the edge of the knoll formed of stone blocks mortared snugly together. No light showed above it or through any of the spy slits. The rain prevented me from sending out a probe to search for watchers, but it would have been useless in any case due to the strength of the taint in the wall. This, more than anything else, assured me that this was Ariel's residence.

We followed the knoll until we came to a corner. I marveled at the fact that the mound was as squared off as the wall atop it. The angle was so sharp that I stopped to examine the knoll, expecting to find that it had been deliberately shaped to match the wall's corner, but there was neither chisel mark nor any sign that nature had *not* shaped the stone. Still pondering this, I rounded the corner and stopped to stare, for the wall that stretched away was at least twice as long as the one we had already paced out. We had not gone far along it before we came to a gate at the top of a set of steps hewn into the knoll.

Through the gate I could see a strange wide building, quite square, with a queer flat roof that ended abruptly at the walls like a giant box. I was reminded of the skyscrapers of the Beforetime laid down on their sides, for the building did not rise more than a single level above the ground. I no longer wondered if Salamander and his crew had stayed here, or if the slaves to be transported to the Red Queen's land were kept here, for why else build such a massive residence?

With no windows in the front, there was no way to see if the building was occupied, but to my surprise, Gilbert withdrew from his pack a Herder robe, donned it, then bade us stay back and went to hammer and shout at the gate. There was no response. Still warning us to keep back, he reached into his backpack and drew out a short metal bar with one end flattened to a wedge and the other tapered to a point. He pushed this into one of the gate hinges and heaved on it. There was a slight grinding sound, barely audible over the relentless hissing of the wind, and then with a snap, the metal gate sagged inward with a creak. Despite the tension of the moment, or maybe because of it, I found myself stifling the urge to laugh, for if faced with the same locked gates, I would have exhausted myself opening the lock, never thinking of attacking the hinge. *There is a lesson there,* I thought as Gilbert slipped through the gap.

When the rest of us would have followed, he held up a hand and shook his head, but Andorra made a clicking sound with her tongue. Gilbert looked back questioningly. She tapped her chest. He considered a moment, then nodded, and she slipped through the gap to join him, drawing a thick, short-bladed knife from a hip sheath and carrying it point down like a great fang. They crossed the yard to the door at the front of the building, and Andorra pressed herself flat to the wall beside it, knife at the ready. Gilbert adjusted his sword and knocked loudly.

There was no response. I saw Gilbert reach for the handle of the door and all at once I remembered the premonition I had experienced at the door to Ariel's chamber in the Herder Compound. I gave a roar and raced across the yard.

Gilbert swung around in surprise, and I gasped out an explanation. Then he and Andorra stood back as I laid my hand over the lock. To my relief, it was merely a rather simple lock, so I focused my mind to turn the tumblers and opened the door.

It was too dark to see anything. I stepped inside and sent out a general probe. Then I turned to Gilbert and

Andorra, who had entered behind me. "Either there is no one here or someone is trying to make it seem so. There are just two places I can't probe."

Gilbert nodded and knelt to remove a lantern from his pack; then he rummaged for a tinderbox with which to light it. Andorra had gone to summon Jak and the Sadorian man, and they arrived just as the lantern wick caught. We all stared about at the room we had entered. There was not a piece of furniture and no rug on the floor or hanging upon the stone walls, but there was a large hearth where a fire had been laid but not lit and three doors other than the front one. Gilbert went to light the fire, for we were all wet and shivering with cold. I sent out a probe again. Still there was nothing, but I had not truly expected to find anyone.

"The place seems empty," Gilbert said, regarding the fire critically before prodding two pieces of wood into different positions. Then he looked up at me and frowned. "You'd better stay here and thaw out a bit. You too," he said to Jak. "The Sadorians and I will take one of those doors each and make a preliminary search of the place?" He phrased it as a question, and the Sadorians nodded as one. After they had gone, I turned back to the fire.

"Take off the coat so the heat can get to you," Jak said through chattering teeth, removing his own. I obeyed, and he took both and hung them on hooks by the hearth. Then he rummaged in his own bag and withdrew a wide metal pan and a small pot, which he carried outside.

"It will take hours to fill them," I protested. "Surely there is a supply of water in this place."

"I have set them under a downpipe from the roof,"

Jak said mildly, squatting down and stretching his hands out to the flames. "We will certainly need something to warm us after we search this building. It is a queer chilly place to call home, I must say, yet mayhap it matches the strange cold shape of Ariel's soul."

I stared down at him, startled to hear a teknoguilder wax poetic. Then I turned, too, and squatted to be closer to the flames. It would be some time before the fire emitted much real heat, but the brightness was heartening. Shortly, Gilbert and the Sadorians returned to say they had found nothing to suggest that the building was inhabited. I was ready to begin searching, but Jak said he would make some porridge, for we would all search the better for eating. I disliked wasting time, but I was hungry, and I was as glad as the others to accept a bowl and devour it.

Warmed inside and out, we were then ready to begin searching in earnest. As we ate, Jak had told us what we ought to be looking for. Now he warned us very seriously to touch nothing and summon him if we found anything that looked like a room a healer might use or perhaps a dye worker or even a candle or perfume maker.

We split into two parties, for one of the passages leading back from the entrance had led only to a door that opened into an enormous rain-swept courtyard. Jak would take one of the other passages with the Sadorian man, named Hakim, while Andorra and I would take the third with Gilbert, who had found a store of lanterns and oil for us to carry.

"What bothers me is where the servants are," Gilbert said as we walked along the hall. We did not bother opening any doors, because he had already checked this area.

"I suppose Ariel dismissed them when he left," I said, "though it seems it would have been too far for people from Cloistertown to travel each day. Maybe they stayed here. There are certainly bedchambers and common chambers enough for an army of servants. He might also have used the nulls. That is what he did on Herder Isle."

We reached a turn in the passage where Gilbert looked back to say that henceforth we must search, for this was as far as he had got earlier. Gilbert moved ahead, saying Andorra should check one side of the corridor and I the other.

To begin with, every door I opened belonged to a bedchamber, but unlike those closer to the front door, these had locks and, therefore, must be slave accommodations. Each chamber was as bare as most of the rooms and halls, equipped with a bed, chest, shelves, and a mat on the floor. I flipped over each mat until Gilbert noticed and asked me why. I told him that I was looking for trapdoors, and he reminded me that the whole place was built on a great raft of solid rock.

As we continued, I found myself thinking of Domick and Rushton, who must also have traversed these halls. Had they been conscious, walking with their hands chained behind their backs, or had they simply awakened in cells? Long ago I had experienced a vision of Domick in a cell, and I was suddenly convinced that cell was here. I shivered, profoundly glad that Rushton was safely aboard the *Umborine*.

Thoughts of the ship turned my attention to Brydda and the Sadorian who had mastered the third ship boat and the rest of Gwynedd's armsfolk ashore. I could only pray that they had merely missed the entrance and had returned to the greatship. How would I tell Brydda's parents if he perished? How would I bear his loss?

Then I thought of Gwynedd, wondering if he and the others had reached Cloistertown safely, and what sort of reception the Per had given them. Brydda had told me that Gwynedd had no intention of revealing that he was kin to the last Norse king unless he needed to induce the Norselanders to help him. I could not help but wonder why he imagined they would believe him, but according to Brydda, the Norselander had no doubts on that account.

Gilbert and Andorra were walking more quickly than I, and a little pool of darkness had opened between our lanterns. I hastened to catch up as the horrible thought crept into my mind that, despite my certainty of Ariel's departure from Norseland, I had no proof of it. I might come face to face with Ariel here as I had done so often in the dark and twisting passages of my dreams.

"Come to me," he had whispered many times. And now I had.

An hour later, I opened a door to a large bare dining chamber containing a long trestle and some twenty unadorned and uncushioned chairs. It was the second I had seen, but the first had been a smaller and far more luxuriously appointed room with a thick red rug on the floor and embroidered chairs. There had also been two sitting rooms, one as large and bare as this dining chamber and another about half its size, with soft couches and embroidered chairs with beaded cushions. It looked as if Ariel used the bare rooms to entertain his official guests and kept the smaller more lavish versions for his own use.

"Come and look at this," Gilbert murmured, beckoning. Andorra and I joined him at an open door to see a lavish bedchamber filled with every conceivable color, texture, and ornament, as well as every conceivable comfort.

"Which of them used this one, I wonder?" Gilbert murmured, gazing at the bed hung with scarlet Sadorian double silk with golden embroidery.

I said nothing, but I thought it must belong to Salamander, for Ariel had always preferred to wear white clothing that set off his pale golden beauty. Whoever had slept in this room had wished to ravish his senses with beautiful fabrics and textures. An array of exquisite cut crystal bottles sat atop the hearth's mantel. I opened one, and the sweet heady smell of pure incense filled the air. Replacing the stopper, I noticed that the fire was made up here just as it had been in the entrance chamber, and I wondered what this meant. The only reason I could think of for the carefully prepared hearths was that Ariel's departure had been sudden and unplanned.

I noticed a book lying half hidden under the golden fringe of the bed covering and bent to pick it up. I was astonished to see that the words on the cover were in the coiling gadi script that I had first seen on the carved panels of Obernewtyn's original doors. Since the Sadorians never scribed in gadi, this book must have belonged to the Gadfian raiders who had preyed upon them. If I was right, this was surely evidence that they had not died out. Indeed, it seemed proof that there were still Gadfians somewhere with whom Salamander had some commerce that resulted in his acquiring a gadi-built ship.

A thought came to me that was so shocking it took my breath away. What if Salamander had not just traded with the Gadfian raiders *but was one of them!* What if he hid his face and form as fanatically as he did, not to keep his identity secret, but to hide the color of his skin! This would explain not only the resemblance between the *Black Ship* and the Sadorian spicewood ships, but also the slaver's relentless viciousness, since ferocity and the need to oppress seemed characteristic of the Gadfian people.

I slipped the book into the bag I carried over my shoulder, thinking that when I was back aboard the *Umborine.* I would show the book to Jakoby and see what she made of my theory.

"Ye gods!" Gilbert muttered.

He had opened the door to a cupboard, and I went to see what had made him sound so astounded. Looking over his shoulder, I saw that the clothes on the shelves were not men's. I reached into the cupboard and drew out a long gown of roughened silk, beaded in an exquisite pattern that mimicked the intricate shadings of some strange large-eared feline.

"One of them must have kept a woman," Gilbert muttered. "An *expensive* woman. I suppose she went with them when they left."

"Sandcats," Andorra said, fingering the silk. "They live in the desert lands, and they are mad."

"There are sandcats near Murmroth, too," Gilbert said. He stooped to pick something up off the floor.

"Here is another one." He opened his hand to reveal a small silver clasp fashioned into the likeness of a sand-cat. It was a pretty, intricate piece and positioned so that only one eye showed—a tiny yellow topaz.

"It is one-eyed, like your cat friend," Gilbert said. "Why don't you keep it?"

I was revolted by the thought of stealing something that had belonged to Ariel or Salamander, but instead of putting it down, I found myself looking at the brooch again. Finally, I slipped it into my bag with the book. It did remind me of Maruman, but it was the exquisite craftsmanship, not the design, that made me take it, for such work might be tracked back to its source.

"You know what troubles me," Gilbert said after we left the chamber. "I can't see any woman leaving all those beautiful, expensive clothes and gewgaws if she was never coming back again."

"Maybe they didn't give her time to pack," I said. "Or maybe she knows there is more where this came from and did not mind leaving it. Whoever lavished all of this on her was hardly going to keep her wanting."

As we continued, I remembered that when Salamander had first appeared in the Land, there had sometimes been mention of a beautiful woman who spoke for him. Perhaps the room belonged to this woman, in which case she might be more of an accomplice than merely an object of love or desire.

I farsent Jak to tell him what we had found, and he told me that he and Hakim had discovered some animal pens, their size and stink suggesting they had recently been occupied by dogs. He sounded subdued and uneasy, and I knew that he was remembering that

Ariel had taken particular delight in using brutal and sadistic methods to train dogs to kill.

As I withdrew from Jak's mind, Gilbert beckoned to me. He looked into a smallish chamber with a single large comfortable chair set facing an enormous window that overlooked the large central courtyard. Just outside the window stood a beautiful ravaged tree, which had either lost all its leaves to the savage wind or was dead.

"Looks like some sort of contemplation room," Gilbert said, nodding to the chair. He shivered and I realized my own teeth were again chattering with cold. Gilbert suggested returning to the entrance chamber to warm ourselves, but Andorra gestured to a small hearth where yet another fire had been laid. I lit it while Andorra went back to raid a clothes cupboard she had seen, and Gilbert found two more chairs. He set all three to face the fire, but instead of sitting down, the armsman went to the window to gaze at the twisted black form of the tree outside. "A grim sort of place to plant a tree," he muttered. "The soil would have to have been brought in, and the tree would never be able to put down deep roots. No wonder it died."

My heart sank as he looked over to where I sat, for his eyes were full of yearning. I had thought our earlier conversation had ended any hopes he might have harbored, but clearly it was not so. I willed Andorra to return, for there was an intimacy in this small room that might better be avoided. Then I decided that it was cowardly to avoid being alone with the armsman, given that I had accepted Gilbert's sincere offer of friendship.

"I meant what I told you aboard the ship," I said, wishing that embarrassment would not render my tone so harsh.

He smiled sadly. "I know it. Only what I feel is not so easily set aside. But I will not trouble you with any declarations. I, too, meant what I said aboard the ship." He hesitated and said, "This might be a good moment to confess that I asked Gwynedd to send me with you."

"Why?" I asked.

He shrugged and said lightly, "Let us say that I am not too proud or foolish to see that half a loaf of good bread is still nourishing." But immediately his expression became serious. "No, I speak too flippantly, a habit I am trying to break. You are far from half a loaf, Elspeth Gordie. What you have done is the stuff of tales told over and over around firesides; they set the hearts of everyone who hears them to racing and dreaming. In truth, I never had any right to aspire to you. What you did before—opening that lock and then reaching out with your mind to Jak—I realize you would never be satisfied with an ordinary man like me."

I felt my face flame and wished he would stop. This was far worse than any declaration of love! I tried to get up, but he caught my hand. "Please, let me speak."

I expelled a breath and said urgently, "Listen, most of my life I have been in danger of being burned for the Talents you seem to feel are special. I don't think that I am better than you."

"I think it," he said flatly, and released me. "Yesterday afternoon, after we had spoken, I thought of my bondmate, Serra. I began to wonder if perhaps the mystery she had wanted from me was no more than the part of me that I had laid to rest when I thought I saw you die. Maybe she understood that I was withholding the best of myself, not only from her but from my children. I had felt myself cheated by life when I thought you had been snatched away from me. I never considered that you had not been mine in the first place. I got it into my head that you had been my shining destiny, and your loss was another example of the ill luck that had dogged me all my life.

"But lying in my cabin last night, with the storm raging outside, I thought of all you had said, and suddenly I saw everything from another angle. I was not unlucky. Indeed, luck has walked beside me constantly. My mother died birthing me, but I lived. My father was a good and honest man who loved me, though I had killed his beloved bondmate. I was away from the Druid's camp when the firestorm struck, so I was one of the few to survive. A plague came to the west coast, but I was not infected, and when there was the possibility of a second plague, which none would have survived, you prevented its spread. What have I to complain about? Nothing. I had acted like a spoiled child who could not have a toy that did not belong to him in the first place. I petulantly locked up all that was good in me. But last night in the midst of that raging storm, it occurred to me that I might die. That was when I realized that it was not too late to become a whole man again."

"What will you do?" I asked to break a silence stretched too thin.

"I will continue to serve Gwynedd, for he gave me a purpose, and I owe it to him to fulfill it."

"Are not children also a purpose that ought to be fulfilled?" I said softly.

He smiled. "They ought to be," he said. "Maybe it is not too late for that as well."

"You will go back?"

"I will see if their mother will give me a second chance. Maybe she will finally meet the man you met in the Druid's camp, if he can be brought back to life."

"I see him now," I said.

He held my eyes a moment, and the silence between us became easy. When Andorra returned, he went out to let us change our clothes. I was grateful for the thick silk shirt and the gray felt tunic and shawl. Once dressed, I farsought Jak again and found that he and Hakim had discovered a kitchen and were also lighting a fire. He added that they had found more yards and some animal pens with bench seats in them. I shivered and withdrew from his mind, chilled at the thought of the hapless people who had been brought here and penned up to await whatever fate had in store for them.

"You are looking grim," Gilbert said as he reentered the room.

I was telling them both what Jak had said when we heard a distant crash.

"What was that?" Gilbert said.

Andorra had drawn her knife and was listening hard, too, her head tilted. "It sounded like it came from the other side of the building," she said.

"Wait," I said. Closing my eyes, I farsought Jak. The probe located tenuously, as if there were too many walls between us or maybe one of the rainy courtyards.

"Did you hear that noise?" I farsent.

"We caused it," Jak told me. "We found a trapdoor in the storeroom beside the kitchen, but it exploded when I tried to open it. I'm bleeding, but Hakim was knocked out."

"What is it?" Gilbert demanded when I opened my eyes.

I told them, and we put a screen around the fire and hurried along the corridors.

"If there was a trapdoor in the floor, there must be some sort of underground chamber," Gilbert said.

"You said that it would be impossible, given that this place is built upon solid rock," I protested.

"I did, but why else would there be a trapdoor?" Gilbert asked. "The Beforetimers might have done it. After all, if they could truly fly through the air, it would be nothing to cut chambers out of stone."

"Why do you speak of Beforetimers?" I asked, slowing to stare at him. "Ariel built this place."

He shrugged. "I assume that this place is built on Beforetime ruins. After all, Gwynedd said his mother told him this knoll was cursed, and that is usually what people mean when they use that word," Gilbert said. "I suppose it was they who honed the knoll to make it square."

· 17 ·

"THIS IS DEFINITELY Beforetimer work," Jak said, his voice trembling with excitement. His forehead and face were badly cut, and one of the gashes was so close to his eye that he was lucky he had not been blinded. Andorra, who had announced that she had some simple training in healing, was examining the teknoguilder, having checked that the still unconscious Hakim was otherwise unharmed. The force of the explosion had knocked him out. Now she announced that Jak had a cut on his shoulder and another on his chest that needed stitches, but he had brushed her away.

"The explosion looks as if it was the result of some sort of Beforetime device, but Ariel definitely knew of the trapdoor, because, as you see, the storage space has been carefully constructed around the trapdoor so it would not be blocked, but in such a way that it would be hard to see if you just glanced in. If I had not been scrounging for food, I would not have noticed it."

I studied the hatch, which, despite being blackened and slightly buckled, remained intact. It looked very similar to the trapdoor that Pavo and I had opened to enter the upper level of the Beforetime ruins on the west coast, and I had no doubt that Ariel knew about the existence of this trapdoor. It might very well be the reason he had constructed his residence here. But the question that remained was if he had ever managed to open it.

As if he had read my thoughts, Jak said, "This could be where Ariel got the plague seeds." He looked at me. "Do you think you can open it?"

"Now wait just a minute," Gilbert protested. "Two people have already been hurt trying to open it, and who is to say what will happen if Elspeth tries. We have heard talk of Beforetime weapons capable of destroying cities!"

I thought of the prickling premonition I had experienced upon Herder Isle when I had touched the door to Ariel's chambers. "I will know if there is that sort of danger," I said. I lay my hands on the lock and was surprised it felt warm. I looked around at the others—Jak's eager face; Andorra, with her inscrutable expression that showed neither fear nor apprehension but only a profound watchfulness; and Gilbert.

"Trust me," I said softly. A nerve worked in his jaw, but he gave a jerky nod. I closed my eyes and probed the lock mechanism, striving to understand it. I had never encountered anything so complex, and it took only a moment to know that it was beyond me. "I can't understand how it works, so I can't open it," I said.

Gilbert expelled a breath and even Andorra relaxed somewhat, but Jak moved closer and knelt down beside me, unaware that blood was running down his neck and soaking into his collar. I had lifted my hand from the lock, and now he laid his own over it. "Go through my mind," he said. "Use my knowledge. Dell has done it before and Merret, too."

I stared at him in wonderment and realized that, of course, it would be possible.

But Gilbert caught my wrist. "What are you doing?" he demanded. "We are here to seek out the plague seeds."

"We are," Jak said. "And this is likely where Ariel found them. It is my guess that the door was not closed when he opened it the first time, but it has been closed since."

I gently but firmly removed my wrist from Gilbert's grip and then lay my hand atop Jak's. I closed my eyes and entered the teknoguilder's mind. Jak had drawn all of his knowledge and experience of complex Beforetime mechanisms to the surface of his conscious thoughts, and I roved over them until I came to something that might work. Instead of withdrawing, I reached from inside Jak's mind to the lock under our hands, drawing his awareness with me. I felt his fascinated attention as I probed the lock, and then I sharpened my focus into a physical force.

"There will be a current of energy that you must break." Jak's voice sounded oddly like the disembodied voice of Ines. This made me realize that there might be another Beforetime complex under the stone knoll, operated by a computermachine with the same Ines program! Jak heard the thought, and his excitement almost dislodged my mind from the lock, but I strengthened my shield, found the current he meant, and broke it.

"That was . . . Your mind is so strong!" the teknoguilder gasped. He broke off as the metal hatch hissed and loosened.

Gilbert breathed a sigh of relief and ordered all of us back while he opened it. He closed his hands around the two grips set into the trapdoor and pulled. It opened smoothly to reveal a ladder going down into darkness. I relaxed fractionally, having been half prepared for another explosion.

"I wonder how far it goes," Jak murmured. He had been looking into the black abyss, and we all froze as his words echoed into the darkness, fading at last to a soft hoot.

"No mere cellar ever gave out an echo like that," Gilbert said.

"I will go," said Andorra. She hooked her lantern over her arm and began to climb down the ladder. We all watched her descend, the lantern light illuminating no more than the section of the ladder before and after her.

"What do you see?" Jak called impatiently after a time. Echoes of his shout filled the air, sounding and resounding for a long time before fading. Andorra had frozen, and at last she looked up, her eyes shining in the immense darkness. "I can see no end to the ladder, but it holds firm, so it must be fixed to the ground below."

She had spoken softly, but the darkness was filled with hissing echoes of her words. She began to descend again.

Jak said decisively, "I'm going after her." He, too, hooked his lantern over his arm and began to climb down. Then he looked up at me. "Are you coming?"

"I don't think this is a good idea," Gilbert said. His face was pale with a greenish tinge about his mouth.

"It's not a good idea for all of us to go," I said calmly. "You stay here and keep watch over Hakim." Then I took my own lantern and went down the steps. Jak was descending slowly below me, and at least thirty steps below him I could just make out Andorra still climbing downward in a pool of lantern light. Our footsteps set up a ringing echo.

On and on we climbed through that vast void of darkness until my fingers ached from clinging to the rungs, and my legs, which were still sore from the climb to the surface of the island, now ached from lowering myself step by step. Eventually I heard my name and looked down to see that Jak had reached a small metal platform fixed to the ladder. Andorra had continued her descent, but I joined Jak, holding tightly to the rails.

"What is this place?" I panted, speaking as quietly as I could. Even so, my voice produced a rustling of whispers.

Jak shrugged, his face shining with perspiration in the light shed by our lanterns. The blood had dried to a line of black against his pale skin. "It could be a missile silo chamber, though I cannot see how, with this ladder cutting through it. Unless the missile was designed to fly out at an angle from the side of the island."

"What is a missile?" I asked.

"It is a Beforetime weapon. A fearsome flying weapon that could be made to go where its master desired and destroy what it was bidden to destroy. Such weapons were capable of destroying cities much greater than Sutrium or Aborium."

"You think we are climbing down to such a weapon?" I asked, feeling a thrill of terror.

But he shook his head. "I think that we are climbing down to a nest devoid of its deadly egg," Jak said. Without further ado, he stepped back onto the ladder and began to descend again. Before following, I glanced up and saw that the opening was a tiny square of light where I could see a movement that might have been Gilbert, watching.

I had just begun climbing down again when there was a shout from below. It was Andorra, who had finally reached the end of the ladder. It took Jak and me a long time to join her and see that she had not, after all, reached the bottom of the void but only a narrow metal bridge passing over the void to darkness in two directions.

"Which way?" Andorra asked.

Jak looked at me. "We could split up and go both ways."

Andorra gave him a look that told me the tribeswoman was trying to decide if Jak was fearless or simply a fool. "What is this place?" she asked.

Jak told her what he had told me, adding, "I think this path will lead us to the place where there are controls that would have propelled the missile from an opening in the side of the island."

"Surely plague seeds would not be kept in the same place as a flying weapon?" I asked, suddenly wishing I could simply climb out of the suffocating chill of a darkness that must surely contain some of the malevolence of the monstrous weapon that once rested here.

"On the contrary, it may be that the weapon was designed to carry plague seeds to some land or city," Jak said. "I'll know more once we reach wherever this path leads." He glanced back at me and grimaced. "It is a pity whoever built this did not consider an elevating chamber."

I controlled an urge to snarl at him for his easy acceptance of such horrors and asked, "Is it likely there would be a computermachine program like Ines running this place? And *if* there is, could you talk to it? Ask it where the plague seeds are?"

"I could if the program was sent to sleep as our Ines was, and if its name is the code to awaken it as in the ruins outside Aborium, but the likelihood of that is so slender as to be almost an impossibility," Jak said. Without waiting for my response, he said firmly and clearly, "Ines, can you hear me?" Echoes of his question rang out and whispered and finally rustled to silence. But there was no answer. "In fact, I do not think we will find such a program here, because Govamen was virtually the only organization capable of affording such a complex program, and I do not think this place belonged to them."

"I thought govamens controlled all of the weapon-machines," I said.

"Most, but certainly not all. And although they usually concealed their most dangerous caches of weapons in remote locations, Govamen weapon stores were always bristling with all sorts of defenses and protections to make sure no one entered unless authorized. Even the attempt to enter such a place could be deadly, for once a person got part of the way in, the system would not allow her to withdraw, and if a person was unable to give all the correct codes and responses, the entry programs might have the capacity to injure or kill."

"Were they so afraid people would wish to steal their weapons?" I asked.

"Not people. Other govamens. You see, each of the great powers had a govamen, and each govamen hated and feared the others. In addition to producing terrible weapons with which to threaten the other powers, they lived in mortal fear that those weapons would be stolen and used against them. What kept them from attacking one another was what they called the 'balance of fear,' which some called the 'balance of power'; that is, the fact that all the great govamens had terrible weapons. You must imagine five warriors who wish to kill one another, but they each have a sword and are skilled in its use, so they can only watch one another, none daring to move on another for fear that one of the others might attack them."

"Madness, for in the end, someone did attack," Andorra said.

I said nothing, knowing that this fear of the govamens had led to the decision to create a computer-machine program that would hold the balance of power over all govamens, with its ability to retaliate against any one of them that aggressed against the rest by summoning up weaponmachines so powerful that they had been called BOT, the Balance of Terror. Their creation had been part of the Sentinel project, run by Cassy Duprey's father, only something had gone wrong. Maybe, as Andorra had suggested, one of the five powers had attacked the other, or maybe there had been an accident and the BOT arsenal had been unleashed, causing the Great White and bringing the Beforetimers and their world to a deadly end. And it was those same BOT weaponmachines that the Seeker was to find and disable forever.

"Elspeth?" Jak said.

"We are wasting time," I said. "Let's go left."

We set off again, Jak and Andorra walking ahead of me, and my thoughts drifted back to what Jak had been saying. I was certain the "keys" Cassy had left were to enable me to negotiate the defenses with which Sentinel would protect the BOT weaponmachines and that once I reached them, I would have to shut down the program that controlled BOT so it could never awaken the weaponmachines. It was even possible that some long-dead human had left Sentinel sleeping like Ines, ready to wake at the right word or phrase, and all I might have to do, once I had reached the right place, would be to command it to sleep or to switch itself off. Would a computermachine be capable of destroying what must effectively be part of itself? A human would be afraid, but a computermachine did not feel; therefore, if the command was put in the correct way, it ought simply to obey.

Jak uttered an exclamation, and I saw that the metal bridge had reached the gray stone wall of the immense cavern, where it joined a metal walk running away in both directions. Right where the bridge ended was a gray metal door set into the stone.

"Raw stone," Jak murmured, laying his hand on it. "This is a natural cavern." He held up his lantern and looked one way and then the other along the stone wall. "The wall curves inward in both directions." He turned to face the bridge we had walked across. "I think that this leads to the other side of the cavern and this walk goes the whole way round the outside."

"But what would be the point of that?" I asked, imagining a vast black hole circled and halved by a path.

"I don't know," Jak admitted. "Let's see if this door can be opened."

The door had no visible lock or handle, but the lantern light revealed a rectangular indentation in the metal. Jak reached out without hesitation and laid his hand upon it.

The door gave a click and then the same long hiss as the latch above before sliding into the wall as smoothly as the split door of the elevating chamber in the ruins complex. Andorra gazed fearfully into the dark chamber it had revealed.

"It is only a door and one without even a lock," Jak told her, and he stepped through it into the chamber, holding his lantern up high.

Heart thumping, I stepped through the door after him and found that the floor was soft and almost spongy underfoot, while around the walls were metal lockers. Jak opened one to reveal a number of suits made of some sort of thin plast, and I wondered if these were the same as the one Jacob Obernewtyn had left for Hannah.

Jak had moved to the end of the chamber, and now he said excitedly, "Another door." As he set his hand to it, I turned to see that Andorra was still standing on the metal path looking in at us. The whites of her eyes showed, and I asked, "Andorra, will you follow the path around and see if there are any other doors?"

She nodded and disappeared, and I turned to follow Jak, pondering limits. Andorra was certainly braver and more stoic than I was, yet she feared entering these chambers of the dead, just as Gilbert had feared to enter the gaping darkness below the latch. *What is my limit?* I wondered.

Jak had entered a chamber that was double the size of the first one, and running its full length on either side were immense bathing cabinets such as the one I had used in the ruins complex.

"You see how it was?" Jak said eagerly. "They would enter and remove their plast suits, and then they would come here and bathe." He looked back and saw my bafflement. "I doubt this place was built as a shelter, but whoever made it felt that it could be used as one."

As he spoke, he went to the door at the other end and opened it. Again it slid away, and he passed through it without hesitation. I steeled myself to follow him. The next chamber had several open doorways that led, we swiftly found, to a kitchen and dining hall and to several small bedchambers. I marveled at the thought of people being so afraid of the weapons they had created that they would build and stock such shelters. Why hadn't they simply opposed the building of the weaponmachines in the first place? Surely all govamens in the Beforetime were not oppressive and controlling? But then I thought of Cassy's Tiban lover, killed because he had been opposed to the closed borders and internal practices of Chinon, and Cassy's mother saying that she would not be permitted to speak out against their govamen, and I wondered how different their world had really been from ours.

I turned to say as much to Jak and discovered that he had vanished. I called his name and heard a muffled reply. I followed him, pointing out crossly that we could not go on exploring endlessly, but my words faded when I found him in a small, shiny black room sitting behind the screen of a computermachine. There were other machines and more screens covering the wall behind the computermachine, as well as panels of levers and colored squares, but all were dark and lifeless. Jak held up his lantern to illuminate the lettered squares, and then he began to tap at them, his brow furrowed in concentration. Nothing happened, and he gave a sigh of anguished frustration. "I might be able to figure out how to make it work, given time, but as it is . . ."

"As it is, we are here to find plague seeds," I said firmly. "And in case you haven't noticed, these lanterns are running out of oil."

Jak looked at his lantern with the startled air of one waking from a dream. Then he got to his feet. "All right, let's split up and make a proper search. If there are plague seeds here, they will be in some sort of secure storage place—a small metal box or some sort of sealed cabinet. It will probably have a symbol on it: yellow and black triangles or a red circle with a slash through it. You try through that door on the left, and I will go through the other one." He gestured to two doors, one alongside the other. Then he opened one and passed through it into the swallowing darkness beyond.

I took a deep breath and went through the other door into another room of shining black surfaces, but instead of being square, this chamber had many sides like the edges of a cut stone. It was empty, and I ran my hand along one of the smooth panels, wondering about the room's purpose. Then I noticed that light from the lantern was penetrating the dark shining wall.

I held the lantern closer and saw that the panel was made of thick dark glass, behind which was an empty compartment. I looked at the next panel and saw that it was the same. I examined the glass surface and found a recessed hand shape. There was one in each panel. Heart beating fast, I held my hand above one of the recesses and listened to my inner self for any prickle of premonition. Feeling nothing, I pressed my hand into the recess. There was a click and a hiss, and the segment of glass slid far enough up that I could see into the compartment behind it. It was empty. I pressed my hand to the same place and immediately the glass slid back into place. I went to the next glass segment and discovered another empty compartment. I stepped back and turned slowly around, realizing the place bore a strong resemblance to the healing chambers in the ruins complex. Perhaps this was also some sort of healing complex, but the compartments were much smaller and lacked beds.

I examined the compartment that I had left open and saw holes in the floor. Not a healing chamber, perhaps, but some sort of cage. The compartments were too small to fit a human, even a human child. Small beasts, then? Maybe whoever had built this place had intended to save some beasts from the Great White. I reached into the compartment and jumped as a dim red glow filled it. As soon as I snatched my hand back, the light was immediately extinguished.

I went after Jak, wanting to show him the compartments. I could not see his lantern light and realized with a sinking heart that I would have to go deeper. I stepped into the next chamber and found it identical to the one I had been in, save that it was bigger and so were the glass panels and the compartments behind them. Still there were no beds, so perhaps these had been intended for larger animals.

I called Jak's name, and when he did not answer, I went through the next door, only to find myself in yet another room full of glass compartments. This was bigger again than the other rooms, and at its center stood a long metal table. Fixed to one end of the table was a phalanx of computermachines and screens. Memory stirred, and I went to the metal table and touched its cold surface. Suddenly I remembered the table I had been bound to when Ariel and Alexi had used the Zebkrahn machine on me in an attempt to learn the location of the weaponmachines that had caused the Great White.

I turned to look around at the glass compartments and was suddenly and absolutely certain that Ariel had been here, and *this* was where he had brought Domick and Rushton. Fighting a suffocating sense of horror, I went to open one of the glass compartments. Seeing the bare space with its holed floor, I suddenly understood. This was not a healing center; it was a torture chamber.

There was another door at the end of the room. I went to it and opened it merely to escape the horror blooming in my mind, but the chamber beyond was little more than a room full of small metal lockers. I was about to turn away when I noticed a door marked with a yellow and black symbol, above which was a circle with numbers scribed on it. I went into the chamber and saw a lock on the door, but there was no need to open it, for there was a panel of glass set into the metal door. I knelt and held the lantern close to the glass, pressing my face against it, the better to see. I fell back at once, for the surface of the glass gave off such a fierce coldness that I felt as if I had been burned. Rubbing my cheek, I leaned close to the window again, being careful not to touch its surface. I lifted the lantern and its light shone on rack after rack of tiny bottles containing glistening liquids of various colors.

I had no doubt that I had found what we had come for, and I sat back on my heels, wondering if all the ghastly weapons and devices that the Beforetimers had created had been no more than the result of the same voracious, single-minded curiosity as that which motivated Jak or any teknoguilder. I had never thought of curiosity as bad, yet if it could quench fear, perhaps it could also quench a person's morality.

The lantern flame began to gutter, and I thought that I must have tilted it, swamping the wick, but when I looked into the reservoir, I was horrified to see that it was almost empty. Suddenly I was horribly aware of the darkness and the many doors and steps that lay between me and the stony, storm-scoured surface of Norseland. I might have panicked if I had not recently been lost in a Beforetime complex. This memory enabled me to control my fear and rise to hurry back through the chambers. If I could find Jak swiftly, we could pool our remaining oil, seek out Andorra, and take hers as well. That ought to be enough to get us back to the surface.

I shouted his name through the door he had taken, but there was no response. Perhaps his lantern had already run out and he had lost his way. I tried farseeking him, but as I had feared, there was too much thick metal between us for the probe to locate and too little oil remained in my lantern to go searching for him. I had to find Andorra. I hurried through the chambers to the metal path and was horrified to remember that I had bidden her investigate the path to see if there were other doors. I peered out into the fathomless blackness, searching for her lantern's telltale glow, but I could see nothing.

Either the light was too weak or she had already run out of oil. Cursing our foolishness, I was about to shout to her when I heard a muffled scream. It had come from above, but it broke into a thousand echoes that filled the void and seemed as if there were hundreds of people screaming for help. Even after the screams had faded to whispers, I still stood rooted to the spot, my heart hammering against my ribs with sickening force. I told myself savagely not to be a fool. Andorra had probably noticed that she was running out of oil and had stumbled on the way up the ladder to replenish her lantern. Or maybe she had seen my lantern light and had called out something that the echoes had transformed into a scream. I gathered myself to broach that black void with a call, but before I could utter it, *I heard a low, rumbling growl.*

Every hair on my body stood on end as I thought of the kennels that Jak and Hakim had seen, for it would be so like Ariel to leave some poor dog here to go mad with hunger and thirst. I backed into the chamber of lockers and searched frantically about the door for a means of closing it, but I could find nothing. The lantern flame was guttering wildly, and again I heard another growl. My nerve broke and I fled back through chamber after chamber, knowing that I could always shut myself into one of the glass compartments. Just as I reached the chamber of large compartments, the lantern went out.

I stopped dead, shocked at the complete blackness that enfolded me. I held my breath and listened, praying that the dog or dogs would not enter the complex. I had just begun to relax when I heard something moving through one of the outer chambers. I told myself that it must be Jak, but I dared not call out. Instead, I groped my way to the nearest compartment, felt for the hand-shaped indentation, and pressed my hand into it. The click and the hiss of the opening door sounded alarmingly loud, and I threw myself into the compartment. Instantly, it flooded with ruby-red light, and I cried out before I could prevent myself. Too frightened to wait and listen again, I tore off my boot, set it in the opening, and reached out to press my hand into the recess in the door. There was a hiss and it slid shut. Or it would have done, if not for the boot.

I forced myself to move quietly to the back of the compartment, where I sat down and made myself as small as possible. As I tried to listen, my red-limned reflection gaped at me in the glass, grotesque with terror, but my heart thundered so hard that it made me feel sick. Or maybe the sickness was merely another symptom of terror. I felt as if ice water were coursing through my veins, yet I was giving out so much heat that the glass inside the compartment was beginning to fog.

I crawled forward to wipe the front panel with my sleeve, and froze.

I could see something moving in the red-tinged darkness outside. Whatever it was looked far larger than a dog. Remaining very still, I sent out a beast-speaking probe but encountered a buzzing static that told me that it wore a demon band. Its size made me wonder if Ariel had captured a wolf and brought it to Norseland to train. It had stopped moving now, and I heard it *sniffing*.

Without warning, it rushed toward me and hurled itself against the glass panel with such ferocity that it rebounded violently back into the shadow with a snarling groan of pain. I had fallen backward, too, in shock, and as I sat up, I heard a loud click and realized that the beast had hit the glass so hard that it had dislodged the boot I had used to jam it open. In that moment, it did not seem bad to be locked away from whatever beast Ariel had left to guard his secrets.

I watched, mesmerized, as it approached the compartment again. Now I saw that it was man-shaped but hunched and shambling as if it were part beast and part human. *A bear?* I thought incredulously. At last it entered the bloody light of the compartment, and I drew a long, ragged, sobbing breath of disbelief.

For it was Rushton.

I spoke his name, and the sound of my voice seemed to madden him. He hurled himself at the glass again with such reckless violence that I cried out. For one second, I looked into his eyes' bottomless black insanity, then he reeled backward, clearly stunned by the impact. But immediately he ran at the glass again. This time when he struck it, I heard the distinct snap of a bone breaking. Rushton gave a howl of pain, and when he staggered back in readiness for another charge, he swayed on his feet for several beats, one arm hanging limp. Seeing the rage in his face, I understood that if he had got to me before I entered the compartment, he would have torn me to pieces with his bare hands. That could only mean that his memory had returned and had brought him back here to the source of his torment. I thought of the cry I had heard and wondered, sickened, if he had killed Gilbert or Andorra.

"Rushton," I whispered.

His eyes fixed on me, and his face distorted with hatred. He gathered himself and ran at the door head down. He struck the glass with a sickening crunch and dropped bonelessly to the floor, where he lay utterly still.

I gazed through streaming tears at his still, crumpled form, praying he had not broken his neck or caved in his skull. If only I could get out to check, but I could not open the door. I crawled to the front of the compartment and peered out at Rushton's prone form, trying to see if he was still breathing.

Then my gaze settled on the demon band fitted around his neck, and all at once I understood everything.

This was Ariel's doing, all of it.

Domick had told me Ariel had made Mika torture Rushton coercively while empathically imposing my face and voice but that he had failed in trying to break Rushton. But Ariel had not failed at all. He had never meant to crush Rushton's mind, because he had a more elaborate cruelty planned. When the healers had treated Rushton at Obernewtyn, they had spoken of a long period in which Rushton had dwelt in a drug-induced nightmare world. But neither Domick nor Mika had mentioned drugs, which meant that they must have been administered after Rushton was shifted to Sutrium. That long, bleak, drugged dream he had endured had been imposed only to serve as a screen to prevent any of us from realizing what else had been done to him here.

Rushton had not been left in the Sutrium cloister by chance. He had been left there specifically so that he would be found and brought back to Obernewtyn, where he would be healed physically of his addiction. But not mentally. Ariel had intended all along that

Rushton would be broken open slowly and torturously by his constant exposure to me. Ariel had wanted me to witness Rushton's love for me turning inexorably to hatred and madness.

It all fitted, save one thing. Why would Ariel set Rushton up to kill me when he had gone to such lengths to keep me alive? For he must know that this would be the result of Rushton's madness. Had he thought I would defend myself? Perhaps he had hoped that I would even be forced to kill Rushton to save myself.

I shook my head, unconvinced that he would take the risk that Rushton might succeed in killing me. But the only other possibility was the most monstrous of all. Ariel had foreseen this very moment: me, trapped safely in a glass compartment with Rushton outside, battering himself senseless to get at me. Yet where would Rushton get a demon band, and why would he put it on, if not at some coerced instruction? And why would Ariel command it if he had not foreseen this?

Nausea rose in me as I imagined the pleasure this vision would have given Ariel, whose need for me made him loathe me and whose defective nature made him take pleasure in cruelty and pain. I could scarcely encompass the idea that Ariel was capable of foreseeing so much, and a deadly, hopeless lethargy stole over me, for how could anyone prevail against an enemy who knew so much?

Then I heard Maryon's cool voice saying that no futureteller, however powerful, could see everything, because even the strongest futuretelling was only the most likely thing to happen. A single, random, unexpected event could change something. And Ariel did not see everything. Domick had said that. Ariel had not foreseen that the coercer would tell me Rushton had been on Norseland. Mika was supposed to have been too strong for Domick to break through. Rushton was supposed to batter himself to death trying to kill me, and I was to be tormented by not knowing why.

Rushton moaned and rolled onto his side, groaning. His face was a mask of blood, and his eyes were vague and bewildered as he hauled himself to his feet. But as before, the second they fixed on me, unstoppable rage flowed into them, and I knew that Rushton would kill himself trying to get at me while I remained safe, locked behind an unbreakable shield of glass.

Shield.

The word echoed strangely in my mind, and I heard Dameon's gentle voice telling me that I must have the courage to believe that Rushton still loved me. The blind empath had claimed that Rushton's rejection was proof that there was love. If he was truly indifferent, he would not have such a violent aversion to seeing me. But he had been wrong. Love had been destroyed by the Destroyer, replaced by bloated lunatic hatred. Yet Rushton's rejection did not fit the plan, because Ariel would not have wanted him to drive me away. That would only have slowed Rushton's mental breakdown. He would have made sure that the hatred was sealed away so Rushton would appear to heal and be normal. This could only mean that Rushton had been rejecting me because somewhere deep inside, he was trying to avoid the fate that had been knitted up for him. *"Do not be a coward,"* Dameon's soft voice whispered in my memory. *"It is not only Rushton's love for you but also his very life that you fight for."*

I licked my lips and thought, *This, this is my limit*. And I watched Rushton marshal his strength for another useless assault on the door, understanding that his rejection was exactly what Dameon had said: proof of love.

There was only one course open to me. Ariel must have striven to futuretell this moment a hundred times, to make sure that it would come out as he desired. He must have looked at this moment again and again, trying to see if there was anything that could go wrong. He knew that Rushton would want to kill me, and he knew that I would be safe. He would watch it again and again, building a web of certainty, just as Dell had done in order to make sure that Domick would reach the ruins complex without infecting anyone. But there was no complete certainty, even in a web forecasting. Some unexpected element could always intervene. My only chance to save Rushton now was to introduce some element that Ariel could not have foreseen. I must do the unthinkable. I stood on legs that trembled.

"Rushton," I said. "Here. Here is where you must put your hand to open the door so you can reach me. Here." I tapped the hand-shaped recess, which I could see through the glass. I mimicked pressing my hand into it. "Look, Rushton. Like this. Press your hand here and the glass will open. Here." Over and over I repeated it as Rushton stood glaring at me with malevolent loathing, opening and closing his fists. Again and again I tapped the indentation and mimicked pressing a hand against it.

At last, I saw his eyes drop to my hand, and I laid it over the recess. Slowly, the blank, black hatred gave way to a glimmer of purpose, and Rushton lurched forward and pressed his hand into the recess. For a heart-stopping moment, our fingers were but the thickness of glass apart. Then there was a click and a hiss that sounded like an indrawn breath, and the glass slid away.

Rushton bared his teeth, and I resisted the urge to step back.

"I love you," I said, letting my hand fall to my side.

Strangely, I was not afraid, for in showing Rushton how to open the compartment door, I had defied Ariel and the power of his futuretelling abilities. Now there were only two possible outcomes: I would die or I would not. And Ariel had done all in his considerable power to make sure Rushton would have an unassailable desire to kill me. If Ariel had foreseen this moment, he would not have taken the risk of setting this is motion, because if Rushton killed me, the Seeker would never come to the weaponmachines to try to shut them down. The Destroyer needed the Seeker to try and fail to stop the weaponmachines before he could take control of them.

Ariel must have foreseen that I would be locked in, and he might have seen Rushton battering himself against the door, but it would never occur to him that I might show Rushton how to open the door.

Of course, the most likely outcome was that I would die. But even thinking this, I was not afraid. I felt only a strange liberating elation at the knowledge that, for the first time in my life, I had acted wholly as Elspeth Gordie and not as the Seeker.

Rushton lifted his fist over his head as if it were a club, his face blank and mindless. I looked into his eyes and said, "I am your shield."

He hesitated. His fist trembled, but it did not descend. Rushton gave a groaning cry and seemed to fight with himself, his fist still upraised. I dared not move, for I had introduced something fragile and random into certainty, and the outcome of this moment was so finely balanced that a single breath would push him to attack.

Suddenly Rushton dropped to his knees with a horrible half-strangled snarl. He lunged at me, but he stopped short of grasping me. His expression in the red light shifted maniacally between mad rage and terror. He snarled and groaned, now creeping toward me with clawed hands, now falling back and shuddering. His dreadful inner battle seemed to go on for hours, and in all that time, I did not move or speak. At last he grew quiet. His head was bowed, so I could not see the expression on his face, but suddenly I could not stay still any longer. I knelt down and reached a hand toward him, palm up. I knew he was looking at it. After a long, slow age, he leaned forward and laid his blood-slicked cheek against my hand.

I gave a gasping sob. "My love! My dearest love." I put my arms around him and drew his dark head to my breasts. He gave a sigh that seemed to come from the depths of his soul, and I felt the rage and strength flow out of him as he collapsed against me in a dead faint. I sat back on my heels, cradling his body in my arms. I loosened one hand and reached up to unclasp the demon band about his neck. Then I held him tight, kissed his head, and entered his mind.

It was as if I had entered the ferocious, keening heart of a storm. All was blackness and screaming chaos. Nightmarish creatures flew around me and over me and under me. The only thing solid in the maelstrom was a stony track leading steeply down. Limping along it was the scarred bear of the shape Rushton had worn inside Dragon's dreams. I had thought that image her creation, but I saw now that this wounded beast was the essence of Rushton. I could see scars and open wounds all over his body. I tried to touch him, but he did not seem to feel or hear me. His whole being was focused on the road. Now, far away, far down at its end, I saw a gleaming thread. The mindstream.

"No," I whispered, but Rushton did not hear me.

Without thinking, I did something I had never done before. I entered the mind of the wounded bear. To my astonishment, I found myself knee-deep in freshly fallen snow. *Was this a memory that I had entered?* I wondered.

Before me was a house formed entirely of ice. It was beautiful, but there was a cruel and deadly coldness in its beauty. Footsteps in the snow led to the house. Paw prints. I ran to the door, and it opened even before I touched it. The bear was vanishing into the vaporous mist that filled the corridor inside.

I went after him, slipping and skidding on the smooth gleaming ice. My feet ached, and I realized that I was barefoot. I ignored the burning cold and went down icy steps into a vast white chamber. It was exquisitely beautiful but deathly cold. Veils of mist hung like scarves in the air. A chandelier of ice crystals glittered like a fall of diamonds, and beneath it stood Ariel, as white and fair and deadly as this house of ice. He was tall, and his shoulders were wide, his neck and chin those of a man now; yet his mouth and eyes were those of the cruel spoiled child I had met at Obernewtyn. His hair hung about his shoulders like a cape of some sleek fur, and he stroked it with evident pleasure.

At his feet was Domick. Ariel was caressing his head as if he were a well-loved hound. "Go, Mika. Go and tend to your kennel mate."

Domick slunk to an alcove where the bear lay, panting and shuddering. He was dragging a whip that left a bloody smear of gore on the shining white floor. I ran past Domick to Rushton, ignoring him, for he was only an image from Rushton's broken mind. I stroked the bear's matted fur, horrified at the depth of some of the wounds, which had surely grown deeper and wider since I had seen him on the road. Then I realized that this bear was within the bear I had seen on the road, and the markings on both bears were only reflections of the damage that had been done to the different layers of Rushton's mind.

On impulse, I probed the bear's mind again.

This time I found myself standing by a sunlit steaming pool. The bear sat on the edge of the pool watching a woman swim. Incredulous, I saw that the woman was me, but this Elspeth was taller and stronger than me and so beautiful as to take my breath away. She was a warrior woman with proud eyes that glowed like jewels. Her hair splayed out in the water like a silken net as she swam, and when she smiled, a radiance flowed from her face and a sweetness filled the air.

I turned to the bear and found Ariel was now standing beside him. He ran a long elegant white hand over the bear's head.

"It is not I who hurt you," Ariel said persuasively. "It is she who will do you the greatest harm. She will teach you the true meaning of pain."

The Goddess-Elspeth in the pool emerged, and I saw that she was carrying a long, thin-bladed knife. I tried to cry out a warning, but no one heard me.

"I do not love you," she said coldly to the bear. "You know that I always meant to leave you."

She lifted the knife. I threw myself into her as she reached out with her other hand to stroke the bear's fur. She/I felt the thick, warm coarseness of fur in one hand and the hardness of the knife hilt in the other. I could not stop her as she drove the knife into the bear. He gave an agonized growl, and she/I felt him slump against me.

I left the Goddess-Elspeth and dived into his mind. The bear was falling away from me. I followed him, stretching myself out, arrowing down. I caught him and closed my arms around him, catching handfulls of his fur. I tried pulling him back up, but the impetus of his descent was too great. All I could do was slow him, but we continued to descend through his deepest mind and through images of torture so horrible that I felt I was in danger of losing my own mind just witnessing them. If Domick and Ariel had not been mad before they tortured Rushton, their minds had surely crumbled under the corrosive insanity of their deeds.

All at once, we were hanging above the mindstream. The bear struggled, but I clung to him, knowing that if I let go, he would surely enter the mindstream. For a long moment, I held him safe, but then my strength began to fade. Bit by bit, we began to drop. I would not let him go, I swore to myself. If he went into the stream, then I would follow.

"You must not go!" I recognized the voice of Atthis.

"Help me!" I cried.

"I cannot. I am still much weakened from the spirit merge, and I have not the strength for what you want," she sent sternly. "You must let him go."

"No! Help me save him or we will both go into the stream."

"Then the Destroyer will win."

"Help me."

"There will be a price," said the bird.

"I will pay it."

"It is not you who will pay," Atthis answered, but I felt a warm flow of energy coursing through me.

"Tell me what to do!" I cried, for the pull of the mindstream was growing stronger.

"To prevent him from seeking death is not enough," Atthis said, her voice growing faint. "If you would save his mind and soul, you must enter his deepest mind." And then her voice and presence were gone.

It seemed impossible that there would be another layer of his mind when we were so close to the mindstream, but I entered the bear. I found myself in a vast shadowy cavern. The bear was curled motionless in a pool of black blood at my feet. Ariel was standing over him, laughing. He spoke to me, over the bear. "Did you think I would not be here as well? There is no part of him that I have not invaded and violated. He will never be free of me until he is dead."

My heart faltered until I remembered that this was not Ariel. It was only a loathsome image he had stamped in Rushton's mind. He was not real. *But I was.*

"You are not real," I said.

I lifted my hand and directed the golden energy from Atthis at Ariel. His pale beauty melted as if he were made of candle wax. Then I was alone in the vast cavern that was Rushton's Talent. Here, a hundred minds could merge and be contained, and still there would be room for more. I was alone in this miraculous secret fastness; alone, save for the bear that was Rushton's soul. Here he had come, seeking sanctuary, and even here had Ariel come, with Mika's help, for Domick had known what lay locked inside the mind of the Master of Obernewtyn. He had once merged with Roland and others inside his mind, to find and save me.

I sat down and lifted the bear's head into my lap, surprised at its weight. I stroked his fur, and the gashes closed and scars healed at my touch. I stroked him until his fur was sleek and beautiful and smooth. Then the gleaming fur shortened and became pale flesh under my fingers, and it was Rushton I held in my arms.

Green eyes opened, and he gazed up at me for a long time, his expression grave and wondering.

"I love you," he said.

Someone was shaking me. I had the queer, unnerving sensation of falling up, and then I was conscious of being in my own body. I opened my eyes and found I was seated exactly as I had been inside Rushton's deepest mind, but the Rushton lying in my arms now was clothed, unconscious, and badly hurt.

I looked up to find Brydda squatting beside me.

"Elspeth?" His eyes searched mine, and I saw relief in his expression.

"How did you . . . ?" I began, and found I had not the strength to finish.

"The ship boat capsized, and we could not find the way into the cove. I was near to drowning when I seemed to hear a voice in my mind, saying you had need of me. It led me to the inlet, and the others followed me. We finally figured out how the rest of you had got up to the surface. I sent Gwynedd's armsman after him and came here with the Sadorian man who had mastered the ship boat. There were signs of fire or some sort of explosion, and Gilbert was unconscious, but Hakim had awakened in time to see Rushton enter the trapdoor, muttering and snarling your name. Rushton must have got off the *Umborine* as soon as it dropped anchor and headed here, though I do not know how he got past the Hedra. I bade Selik take care of Gilbert and Hakim, and I came down after you."

"Ariel planned it all," I said hoarsely. "He would have made sure Rushton knew exactly how to get here. He must have left orders to the Hedra guarding the path up from Fryddcove not to hinder him."

"You think Ariel knew he would come here?"

"I think he foresaw our coming here and intended for Rushton to die trying to kill me."

"He must have a black hate for Rushton," Brydda said grimly. "The voice—"

I cut off his words to ask about Andorra, Jak, and Hakim.

"Andorra was knocked out on the metal walkway. I roused her, and she was with me when we found you two here. I left her to watch you while I went and helped Selik move Hakim and Gilbert to a little chamber facing the courtyard where a fire had been lit. I fetched blankets and so forth, and then I left Selik again to come back down here."

"What about Jak?"

"Andorra and I could not find him, but Jakoby searched and found him wandering in darkness, lost in the labyrinth of this place."

"Jakoby!"

"You have been here for a long time, Elspeth, and much has happened as you slept. If sleeping it was," he said. "Dardelan guessed that Rushton would come here, so the moment she could, Jakoby came ashore, borrowed a horse, and rode here."

"The . . . the battle is over?"

"It was in the process of being won when Jakoby rode from Covertown, but leave that for now. We need to get Rushton out of here. He is cold and shocked and battered, but aside from a dislocated arm and a gash on the brow that needs stitching, I do not think he has taken any mortal wound."

I heard footsteps and turned my head to see Jakoby. Behind her came Jak.

"I am so sorry, Elspeth," the teknoguilder said, looking down at Rushton with horrified pity. "I should have come back sooner, but I found a whole lot of storage rooms filled with what I think are weapons. I was looking for the plague seeds when my lantern went out. I tried to grope my way back to the entrance and got lost. I had truly begun to despair when I heard Jakoby shouting out my name. Never have I heard a sweeter sound in all my life."

Jakoby acknowledged his declaration with a faint smile, and then she squatted down and looked into my eyes. "All is well?" The gravity in her voice struck me, but I had no strength for questions. I nodded, and then she and Brydda gently lifted Rushton onto a stretcher, explaining that they had rigged up a basket to raise him to the hatch but had not wanted to touch him or me until I woke.

"Can you walk?" Jakoby asked.

"I can manage, but take Rushton up," I croaked. "I need to show Jak something."

Jakoby and Brydda carried Rushton out as Jak helped me to my feet. I cried out at the stiffness of my legs and back. Jak knelt and began to massage my legs vigorously. "No wonder you are stiff. You were sitting there for an entire day and night," he said. "I wanted to lay you down at least, but Brydda said he had a strong feeling you ought to be left to wake naturally."

I managed to smile, despite the pains shooting up my legs and back, wondering if Brydda would ever acknowledge that his feelings and hunches were Talent. Perhaps it does not matter how he defines them, so long as they serve him. It took some time, but finally I was able to stand straight. I bade the teknoguilder help me walk and directed him where to go. Soon we were in the tiny chamber off the torture room. I pointed to the little black and yellow symbol, and he drew a swift breath.

"I see no seeds and yet . . . ," I began.

"This is it, Elspeth," Jak said, kneeling and holding up his lantern as I had done to cast light through the window. "These will be sicknesses. This is how the Beforetimers stored them. Ines showed me pictures of cupboards like this. Ah!" he cried, and I knew he must have touched the glass. He touched it again and bent to examine the round knob surrounded by numbers. "This is how the coldness is controlled. See how the numbers go from red to blue? The Beforetimers used blue to symbolize cold and red to symbolize heat.".

"Do you want me to unlock the cabinet?" I asked.

He smiled and shook his head. "That would be dangerous, and there is no need, for it is the cold that keeps the seeds alive. They are not truly seeds, of course, but the word serves well enough. Making them hot is enough to kill them." He turned the knob in the direction of the red numbers. Then he stood up. "Strange that something so deadly is also so delicate."

"Are you sure they will die?" I asked.

"There would not be such careful control of the cold if it was not important. Now let's get out of here."

I was startled to hear a teknoguilder so willing to leave a Beforetime place full of ancient knowledge, but perhaps being lost in the darkness and finding bottles of plague had soured his appetite for knowledge, at least for the moment.

✦ 18 ✦

THE GRAY CLOUDS that clogged the sky and shadowed our dawn departure from Norseland had dispersed by midmorning, and a fresh steady wind blew, so the *Umborine* seemed to fly over the waves.

I kept to my cabin for the day, watching over Rushton and talking quietly to Jak and Jakoby and to Brydda and Dardelan, all of whom called in briefly to check on him. Aside from being bruised and cut, with a broken wrist and several gashes in his scalp deep enough to need stitches, Rushton showed little sign of the ordeal he had endured, save for the depth of his sleep. He had not awakened during the journey across Norseland to Fryddcove, nor did he wake aboard the *Umborine* until deep in the night.

I was sitting vigil, curled in a chair reading, when a soft movement from Maruman drew my attention. I looked over to find the old cat peering intently into Rushton's face. Laying aside the book, I moved swiftly to the bed, thinking that he was suffering another of the nightmares that had racked him on and off through the day and night, for he was grimacing and his face shone with sweat. I was about to touch his hand to rouse him when Maruman leaned down and touched his nose gently to Rushton's. I caught my breath as Rushton's eyes opened. For a long moment, green eyes gazed into blazing yellow, and then Maruman curled back to sleep.

Rushton turned his head and saw me, and I was relieved that his eyes were clear, his expression calm. "How do you feel?" I said.

He smiled. "Emptied out. Weary. A little confused," he said. "We are aboard the *Umborine*?"

I nodded. "We are bound for Sador with a fair wind filing our sails and triumph behind us," I said, reaching out to touch his cheek.

"What happened with the . . . Hedra?"

I saw that he would not rest until he knew something, so I told him that Gwynedd's arrival in Cloistertown had galvanized the Norselanders. The news he shared about the Faction's fall on Herder Isle had spread like wildfire and roused the Norselanders just as he had predicted. His impromptu army had swelled as people joined him from every farm and small village, despite the storm that raged. By the time they reached the Hedra encampment, situated atop a plateau some five leagues before Covetown, there was such a horde that the only reason they had not been spotted was the foul weather and the fact that columns of Hedra were marching from the camp in response to Jakoby's demands signaled from the *Umborine*.

Gwynedd later learned that, as he had anticipated, the Hedra had marched straight to Covetown and stationed themselves all along the cliffs, from the top of the path up from the beach to the gates of Norseland's sole remaining cloister. The Hedra left behind in the encampment had been completely unprepared when a ruse caused them to open the gates and hundreds and hundreds of Norselanders had poured in. There had been no time for them to open the armory and use its weapons, but as it transpired, there had been none of the worst sorts of weapons I had seen on Herder Isle. The Hedra who had remained in the camp, though numerous, were mostly boys and unseasoned young men.

Meanwhile, unbeknownst to Gwynedd, the Per of Cloistertown had led a small group of young women and boys directly to Covetown to rouse the Per there. By the time Gwynedd and his armsmen and a small force of Norselanders arrived on the stony rises outside Covetown, hundreds more Norselanders were waiting for them, fresh and eager to fight to open the way to the beach. It was clear to Gwynedd then that it was not a small secret sortie he was involved in, but a coup. Thus, he had not waited for us to arrive as planned but had led an attack on the Hedra, from the rear, after signaling to tell Dardelan what he intended to do and asking him to send three large ship boats ashore. The Hedra were caught between the two forces and outnumbered, yet by the sound of it, they had fought with savage skill.

During the hours of fighting that followed, Jakoby had slipped ashore to seek Rushton. By then, of course, she and Dardelan had learned that Ariel was not on Norseland; nevertheless, they felt certain Rushton would make his way to Ariel's residence.

"Do you remember leaving the *Umborine*?" I asked Rushton.

"I remember diving overboard," he murmured. "I remember as soon as I saw the cove and the path going up, feeling the compulsion to . . . to find you. I swam to shore and went straight up the track that runs alongside the road to the top of the cliffs. The Hedra there took one look at me and let me through. They . . . recognized me, you see. 'Ariel's wolf' they used to call me. I knew where to go, because I had crossed the island on foot many times before. Ariel had me do it over and over, harried by his dogs. 'Let us hunt the wolf,' he would say and laugh. . . . I think that was real."

"It doesn't matter," I said, not wanting him to dwell on frayed places in his mind. "However it happened, Ariel made sure you would know the way to the residence and that you would go there and put on the demon band before coming to find me."

Rushton shook his head. "That he saw so much . . ."

"I know," I said. "But he does not see everything, else he would have seen this." I leaned over to gently kiss his bruised lips. They curved into a crooked smile, but I noted the dark shadows beneath his eyes and sat back to finish my tale. "While you were coming to me, Gwynedd was meeting with the Per of Covetown in the stony rises, and probably about the time you reached Ariel's residence, he was leading an army of Norselanders against the Hedra on the cliffs. By the time we arrived back at Covetown, the fighting was over."

"It is strange to think of a war being fought so close at hand, yet for me it is no more than a tale," Rushton said.

"We do not need to be the center of all wars and all strife," I said gently. "I am very content for the Battle for Norseland to be a tale about other people told over a campfire. And now it is very late. Sleep."

Rushton drew a long breath and sighed before asking, "What were you reading?"

"A book of Sadorian poetry. Jakoby gave it to me when she came to see how you were."

"Read to me. I would like to hear your voice in my dreams," Rushton said, and closed his eyes.

I took up the book I had laid aside and opened it, blinking to clear a mist of tears from my eyes.

Rushton slept for the remainder of the night and most of the next morning, and I did not leave his side, but when a Norseland herbalist, who was aboard as part of the Norse delegation, appeared with a gift of some special nourishing soup she had concocted, I went to wash my face and eat a meal in the saloon.

The first person I saw when I entered was Gwynedd, surrounded by the delegation appointed by the Norseland Pers to serve their king. Neither Dardelan nor Brydda were there, so I sat at an empty table by the door and helped myself to some buttered mushrooms from a heaped platter and sliced some of the heavy Norse bread and ate. I marveled again at how readily the Norselanders had accepted Gwynedd's claim to have king's blood flowing through his veins.

Contrary to my expectations, he had not told the Norselanders of his lineage in order to gain their trust. The news that the Faction had been overcome in the Land and upon Herder Isle had convinced the Norselanders to fight their oppressors. That, and the fact that the forceful if diminutive Per Vallon of Cloistertown had declared Gwynedd's arrival to be a sign from the goddesses.

Although the Faction had been overcome, I had not told Rushton that the death toll had been horrific. Over a hundred Norselanders had fallen in the first half hour of the brutal battle on the cliffs and double that again before it was over. Many more had been wounded.

There had been even more deaths among the Hedra, especially in the encampment, for many of the warrior priests had been young novices and acolytes, and this was their first true battle. Whatever glory they had thought to find in fighting for their Lud was eventually lost in blood and mud and screams of pain, and they began to throw down their weapons. Some were slain by their own captains, true fanatics who believed that the only honor in defeat lay in death.

I shivered, remembering the ferocity and fanaticism of the Hedra master on Herder Isle.

As if he had heard my thoughts, Gwynedd looked over and saw me. He immediately excused himself from his followers and came to join me, apologizing for not yet visiting Rushton.

"He is still very tired," I said. "You look tired, too."

He sighed heavily. "In truth, I am weary to death of fighting. Yet there will be fighting in the Westland before the Council and the Faction are overcome, and if Rushton wins the aid of the Sadorians, we will sail across the sea to wage war on these slavemasters. Ye gods, I wish I could disbelieve the prediction of this Futuretell guildmistress, but I have seen for myself the power wielded by Mistress Dell, and I have heard her say more than once that the guildmistress of the Futuretellers is far more gifted than she."

"I am not sure that would be true anymore," I said. "But Maryon would never announce such a future-telling unless she was certain that it would come to pass."

Gwynedd ran his hands through his long blond hair, and I noticed for the first time the glint of silver in the gold. "You know, I ought to be celebrating our victory, and it was a victory, despite leaving the cloister under siege. But I keep thinking of the dead Hedra laid out in rows in the encampment. Most of them were young, and some seemed no more than children to my eyes. They would have grown up to be vicious fanatics, but seeing their youth, I understood that most of them would have been given no choice about what they would become. It was all I could do not to weep."

"I am sorry for their deaths," I said, "but I do not know what else you could have done."

"That is what I tell myself, but it is a convenient answer, is it not? I fear the faces of the dead boys will haunt me."

"They should," I said, and he looked up at me, his blue eyes questioning. I shrugged. "I mean only that if we kill, we ought to be haunted by it, else we are monsters."

He held my gaze. "You are wise, Guildmistress, for all your youth."

I laughed ruefully. "I feel as if I am a hundred!"

He smiled, but his eyes were serious. "One thing I would tell you. This 'victory' has taught me how much I have come to rely on the Talents of Misfits like you, not only to help me win battles but also to win them with as little violence as possible. This battle seemed utterly brutal, yet all battles were once thus. I have changed, because I have seen that battles need not be bloody and full of death. I have lived with the constant gentling desire of your people to cause as little harm as possible, and I find that is my desire, too. Because I have had around me Blyss and Dell and all of your people in the midst of battle, I was struck by the terrible waste of it, for nothing can be learned by corpses. The truest victory is the winning of hearts and minds."

"*That* is a true victory," Rushton murmured when I returned to my cabin and told him what the Norselander had said. To my consternation, he was dressed, but in truth he seemed much improved, and when I told him about the maps I had seen, he grew excited and sent me to ask Jakoby for permission to visit the map chamber. Gwynedd had not managed to obtain a good clear map of the way to the Red Queen's land on Norseland, which meant that the information that could be culled from the ship's map collection might be vital to the success of the journey to the Red Queen's land.

On my way back from speaking with the tribeswoman, Brydda hailed me. Joining him at the side of the ship, I related the substance of my earlier conversation with Gwynedd. Brydda told me that the Norselander had been appalled by the number of his countrymen killed, all the more because the Pers of Covetown and Cloistertown had praised him for defeating the Hedra with so few dead and injured. He also said that the Pers had been on the verge of commanding the execution of their captors, for this had been the sole punishment dealt out to them by the Hedra for any misdeeds. But Gwynedd had forbidden it, saying only that the Hedra must be shackled and made to labor, for soon enough they would be needed. He had told Brydda that there was no use in pointing out the youth of most Hedra from the encampment or suggesting the possibility of redemption to the Norselanders. He had said only that the Hedra were

406

going to be coerced and used to fight the slavemasters. That was a reason the Norselanders could accept.

I did not envy the fate of the priests who had shut themselves up in the cloister, for in refusing to surrender to Gwynedd, they had ensured that they would be judged and dealt with by the Pers, unless they managed to hold out until Gwynedd returned.

"And will he return?" I asked.

"He must, for he is their king," Brydda answered.

"He agreed?" I asked as Dardelan joined us.

Brydda shrugged. "I do not think they see kingship as a question. Gwynedd is the Norse king, and that is that. It does not matter to them that Gwynedd announced his lineage only to ensure obedience when he forbade anyone to enter Ariel's demesne."

"How can he be king of Norseland *and* high chieftain of the Westland?" I asked.

"Gwynedd told the Pers that he had just sworn to serve a year as high chieftain of the Westland and that even before that year ended, he must travel to the Red Land with us to prevent the slavemasters from invading our lands," Dardelan said. "Per Vallon merely told him blithely that kings were not ordinary men whose doings could be ordered by their people. Kings were always going hither and thither on kingly business, and it was left to the Pers to deal with the day-to-day ruling of the king's land and his people."

Gwynedd would come to them once he had fulfilled his oaths in the Westland and achieved victory over the slavemasters of the Red Land. In the meantime, he must choose a *kinehelt* to rule in his stead. *Kinehelt*, Dardelan explained, was an old Norse word for "king's hand." So Gwynedd had appointed Per Vallon of

Cloistertown and Per Selma of Covetown as his kine-helt, saying a king needed two hands. Just before he had boarded the *Umborine* for Sador, the stooped and balding Per Vallon had produced the crown of the last Norse king, which his family had kept hidden through the generations. Dell's foreseeing came to pass as Gwynedd knelt in the pebbles to be crowned.

I had not known this, and I pictured it as we were all silent for a time, gazing out over the sea. Then I saw that the water was so still it might have been made from glass, for the wind had fallen away utterly. The only thing that marred the glassy perfection was the spreading ripples running out from the hull of the *Umborine* as the deep currents of the strait drew it slowly along.

"We are becalmed," Rushton said as I reentered the cabin. "What did Jakoby say?"

"She will bring some maps here later, though she says none shows the way to the Red Queen's land. We will have to hope that Gwynedd is right in believing that maps will be found in the cloister, once it is surrendered."

I hesitated, contemplating whether to tell him about Dragon now or wait till he was stronger, but he limped across to the window and opened it to stare out moodily.

"You should lie down," I chided him.

"I feel better than I did last night. It is just my head. The ache is constant, but Jakoby says that Andorra is mixing up a potion that will ease me." He gazed out the window for a while longer, and then he came back to sit on the bed beside me, saying, "I mislike this stillness. I must not miss that meeting."

"Jakoby says we will be there in time. Why not let Dardelan address the tribes?"

"I think it is important that I speak as Master of Obernewtyn, since it is Maryon who foresaw what will come," Rushton said.

I did not argue, for I could see he had no strength for it. I coaxed him to lie down with me, and he slept a while then. I dozed, too, until Jakoby came bearing the promised maps and Andorra's potion. The ship was still becalmed, but she assured Rushton that we were not far from the Sadorian coast, and even if we were becalmed all night, we would still reach Sador in time for him to make his request, for there was one full day of the conclave remaining. Only an hour later, the wind rose again. Spurred on by it, Rushton got up and asked me to fetch Gwynedd, Brydda, and Dardelan, for they must speak of what to say to the tribes. I knew him too well to suggest he ought to rest while he could, and when the others arrived, I slipped out with Maruman for a breath of fresh air.

The wind whipped at my hair as we made our way aft to the holding yard, and I glanced up to see the sails billowing scarlet against a bright blue sky. Once again, the *Umborine* was flying.

Reaching the holding yard, I saw that Gahltha and Calcasuss were at the other end attempting to instruct a group of small, hardy Norseland ponies in the rudiments of Brydda's fingerspeech. I did not wish to interrupt them, and sunlight lay so enticingly on a bench alongside their pen that I sat down on it to wait. I was not there long before Maruman leapt onto my lap. When I thought he was asleep, I allowed myself the illicit pleasure of stroking him, acknowledging that it had been the right impulse to ask him to look after Gahltha, for he had spent most of the time I was on Norseland comforting the black horse and taking his mind off wave-sickness and terror, which had kept him from fretting about me.

Gahltha put his head over the barrier to nuzzle at my shoulder.

"You seem in good spirits," I told him fondly, reaching up to stroke his nose.

He answered that he had liked the ship's being becalmed but that he was also glad the wind had begun to blow again so his time aboard the ship would end soon. "My hooves want to feel proper steady earthfastness under them," he sent.

Without opening his eyes, Maruman pointed out languidly that sand was none too steady under paws, let alone inferior hooves, which was why kamuli were called "ships of the desert." Gahltha ignored this to ask about Rushton.

"He is bruised and battered, inside and out. But he will heal—is healing." I looked into the black horse's lustrous eyes with a rush of tenderness so potent that my eyes filled with tears. "I am glad that you and Maruman are with me."

"We will always be with you," Gahltha sent.

He withdrew his head, and I lay back and closed my eyes, enjoying the slight warmth of the sun on my face and the soft weight of Maruman on my lap. It was strange that, having faced certain death, my spirits were now as calm and glassy as the sea had been. *I am becalmed*, I thought, closing my eyes. Maybe I could hear the song of the waves so clearly now that its vast, encompassing serenity made me feel very small and insignificant. It was odd how some people longed to be important, people like Chieftain Brocade. Everything about the man, from his immense size to his manner and arrogance, spoke of his hunger for importance, yet what, truly, did he desire? To be significant? For what purpose? Did he understand that with significance came a terrible weight of responsibility? I felt that weight as the Seeker, but for the moment, I was utterly content to let the song of the sea show me how small I was.

A shadow fell over me, and I squinted against the sun to see Gilbert, whom I had not set eyes on since we had reboarded the *Umborine*. Like Rushton, he had been sleeping and healing. Now the wind tossed his side plaits and blew his thick red hair back from his handsome face, revealing an ugly purpling bruise on his forehead. But his eyes were clear and his expression tranquil, and I thought his was a face that a woman might easily love. I hoped for both their sakes that his Serra would see the change in him. Or that she would at least let his sons come to know their father. Gilbert was a man who would grow for having children. It would bring out his tenderness, which had begun to curdle.

"Jakoby sent me to tell you that we will see Templeport on the horizon within the half hour," he said. "Is it true that not a single tree grows there?"

I hid a smile at the boyish curiosity in his voice. "There are trees in the isis pool rifts, and there are the ancient giant trees of the spice groves, which I have never seen but from which the *Umborine* was made. But other than them, there is not a tree or a blade of grass in all Sador. It is a true desert land and hotter than any place I have ever been. Jak says the heat comes from the land underneath, as in the Westland. He believes that great pools of molten rock lie at the burning heart of the world and that in the Great White, cracks opened that let molten rock flow close to the surface."

"Do you believe the world has a heart of fire?" Gilbert asked, looking at me curiously.

"I do not know how something with fire inside can have ice and snow upon the surface, but the longer I live, the more it seems that life is full of the unexpected and impossible. Why should it not be so of the land as well?"

"That is neither a yes nor a no," the armsman observed dryly.

I laughed. "I suppose the answer is that I don't know. But the teknoguilders seem very sure."

"You sound as if you don't think their certainty is a good thing."

I sobered. "Let us say that I have too often seen certainty as a sort of blindness."

"How did one so young become so wise?" Gilbert asked.

"For the second time today I have been called wise, but I do not think myself so," I said wryly.

He did not smile. "Perhaps *not* thinking oneself wise is the modesty that must form the heart of all true wisdom. On the other hand, my father used to say that fools and wise men were made so for a reason." I made no response, and he continued in a soft, distant voice. "Last night, I dreamed of you standing in a black and barren place surrounded by snarling wolves."

"It was just a dream," I said, though his words sent a trickle of ice along my spine, for the previous night, I, too, had dreamed of wolves, though I had attributed it to Rushton telling me that Ariel had called him a wolf.

A burst of laughter made us both turn to see Dardelan holding open the door to my cabin for Brydda and Gwynedd, who were supporting Rushton between them. They were all laughing at their awkwardness, but even from this far away, I could see the knotted black line of stitches that ran almost to one brow. Rushton was smiling, but this faded into an intense seriousness as he leaned closer to hear something that Dardelan was saying. A fierce love for him rose up in my breast as I thought how I loved that look above all others upon his face, that grave solemnity.

Seeming to feel my gaze, he turned to look in my direction, and our eyes locked and clasped for a long moment. I had a sudden dizzying memory of the first time I had seen him coming from the pigpen at Obernewtyn. He had looked at me in the same way, unsmiling, intent, as if there was nothing else in the world but me. Then Dardelan reached out to clasp his shoulder, and he turned away.

I sighed and then started when Gilbert said softly, "He is the one you love. The Master of Obernewtyn. I do not know why I did not see it before."

Whatever response I might have made was lost in the ululating cry from the lookout and the commotion that followed as everyone on deck crowded to the side of the ship. Gilbert offered me a hand, and I let him heave me up, lifting a grumbling Maruman onto my shoulders as we went to gaze at the long purple shadow on the horizon. Gwynedd called out to Gilbert, and the armsman smiled at me and went to his chieftain.

Maruman demanded tersely to be put down, and I realized that my heightened emotions were irritating him. I lifted him to the deck, turned to lean on the edge of the ship, and gazed out at Sador.

I felt a hand on my shoulder and did not need to turn to know that Rushton had come to stand behind me. He stepped closer and I trembled, feeling the heat of his body through the linen shirt he wore and through the silk and woven vest. Softly he said, "When last we came to Sador, you told me that you loved me. I will never forget how it felt to hear you say those words for the first time, for I had believed that you could not love one whose Talent was locked uselessly inside him."

"You were wrong," I said.

"It would not be the first time," Rushton murmured, a smile in his voice.

The white-haired tribal leader Bram was at the front of the crowd that had gathered to meet us on the sand-covered point of rock that extended a little way out and then dropped off steeply at one side, allowing even greatships to anchor very close to shore. A ramp was laid down to allow the horses to leave, and I led Gahltha across it with Maruman draped about my shoulders. The minute his hooves touched the sand, Gahltha announced a powerful need to gallop. Laughing, I bade him go. The crowd parted for him and the other horses and then closed about us again. I looked at them uneasily, fearing their presence had some connection to Jakoby's trip to Sutrium and my quest, but I need not have worried, for Bram greeted us fulsomely, explaining that the fall of the Faction and Council in the West and the Norselands had been foretold by more than one kasanda, as well as by the Earthtemple's over-guardian. He made a long, effusive speech about the value of freedom and then called for a strange evil-smelling brew, which we all drank to celebrate our victory.

Maruman hissed at the strong acrid scent of the brew and insisted on being put down. I was not troubled, for he disliked crowds and would sniff his way to me in a while.

Once the toasts had been drunk, Bram announced that tents had been set up in expectation of our arrival, and we were to be shown to them so we could rest in order to be fresh for the feasting that would begin when the moon rose.

As we made our way along the sand spit to the road to the desert lands proper, I noticed Jakoby speaking to Bram. From his grave expression, I guessed that she was telling him of Maryon's futuretelling, and it occurred to me that some of the Sadorian seers or the over-guardian might also have foreseen the slavemasters' coming. I said this to Rushton, who agreed that Bram might already know why he had come; nevertheless, if he had understood Jakoby, he would still have to put the matter of the ships formally before the tribes. I asked him exactly what Zarak had told him of Maryon's prediction, but he had no more detail to offer than Brydda had shared. I would have to wait to learn more from Maryon herself. Again I was tempted to tell Rushton about Dragon, but I could not do so while hemmed in by tribe children and adults chattering in gadi and in the common tongue of the lands. Hearing that language reminded me that I still had not shown Jakoby the book and the brooch from Ariel's residence.

"It was fortunate that the *Umborine* had not left when Zarak rode up. Indeed, at the time, it seemed so suited to my need that I hardly questioned it, yet I do not know why Jakoby came for you with such urgency."

"She has not told me clearly, but I think the over-guardian wishes to speak with me," I said. We reached the noisy trade area, and I sniffed the scents of spices and perfumes and frying fish with pleasure, regretting that I lacked coin to exchange for the temple tokens used as currency in the desert lands. Nevertheless, later I would walk through the trade tents and stalls, for I liked the market here.

It was hard to imagine how the area must look outside the annual period of conclave, which included the gathering and drying or smoking of the schools of fish that once a year mysteriously cast themselves upon the sandy spit. Yet the Sadorians believed deeply that they must leave nothing of themselves upon the earth when they moved on. So the tribes would take their tents and their kamuli and leave Templeport to go wandering in the desert or take their turn at tending the spice groves, and their departure led to the traders' departure. In no time, Templeport would be deserted, save for a few traders who would trade with the occasional small shipmasters, who put in at Templeport to take on fresh water and do a little trading with the Earthtemple, which was built into soaring cliffs honeycombed with tunnels and chambers, its stony face carved into a thousand faces that looked out to the sea.

At last we reached the area where dozens of white guest tents rose up from the pale gold sand like an armada of tethered sails fluttering in the wind and the warm, clear light of dusk. Bram made another short speech, this time welcoming the Norselanders, and then he once again bade us rest before the feasting. Once the speech was done, Jakoby drew Rushton aside, and I left them to it, hoping he would not overtax himself. I moved through the tents until I found one tethered with its flap facing the empty undulating dunes and crawled into it. I had just let my pack slide to the floor when Rushton came in and stretched out on the bedroll that had been so neatly laid out.

"What did she say?" I asked.

He sighed and rubbed his eyes. "She told Bram about the slavemasters and my intention to request the use of the Sadorian greatships. It seems their kasandas made some prediction that would fit the coming of these slavemasters, and for this reason, I will be heard with sympathy. But Bram told Jakoby that the Sadorians will not simply hand their ships over. They will regard my request as an invitation to take part in a war. This will likely result in a vote to extend the conclave a sevenday so the matter can be examined thoroughly before a vote is taken."

"A sevenday," I said, my heart sinking.

Rushton turned his head to look at me, and he might have read my mind. "I, too, ache to return to Obernewtyn, but gaining these ships is too important a duty to shirk, and it will be worth the time, if they agree. Meanwhile, Dardelan, Gwynedd, and I will begin to plan the journey to the Red Land and all that must be done before it." He was silent for a little, and then he said, "Jakoby also told me that I must present my request in gadi."

I stared at him in disbelief. "But you cannot speak gadi."

"I do not have to speak it, only to announce my request in it. Apparently, that request can be stated very simply. But it is a formal requirement and cannot be waived. Bram has agreed to teach me the words, and my tuition will begin tonight, at this feast." He sighed again. Then he looked around and said I had clearly been given preferential treatment, since my tent was larger and more luxurious than his.

I told him he was a fool, for all tents were exactly alike, and I had chosen my own at random. He complained that I lacked the proper respect for my chieftain. Then he caught my hand and pulled me down alongside him, wincing as he jarred his splinted wrist. I tried to sit up, scolding him for failing to mind his wounds.

"You mind them for me," he said. "I have other matters to mind." Then he pinned my legs under a knee, ignoring my laughing protests that he was being unfair, since I could not wrestle an injured man.

"Of course not," he said loftily. "The only honorable thing to do is to surrender immediately."

Laughing, I tried to wriggle away but froze when he winced. I drew back from him in dismay. "We should be careful."

"Maybe so," he sighed, and lay back against the rumpled bedding. "I am not completely healed, it is true, but I am healing. Inside as well as out, this time." It was the first time he had referred directly to what Ariel had done to him. Not that we had avoided the matter or feared to speak of it; we just seemed to have come to some unspoken agreement to put it off for a time. His eyes met mine, jade green and gravely tender. He said, "You risked your life to save mine."

"I saved myself," I said fiercely, and reached out to brush the thick silky fall of black hair from his brow. I frowned at the great puckered gash there. "That will leave a scar," I said.

He took my hand and kissed the palm. "Each scar is a wisdom learned. My grandmother told me that."

"I have never heard you speak of a grandmother," I said, relaxing beside him. This mood of his, which allowed laughter and childhood confidences, was so welcome after his long, relentless coldness that I wanted to prolong it.

"My grandmother died before my mother became ill and sent me to Obernewtyn in search of my father. But I remember her very well, because she was strange and embarrassed me dreadfully with her eccentricities. The other boys in my village whispered that she was a witch, and oft times I thought so, too."

"What did she do?" I asked curiously.

He laughed. "Not much. It does not take much in a village to be thought peculiar."

"But what?" I persisted.

He shrugged. "She liked to walk about the forest at night, and when the moon was full, she would go out and glare up at it. 'Moonhater,' they called her."

It was an odd coincidence that Rushton's grandmother had hated the moon, for Maruman hated it as well. "A strange distant thing to dislike so much," I said tentatively. "Did she ever say why?"

He shook his head. "She talked to herself, and she had many queer dislikes."

"Had she any Talent?" I asked.

"My mother definitely had a touch of empathy. That is what made her such a good herb lorist. Perhaps her

419

mother was the same. The Twentyfamilies gypsies who passed through our village each year on the way to tithe the Council made a point of visiting her to pay their respects." He laughed ruefully. "I remember their bringing her gifts: little carved creatures or some special fruit or sweet. My mother was convinced they made my grandmother worse. I think it was true, because sometimes, after they had come, my grandmother would walk through the forest to the mountains and stand staring at them for hours as if they were a puzzle she must solve. Back then, they were still so dangerously tainted that most people avoided going anywhere near them. People in the village said my grandmother's habit of staring at the black mountains was hereditary and came from a queerness in our bloodline. Once I asked my mother about it, and she said we had another ancestor who had been just as fascinated with the mountains. But she had believed there was a marvelous settlement of wondrous shining people living beyond them and was always yearning to go to them. She vanished one night, and people said she must have just walked into the tainted mountains and died." Rushton suddenly smiled. "I remember that I asked my mother if *she* was planning to go mad, and she said she would endeavor not to do it, for my sake."

His voice trailed away, and I stared at him, wondering.

Rushton went on, "After I came to Obernewtyn and Louis told me who my father was, I remember wondering if my mother falling in love with Michael Seraphim was just another form of our ancestral fascination with the high mountains."

I drew a breath and said as casually as I could

420

manage, "Louis Larkin once told me that Lukas Seraphim had been determined to build a home in the mountains, because he had dreamed of a wondrous settlement of people living there. Apparently, he was bitterly disappointed to find only a Beforetime ruin."

"Perhaps Lukas Seraphim heard a tale that arose from the mad notions of one of my ancestors."

"But it wasn't just a tale or mad notion," I persisted. "There *was* a settlement in the mountains that some might call miraculous, only it existed in the Beforetime."

"Are you saying that my ancestor and Lukas Seraphim both had true dreams of the Beforetime Obernewtyn?" Rushton asked skeptically.

"They were both your ancestors," I reminded him. "But it was not dreams I meant. What if Hannah Seraphim started the rumor about the settlement in the mountains? She was not at Obernewtyn when the Great White came, as we now know, so maybe she was in Newrome and escaped before it collapsed. If she did, she would have been unable to return to Obernewtyn, because the mountains were now a deadly barrier. What if she just stayed there and waited, watching the mountains and longing to go over them, knowing it was impossible?"

Rushton gave me a sleepy-eyed smile. "Do I hear one of Zarak's theories?"

I laughed. "Now that you mention it. But really, it makes sense. She gazed at the mountains and talked about Obernewtyn, and that was how the rumor of the wondrous place there began." I was silent a moment, thinking hard. Then I drew in an excited breath. "What if she remained up in the highlands and eventually bonded and had children? Might they not have talked of her obsession with the mountains, even generations later?"

"You think my illustrious ancestor Lukas Seraphim built Obernewtyn because of stories told to him by *his* ancestor, and then my mother's mother came to hear of the tale and took to staring at the mountains, too? A very convoluted theory," Rushton laughed, yawning.

"Rushton, I know it sounds strange, but think of it. If Hannah Seraphim lived through the Great White and had children, they could be your ancestors *on both sides!* Hannah would have been trapped on the other side of the mountains during the Age of Chaos, and while the worst of the madness was happening in the cities, we know that it was much calmer in remoter regions. Just the same, people from the cities came to the Land, and they brought upheaval and fear enough that a family might easily be scattered and lose one another. If I am right, it would explain your name, Lukas's determination to build Obernewtyn, and your great-grandmother's fascination with the mountains."

I looked at Rushton to see how he had taken my revelations, but his eyes were closed. The slow rise and fall of his chest told me that he was asleep. I glared at him indignantly for a moment and then laughed softly. No matter, for I could not tell him the last part of my speculations: that the main reason Hannah would have yearned to cross the mountains was because she knew her bones were supposed to lie with Jacob's and with the key Cassy had given her, for the Seeker to find.

Rushton stirred, and I realized he had woken from his drowse when he reached up to capture a strand of my hair in his fingers, distracting me from the wild tumble of my thoughts. "Like silk," he murmured, stroking it between his fingers. "Black silk." He reached out, and this time I did not resist as he drew me onto his chest. He studied my face with a hungry longing that made my blood sing.

I said unsteadily, "We are supposed to be preparing for a feast."

"That is exactly what I am thinking," he said very purposefully, and his mouth closed on mine.

✦ 19 ✦

THAT NIGHT WHEN the moon rose, as ripe and golden as a peach, a desert horn sounded, announcing the start of the night's festivities. A Sadorian tribeswoman named Kaman had been sent to bring me fresh clothes and desert sandals, saying they were gifts from Jakoby. She had imperiously shooed an amused Rushton out to make his own preparations and sent a boy running off for hot water so she could help me bathe and dress. I had tried to tell her I needed no help, but very politely she made it clear that my wishes were irrelevant, since they conflicted with Jakoby's command. Seeing no other course than to submit, I had allowed myself somewhat self-consciously to be disrobed, sponged down, and toweled. Then she had oiled my skin in a massage so delicious that I had actually fallen asleep. Which was just as well because the hairdressing that followed had been a very long and wearisome business. I had managed to endure it only because Kaman had begun describing the process of smoking and drying and salting the fish they gathered each year.

It was fascinating, though I asked if she did not fear to eat fish that had washed up dead on the beach. She answered that the fish were not dead when they washed up and that even if one threw a fish back into the waves, it would swim ashore again. I was pondering this, wondering what Ari-noor or Ari-roth would say of this determined suicide, when Kaman went on to tell me that the tribes believed the fish were regarded as a promise that one day the earth would be healed and that the feast on this night was a thanksgiving for the sea's bounty, without which the Sadorians would not survive. This was a night, she added, when tribesfolk bestowed gifts upon one another to echo the gifting of the sea.

At last, Kaman pronounced that my hair was finished. At her command, I removed the light wrap I had worn to soak up any excess oil, and she helped me dress in the exquisite blue and green silken robes that Jakoby had sent. They felt beautiful against my skin.

Kaman bowed and departed, which was when I heard the desert horn. I took a deep breath and emerged from the tent. The desert looked like a frozen sea, with waves and troughs filled with greenish shadows running away into the indigo night, and the stars sparkled, despite the moon's brightness. I drew a long deep breath of the sweet desert air and turned to look at the tents glowing white and billowing slightly. A number of people were walking among them and back toward the trade stalls, and I began to move in the same direction, farseeking Maruman, but he was either sleeping or had boarded the ship. I strove for Gahltha and, finding him wooing a Sadorian mare, withdrew at once, not wanting to interrupt.

"Elspeth?" said a voice. Seely stood with Jakoby and Jak, clad in brown and gold sandsilk robes. Like mine, her hair had been elaborately plaited, and seeing the lovely and intricate design woven into it, I felt less self-conscious about my own hair.

"Both of you look well in desert attire." Jakoby approved so maternally that I guessed she must have gifted Seely, too, and I thanked her for my own clothes and for sending Kaman. I wanted to ask if she had any news of Bruna, who must surely be in Templeport, but before I could speak, Jakoby said briskly that we ought to go to the feasting ground, for Jak must make his speech to the tribe leaders before Bram spoke. She took Jak's arm and drew him a little ahead with her as she began explaining the formalities that must be observed when presenting his gift of taint-eating insects. Jak said it was not so much a gift to the tribes as to the earth.

"Nevertheless," said Jakoby, "you must present the insects in this way, for what you propose to do will change the earth, and that is a very serious thing in our eyes. Indeed, you must present your gift specifically to the Earthtemple."

It dawned on me belatedly that Jakoby intended the teknoguilder to present his gift this night, and Seely confirmed this, saying that Jakoby had suggested it, for this was a night of gift-giving, and was not the bestowing of Jak's insects a gifting?

We were now passing through the trading area where numerous stalls and tables were laden with everything from oranges to glimmering stones, perfumes in tiny bottles, feather sunshades, and great soft bolts of sandsilk. Surprisingly few people were buying and browsing, but when I saw the number of people crossing the stretch of sand to our same destination, I realized that all Sadorians would attend the feast. The distance was not great, and soon I could see fifty enormous bonfires dug in a semicircle facing a long semicircular table at which sat all the tribe leaders. Fire pits and tables formed a complete circle, with two halves facing one another, and people sat about the fire pits on woven mats. The smell of cooking food was strong, and I realized that much of it was buried in the embers of the fire pits. But there were also young Sadorian boys and girls, beaming with pride, moving around the fire pits with trays of cold food and ceramic mugs of fement.

"Come," Jakoby said to Jak, and the teknoguilder smiled reassuringly at a suddenly anxious-looking Seely, saying he would join her soon.

We were close to the last fire pit, and there were plenty of empty woven mats set down. Just as we took our places, Jakoby called for silence. Seeing Jak standing nervously beside the tribeswoman, I realized that the teknoguilder would speak immediately, and my stomach clenched in sympathy. To his credit, Jak looked pale but composed as Bram rose to present him to the tribes as a senior Misfit of Obernewtyn, explaining that on this night of thanksgiving, Jak wished to present a gift to the Earthtemple on behalf of his people, the Misfits.

Then the old man took his seat. I knew Jak had no taste for speaking nor any particular skill at it, but he spoke without pretense and with care, and although his voice shook at first, it steadied as he became absorbed in explaining his interest in the shining insects that inhabited dark wet caves in the Land and his discovery that the tiny creatures could consume tainted matter and transform it within their bodies so that it was harmless. He told how he had conceived a plan to breed the insects until they were capable of surviving in the open, in the hope of being able to set them loose on the edge of the Blacklands to begin the massive task of undoing the damage that had been done to the earth. But all Blacklands were arid, and the tiny insects needed cool, dark, damp surroundings to thrive in their natural state; therefore, they would have to be bred to tolerate dryness and even heat. His research had been completed during his exile in the West land when he had finally succeeded in breeding a hardier if less long-lived form of the insect.

"Given your reverence for the earth and your belief that healing is possible," Jak said, "it seems more than fitting to me that this is where I will release my insects. Therefore, I offer my insects and my skill in settling them here in the desert lands as a gift to the Earthtemple."

The wording was formal and careful, and there was almost no response to his speech, save that the silence seemed very concentrated. Jakoby rose smoothly from the place she had taken at the end of the table and went to stand beside Jak, saying, "I would like to thank the teknoguilder Jak, who has brought to the desert lands a gift of even more extraordinary importance than he can guess, for his gift fulfills an old prophecy that says a day will come when the earth begins to heal itself, and from that day, no woman shall immerse herself in an isis pool. For once Jak releases the insects, it may truly be said that the earth has begun to heal itself."

I saw by Jak's expression that he had not expected this announcement, and I suspected it was the same with Bram, though he was too canny to show his reactions openly. Other tribal leaders muttered and scowled to one another. Then a woman's voice shouted out to accuse Jakoby of deliberately misinterpreting the prophecy because of her obsession with ending the practice of immersions.

"It does not matter to you that other women do not fear the immersion, Jakoby, for in suffering, we show our allegiance to the wounded earth."

"The earth did not choose to be poisoned, Galia."

There was an uproar at this, with cries of anger and distress from the audience, and shouts that the immersions did not signify choosing to be poisoned but a sharing of the earth's pain.

Jakoby heard the latter and swung on the woman who had spoken. "And what of the babes who are deformed by this wondrous sharing, for it is they who must bear the burden of their mother's choice," she said icily.

There was another outcry, and then a man called out to ask how the Earthtemple would survive if there were no more deformed babies to serve as Temple guardians.

Jakoby's eyes flashed, as if she had been waiting for this question. She said grimly to the man, "And now the truth comes to show its face. Are there no whole Sadorians who will offer themselves in service to the Earthtemple? Only those born maimed and crippled are worthy to serve the earth?"

The ensuing hum of talk was less angry and more confused, but now Bram rose to say with authority and finality that this was a night of thanksgiving and not for angry debates. The gift offered by Jak had been properly announced, and the overguardian of the

Earthtemple would either accept or spurn it. There was some low muttering, but Bram called to the chanters to offer the Song of the Fish in praise of the sea, and soon their voices drowned out any protest.

"What was all that about?" Seely whispered worriedly when the chant ended some minutes later and we had both been served mugs of a sweet light fement.

"The Sadorians feel it is an honor for a woman to offer herself to the isis pools once a year. They are tainted, and by risking the health of any child they might be carrying, many Sadorians believe that they are showing their solidarity with the wounded earth. Any child born with deformities is given as a gift to the Earthtemple, where it will be cared for and trained up as a guardian," I said.

"And this prophecy Jakoby spoke of. Who made it?"

"I do not know who prophesied it, but no doubt it was one of the kasanda. It is only Jakoby's opinion that Jak's insects fulfill the prophecy."

"You would think that the people here would be grateful that they need not risk their unborn children," Seely said indignantly.

"Some probably would be, but the immersions have become tradition, and people do not like breaking traditions. And, of course, they fear what will happen to the Earthtemple. For them, the deformities are natural in the guardians. They revere the guardians and are guided by them. A person deformed by reverence to the earth is no ordinary person. But to have an ordinary man or woman as a guardian or even an over-guardian?" I shook my head.

"A tradition based on harming unborn children is wrong," Seely said.

"So my mother says," said a clear husky voice, and I looked up to see Jakoby's lovely, long-limbed daughter, Bruna. She was clad in violet silks, and she sat beside Seely with the fluid grace of a silk cord, adding, "I think it is her greatest desire to see the practice of immersions end."

"Bruna!" I said. "I am glad you arrived safely. I did not see you when we came ashore, and I feared that something might have befallen you on the coast road."

"I did not go down to the ship, but I sent word with a friend to tell my mother where I had placed her tent."

I did not ask why she had not come to the ship, for it was obvious. "Why is Jakoby so opposed to the practice of immersion when the rest of your people see it as an honor?" I asked.

Bruna turned her slanted golden eyes on me. "You must ask my mother that question, Guildmistress, for it is at the heart of her deepest sorrow."

I was startled by her words, for if I remembered correctly, the overguardian of the Earthtemple had told Jakoby that before she returned to Sador on the *Umborine,* she would encounter something that touched upon a deep sorrow. Did that mean that she had been sent out by the Earthtemple to bring back Jak and his insects since they would heal the isis pools and put an end to the practice of immersion? If so, then surely the Temple guardians would approve Jak's gifting.

I realized that Bruna was watching me, waiting for me to respond to her rebuff. In truth, I had half expected it, for the question had been an intimate one. But Bruna had dealt firmly and gracefully with me, and as she turned back to answer some question of Seely's, it struck me that the young tribeswoman had lost her characteristic arrogance. There was no longer any haughtiness in her face or judgment in her eyes. Indeed, the last time I had seen her in Sutrium, Bruna had been a girl, lovely and half wild, but now she was a woman.

Bruna remained with us for the length of two chant songs, singing exquisitely when everyone sang and between songs helping us get food from the embers to sample, recommending some and rejecting others. In the break between the chant songs, she asked numerous questions about Sutrium and events in the Land with an eagerness that surprised me. Yet she did not ask about Dardelan. Then she rose and departed as abruptly and unexpectedly as she had joined us.

"She is very beautiful," Seely said wistfully, gazing after her.

My attention was not on Bruna but on Dardelan, who was approaching our fire pit from the other direction with Jak and Brydda. Obviously, Bruna had left because she had seen him, but from the tranquility on Dardelan's face, either he had not seen Bruna or he truly cared nothing for her.

As they sat down, Dardelan told me I looked splendid, and it was a pity that Rushton would not join us to admire my finery. He nodded toward the tables, and I turned to see that Rushton was now seated beside Bram, and the two men were speaking closely together. Rushton had a parchment before him and was now scribing something upon it. Not envying him, I turned back to find the others talking about Jak's insects and the furor they had roused. The teknoguilder insisted he had not had any idea that his gift would be so controversial, and Dardelan asked what was involved in releasing the insects into the desert lands. Was it simply a matter of tipping them onto tainted earth? Jak shook his head, explaining earnestly that it would take him and Seely at least two moons to settle the insects, for they had to be carefully established as a colony somewhere near the edge of the Blacklands, and from there, they would gradually spread out.

"I look forward to hearing of your progress, for I cannot truly see the Sadorians refusing your gift. It seems their objection concerns whether these insects mean the process of immersion is to end immediately or die out naturally as the isis pools lose their taint," Dardelan said. "How do you plan to return to the Westland when this work is done? If you will travel by sea, I would be glad if you would stop a night at Sutrium and give us your news."

"Seely and I mean to travel by the coast road to Obernewtyn after we have finished here," Jak said. "But it will be no hardship to stop a night to exchange news in Sutrium on our way back to the Westland."

"You will be my honored guests," Dardelan promised. "But perhaps you will decide not to go back to the Westland, once you have been at Obernewtyn again."

"There is a lifetime's work for me in the Beforetime complex," Jak said simply.

"What will you do with the knowledge you gain of the Beforetime?" Jakoby asked. The glint in her eyes as she joined us made me think that she had been engaged in more than one fiery discussion following her speech.

The teknoguilder met her gaze steadily. "I will use what I learn as best I can, to serve our time."

"Are you sure the knowledge of the Beforetime will serve this world?" Jakoby countered. "Some say that it is enough to live in the aftermath of the mistakes made by the Beforetimers, without courting the danger of dabbling in their knowledge."

"So said the Council," Jak replied, "but knowledge is no more evil than a knife. It is how knowledge and knives are wielded that makes them evil or not."

"I do not doubt you or your motives, my friend," Jakoby said. "But like a knife, knowledge can all too easily fall into the hands of those who will have no scruples about using it."

The teknoguilder sighed a little. "This is a dance of words I cannot win. Let me ask you a question instead. My hunger for knowledge gave me the gift that I offered tonight to the tribes. Do you say I should not have sought that knowledge or brought it here to put into practice?"

Jakoby held his gaze and finally said, "No, I do not say that." She laughed then and seemed to relax. "For one who does not dance with words, my friend, you have a quick-stepping mind."

Seely gave me an expectant look, and I knew she was willing me to ask why Jakoby had been so determined to end the practice of immersion. But instead, I said lightly that we had seen Bruna and that she looked well. I was watching Dardelan covertly, and I saw him stiffen and then master himself. His reaction made me feel gleeful. Jakoby merely answered equably that she did look well. "I only wish she had not decided to work for a season in the spice groves, for I had hoped to spend some time with her." She did not look at the young high chieftain at all, as if she had forgotten there was ever anything between him and her daughter.

I asked, "When will she leave?"

"Tomorrow," Jakoby said. "Those who will serve always leave before the final feast of the conclave, for the grove cannot be left unattended for more than a five-day. She will leave at dusk."

"She will be happier in the desert than she was in the Land," Dardelan said flatly.

"If you think it, then I know it must be so," Jakoby said to him coolly. She rose with the same sinuous grace as her daughter and looked at me. "Guildmistress?"

I stared up at her stupidly before realizing that she was asking me to accompany her. I got to my feet with clumsy haste, mumbling a farewell to the others, and followed her through the throng. She led me away from the feast site and toward the trade stalls. A silky breeze blew, carrying the scents of cook fires and perfumed oils and salt to us, and I asked if Bruna really meant to leave for the desert so soon.

Jakoby's laughter echoed merrily over the moon-drenched sand dunes. "Did you see Dardelan's face when I said she would leave tomorrow?"

"Then it is not true?"

"It will be true, if I have not lit enough of a fire in Dardelan's belly to hunt a mate," Jakoby said crisply.

"Hunt?" I echoed.

"Three hours before dawn tomorrow, any man may hunt any woman whose name he has scribed on a stone and set into the bowl that stands before the tent of the tribal leader of the woman he desires, so long as she is not mated to another or deemed too young. The woman is given the stones at midnight as a warning, and she has an hour's start on her hunters. She may favor the man when she glimpses his face, but still the man must catch her. The hunt ends at dawn."

"That is barbaric," I said, appalled.

She grinned. "It would be, if those hunted were not tribeswomen."

"Dardelan is no tribesman," I said.

"For this night, he must become one if he would have Bruna. He let her flutter from his fingers when she had given herself to him like a tamed bird, and now she has returned to the tribes. So now he must hunt her in the desert way. Right at this moment, several of my tribesmen are telling Dardelan of the hunt, and one of them will boast that he means to hunt Bruna. He is a strong, handsome warrior whom any woman might desire for a mate."

I did not know whether to be shocked or to laugh. "Does Bruna know?"

"Of course not. She is all sad dignity and restraint since her return from the Land. She has told me that her love for Dardelan is dead. Maybe she even believes it. Yet in an hour or so, I will send someone to her with the stones that have her name scribed on them, and she will have no choice but to take part in the hunt." Jakoby laughed wolfishly.

"What if Dardelan does not put in a stone? What if the other hunter catches her?"

"My daughter will not be caught, save if she desires it, and Dardelan will have to prove himself by catching her," the tribeswoman said proudly. Then she smiled. "I do not doubt that I will go now and find there are two stones in my bowl for Bruna."

"I thought you were opposed to their match," I said.

"I was in the beginning, but there is true love between them, and recent events tell me that the days in which Sador stood apart from people of the Norseland

and your land are coming to an end. Yet, they will still decide the matter between them, the boy chieftain and my daughter. I am done with a mother's meddling."

Jakoby stopped, and I realized where she had been leading me; the Earthtemple loomed ahead.

"The overguardian has summoned me?" I asked, looking into the dark cleft in the earth that was the entrance to the Earthtemple.

Jakoby nodded, and we walked in silence down into the dense pool of moonshadow where the Temple entrance lay. The last time I had come here, I had entered this rift in broad daylight. Long lines of petitioners had waited in the shade of the rift walls—people wanting prayers said for them or a futuretelling, healing or medicines, or those needing to exchange coins from the Land for tokens. The veiled guardians had gone up and down the lines dispensing advice, exchanging coin for tokens, accepting gifts, and handing out medicines and, occasionally, reproaches.

Tonight the rift was empty.

"We must wait here," Jakoby said, a grim note in her voice.

"Jakoby, do you dislike the Earthtemple because it allows the immersions?" I asked softly.

She glanced up at the star-specked sky and said almost wearily, "Do you know I might have served here as a guardian, for my mother entered an isis pool when she was pregnant. Though she did not know it at the time, there were two inside her belly. Both of us were born perfect, save that my sister had a deformed jaw and mouth. Seresh remained with me and our mother until we were five, for my sister needed no special care such as the Earthtemple offers. My father disapproved, for deformed babies were generally given immediately to the Temple. I do not know what motivated my mother to diverge from tradition, but she left my father and lived apart from our tribe, so neither my sister nor I knew that she was deformed. I only knew that I looked like my mother and my sister did not, but we supposed that she resembled my father, whom we believed to be dead.

"You would think I would have known she was terribly deformed in the face, but the ideal of beauty is learned. Despite the difference in our faces, my mother adored us both and lavished us with affection and tenderness, telling us over and over that we were beautiful. Then one dark-moon night, she brought us to Templeport. We came here and waited until a Temple guardian emerged. I do not know how, but it had been arranged in advance. Only at that moment did we realize Seresh was to stay, but not I. We wept and clung to one another, for there was great love between us, and we did not understand why we must be parted. "It is an honor!" my mother cried to my sister, and tore her fingers from mine and dragged me off.

"I ran away as soon as I could and came back here, but the Temple guardians would not let me see my sister. They said she needed time to become accustomed to that life. When I was older, my mother told me everything, but I came here many times against her wishes, seeking Seresh. I wanted to see that she was happy, as I had been promised. Finally, they allowed me to see her. She was veiled, but when she drew back her veil, I gasped, for I had not seen her since we were children, and I saw that her face was ghastly. . . ."

Jakoby's eyes glittered with tears. "Seresh saw my

reaction, of course, and she asked me in a bitter voice what hurt she had ever done to anyone that I should have beauty and she a monster's mask. I did not know what to say, so I asked foolishly if she was not happy serving in the Earthtemple. "I am a monster among monsters," she answered.

"What happened to her?" I asked, full of pity.

"She ran away from the Earthtemple. The guardians said she drowned herself, and I believe that is truly what they thought. But when I was older and had been made tribe leader, an overguardian who was a kasanda summoned me and told me that Seresh had not died but had stolen coin and escaped upon a ship that had berthed here to collect water and food. The overguardian had dreamed it and dreamed that I must be told. She did not tell me why. Perhaps she did not know."

"But . . . where could she go and what could she do?" I asked.

"There is not a sevenday that passes when I do not ask that myself," Jakoby said. "Needless to say, when Bruna lay in my belly and my bondmate said it was dark-moon and time for me to go to the isis pools, I refused. He left me, saying I was no true woman. You saw tonight how many of the tribesfolk revere the practice of immersions." Her expression was cold and dreamy. "You know what I remember most? Seresh loved pretty things. She dressed in my mother's silks and jewels and danced with such grace that it was pure beauty, and neither of us ever knew she was hideous to behold. How she must have hated it in the Earthtemple where they wear only rough white weaves and never dance."

At the sound of stone grinding on stone, Jakoby's face became a blank mask. "Go. The overguardian awaits you." She turned and strode away without looking back.

"What do you seek of the earth?" asked the veiled girl who had emerged from the narrow gap beside the great pivoting stone that was the entrance to the Earthtemple. Her form was slight and not visibly deformed, but she limped when she walked.

"I seek that which the seer Kasanda left for the Seeker, as promised to me by the last overguardian of the Temple," I replied.

"May you nurture the earth and find harmony," the guardian said. It was no true answer, for these were words of ritual offered to all who came to the Earthtemple. The guardian gestured for me to follow her, when suddenly I remembered that Maruman and Gahltha were supposed to come here with me for the fifth sign and one of Kasanda blood as well! Was it possible that I was wrong in thinking I had been brought here to get what Kasanda had left me?

"Come," said the Temple guardian, for my doubts had slowed me almost to a stop. She led me deep into the many-layered labyrinth of tunnels and caves that was the Earthtemple. The air was cold and strangely scentless, though outside the night was warm and fragrant. As I followed the steady, padding footsteps of the silent Temple guardian, I thought of Jakoby's twin sister, Seresh, dragged weeping and terrified from her beloved sister's arms. She had been only five, younger than I had been when my parents were burned. How terrified she must have been to be brought into these

cold stone corridors and informed that she must henceforth live veiled among men, women, and children all
deformed in their own ways. Were the veils ever removed? If so, the deformities of the other Temple
guardians would have frightened the little girl, for she
had not known that she was deformed. No wonder
Seresh had run away, but where could she have gone,
for she could not run away from her deformed face?

The Temple guardian stopped and turned to me,
lifting her lantern, allowing me to see the shadowy
darkness of her eyes and hair through her veil's thin
gauze. She indicated a narrow doorway cut into the
stone behind her, saying, "You must go through this
door into the chamber beyond it and wait. I will tell the
overguardian that you have come." She unhooked a
lantern from the wall and gave it to me.

I did as she had bidden, knowing what I would see,
for I had been here before. Soon I was gazing upon the
panels that Kasanda had created and that I had been
shown on my previous visit to the Earthtemple. It was
strange to think that they had been carved by the laughing, dark-haired, dark-skinned Cassy of my dreams,
who had laughed with her Tiban lover and argued with
her mother and father.

I went to the first panel, which showed a Beforetime
city. I had thought it the city we now knew as
Newrome under Tor, but maybe it was another. The
city was very beautiful in its queer, angular way, a forest of slender square towers rising impossibly high into
the sky. The panel depicting it paid homage to the art
and power of the Beforetimers and was in stark con-
trast to the next panel, which showed the city again, but
as a great, soulless, devouring beast that smothered the

earth and befouled the waters, killing all living things other than humans. The third panel focused on the skies, showing them clogged with the filth that spewed from hundreds of pipes rising from human buildings. I noticed, though I had not noticed before, that in one corner, the carved black smoke parted to reveal a full moon peering through a torn patch, almost like an eye peeping through a spy-hole. This sly moon eye made me think of Rushton, his moon-hating ancestor, and my theory.

Later panels showed forests, waterways, the sea, wetlands, and mountains, all damaged and besmirched by humans and the scabrous outcroppings of their cities. The panels' message was as simple and starkly clear as it had been when I came here the first time: The Beforetimers had used the earth ruthlessly, disregarding everything but their own immediate desires. Their heedless greed and arrogant desire for power had brought the Great White upon the earth. The last panel showed the Great White, and I gazed at it, thinking of Cassy's father, who had believed the Sentinel project would save humans from themselves, even though his own bondmate had left him because she could not believe it.

I heard a step behind me.

A tall, slender, veiled figure entered the chamber, and I knew it must be the woman who now served as overguardian of the Temple, but I gaped to see Maruman prowling by her side, his yellow eye gleaming smugly.

"Greetings, Seeker," the overguardian said before I could beastspeak Maruman. It was a young voice for all its cool poise, and I remembered that the previous overguardian had been little more than a child as well. How was it that the guardians chose a child to set above them?

"Most overguardians are children," said the thin formal voice. "Age brings experience, it is true, but experience does not always bring wisdom. Often it brings complacency or confusion or anxiety. But you are mistaken in thinking that the overguardian of the Temple is chosen by the previous overguardian. We are not chosen. We are foreseen."

With a little shock, I realized the overguardian had answered a thought that I had not voiced!

"I am a kasanda," she said composedly.

"Do you think it courteous to listen to my private thoughts?" I asked aloud, a little sharply.

"I would think it discourteous, if I had the means to prevent myself," she said tranquilly.

There was nothing to say to that. I drew myself up and said, "Why did you have Jakoby bring me here? Is it because I am to collect whatever Kasanda left for me, because if it is, the last overguardian told me I was supposed to come here with Gahltha and a companion who has Kasanda blood, as well as Maruman. Perhaps he meant you, when he spoke of a Kasanda blood, and Maruman came here before me, but even if I summoned Gahltha, he could not fit in here."

"By here, the overguardian may have meant Sador, rather than the Earthtemple," she responded mildly.

I clenched my fists, feeling almost as irritated as when I spoke with the Futureteller guildmistress at Obernewtyn. I did not want speculations and guesses; I wanted clear answers! "The overguardian made it seem like it had been predicted that I would come here, but in fact, you sent Jakoby for me. Why didn't the last over-guardian tell me that I would be summoned?"

"Perhaps when he foresaw what he did, the strongest likelihood was that you would come here of your own accord, but something changed, which brought to me the revelation that Jakoby must be sent after you."

"Why didn't you just send her to find me?"

"I knew that you would come here and that Jakoby had some part to play in your future that was vital and important, but much in my foreseeing was unclear. It seemed safest to do as I did, sending Jakoby to the Moonwatcher and allowing the rest to unfold as it would, thereby leaving you free to come here if you chose."

"What is the fifth sign?" I asked, suddenly weary of mysterious talk.

"It is not a thing to be told," the overguardian said. She reached out and laid her hand on the final panel showing the Great White. With a faint grinding sound, the whole panel suddenly swung outward on a pivoting stone to reveal a narrow passage behind it. The over-guardian made a gesture for me to go through. I did so and Maruman followed, but the overguardian did not. Seeing or maybe hearing my puzzlement, she said, "None may walk here, save the seer who made this place, the Seeker who seeks it, and the Moonwatcher."

There were a thousand questions to ask, yet I knew that I would receive no proper answers here. As I turned to follow the narrow passage, my heart quickened at the thought of finding some communication from Kasanda awaiting me.

"What made you come here?" I asked Maruman as we made our way along the narrow tunnel.

"I came because I dreamed I came," Maruman said dreamily.

The passage ended in an entrance to a large cave with nothing in it, save a slitlike opening in the wall opposite the passage. Maruman was already moving toward the opening, and I hastened to catch up with him, wondering what the overguardian had meant by saying "the seer who made this place." Surely she did not mean that Kasanda had literally carved out the passage and the cavern. The opening was truly more a slit than a doorway, and I had to turn sideways to get into it. Feeling uneasy, I pressed forward, and two steps later, I stumbled into a wider space that immediately blazed with a shimmering, coruscating purple radiance that completely blinded me. After a moment of blinking and squinting, my eyes began to adjust, and I realized that the blaze of brightness was nothing more than the light of the lantern I carried, reflected from a thousand shining jagged surfaces.

Fian had once shown me a small dull-looking boulder, which, when cracked open, turned out to be a hollow stone shell lined in tiny perfect crystal spikes. He told me that the Beforetimers had called such a thing a *thunder egg*. What I had entered now was part of a giant thunder egg lined not in white quartz crystals, but in dazzling purple amethyst. Some seemed to reflect the lantern light blindingly, and only after studying the walls for a moment did I realize that some had been cut into diamond-like facets. Indeed, it seemed there was a pattern in the polished stones. So absorbed was I in trying to make out what it was, I did not at first notice something gray and square sitting on the floor.

I knelt down and gazed at a flat rectangle of plast the size of a tea tray and as thin as two of my fingers. Atop it was a black glass panel like a window, but I could see nothing through it. Setting the lantern down carefully, I leaned closer and noticed that there was scribing on the plast. Not gadi words, but some language that I did not recognize. There was also a join all about the edges, which suggested that the rectangle was some sort of case, but there was no lock or keyhole or any sort of handle to open it. I touched the case warily, but it felt merely cool as anything kept long in a cave would feel. I touched the glass, and when nothing disastrous happened, I tried simply prizing the case open with my fingers.

It would not budge, but the case was very light. I sat down cross-legged, lifted it onto my knees, and examined it minutely. I had not noticed before a small recessed shape, almost invisible in the side of the case, alongside a small square gap. Remembering the recessed hand shapes on Norseland and in the Westland, I pressed a finger carefully into the space. Nothing happened, and the sickening thought came to me that perhaps the key that was supposed to have been left in Jacob Obernewtyn's tomb, along with his and Hannah's bones, would have opened this case. That was the first time it occurred to me that just as Ariel could not see all, neither must Kasanda have been able to do so. I set the case back on the ground and stood up, wondering if all of Kasanda's careful plans and sacrifices had come to nothing because she had failed to foresee that Hannah would not be at Obernewtyn when the Great White came.

Maruman gave a snarling hiss, and I turned to see that his fur was standing on end and crackling with static energy in a way that would have been comical had it not been so unnerving.

"What is it?" I asked him, and then shuddered as I felt it too—a frisson of prickling power that ran about the glittering chamber and over my skin till I felt my own hair stand on end. A low-pitched hum filled the chamber. It took me a moment to realize that it was coming from the plast case, and I saw with a shock that the glass panel on the top now glowed with a greenish light. Then there was a faint click. I knelt down and looked closely at the case. The recessed place had now come level with its gray surface.

Heart pounding, I touched the recess. There was another distinct click, and the case split open at the join and lifted open smoothly of its own accord, revealing a set of small raised squares scribed with letters in the bottom half of the case and a glowing white screen in the top.

Seeing the now familiar rows of small squares and the screen, I realized with incredulity that I was looking at a small computermachine! And unlike the computer-machines under Ariel's residence, this one was working. Or at least, it was being powered, somehow, by the amethyst chamber. But how to learn what it contained? I studied the little squares, which Reul had once told me were also called *keys*. He had shown me how to tap on them to create scribed commands that the computermachine would obey if it could. More recently, Jak had shown me that a computer could be questioned as well as commanded, but he had added that communications with a computer must be framed in a way and in words that the computer would understand.

I licked my lips and realized my head was beginning to ache. I forced myself to concentrate on the computermachine as I carefully tapped in letters to ask what was required of me. The words appeared in neat perfect black letters on the white screen, but nothing else happened. I tried several other questions, and they appeared one after another on the screen, but the computermachine offered no response. Perhaps the computer needed a code word or a series of numbers that would allow me to communicate with it. Another sort of key. I chewed my lip and then tapped in my name. That produced no effect, and I thought of Jak saying that it would be impossible to guess the code word of any Beforetime user of a computermachine, for they and their world were utterly unkonwn to us. Except that Cassy was not unknown to me. I typed in HANNAH and JACOB, and when they did not work, I racked my brain for the name of Cassy's Tiban lover and wrote SAMU. Still nothing. I tried CASSY DUPREY and nothing happened.

Defeated, I set the case down again, reminding myself that Jak had said that it would be virtually impossible to guess a stranger's code word. But Cassy was no stranger to me after so many years of dreaming of her, and she would have known that I had been born in an age beyond the computermachines of her time. She had lived into that time, and she might have foreseen that I would come to learn something of computermachines. But if she had set a code containing a message to me, would she not have made very sure that it was something I could guess?

I took up the computermachine again and tapped in KASANDA. Nothing happened. I tapped in CASSANDRA. Again nothing happened, but it was possible that I had scribed it incorrectly. I tried several versions of the name, but none caused anything to happen. I stared at the screen glumly and thought of Dell, wakening Ines by speaking her name aloud. Would the program in this computermachine hear me as Ines had?

I licked my lips and said in a stilted voice, "Kasanda, can you hear me?"

Nothing.

"Kasanda, can you hear me?"

Nothing again. I thought for a moment, and then said, "I am the Seeker."

The light in the chamber seemed to dim, and I listened eagerly, awaiting the voice of the computermachine, but to my disappointment, there was no response. I glanced back down at the computermachine and gasped, for all of my laboriously typed questions had vanished, and now words were scribing themselves rapidly in lines on the screen.

I read them, heart thundering.

MY FRIEND, I read. I CALL YOU FRIEND, SEEKER, THOUGH WE HAVE NEVER MET, FOR I HAVE KNOWN YOU A VERY LONG TIME. TO YOU I KNOW THAT I WILL ONLY EVER BE A STRANGER WHOM YOU HAVE SOMETIMES GLIMPSED IN DREAMS OF A TIME THAT YOU WILL CALL THE BEFORETIME.

THERE ARE SO MANY THINGS THAT I WISH I COULD TELL YOU, EXPLANATIONS I MIGHT MAKE, BUT THERE IS NO TIME.

How strange it is to speak of time, when I have defied it more than once and in more than one way in my life. Yet time is truly of the essence, for I have no reliable way to regulate the power of this crystal chamber. I used the knowledge of my lost world to prepare it as best I could, but I know the power of the crystal resonances is too strong and that very soon it will destroy the workings of the computer. Therefore commit to memory all I have written here, for there will not be time for you to read my words again.

If you are reading this, then this portable computer is being powered by the crystals in the amythest chamber, which your lantern light will have activated after a short time. I cannot explain the science of crystal resonances as an energy source, for that is knowledge lost to your world, but I pray that this computer, for which I paid long and dear, will last long enough to do what it must do now.

Inside it is a small device, which you will take away with you from this place. But before I explain how to get it from the computer, you need to imprint it with your voice.

Press the A key.

I looked at the little squares until I found the A and pressed it.

The humming changed pitch again, and all the words vanished, to be replaced by two new lines of scribing.

Speak your name and say what you are, simply and clearly.

PRESS C AND REMEMBER EXACTLY WHAT YOU HAVE
SAID.

I cleared my throat and said, "I am Elspeth Gordie. I
am the Seeker." Then I pressed C.

The line of words on the screen vanished, and new
words appeared, letter by glowing letter and far more
swiftly than any hand could scribe them.

PRESS B AND LET MERIMYN SING.

PRESS C.

"Merimyn?" I read, baffled.

Maruman padded forward and sniffed at the
computermachine, and I suddenly remembered a vision I had had of him as a kitten, playing on the dreamtrails with a young woman who had seemed vaguely
familiar to me. She had called him Merimyn! My mind
surged with questions, but I dared not waste time in
questions lest the computermachine be destroyed before it could serve its purpose. So I found the B square.
Bidding Maruman sing, I pressed it. He gave a long
warbling yowl that would have made my hair stand on
end, if it was not already doing so, and when he
stopped, I pressed C.

The humming changed pitch again, and when I
looked back at the screen, large red letters were flashing
there: WAIT. IMPRINTING VOICE CODES TO MEMORY SEED.

The humming dropped in pitch, and the words
were replaced by other words.

THE MEMORY SEED IS NOW ENCODED.

PRESS THE EJECT KEY AND THE DEVICE WILL APPEAR
AT THE SIDE OF THE COMPUTER. TAKE IT AND KEEP IT
WITH YOU AT ALL TIMES.

It took me so long to find the tiny word *Eject* scribed

above the square marked with an O that I was beginning to panic, for I was sure I could now smell a faint burning odor, and I feared that the computermachine might suddenly explode or burst into flames. I pressed the O, and a small round shape protruded from the side of the machine. Gingerly, I pulled it out. It looked indistinguishable from thousands of similar small bits and pieces of plast that the Teknoguild had brought up from the levels they were continually excavating. I had no idea what it was or would do, but clearly the tiny tablet played some vital part in my quest. I slipped it into my inner pocket and buttoned it before turning my attention to the screen, where new words had scribed themselves.

THE MEMORY SEED CONTAINS WHAT YOU NEED TO GAIN ACCESS TO ALL LEVELS OF THE SENTINEL COMPLEX. YOU NEED ONLY LOAD THE SEED INTO ANY PORT ONCE YOU ARRIVE. EVEN A MAINTENANCE PORT IN THE AUXILIARY BUILDINGS WILL DO BECAUSE ALL ROADS LEAD TO SENTINEL, AS MY FATHER USED TO SAY. NO ONE WITHOUT THE MEMORY SEED WILL BE ABLE TO ENTER WITHOUT CAUSING SENTINEL TO SHUT DOWN ALL ACCESS AND DEFEND ITS PERIMETER, AND THE MEMORY SEED IS NOW NO USE WITHOUT YOU AND MERIMYN, FOR YOUR VOICES HAVE BECOME PART OF THE KEY CODE.

THERE IS VERY LITTLE TIME LEFT NOW. I WISH I COULD HAVE HELPED YOU MORE. ONLY REMEMBER THAT . . .

There was a crackling buzz, the smell of burning, and the computermachine screen went black.

Remember what? I wondered, horrified to think that something vital had been lost. Then I swiftly ran over what I had read, committing it to deeper memory, for there were many words I had not understood, and I would have to find out what they meant before I could properly understand what I was to do.

I turned to look at Maruman, whose fur still stood out in a ruff about his head, making him look like a small fierce lion. "Who called you Merimyn?" I asked. It was a mistake, of course. Maruman glared at me with his one baleful eye and turned to stalk out of the amethyst chamber. I rose with a sigh, wondering if the reason he hated questions so much had less to do with the mess of misconnections in his mind than the fact that curiosity was a form of desire, and desire was an emotion.

I looked down at the gray case with its dead black screen, hardly able to believe that it had enabled Kasanda to communicate with me. It was astounding, but at the same time I had a queer feeling of anticlimax. There were so many questions I wished I could have asked, not just about Kasanda's message but about her life and her knowledge of me and my visions, about the Great White and Hannah and Jacob Obernewtyn. Of course, I knew that Kasanda was long dead and could not answer any questions, yet the queer intimacy of what had effectively been a letter to me made it seem eerily as if she *was* alive, as if all times were existing at once.

I touched my pocket and felt the small hardness of the memory seed as I rose and looked one last time at the amethyst chamber's glittering splendor, marveling that Kasanda had been able to use it as a power source. I took up the lantern, and as I left the chamber, the blaze of light was extinguished and I almost stumbled in what seemed darkness, until my eyes had readjusted. I made my way along the narrow passage, my eyes gradually adjusting to the dim, unaugmented lantern light. I crossed the empty cavern and returned to the chamber of carved panels, where the over-guardian waited, Maruman sitting by her feet.

"There is one more thing Kasanda left you," she said.

✦ 20 ✦

WE ENTERED A long sloping walk up the side of an enormous cavern. The faint sea-scented air blowing toward us told me that we were close to the front of the Earthtemple. At length, we entered a small chamber where the wind blew so hard that it immediately snuffed out the lantern flames. But there was no need of them, for nearly palpable beams of silver-white moonlight streamed though a number of irregular openings in the stone. Through them, far below, lay Templeport and all about it as far as the eye could see, the vast, moonlit ocean. I crossed to look out one of the windows and became aware of the drumming of the sea on Templeport and the skirling of the wind against the stony faces carved into the cliff.

The overguardian spoke my name, and I turned. Standing in a shaft of moonlight, her veils whipping and fluttering in the wind, she made such a mysterious, striking vision that it took me a moment to notice that she was pointing to the stone wall behind her. Then I noticed a long vertical crevice in the rough stone too regular to be natural. I went to it and saw something long, narrow, and white standing in it.

"Take it," said the overguardian.

I reached into the niche, and my hand found a long,

hard, linen-wrapped bundle. It was much heavier than I had expected from its thinness.

"Open it," said the overguardian.

I knelt to lay it on the ground so I could untie the thongs of hemp binding the cloth tight. When I had unwrapped what lay within, I stared, for it was a sword such as a soldierguard captain might wear or a Councillor who fancied himself a warrior, but this was carved from stone inlaid with silver or some pale shining metal in a scribing that seemed to be the same atop the ruined computermachine. It was a beautiful, ambiguous object and unmistakably Kasanda's work. Indeed, it might be the finest she had ever created, as well as being the last.

"What is it for?" I asked, looking up at the overguardian.

"You are to take it and keep it with you until you find the one to whom it rightfully belongs."

"Who is?"

"That was not given to me to know," she answered serenely.

"It that all?" I asked tersely.

"What more do you want?" she asked.

"I don't mean I want something more. I mean, is that all you can tell me. What is this sword that is not a sword? Why was such a thing made and for whom?"

"I do not know the answers to these questions. I know only that she who placed no value upon possessions valued this and named it the key to all things."

I sighed, suddenly exhausted by puzzles and intrigues. Would there ever be an end to them? I rewrapped the stone sword, retied the thongs, and stood up.

By the time I had climbed from the cleft that led to the pivoting stone Earthtemple entrance, my arms were aching from the weight of the sword, and I headed straight for my tent to rid myself of the unwieldy thing. There was no sign of Jakoby, but I did not need her to guide me. It seemed as though hours had passed while I was in the labyrinth of stone, and I felt chilled to the bone, but the night air was balmy and warm, and when I reached the path leading up from the spit, I saw that a good deal of activity still centered on the trade stalls. In the distance beyond them, the frenzy of movement about the fire pits suggested feasting had given way to dance. I could have gone back and joined the others, but suddenly I knew that I would not. What had happened in the Earthtemple had severed the warm connection I had felt to everyone and everything earlier in the evening, for it was a reminder that however much I might feel or long for it, I was the Seeker, which meant I was alone.

In my tent, I lit a lantern and unwrapped the sword to study it again, wondering why Kasanda had made such a useless if lovely object. It was not a statue that could be set up and admired, and it would never cut anything. The overguardian had called it a key, which made it seem as if it must be connected to my quest as the Seeker, but she had also said it was to be returned to the one it belonged to, and who could that be? Besides, if Kasanda had made it and left it for me, it had never belonged to anyone but its maker. Unless she had made it *for* someone. But how was I to discover who? I wrapped up the sword, something else nagging at me. The words in the computermachine said that the memory seed would give me access to all levels of the

Sentinel Complex, which confirmed that this was my ultimate destination as Seeker, but if it was to open all doors, then why did I need the other words and clues that had been left for me: the key Jacob Obernewtyn had carried into the Blacklands; the words on Evander's cairn; whatever had been carved into the statue that marked the Twentyfamilies' safe-passage agreement; and whatever awaited me in the Red Queen's land.

I lay back on my bed. Kasanda had said that she had defied time twice and in more than one way. What could that possibly mean? And what had she meant by saying it had cost her much to obtain the small computermachine? I could only imagine that she had brought it with her on her journey across the sea to the Red Queen's land, but if so, how had she managed to keep it with her when she was taken by the Gadfian raiders? Unless she had obtained it while she was their captive. Indeed, it might even be the reason she had allowed them to take her.

I rolled onto my stomach and looked at Maruman, who had curled to sleep on the end of my bedroll, and I wondered again about the young woman who had called him Merimyn and how Kasanda had known that name. She must have foreseen his play on the dream-trails, but why use that slight distortion of his name?

I pushed the stone sword out of sight between my bedroll and the side of the tent. I had no fear that it would be stolen. The penalties for theft were very severe in Sador, because all crime was regarded as theft. I lay staring up into the darkness of the tent roof, feeling more and more awake. Finally, I gave up trying to sleep and decided to bathe in the clear pool at the base of the cliffs. It was but a few minutes' walk away, and the moment the idea came to me, I yearned to feel water on my hot sticky skin. I stripped off my silken clothes, drew on the wrap Kaman had given me earlier, and walked barefoot from the tent over sand still warm from the day, Maruman padding lightly beside me.

I had thought to swim alone, and I was startled and disappointed to see a large crowd of young women already swimming. Their easy nakedness, the lack of men, and the giddy horseplay puzzled me, given the lateness of the hour, but the thought of a swim was too enticing to turn back. I walked to the edge of the pool, shrugged off the wrap, and entered the water. Its embrace was like cold silk, and I sighed with pleasure.

"Greetings, Elspeth," called a voice, and I opened my eyes to see Bruna swimming languidly toward me.

"An odd hour for so many to swim," I said.

"You might call it an informal ritual," Bruna said. "You see, in an hour or so, many of these women will be hunted, so they cool their blood in readiness to make themselves elusive."

I remembered then what Jakoby had told me and said as lightly as I could, "Will you take part in this hunt?"

"I must, for three stones in my mother's bowl had my name on them," she said, tossing her sleek braided head, the beads and silver cuffs giving out a silvery music. "Probably it is no more than curiosity on the part of the men who scribed my name, for I have been away a long time." Her tone was cool and certain, and I wondered what she would say if I told her that Dardelan may have left one of the stones.

Of course I did not, for it was none of my business

459

to meddle with a mother's meddling. Besides, maybe Dardelan had *not* put a stone in the bowl. Indeed, when I thought of him, he was always surrounded by maps and books and laws and quills, serious and preoccupied by the weighty business of governing the Land; I could not imagine anyone less like a hunter than the bookish young high chieftain.

We swam together companionably for a time, and I asked if she had heard anything of Miryum and Straaka. Being in Sador had made me wonder again what had become of the Coercer guilden and the body of her Sadorian suitor since their disappearance after Malik's betrayal in the White Valley. Bruna said she had asked about the pair upon her return to the desert lands, for Straaka had been one of her tribesmen, but no one had seen them. One of the kasanda, however, had told her that the pair walked together still, though not under the moon or sun. I asked what this meant, and Bruna said she deemed it to mean that they walked together in death. This thought sloughed away the languid mood I had fallen into, and I climbed out to find Maruman curled on my robe, his yellow eye fixed on the full moon. Bruna climbed out, too, and stretched out unself-consciously on the warm sand.

"Lie down," she encouraged. "The warm sand is very pleasant, and once you are dry, you brush it off and your skin is gently scoured to silk." Other women lounged all about the pool, and after a slight hesitation, I lay down alongside Bruna. As she had promised, the sand felt wonderfully warm and soft, and I relaxed. Beside me, Bruna sighed and closed her eyes. I slept for a time and woke when Bruna rose and began to brush off the sand. I bestirred myself and did the same, judging from the moon that almost two hours had passed.

When we had both dressed, she suggested I come with her for some food. "The tents will be serving food all night tonight because of the hunt," she said.

The tents and cook fires were busier than ever, but as we approached them, I realized I had no tokens or any coin to exchange for them. Bruna waved aside my confession and brought us both hot berry pastries and minted water. We ate and drank standing, watching two very small women with honey-colored skin and deeply slanted eyes tumble and roll with an agility that Merret would have gasped to see. We were interrupted by a long mournful note that swelled in the air.

"That is the signal to tell the hunted that they have an hour before the hunt begins. An hour before I teach some warriors to eat my dust," Bruna said, her golden eyes glimmering with contempt. Fleetingly, I saw the wild, haughty child-woman who had first come with her mother to the Land. Then she smiled. "I have enjoyed your company, Elspeth."

"And I yours," I said, wondering if Dardelan would take part in the hunt and how she would feel when she discovered it. "Good luck," I added, but she was already sprinting away on long lean legs.

"You ought to have said, *Run wild and never submit unless you choose*," said a voice.

It was the Druid's armsman Daffyd, standing beside me clad in loose Sadorian robes.

"Da-Daffyd!" I stammered, gaping at him. "What are *you* doing here?"

His smile faded into a grim determination. "Doing

what I have been doing since Ariel sold Gilaine, my brother, and Lidgebaby to Salamander."

"But Salamander has never been here," I said.

"I am not so sure," Daffyd said darkly, glancing around.

I stared at him, taking in his gaunt look and haunted eyes. "Why do you think he would come here?" I asked gently.

Instead of answering, he said, "I have just been speaking to Rushton. He told me what has been happening on the west coast and in the Norselands. That was a fine set of victories. He told me, too, about Domick. It aches my heart to think of it."

I sighed heavily and told him it ached mine, too, but I did not want to speak of the coercer. The hours I had spent with Bruna had lightened my heart, and I did not want to plunge into grief again so soon.

So I said, "Why would Salamander come to Sador knowing he would be despised as a thief of freedom, captured, and sentenced to the desert walk?"

"I don't think he came here as a slaver," Daffyd said with such certainty that I was taken aback.

"You think he came in disguise?" I asked.

"I think if he came here, it would not be in any disguise, because what he wears the rest of the time is a disguise. I think he came as himself. *As a Sadorian tribesman.*"

"You think Salamander is *Sadorian*?" I demanded incredulously. "The Sadorians despise slavers even more than murderers."

"True, most Sadorians hate slavers as they hate murderers," Daffyd said. "But do you think there are no Sadorian murderers?"

"I see what you are saying," I said more moderately. "But what makes you think Salamander is a tribesman?"

We went to sit on a dune slightly apart from the press about the stalls, and Maruman slipped from my shoulders into my lap.

"I didn't come here originally to find Salamander," Daffyd said. "I came here because there was no way to reach the west coast from the Land after the rebellion. My plan was to board one of the vessels that fish the waters along the edge of the strait and bribe the shipmaster to let me slip overboard and swim to the west coast."

"But you could not find a ship that would take you?" I prompted, weary enough to feel impatient with the circumlocutions of his tale.

"The rumors that fishing boats went that far from Sador proved untrue. Once I realized there was no way to reach the west coast from here, any more than from the Land, I was disheartened. There seemed no reason to go back to the Land as long as the Suggredoon remained closed, so I worked as an aide to one of the traders who stays here all year round, serving the odd seaman and trading with the Sadorians who wander by. I was so much into the habit of thinking about Salamander that I went on doing it, and gradually I started to wonder why he had never attacked any of the Sadorian greatships save the one he destroyed at Sutrium, and why he had never come here."

"Because he is a slaver and the Sadorians loathe slavery," I said.

"Listen," Daffyd said, and now he suddenly changed the subject and began to tell of a good hire he had been offered to go into the desert with a kar-avan. The story was fascinating enough that I did not interrupt, but finally he said that on this trip he had heard something that made him question the prevailing belief that Salamander was from the Red Queen's land.

This startled me out of my irritation, for I had always assumed Salamander had come from the Land until recently, when it had occurred to me that he might be of Gadfian stock. I advanced my own theory, but Daffyd merely shook his head and went on with his kar-avan tale. He said that halfway through the trip, he had become friendly with the bondmate of a Sadorian who had eventually confided to him that she was originally from the Land.

"I asked how she had come to be bonded to a tribesman. I suspect she had never told her tale, and maybe my being from the Land led her to confide it. She said she had been a shipgirl aboard one of the small vessels that the *Black Ship* had attacked. As was usual in those days, Salamander boarded the ship and took all passengers and shipfolk aboard the *Black Ship* to sell as slaves, save one, who was blindfolded and put into a ship boat with the tiller tied so that it would eventually reach land if it did not capsize. The aim, of course, was that, if the man did reach the Land safely, he would tell his tale and spread a terror of the *Black Ship* to make other ships much more inclined to surrender at once. Sometimes Salamander claimed the ship he had captured, but more often than not he simply scuttled it, as he had done this time, and departed.

"Unbeknownst to Salamander, the woman from the kar-avan had climbed over the edge of the ship on a dangling rope, and she clung to it grimly through the battle. She knew it was Salamander's practice to release a single person in a ship boat, and her idea was to swim after it and climb aboard. But she didn't dare swim to it at once, for fear of being seen. She waited until the *Black Ship* was far away before she dived from the last bit of the ship poking up from the water and swam after the ship boat." He shook his head and added that it had been carried almost out of her sight, and from the woman's account, it had been a long, desperately hard swim to reach it. The whole time, she had been in mortal terror of sharks or of losing sight of the ship boat in the gathering darkness and the high waves. But luckily the moon had risen, and knowing she would die if she did not reach the boat had given her strength and determination. Reaching the ship boat at last, she had dragged herself into it, untied the man, and between them they managed to paddle the boat into a coastal current that brought them here. The man went back to the Land, but the woman stayed in the desert lands and changed her name, terrified that the vengeful and fanatically secretive Salamander would come after her.

"You see, when she was dangling from that bit of rope, the two ships were side by side for a time, and right after the battle, when her shipmates were being marched across a plank onto the *Black Ship*, she saw a queer thing through a porthole in the *Black Ship*. Salamander strode into a cabin, gloved, masked, and swathed in trousers and greatcoat as usual, clutching at his belly. When he took his hand away, his vest was red with blood. The great half-naked slave who tends him took out a needle and thread, and Salamander lifted up his shirt to let the man sew the gash. It was a bloody wound but not a mortal one, but here's the thing: the woman said Salamander's *belly was as brown as choca.*"

"He is Gadfian," I murmured, imagining the woman hanging precariously between the ships, holding her breath, and praying not to be crushed or noticed.

Daffyd went on. "My first thought on hearing he was brown-skinned was that Salamander must be Sadorian, but I could not understand why he would be so fanatically secretive if he was, given that the *Black Ship* never visited here. That is when it came to me. He would not care that he was seen and recognized as a Sadorian *unless he wanted to be able to come back here.*"

I asked breathlessly, "Have you told this to any of the Sadorians?"

He shook his head impatiently. "I did not care about accusing Salamander to the tribe. I just wanted to use him to go to the Red Queen's land to rescue my brother, Gilaine, and the others. If I could find out who he was, I could slip aboard his ship. I figured he must use one of those vessels he had taken in the strait, since he could not simply come sailing up in the *Black Ship* without being instantly identified as a slaver. I set myself the task of learning if there were any Sadorians who vanished for periods and then reappeared. It was a near impossible quest given that the Sadorians are nomads, but what else had I to do?

"Then not an hour ago, I bumped into Rushton, who told me he is here because he is trying to mount an expedition to the Red Queen's land before the next wintertime. I asked if I could join, and he said that he saw no reason why I should not come but that I must present my request to Dardelan and Gwynedd, who are high chieftains of the Land now, for they would be the masters of the expedition. Rushton told me that he is to address the tribal council tonight, and he wants me to come with him and tell what I have learned of Salamander. He believes the Sadorians' profound loathing of slavery might sway them in favor of this expedition, since they would protect their land from the slavemasters by participating, and they would have the opportunity to capture Salamander and learn who he is." He frowned. "I suppose you know that the slavemasters are Gadfians?"

I frowned. Once I had dreamed that the slavemasters were Gadfian, but I had not taken it seriously until I had begun thinking that Salamander had got his ship from them. "It is hard to imagine the Gadfians described by the Sadorians could have increased in such numbers."

Daffyd nodded. "From what I have gathered, the Gadfians who stole the Sadorian women died out long ago. Those who invaded the Red Queen's land were another group, and wherever they settled, their fertility was not affected."

"But how could one people live so far apart?"

"The land of the Gadfians was vast, so perhaps after the Great White, some of its people fled in one direction and thrived while the rest settled on the tainted land, which destroyed their ability to bear healthy children."

"You have learned a good deal about Gadfians," I said.

He shrugged. "The Sadorians teach their children about them and the lost Beforetime."

At the sound of an explosion and a flare of golden light, I looked up to see a cloud of shimmering gold snowflakes against the dark sky.

"That is the signal that one successful hunt has ended," Daffyd murmured.

"What happens if the woman doesn't let herself be caught?" I asked, thinking of Dardelan and Bruna.

"Nothing. The hunters who strived for her will have their stones returned."

"Daffyd!" It was Gilbert, hurrying across the sand. He smiled warmly at me as I struggled to my feet with Maruman in my arms. Daffyd had leapt to his feet at once, and the two men greeted one another with warm handclasps and many questions. Daffyd expressed surprise at Gilbert's Norselander hair, and Gilbert laughed and said he was armsman to Gwynedd, king of the Norselands. Daffyd demanded to know how that could be.

"Come with me, and Gwynedd will tell you his own tale, for he has sent me to find you," Gilbert said.

"Now? But it is not even dawn. How does he know of me anyway?" Daffyd looked almost comically alarmed.

"Rushton spoke of you just now, and when I said I knew you, I was promptly dispatched to find you. As to the time, it seems we have given up on sleep for now. Will you come?"

Daffyd looked at me apologetically. "I should go, for I can ask at once about joining this expedition to the Red Queen's land. We will continue our conversation later."

"Just one thing," I said to Gilbert. "Is Dardelan with Gwynedd?"

The red-haired armsman shook his head. "I think he is the only one among us sensible enough to have gone to his bed, for I have not seen him since the feast ended. Shall I find him for you?"

I shook my head and said that I would see him at firstmeal. I bade Daffyd farewell for now, and Gilbert smiled at me as they moved away. Not until they had vanished into the crowd about the trade stalls did I remember my dreams of Gilaine and Daffyd's brother, Jow, in the Red Queen's land. I should have asked Daffyd if he had dreamed of Gilaine, since my dream indicated that she had dreamed of him. That would have to wait until later. I yawned.

"I/Maruman am tired," Maruman sent.

"I am, too," I admitted, draping the old cat about my neck. Yawning again, I made my way slowly across the sand to the cluster of sleeping tents, hardly able to believe that only a few hours before, I had been inside the labyrinthine Earthtemple receiving a mysterious communication from Kasanda. I reached into my pocket and felt the little memory seed, but I was too weary to begin another whirl of speculations. It was enough, for now, that I had gained what Kasanda had left for me.

By the time I crawled into my tent, I could hardly keep my eyes open. I stripped off the loose robe I had worn for my swim and stretched out luxuriously on my bedroll, lying gingerly on my beaded hair and pulling the cover over me. Maruman turned in several intent circles before settling against my waist, and in moments, I could hear his soft, purring snore.

I was so weary that I felt dizzy, but something kept me from actually falling asleep. Almost of its own volition, a probe formed and ranged, first over the tents, touching a few minds lightly, then moving out beyond the fires and press of people to the open desert. As had happened very occasionally before when I was extremely tired, my mind spontaneously produced a vague spirit shape, and suddenly I was seeing the desert with spirit eyes. The desert's aura was a shifting, liquescent yellow-gold and white.

I saw a dark form running across it, and curiosity sharpened my wits and bade me send my probe toward it. I could not make out the face of the shadowy human form with my spirit eyes, but I reached out to touch the person's ice-blue aura and realized it was Bruna. My curiosity about her was strong enough to have directed my unfocused probe to her. I felt her surprise as she stopped abruptly, and I realized she had heard someone running toward her. She turned and ran on, and I followed her effortlessly.

Then the desert changed, and Bruna seemed to enter a cave. When I saw the glowing aura of plants, I realized she had entered one of the rifts. She was moving deeper into it, and my curiosity was so intense that it drew me deeper into the merge so that, suddenly, I saw through Bruna's eyes just as I had once been able to do with Matthew. I was elated, for it was rare to find someone compatible enough to manage this, but I was shocked, too. For standing before Bruna was *Dardelan*, but Dardelan as I had never seen him! Through Bruna's eyes, I saw that he was naked but for a Sadorian loincloth and a dagger strapped to his leg. He was pale and slim, yet there was a wiry strength to his body not evident when he was clothed. But the most fascinating thing was his aura, visible to my spirit eyes as an overlapping glow. It was a blaze of yellow and gold with flashes of diamond white so dazzling as to be nearly painful. I had never seen an aura quite like it, and I wondered if it was why people had always found Dardelan so charismatic.

"You!" Bruna whispered. "What are you doing here?"

"Hunting you," Dardelan answered. "You spoke once of loving a particular isis pool. So I begged Andorra to lead me here, and I asked Hakim to place his own stone in the bowl and drive you in this direction. I do not know who the other man was, whose stone was in the bowl, but I claim victory. Yet I did not hunt you as a tribesman would have, so I will not send up the golden sign unless you will it."

"You . . . have hunted me?" Bruna's voice trembled with doubt, with grief, with anger. "Why would you bother? I am the same woman you let walk away in Sutrium without a second thought. I have not changed. I will never sit tamely at home while you go to fight. I will never obey orders without question."

"I treated you as I did and said what I said not because I desired you to be anything but what you are, but because I believed that your mother was right in feeling you would be happier here in the desert lands. But after you left Sutrium, I realized that I had never given *you* the choice."

"You let me leave." Bruna's voice had hardened, and I sensed her implacability. The ice lume of her aura shimmered around us.

"I did not let you leave. I deliberately drove you away and only then discovered that I had sent the sun into exile. I love you."

I felt her shock reverberate through our merged

aura, and a wave of hot dazzling red suffused the ice blue. "You . . . discovered that you loved me after I left?"

Dardelan laughed, but there was no humor in the sound, and bruised purple ran through the golden aura. "I was dazzled by the fire in you when you were nothing but a child, as sweet and golden and full of stings as fresh honeycomb. You shone like a flame before my eyes. I went about my duties, turning my eyes resolutely away from you, but I seemed to see the after-image of your face and form everywhere. Maybe it was because you made such a strong impression when you were still a child full of tantrums and willful pride that I failed to perceive that you had grown into a woman. Only after you rode away from Sutrium did I see you clearly, and when I thought of your last words to me, I was shamed. But even amid the shame, I felt pride in the lovely dignity you had shown. I knew I must come to you and beg your forgiveness."

"My mother told me that you came here to ask the tribes for the sacred ships," Bruna said in a stony voice, but I could feel that she was trembling from head to toe.

"I had made up my mind to come here the first moment I could, within a day of your departing Sutrium. But I am high chieftain, and I could not leave on the eve of the great ruse. As Jakoby's daughter, you understand that a leader has a duty to those he leads that he must set above his own desires. My duty took me to the west coast, but then Gwynedd asked your mother to bear him to Norseland, and Rushton asked your mother to bring us here afterward. My duty required me to go with them, but I rejoiced, for there was nowhere else I desired more to visit. I was determined to find you and speak with you before I left the desert lands. But then ... last night I heard some tribesmen speak of this hunt ... One talked of hunting *you* and I ..." He broke off and laughed, looking all at once younger. "I was filled with jealousy, and I put a stone into the bowl with your name upon it. I feared I would lose you to your unknown Sadorian suitor, and I knew it would serve me right, for I had been a fool and did not deserve you. Yet here we stand." Dardelan took a deep breath. "And now all that remains is for you to tell me whether the love you once felt for me is utterly quenched, or whether there is a spark I can fan to life."

Bruna gave a choked laugh, and her icy aura blazed hot red-bronze. "My love for you could as easily be extinguished as the sun!"

"Then you will be hunted?" There was humility and overwhelming relief in Dardelan's soft question, but now his aura blazed red and gold, like flame, and even though Bruna could not see it, she swayed back, as if from heat.

"I was caught long ago by this hunter, my ravek," she whispered, and she stepped forward and spread her long fingers on Dardelan's chest. He stood immobile for a moment, and then he groaned and gathered her to him.

I wrenched my spirit form from Bruna, mortified to have eavesdropped on her and Dardelan, yet deeply touched by what I had seen and heard. This desert land was a fruitful place for love, I thought, perhaps because there was a nakedness to its bare undulant beauty that demanded truth. Suddenly I longed for Rushton to come to me. I was tempted to farseek him, but I resisted, knowing that he, too, had a duty to fulfill.

473

The lemon light of sunrise was now filtering through the tent, but perversely, I fell asleep at last. Instead of sinking into dreams, my spirit was so enlivened by what I had witnessed between Dardelan and Bruna that it rose, and all at once I was on the dream-trails. All about me, the world was a shifting mass of shadow and light, waiting for me to summon up a memory or a dream to give it shape. But before I could do anything, a shadow fell over me, chilling me.

"ElspethInnle must not seek the dreamtrails alone," said Maruman, appearing in his tyger spirit form beside me, tail snaking.

"I did not exactly choose to come here," I sent, exasperated.

"ElspethInnle must choose *not* to come here," Maruman responded sharply. "Return to your body, for the oldOnes summon you to the mountains."

I stared at him, wondering if this was the summons I had spent half my life awaiting, the moment in which the Seeker set off on the dark road. But then I realized it was impossible, for the ships would not journey to the Red Land for many months, and no one yet knew if the Sadorians would agree to take part in the expedition at all.

"Why?" I asked.

"Maruman does not know. The oldOne's voice said that ElspethInnle must return at once to Obernewtyn. The oldOne's voice was very weak."

I shivered, suddenly remembering Atthis's voice inside my mind when I had been trying to hold Rushton back from the mindstream. She had bidden me release Rushton lest I perish with him. I had refused and had begged her to help me.

"There will be a price," Atthis had warned.

"I will pay it," I had sworn desperately.

"It is not you who will pay," Atthis had answered.

All at once I was aware of the formless matter about me, darkening.

"ElspethInnle must leave the dreamtrails," Maruman sent urgently, looking up, ears flat to his skull. I looked up and saw that the unformed matter of the dreamtrails had not darkened but that something enormous was circling overhead, casting a vast black shadow.

"What is it?" I asked, aware of an unfocused malevolence emanating from it.

"The Destroyer seeks ElspethInnle," Maruman answered. "Fly before it sees you!"

I obeyed instantly, leaping from the dreamtrail and letting myself fall like a stone. I fell so fast that rather than waking, my spirit form shredded and dissipated as I sank into the depths of my own mind. Before I could shield myself, a dream snared me.

It was a queer dream, for although it felt like a true dream, it could not have been so, for in it, Matthew was running along the tunnel that had appeared repeatedly in my dreams for as long as I could remember. It was filled with a thick, yellow mist, and through it, I saw the dull regular flashing of the yellow light and heard the familiar dripping of water into water.

"Elspeth?" Matthew called urgently. "Elspeth?"

There was no answer but his own voice whispering my name back to him over and over, growing softer and softer, until it faded into a barely audible sibilance.

I slipped free of the dream, but as I rose to wakefulness, I heard the infinitely mournful howl of a wolf.

❖   ❖   ❖

I opened my eyes to sunlight and Rushton smiling down at me. He might have been a dream summoned by my longing, save for the utter weariness in his jade-green eyes and the mottled bruises that marred his face.

"You were with Bram all night?" I asked.

He yawned and lay down beside me with a heartfelt sigh. "A good bit of it. I know what I am to say now, but the way of speaking gadi is so difficult. I feel as if my tongue has been turned inside out. I fear that I will never manage to speak it well enough to be understood." He rubbed his red-rimmed eyes and yawned again. "These last few hours I was with Gwynedd and Daffyd; he said he had spoken to you."

I nodded. "Do you think he is right about Salamander being Sadorian? Do Bram or Jakoby know?"

"I spoke of it to Bram, and he says that if the tribe leaders accept Daffyd's argument, it will definitely make a difference, though he believes it is only a matter of time before the tribes agree to participate in the expedition."

"That's wonderful," I said. Then I remembered the dreamtrails: Atthis bidding me through Maruman to return to Obernewtyn immediately; the Destroyer shadowing my dreams. "I must return to Obernewtyn," I thought, and then realized I had said the words aloud.

Rushton's smile faded. "You are serious?"

I looked into his green eyes, trying to think how to explain why I had to go without speaking of my quest and without lies. But before I could speak, he sighed and the tension in his body seemed to flow away as he reached out to cup my cheek. "You have had a premonition?"

It would have been so easy to nod and leave it at that, but it was hard to lie to him. Yet I might as well have lied, for while I dithered, he took my silence for an answer, saying, "Gwynedd has asked Jakoby to take us all to Sutrium, to drop Dardelan, Daffyd, and Brydda there before going on to leave Gwynedd and his people ashore at Murmroth's Landing. He is hoping that by the time we get to Sutrium, Shipmaster Helvar will have sent word with the *Stormdancer* to agree to take part in this expedition. If that is so, it will mean all parties concerned will be in one place, and the opportunity to have a proper meeting to plan it all out is too important to miss. I feel I must go along for this reason. But that is not the only reason. There is so much that can be achieved now, while the Land and the Westland are being forged anew, that will better the lot of Misfits."

He was thoughtful for a moment. Then he continued. "Gwynedd has the notion that we ought to set up some Misfit schools in the Westland and upon Norseland to allow anyone who might have Talent to be tested and to seek training locally, rather than being forced to travel all the way to Obernewtyn. And both he and Dardelan are speaking of there being two beasts apiece on each Council of Chieftains. There will be opposition from the likes of Brocade, of course, but if the practice can be introduced in the Westlands, it will be hard for him to make a strong case. Besides, did not beasts play a vital part in our battle for freedom? Brydda is longing to return to Sutrium to tell Sallah, and I want Guildmaster Gevan to know so he can raise the matter with the Beastguild as soon as possible. Also, you will need to ask Roland to appoint some healers to travel to the Westland to help establish healing centers in the cloisters. Of course, there is still much to be done before the Westland is secure."

Suddenly he laughed sheepishly. "What I am trying in my long-winded way to tell you is that although I meant to ask you to come with me aboard the *Umborine*, it being nearly impossible to imagine being parted from you so soon after all that has happened, in truth I would be glad to know that you were at Obernewtyn. Do you know the meaning of this premonition? Is it Dragon's disappearance? Or Angina?"

"I do not know why I must go back," I said truthfully. "Only that I must and immediately."

He sighed. "Well and good. Yet it is hard to let you go, and the coast road is no pleasant afternoon ride."

"I have been along it before, and Gahltha will not stumble," I said, utterly relieved not to face disappointment or anger, or worse, hurt at my announcement that I would return at once to Obernewtyn.

"When would you leave?"

"As soon as I have provisions for the journey. If I must go, then I might as well be gone swiftly."

He sat up, and I did the same, noting dark circles under his eyes. "I feel as if I have been away from you for years and that I have only just found you again, and now we must part."

"We are not only ourselves and our desires," I said. "You are the chieftain of Obernewtyn and leader of the Misfits, and I am . . ." I stopped, shattered at the realization that I had almost named myself the Seeker.

"You are mine whatever else you are and wherever you go," Rushton said with an intensity that made me want to weep. I kissed him softly and would have drawn back, but his arms closed fiercely about me and the kiss deepened, drawing us both to passion's breathless edge. Finally, he broke away, his breathing ragged. "If you would go, then you must go now, for I am not made of stone."

His words summoned to my mind an image of the strange stone sword that Kasanda had left me, which the overguardian of the Earthtemple had called the key to all things.

Rushton touched my lips, drawing my mind and heart back to him. "You have left me already," he said. His eyes were sad.

"I may leave you, but my heart has ever been in your keeping," I whispered, and this time I drew the Chieftain of Obernewtyn into a fierce embrace and rained kisses on him as I had so often longed to do until he laughed in delight and gave me kiss for kiss.

✦ EPILOGUE ✦

"THE RAIN SMELLS of the sea," Gahltha sent.

"I/Maruman hate the rain," sent the old cat, sinking his claws into my shoulder to let me know that he blamed me for the weather.

I looked up into the brooding cloud-filled sky and thought of the enormous beast that had flown over Maruman and me, emanating malice on the dream-trails the night before I had left Sador. The Destroyer, Maruman had named it, yet what had he truly meant? Ariel was far away in the Red Queen's land, but my communication with Matthew had shown me that it was possible to reach someone over such an impossible distance. Yet Ariel had never taken such a form before. He had only ever been himself, even if he had occasionally projected a younger version of himself.

My eyes sought the gray sea that heaved and churned far below the coast road, the black jagged rocks rising above the froth like dark fangs. I let my gaze run away to the horizon, lost in sea mist and veils of rain, thinking of the *Black Ship*, which was even now sailing to the Red Queen's land, and of Salamander, its master. Was he a Sadorian? I had felt convinced, hearing Daffyd, but in truth, the man might be a Gadfian, especially if it was true that the slavemasters were

Gadfians. I thought, too, of the woman who had slept in a lavish chamber in Ariel's residence, wondering if she was Salamander's woman or merely a woman showered with Sadorian luxuries.

In a few months, I had no doubt four ships would follow the *Black Ship* out into the dangerous sea. And Gahltha, Maruman, and I would be aboard, as would Rushton and Daffyd. And Dragon.

"ElspethInnle gnawing and gnawing," Maruman complained irritably.

I laughed ruefully. "You are right, Maruman. I do gnaw horribly at things, and I wish I would stop as much as you do."

"Soon we will come to the end of this weary/narrow way, and we will gallop instead of plodding," Gahltha sent.

"That gallop will help ElspethInnle, but it will give Maruman pain," the old cat said grumpily.

"To ride swift is to arrive soon," Gahltha sent with callous good cheer.

"I fear we cannot gallop, even if Maruman would agree to it," I told Gahltha regretfully, thinking of the stone sword we carried, wondering again who its rightful owner was.

"Maruman wearies of this long journeying," Maruman sent, so wistfully that I could not resist reaching up a hand to stroke his head. He stiffened but suffered the caress.

"It is not so far now," I promised. I glanced ahead as I spoke and was startled to see the faint shapes of mountain peaks just visible through the constant haze of rain. "Look! You can see the mountains already. Our journey will be over by tomorrow morning."

"The mountains are only the beginning of the journey," Maruman responded, and his mindvoice now had a fey quality that sent a prickling premonition across my mind and skin.

And somewhere, a wolf howled.

✦ ACKNOWLEDGMENTS ✦

This book was written in La Creperie in Janovského, Prague, and in The Bay Leaf, Seagrape, and Cafe 153 in Apollo Bay, Australia. Thanks to Cathy Larsen for her persistence and generosity in her quest for a new look for the Obernewtyn Chronicles and for the new map, and to Nan for being all that she is, editor and friend. Gratitude to Mallory, Nick, and Whitney for their help in bringing this book to America. And a special heart-felt thank-you to the faithful readers of this series for waiting, patiently and impatiently, for what turned out to be, after all, not quite the last book.

✦ ABOUT THE AUTHOR ✦

ISOBELLE CARMODY began the first of her highly acclaimed Obernewtyn Chronicles while still in high school. She continued writing while completing a Bachelor of Arts and a journalism cadetship. This series and her short stories have established her at the forefront of fantasy writing in Australia and abroad.

She is the award-winning author of several novels and many series for young readers, including The Legend of Little Fur, the Gateway Trilogy, and the Obernewtyn Chronicles.

She lives with her family, and they divide their time between homes in Australia and the Czech Republic.

Discover an all-new heroine in this tale of romance, suspense, and the paranormal!

Turn the page for a sneak preview of ALYZON WHITESTARR— available June 2009!

"WHAT THE HELL is going on?" I whispered.

It was wild to imagine that thoughts and feelings could give off scents, but the more I thought of it, the less crazy it seemed. Dogs always seemed to know when you were sad, and how could they know? It had to be that they could smell your sadness because their sense of smell was much better than a human's.

The coffee-grounds smell I experienced when I was close to Da seemed to be permanent, so maybe it came from something in his essence that didn't change. But his pine-needle scent came and went, as did the smells of ammonia and caramelized sugar, so they might come from things he was thinking or feeling at certain moments.

I debated ringing Dr. Reed to tell her what I had figured out. But I was pretty sure I would just sound like someone who sees Martians and has this whole rational-seeming theory about why no one else can see them.

Anyway, I wasn't sick, so why talk to a doctor? I was positive that the accident had done something to the part of my brain connected to my five senses, extending them in some way. All I had to do was to find an efficient way of controlling input before I blew a fuse.